D R Beavers

Save America

SAVE AMERICA

This is a work of fiction. All of the characters, names, incidents, organizations, and dialogue in this novel are either the products of the author's imagination or are used fictitiously.

iUniverse books may be ordered through booksellers or by contacting:

iUniverse
1663 Liberty Drive
Bloomington, IN 47403
www.iuniverse.com
1-800-Authors (1-800-288-4677)

ISBN: 978-1-4917-5896-0 (sc)
ISBN: 978-1-4917-5895-3 (e)

Library of Congress Control Number: 2015901034

Printed in the United States of America.

iUniverse rev. date: 02/17/2015

Chapter 1

William's administrative assistant told him Senator Jones was on the phone. She had called the Senator earlier to set up a time for the call.

"Hello, Senator Jones. How are you today?" William started the conversation with a friendly greeting.

There was a short silence and then the Senator said, "Hello, Jeremy. What did you need to talk to me about?" The pause was probably to see the name on his phone message. The message said the call was from Jeremy Walter.

The Senator had a gravelly voice with a New York accent. He enunciated his words as if he was making a speech and the press was listening. William expected there was at least one person listening and the call was being recorded.

William allowed a short silence to elapse. "I believe you need to talk to me."

William's voice wasn't gravelly and it had a southern twang. He didn't enunciate as well as the Senator since he didn't make speeches and have the press quoting him. The press had left messages at the Save America call center many times but William hadn't returned any calls.

"Why do I need to talk to you?"

"Because you're on our website today and you need my help to get off."

"What website?" he asked, although William was sure he knew the answer.

"I guess you don't need my help if you don't know about the website. Goodbye, Senator Jones." William hung up the phone without waiting for his reply. He knew his administrative assistant had included the fact that the call was from Save America. Senator Jones had been on Capitol Hill for five terms and was a fixture in the Senate. William was sure there were very few people that ever hung up on him.

In about fifteen minutes, William's administrative assistant told him Senator Jones was on the phone again. William answered and repeated his earlier greeting, "Hello, Senator Jones. How are you today?" He was sure someone checked the website, saw the Senator's picture prominently displayed as the most fiscally irresponsible representative, and told the Senator.

This time there wasn't a short silence and the Senator spoke, "We must've been cutoff. I suppose I may need your counsel." His voice wasn't as gravely this time and he sounded slightly more sincere.

William paused before he answered, "My advice is that you should demonstrate that you're truly interested in a fiscally responsible federal government."

The Senator attempted to be coy again, "I'm just one Senator, and I'm limited to what I can do."

William took the same tact as before and said, "I guess you don't need my help. Goodbye, Senator." William hung up the phone.

The administrative assistant told William, with a snicker this time, that Senator Jones was on the phone. William figured the Senator didn't need to consult with the listeners this time before making the call.

"Hello, Senator Jones." William was grinning.

"Let's cut through the crap. What do I need to do to get off the website? My office is getting hounded by calls from the press and my wife is getting calls. Several news trucks are parked outside my home."

William wanted to remind him that he didn't know about the website a short while ago, but didn't think it was productive. William answered in his sincerest voice, "There are two things I need you to do. The first one is to cut your staff by one-half in the next week. Can you do that?"

The Senator responded after a pause, "I can make a few reductions in my staff but it may take more than a week." The pause was probably to get concurrence from the listeners.

"If you don't think you can cut your staff in half within a week, I don't need to tell you the other request. Goodbye, Senator ….."

Before William could say Jones, the Senator interrupted, "I can do it and in a week. What's the other item?"

"I'll need verification. You'll need to send me the positions you have now and the ones being cut. I'll need to approve them. It's expected the cuts will be across the board and not just interns."

He was sure the Senator's face was quite red and he probably had his fists clenched. William heard a fist hit the desk before the Senator spoke so he was right, "Wait just a minute. I'm not going to let you approve the staff cuts. You're not going to tell me how to run my office!"

"If that's your position, I suppose we have nothing more to discuss." William was prepared to hang up again.

"Wait just a cotton picking minute! I've been in the Senate for thirty years and don't need help running my office. I'll call you back in an hour and let you know what's possible." He threw in a little southern saying to endear William. William figured he needed the time to cool down so he didn't object. Talking to Senators in this manner was quite new to William. In fact, talking to Senators at all was new.

William also had folks listening on the call and they huddled in his office to talk.

William took a few deep breaths and then said, "Well, that didn't go too bad. I thought I would be cussed out at some point."

"I'm sure he was mindful of his listeners and didn't want to act too ornery," said Thomas Wingate. Thomas had joined the group at the beginning, when the idea of Save America became a reality. His computer skills were essential to getting started. He was in his middle sixties, about six feet tall, and still had all of his hair, although it was gray. He was trim for someone who was addicted to computer technology. Thomas and William lived in the same neighborhood and were good friends when Save America was formed.

Charlie Yates spoke next. "The Senator isn't used to having anyone dictate what he does. It'll be hard for him to swallow his pride."

Charlie had joined the group about two weeks ago after Save America was started. He volunteered through the website, not knowing Save America was in Aiken, South Carolina, and in his hometown. He was a retired CPA. His efforts were needed to manage the gads of donations being received. Charlie was about five feet eight inches tall, bald on the top of his head, slightly overweight, clean shaven, and wore horn rimmed glasses. William could picture him as a CPA.

"His advisors will straighten him out and he'll be more amenable when he calls back. Who else should we call today? Who's the next candidate for the website after Senator Jones?" William was now inspired to make more calls.

William was considered to be a quite handsome man with dark hair and chiseled features. He was about six feet tall, in his early thirties, and the youngest of the Save America volunteers.

Thomas answered, "The next one will be Congressman Randolph. If you agree, it wouldn't hurt to let him know he'll be on the website next."

From the beginning, they only showed one Senator or Congressman on the Save America website as the most fiscally irresponsible representative. They figured it was best for the remaining to guess whether they would be next. Senator Jones had been the fourth one who was shown on the website. Two of the three previous ones had agreed to the demands and were taken off the website. The first one, Congressman Williams, wasn't as lucky. He was involved in a serious auto accident within a week of being on the website. The auto accident was ruled an accident, although there continues to be implications that the Save America group was involved. The website's posting for a million-dollar reward to the individual or individuals who helped replace Congressman Williams probably contributed to the accusations against the group. Nobody had asked for the one million dollars yet. The publicity did help foster a lot of donations and supporters. All of the networks and news channels included the Save America website in their reports about the death of Congressman Williams. This led to an overwhelming response from the public to contribute lots of money to Save America.

Within two weeks, over ten million dollars was donated to help the Save America endeavor and donations kept coming in. The other benefit was the leverage that could be placed on the next Senator or Congressman that made the website. Although pressured to shut down the website, the million-dollar reward remained on the webpage. A caveat was highlighted that stated the reward applied only to an election replacement but the caveat was probably not very convincing after Congressman Williams's death.

Thomas asked, "Have you called the Governor of Wisconsin to discuss the replacement for Congressman Williams?"

"I haven't yet, and I'm not sure I should. He doesn't know who I am. What are the group's thoughts on the matter?" William didn't think getting involved with state politics was the right thing to do.

Charlie suggested, "I think you should talk to him. I'm not sure you should ask him to let you approve his choice. Maybe you could give him suggestions."

"Maybe we should just stick to the Senators and Congressmen." Thomas also thought the Save America effort shouldn't get involved with state politics.

They sat silent for about a minute and then William said, "What do you think, Cal?"

Cal had joined the group at the same time as Charlie and was a security specialist. He had retired from the FBI and offered his services as soon as Save America was in the public light. He also didn't know the group was in his hometown until he called to offer his help. Cal was built like a tank with a crew cut and salt and pepper hair. He was about five feet nine inches tall and worked out to stay in shape. He had reminded the others that he was always armed if protection was needed.

Cal always made thoughtful comments and he finally said, "I think we've created enough turmoil already and don't think we should get involved with the Governor."

"I agree. Let's stick to our present agenda." William was now calmed down after his dialogue with the Senator.

Amy Adams, William's administrative assistant, came in and said Senator Jones was on the phone again. All departed from the room to get on a line to listen. William picked up the phone when he thought all were back at their desks. "Hello, Senator Jones."

"After some thought, I've decided to let you help me decide on the staff cuts. Now what's the other item?"

William said, a little bit sarcastically, "Thank you for allowing me to help. Item number two is for you to support the balanced budget bill being submitted by Senator Carlisle."

Senator Carlisle was number two on the website as the most fiscally irresponsible. His picture and voting record were posted on the website for four days before William returned his call. He pleaded with William to get him off the website. He told William he hadn't left the House of Representatives for four days and his family had moved to a relative's house. It turned out the press was helping the cause again since all the networks and news channels had located trucks outside Senator Carlisle's residence. They had been there night and day since Senator Carlisle's picture was the main attraction on the website. The press had also hounded him for an interview. In the end, the Senator had agreed to reduce his staff by one-half and to submit a bill to balance the budget in three years and pay the deficit down in the following years.

"What's the bill? I need to know so I can decide whether to support it."

"The bill will require the budget to be balanced by the third year and will begin paying down the debt after the third year." William knew it wouldn't be passed and probably wouldn't make it out of committee.

"I'm not sure I can support that. It's going to be difficult to get to a balanced budget. Taxes will need to be raised and that won't sit well with my constituents." The Senator was thinking of his next election. He knew his votes resulted from getting government funds for his state.

"The bill will require cuts from the federal government rather than tax increases."

"I don't see how I can support cuts to government spending. My state depends on these funds for jobs."

"Well, I guess we can't agree so I hope you have a great day. Goodbye, Senator."

"Wait a second. I thought we'd discuss the balanced budget more. I'm sure I can make you understand that it's impossible to have a balanced budget."

"Why don't you think about it for a couple of days and get back with me. I don't think you'll convince me, so you shouldn't try."

"I'll talk to Senator Carlisle and see if I can support his bill."

"Let me know." The Senator hung up as William was speaking.

The three others came back in the office and Thomas said, "I guess we should have waited a few days before calling Senator Jones."

"If we'd called him later, he still would've played hardball." William was tapping his desk with his fist.

"I agree. I don't think it would have mattered." Charlie was sitting with his arms crossed on his chest.

William was thinking that the group had been moving pretty fast since starting the website. He had planned to put up the first million but they now had over ten million with another million coming in each day.

"What about changing the reward to two million on the website?" William asked.

"If we do, let's do it tomorrow or the next day. We have plenty of publicity from Senator Jones being on the website. We'll get added publicity when we go to two million," Thomas responded.

"Let's talk about it after Senator Jones calls back." William wanted to see if Senator Jones became more agreeable first.

Chapter 2

It was six o'clock and the four principals for Save America sat down for dinner. Since the venture began, William didn't go out in the city as much. Even though he was quite sure no one in the city knew he was one of the persons who created Save America, he decided that he'd have the daily meetings while having dinner at his house. This time, Thomas's wife had packaged ingredients with cooking instructions. William's restaurant experience had left him with decent skills for their other meals. On some occasions, he had one of his restaurants prepare the meals.

Dinner was also the time when the four discussed issues. Since developing so fast, there were a lot of them. One of the first issues was to establish a call center. They were lucky to find a location in town. They recruited volunteers and hired personnel. Thomas and William worked at the call center when the center was understaffed and starting up. Thomas set up a system for contributions online, but lots of folks wanted to talk to a person.

Concerns had grown about security. There'd been threatening calls and letters. Precautions were taken in the beginning to protect identities. Jeremy Walter was William's Save America name and the others also used fake names for Save America, except for Amy who wasn't known in Aiken, South Carolina. Amy didn't attend the evening meetings and was the only paid employee. She worked for William helping him manage his real estate ventures before Save America was started. Since Amy lived in Augusta, Georgia, a post office box in Augusta was being used for the contributions that were mailed in. Amy was five feet five inches tall, was a natural blonde, had blue eyes, and was very attractive. She was the youngest of the group at twenty four years old.

When all had plated their dinners, William said, "Let's get started. The first subject is space. Cal, tell us what you're doing."

"It's nice to be in your house, but it's time to look for something different. There's a building in Augusta that I believe meets our needs. Here are pictures. I told the real estate agent that we'll probably buy the property. We can decide after you see it. The property has fencing all around, an electric gate, and we can park in the rear. It was used as a tractor and farm implement store, has several offices, and has lots of space. I've got the keys, so we can go look at it anytime."

William was always open for a road trip. "Sounds promising. Let's do a field trip first thing in the morning. We can leave here at seven a.m. Is that okay?"

Thomas answered, "Good by me."

Charlie responded, "Me too."

"Anything else, Cal?" William asked.

"I'm still worried about the threatening calls and letters. I'm following up on those that left their names but I suspect they aren't leaving their real names."

"How about you, Thomas?" William asked.

"Nothing new."

Charlie was in the middle of chewing so William waited until he was finished. "Any updates, Charlie?"

"Nope. We still have a lot of money coming in so I'll need to set up more nonprofit corporations to separate the funds."

Thomas and William had met every day for the past month and Charlie and Cal had joined the daily dinner discussions when they were added to the group. A lot had happened in a month.

It all started as a bet between Thomas and William. Thomas was at William's house for dinner when the discussion turned to politics. Both of them had similar views on the federal government's role and the need to have a balanced budget. Both of them agreed that the government couldn't continue to borrow money to fund itself. William knew the strategy of always borrowing money typically led to disaster. William knew he could shut down a losing business and take the loss. In the case of the government, they couldn't shut down and take a loss.

Thomas was retired and was sixty years old. William was only thirty three years old and was still working in his business ventures, with most being real estate, along with some restaurants. Both of them had made a lot of money in real estate investments and other businesses. William still had properties that were rented or were for sale. Thomas didn't buy houses to fix, while William did. Thomas had owned a software firm before selling it and moving to Aiken. They first met at a real estate auction and became friends. Both of them were known in the community so they used different names for Save America. William owned businesses in Aiken so it was important not to use his real name, which was William Bradford.

The conversation at dinner turned to other subjects but they tried not to talk about politics, except as it related to Save America. Thomas finally breached the subject of Senator Jones. "I think we should just play a waiting game with Senator Jones. I'm sure he'll eventually get pressure from his family and staff to get his photo off the website after Congressman Williams's demise."

Cal typically didn't jump into a conversation unless asked, but did this time. "I'd feel more comfortable from a security standpoint if we didn't pressure the Senator. I don't trust him, and he seems like someone who'd retaliate."

"You're probably right. We've moved pretty fast lately and slower may be okay. It took years to create the mess in the federal government, so we can wait a few days on Senator Jones," William agreed.

"We can use the time to set up the space in Augusta. A lot of work will be needed to move the call center and set up the computer systems." Charlie suggested.

Thomas had set up the computers so that the IP addresses were hidden and had routed the phones through the computers. He had

Save America on the Tor Network for communications. It was affectionately called an Onion Router. They were careful not to use personal cell phones for anything dealing with Save America. The plan was to be even more sophisticated when they moved to the Augusta office. William expected the offices in Augusta would be a great improvement.

They ended the dinner and the others prepared to leave. They offered to help clean up but William refused their help. While William was cleaning the kitchen and the dining area, he contemplated his situation. He knew they were in over their heads attempting to change the course of government. He was still in his thirties but thought about his children and his grandkids suffering with the growing debt. William thought he should probably just stop the ridiculous effort, but there was the ten dollar bet. His life had been pretty complete, as he'd been involved in a lot of business ventures, traveled plenty, and still had his health. He thought his health would suffer significantly if someone decided to end it. William was just finishing cleaning the kitchen when Jessie came through the door.

"Hello, sweetie. How was your day?" William smiled at her.

She answered after she came over and gave him a hug and wet kiss that lasted a couple of minutes, "It was a great day. I solved a murder today and it may provide leads for a cold case. How was yours?"

Jessie was a detective with the Aiken County Sheriff. She was on loan from the Chicago Police Department while her parents were recovering. They were in a horrific auto accident in Aiken. Jessie was about William's age and had made his life more interesting since coming into it. Jessie Barnes was tall, slender, athletic, and could hold her own when they practiced martial arts. She tried to hide her Chicago accent, but it was still apparent.

"Not the greatest day. I'm not sure I should continue with this latest venture to improve our federal government." William hadn't planned to blurt it out right away. He thought that maybe Jessie could talk him out of the Save America foolishness.

"What happened today that made you think differently?" She *was* a detective.

"Senator Jones."

"Did you think the Senator was going to be a pushover?"

William had told her about the Senator when they displayed him on the Save America website.

"No. I didn't think he'd be a pushover but I thought he'd have a little common sense."

"The federal government didn't get in the predicament it's in from people having common sense. I'm sure Senator Jones is one of the worst."

"I wanted you to talk me out of this mess."

She got a thoughtful look on her face and William let her think. He knew she was searching for the right words. "I'll listen, but I've found out hasty decisions usually aren't the best—unless I'm shooting someone."

"You're probably right. I won't quit—at least for now." William knew it would worry him and he knew he'd think about it a lot. Jessie was right about not making sudden decisions.

"Did you save me any dinner?"

"There's food left in the fridge."

"Did you feed the others?"

"Yes. All of them had dinner. We're leaving early in the morning to look at a property in Augusta. I'll only need one round of sex tonight." William said with a devilish smile. He had convinced Jessie to stay with him most of the time before her mother was released from the hospital. Now that her mother and father were both out of the hospital, they needed lots of physical therapy and it'd be a while before she was independent again. Now Jessie only spent the night occasionally and William was hoping tonight was one of those occasions.

"I'll just sleep in another room so I won't keep you up late."

William's house had lots of rooms. It was in a prominent neighborhood in Aiken with many other large houses.

"I have plans for you tonight. You haven't been over for several days and I feel deprived."

"I'll tell my mother that your needs are more important than her needs."

William said with a little sarcasm, "I'll stop by and tell her myself. Your mother and father must have had sex once, unless you're adopted."

"I don't think my mother would appreciate a discussion about sex," Jessie said as she was still eating her dinner.

William went over and massaged her shoulders and back. There was a knot in her neck so he worked it out. He rubbed her head and she leaned her head back.

"If you'll do more of that, I'll consider sleeping with you."

"I'll do your head, shoulders, and feet after my needs are met."

"You'll probably go to sleep after you get your rocks off. I need to get up early too, so I have time to check on my parents before going to work."

William kept rubbing and massaging until Jessie finished eating. He led her into the bedroom pulling her clothes off as she walked. Jessie typically wore black T-shirts and jeans which were easy to get off. By the time they were at the master bedroom, he had undressed Jessie down to her black socks. He kissed her all over her body while he undressed himself. Jessie took charge when they were in the bed and straddled him. He didn't resist and put his arms above his head in submission. They cuddled as Jessie fell asleep. He got up and cleaned the kitchen, washed his face, brushed his teeth, and joined Jessie in her slumber. At two a.m., he woke Jessie up and took control temporarily until she woke fully. They battled to see who stayed on top until both were exhausted, and both were spent.

At seven the next morning, William met the others outside as he followed Jessie to her car. She had her black Impala that matched her black hair and black attire of jeans and T-shirt. Augusta was about thirty minutes away and they talked about the building during the trip. Cal was very excited about the building and thought it would be perfect. He reminded them that it was also innocuous enough that it wouldn't draw attention.

When they arrived and went through the coded electric gate, the building certainly didn't look like a typical office structure. It was an older metal sided building with a metal roof. There was a loading dock on the side and one double entrance door in the front. Cal drove to the back and parked. The rear had a rollup door and two other standard personnel doors. The inside had several offices, a room that could be a conference room, bathrooms, and a break room with a refrigerator, stove, microwave, and tables. The rooms looked modern so someone had updated them. A door to a small basement area was located near the offices. It looked like a boiler room for an oil or coal furnace. Cal told them the building had been used by several people and for different purposes with the last being the tractor business.

They went into the front part and there was an open area which was probably the showroom for the tractor business. At the side of the building near the loading dock, there was another open space. The concrete floor had greasy spots so it was probably the repair area. There weren't many windows, which was also beneficial. They concurred that the building would work and Cal would tell the real estate agent that they would buy it. William agreed to research the properties nearby in Augusta and decide on a fair offer. They decided to begin leasing the building right away as long as the offer to purchase was accepted.

On the drive back to Aiken, the discussion was about the items that were needed for the building. All of them would be involved as they got the building ready, so they divided up the work.

They made it back to Aiken about ten. Amy was at her desk. The desks were spread throughout William's house in the six bedrooms and the office. He would be glad to have his house back. He couldn't invite anyone over for poker games, dinner, or drinks. Thomas was married so William's house was the logical choice when they started the idiotic endeavor.

About ten minutes after returning, Amy told William to turn on CNN. She also told everybody else to come into William's office.

William turned the TV on and was shocked. He couldn't believe what he was hearing. The anchor was saying that Senator Jones was found dead in bed this morning. The anchor said the announcement was delayed because Senator Jones' wife had just been notified. She had been on a flight to the west coast and couldn't be reached.

They sat stunned and none of them spoke as the anchor kept talking about Senator Jones. In a few minutes, the Save America website was shown on the screen with Senator Jones's picture and the information that was uploaded about him. The anchor then talked about the million-dollar reward. Thomas got up and left the room without speaking.

Cal said, "We should take Senator Jones off our website."

"I think that's what Thomas is doing now," William responded.

Charlie said, "I think I'll go over to the call center. The number of calls will probably increase and they'll need help."

When they went to the call center, they went over as volunteers, except for Thomas. The two managers knew Thomas but didn't know he was one of the principals of Save America. On paper, Thomas was the owner of the call center contracted to Save America.

"I'll be over shortly after Thomas finishes working on the website." William was now wondering whether Save America caused the death of Senator Jones.

Thomas came back into the office and sat down. "I've shut the website down for now. I thought about putting up a message with words about our sympathy for Senator Jones but decided the best thing to do was to shut it down."

Cal said, "Shutting down was the right thing to do."

"I agree. Charlie went over to the call center to help. The calls should increase and I think I'll go over shortly." William wanted to say that he needed to go over so he didn't have to think about Senator Jones and about quitting the Save America effort. The call center involved a lot of talking on the phone, allowing little time to think.

"I'll come over in a little while too." Thomas also thought the call center would keep him from thinking about the death of Senator Jones.

"I'm staying here. I'll make a few calls to see if I can find anything more about Senator Jones." Cal still had his contacts the FBI.

William called Jessie and told her he'd be at the call center. She told William she'd heard about Senator Jones and felt bad about it. She also asked if Save America was involved. William assured her they weren't directly but didn't know if they incited someone to kill the Senator.

The call center was in an old shopping center in Aiken and William got there in about twenty minutes. He took a seat at an open desk and starting taking calls. About one out of ten calls was a call to criticize Save America for being involved in Senator Jones's death. About one in ten calls was from news people wanting comments. Everyone had a script for answering questions from the news people. The script wording was that they didn't have any affiliation with Save America and were just a call center. The other eight in ten calls were from people thanking Save America for their efforts, wanting to contribute, or just wanting to state their appreciation. For some, they had already donated online and were calling to say thanks. For others, they wanted to have a person take their credit or debit card information since they didn't trust the internet. It was a mindless task and certainly kept William's mind off the present situation. He took calls as fast as he could and there was always a line waiting. Food was brought to the desk and he continued to work. At five, he walked out back. The call center closed at five. A recorded message then started directing everybody to an automated service or telling them they could call back tomorrow between nine and five eastern time. Although there were still a lot of calls coming in, the staff and volunteers still left at five.

It was time for William's next mindless task, which was cooking dinner. He opened a couple of bottles of red wine and started dinner. Amy had left for the day and left him phone messages and instructions for tomorrow. He turned on the Save America cell phone and checked messages. There were two messages from the FBI. They must have seen the number he left with Senator Jones. It was a throw away phone, so he turned it off and threw it away. He started cooking dinner and tested the wine while he cooked. The other three guys began showing up about five thirty and asked to help. Charlie was first and William asked him to set the table. The kitchen and dining area were connected to the living area, and he could have turned on the sixty inch TV but didn't. He figured he'd watch after dinner.

All four of them sat down for dinner and all were drinking wine. William made tea but there weren't any takers tonight. William started the conversation by asking everybody about their thoughts.

Thomas spoke first, "This has been a strange day. I know you haven't listened to the news but they keep talking about us. They've mentioned that the website was closed down and no one from Save America was answering questions. Our website showing Senator Jones has been on the news all day."

Cal spoke next, "I made a few calls and found out that there was no sign of foul play. An autopsy was conducted today and the FBI is waiting on results. It appears Senator Jones may have died from natural causes."

"That would be good news but we'd still be blamed since we had him on our website." William remembered the allegations against Save America that were made when Congressman Williams was killed.

Charlie was next. "I know it won't make you feel any better but it was a record day for contributions. Between the call center and the automated system, there was over two million contributed today."

"You're right. I'm not sure it makes me feel any better."

William then told Cal he had calls from the FBI before he turned the phone off and tossed it. "Do you think I should return the calls?"

Cal thought for a second and answered, "They're probably from the Washington FBI. I don't think you should talk to them."

"I agree, especially since I don't want to talk to them." William already felt like quitting the venture and didn't need to talk to the FBI. That would probably convince him to do so.

Cal handed out sheets of paper. "I spent the day making a list of all the things we need to do to the building. Thomas also added his items. I thought I'd get the utilities turned on tomorrow and start buying the computers and furniture. We can move ourselves over first and then move the call center."

Cal didn't work at the call center. He didn't feel comfortable doing it so the others didn't push him.

"I'm looking at the option to contract out the call center. It may be a better choice for us." Thomas knew this was the right time to make the change.

William asked, "Do we need the large building in Augusta if we don't include the call center?"

Cal answered, "I could work on my Cobra in the building if we don't have a call center. Maybe we can have a restoration shop. That would be a great front for us and it'd be fun."

Charlie added, "I'd like a place where I could get my cars worked on."

"Let Thomas figure out whether he wants the call center in Augusta. If not, I get all my cars worked on first." William thought that it'd be nice to have a place to work on cars where there's plenty of room.

Discussing a business venture made William think of money. "What are we doing with the contributions, Charlie?"

"I've set up several nonprofit tax-exempt corporations with no paid employees. All of the funds are in these corporations."

"What can we do with the funds?"

"A lot of things. I'll bring a list tomorrow for the dinner meeting. I guess we'll probably use some of the money to buy the building in Augusta."

"Let's talk about that. I'd like to keep our location secret."

One thing William wanted to be sure of was that everything was within the tax system, but he also didn't want to pay taxes on the contributions. They were getting a lot of money donated and maybe it should all go to candidates opposing the fiscally irresponsible representatives. William figured he'd know more tomorrow at dinner.

"I know you'll keep us out of trouble with the IRS but there's a lot of money coming in and we need to be sure we use it within the rules," William advised.

"I'll make sure. I'll research everything thoroughly before we do it."

"I know you will. There's just a lot going on right now. Any more thoughts?"

"I'll keep checking tonight and tomorrow to see if there's any new information on Senator Jones." Cal had already called his contacts and would follow up with them.

"I'm going to the call center tomorrow and will be working some on my own business ventures," William told the others his plan for tomorrow.

"I'll be working on the location of the call center tomorrow. I've already narrowed the list of potentials and hope to make a decision soon." Thomas had already decided to farm out the call center and just wanted to firm up the details before telling the others.

"I'll be here working on the accounting stuff if anybody wants to help," Charlie said, already knowing everybody's answer about helping with the accounting.

The three left as soon as they finished eating and William spent more mindless time in the kitchen cleaning and putting away the leftovers. He nursed his glass of wine while he researched the properties near the building they wanted. William thought the monthly lease was reasonable prior to the closing. He came up with a reasonable offer to buy the building that Cal could present. He expected he'd have a restless evening, especially since Jessie wouldn't be at his house to console him. He liked it better when she spent every night with him. Tonight would have been a welcome night with Senator Jones's death.

Chapter 3

After a sleep deprived night, William was still up early as usual. He wanted to avoid the news but figured he needed to stay informed. He started with CNN Headline News and Senator Jones was still the top story. The Save America website was still prominently displayed along with Senator Jones's picture. None of the Save America principals' names were included and William was relying on Thomas and Cal to keep their identities secret.

Cal called William while he was eating his oatmeal. "I've been checking since last night and there's no new information. The autopsy results aren't public yet."

"Keep me posted. I'll be here working on my own stuff until lunch and then I'll go over to the call center. Have you given any more thought about responding to the FBI?"

"Let's wait until we hear about the autopsy results and then decide."

"You're the expert. Thanks."

William was finishing eating when Amy arrived. She was a little early and said when she came in, "How are you doing? You look like you didn't sleep."

"I didn't sleep much but I'm okay. Maybe a nap later will help."

She knew William didn't take naps and responded, "I'll fix a pallet for you this afternoon."

"Thanks. That would be nice. I'd also like some juice before my nap."

"Any other special requests?"

"None, but I do have a few things you can help with this morning."

"What specifically?"

"I've got a few properties I've been thinking of buying. If you'd research them and give me your opinion, it'd be helpful. I put the list on your desk. The list also includes properties I'm thinking of selling. Could you look at them too?"

"I'll start on them right away."

"I'll be here this morning if you have any questions. I'll probably go to the call center this afternoon."

Amy was actually hired by William to help with all of his investments. He had a lot of rental properties and investment properties. When Save America started, he asked her if she'd help and she agreed. Her job became bigger but she didn't mind.

William did more research on his own while Amy worked on the list. There were a few auctions coming up soon. Normally Amy would be doing it but it helped William to stay busy. He also had several houses being renovated and made a few calls to check on the progress.

William had lunch at home consisting of leftovers. Amy and Charlie partook as well and thought he did a good job heating up the food. Amy and William talked at lunch about the list of properties he gave her. For those they decided to buy and sell, she would take the actions needed to make offers or list the properties. He told her about the upcoming auctions and asked her to do more research.

After lunch, William went to the call center. He found an empty work station and started answering calls. There were a few calls from people who blamed Save America for Senator Jones's death. Most of the calls were from folks wanting to donate and told William that they supported Save America. The donations continued to flow in.

About three o'clock, he answered the phone with the same message, "Thanks for calling the Save America website. Would you like to support our efforts to make America a better place to live?"

The female voice on the other end of the phone said, "We don't want your reward for Senator Jones but we wanted to thank you for your efforts."

She had William's attention quickly when she mentioned the reward on the website.

"Do you have information about Senator Jones?"

She responded, "I know what happened to him."

"So you've seen the autopsy report?"

"No. I know what happened to him because I helped him die."

William figured it was a crank call and decided to try to end the call as quickly as possible. He was already stressed out enough and didn't need someone pulling his chain.

"Thank you for calling and giving us your support. We're very busy today so I need to get to other callers."

"Don't you want to know what happened to him?"

"I do and I'll wait for the autopsy report. Thanks again for calling." William was now sure it was a crank call.

"We killed Senator Jones."

William was a little sarcastic when he said, "I'm sure you did. Thanks again for calling."

She spoke louder, "He raped us when we were his interns fifteen years ago. We've been waiting until now to get back at him."

Another female voice came on the phone. "We've been planning this for years and it's unfortunate that it happened while he was on your website."

"Are you just stirring up trouble?" He was ready to hang up the phone and go home. It'd been a long day.

The first woman answered, "No. We're telling you the truth. We've waited fifteen years and the opportunity presented itself so we took advantage of it."

William asked when he should have just hung up, "Why didn't you report him fifteen years ago?"

"We didn't think anyone would believe us. He was a powerful Senator. We went to his beach house voluntarily and the Senator and his staffers would just say it was voluntary sex."

"Why didn't you go to a hospital?"

The second woman answered, "We were scared and he kept us in the beach house for two extra days. We both grew up in poor families and didn't comprehend the situation. We did quit as interns right away and vowed to get back at the Senator."

"So why did you wait fifteen years?"

The first woman responded, "It took fifteen years to get in the positions we're in."

"I don't understand." William was actually confused and couldn't comprehend why they waited fifteen years if their story was true.

The second woman said, "We've probably told you enough."

Now he wanted to know more. "I'm now very confused. Tell me how the Senator died." He hoped they wanted to talk more. They must have wanted someone to know if the story is true.

The first woman said, "That's enough for now. We'll call back later."

"When?"

"We don't know."

"When you call back, ask for Jeremy."

"We will," they answered in unison and they ended the call.

William sat still for a long time and stared at the other people in the room. He looked at his call log and confirmed that he'd written down the call time and short summary. He'd check later to see if there was a phone number associated with the call. He suspected there wouldn't be. The light on his call center phone was blinking alerting him there were other callers waiting. He waited another couple of minutes and then started answering calls again. The callers were primarily people who wanted to donate but there were a few critics. He was polite to all the callers.

At five, William left the call center and headed home. He was cooking for the others and needed to get started. Cooking would take his mind off of the day's occurrences.

William opened a bottle of wine and poured a full glass. Dinner was in the fridge and he began the preparations. He had decided earlier to wait until the others arrived for dinner before discussing the women and Senator Jones. He didn't look forward to the discussion. He was sure they didn't want to hear the discussion either. Dinner was chicken breasts with salsa, rice, and mixed vegetables. William also made a mixed green salad.

Charlie arrived first and said as he came through the door, "Something smells good. I need wine."

"The wine's in the fridge." William actually matched the wine to the food tonight although usually he didn't care.

Thomas came in next and filled a glass of wine and Cal was right behind him. The three of them left William alone finishing the meal and went to the living area. Charlie turned on CNN and the first news was about Senator Jones. The Save America website was also shown. William stopped watching and concentrated on the food. He set the table and told the group it was time to eat. He also asked that the TV be turned off. He was depressed enough and didn't need to ruin his dinner. The four of them sat in their usual places and filled their salad bowls while also filling their plates.

Cal was first to speak, "I did more research on the property in Augusta. There's a security system already installed and it only needs a little work to meet our needs. We'll need to have a system that has zones we can control. Our offices will be in one zone. The call center will be in another one and the other offices will be in a third."

Thomas spoke next, "I'm probably going to farm out most of the call center and don't need the whole space."

"Maybe we can have a smaller call center and a car business too. I don't want anyone to steal my Cobra so we'll have zones for the call center and the cars." Cal wanted a car business.

"What about the perimeter?" William poured more wine in his glass.

"The system will cover the perimeter. The entrance gate is already coded. I don't think we'll need a security guard since that would make us look suspicious."

This was the most talking Cal had done. William guessed he was in his zone when he was talking about security. He was thinking he needed better security at his house if anyone found out he was part of Save America.

"When can the security system be changed for our needs?"

"I can have the system ready in a week. I called the company that installed the system and they can come out this week to modify it for us. They'll also do the monitoring for a reasonable monthly fee. I'd prefer the security system call our phones rather than a subscription service."

"Unless someone objects, Cal can get the security system installed this week. You can have the system call my phone too." William assumed Cal would have the system call his phone.

The four of them were all outspoken so someone would speak up if they objected to Cal handling the security system this week.

"Did you find out anything about Senator Jones's autopsy?" William was more interested now after the conversation with the two women.

"Not yet. I made several calls today but didn't find out anything. I'll keep trying tonight and tomorrow."

"Let us know what you find out," William said and then looked at Charlie. "What about our finances?"

Charlie handed out copies of a spreadsheet. "The sheet I handed out shows the different nonprofit companies I've created and the funds in each. The totals include all funds up to two days ago. The last two days brought in a lot of donations and I'll have new totals at the end of the week. The building in Augusta will be a separate company from the company we're using for the call center. If we start a car business, I'll set up a for-profit business."

"What are the chances anyone will figure out the for-profit business is tied to Save America?" William wanted to ensure the principals for Save America couldn't be tracked down through a for-profit car business.

"There's always a chance, but it'd be pretty slim."

William looked at Thomas. "What kind of call center will you have in Augusta?"

"I'll farm out everything except for a small call center in the Augusta building that we can man and maybe have a few employees. I expect that eventually a small call center is all that we'll need. I'd like to set it up as a rented business space separate from the car business and us. I'm thinking we'll probably need a corporation that owns the building and then leases out all the space. That'll make it harder to trace it to us. Charlie and I can work on it. The corporation can be the car business so it's not connected to Save America."

"Can this be done in a week?"

"I think it can, except for closing down the Aiken call center. I'd like to give everybody a two-week notice. If there's no objection, I'll start tomorrow. The farmed out call center and the Augusta building should be ready in about two weeks."

"You agree, Charlie?" William asked.

"Yes. I can set up everything up with the businesses."

"I researched the building and drew up a contract to present to the Augusta real estate agent. It's a reasonable offer so it should be accepted. The building has been vacant for a while, so that should help. Cal can present it tomorrow. It also includes a lease that allows us to add nonstructural items until we close on the building. Charlie needs to come up with a name and create the corporation that owns the building. I left the name blank on the contract so it can be added." William handed copies of the contract to the other three.

Save America was moving fast and it looked like there'd be no turning back. Soon Save America would own a building in Augusta, have offices in Augusta, and would have a car business. William was looking forward to the car business.

William continued, "I have another topic. I manned the phones this afternoon and had the usual positive calls and some negative calls. There was one call that disturbed me. There were a couple of women that called today that said they killed Senator Jones. They said the Senator raped them when they were interns with the Senator about fifteen years ago, and they had planned to get even with him. I don't know if it was a crank call or not. I haven't had time to research their claim about the rape."

"Did they give you any clues about who they were?" Cal asked.

"They didn't other than they said it happened when they were interns."

"Did you believe them?"

William thought about the conversation with the women. "They sounded believable but they could have easily been lying. It could've been just a ruse."

"Did they say how they killed the Senator?"

"No."

"Did they tell you where they lived?"

"No."

"Did they tell you what kind of work they did?"

"No."

"Did they tell you where the Senator raped them?"

"At the Senator's beach house."

Cal kept asking questions and William kept answering. William knew Cal was trying to decide if he could be charged with aiding and abetting. William certainly didn't know so he was depending on Cal to advise him.

When he stopped asking questions, William asked, "Do I need to call the FBI and tell them what I heard?"

"Let's wait for the autopsy results. If it's determined that it's a homicide then you should call. If not, we'll assume the call from the women was a prank."

"Can you see if you can find out anything about the Senator raping a couple of women? I'll research the internet, but you may have better resources."

"I will," Cal answered.

"Have you thought anymore about responding to the calls from the FBI? We had more calls today."

"Let's wait until the autopsy results. If it's a homicide, we'll have to answer questions in person, although I'd prefer not."

They didn't talk any more business and finished dinner. Dessert was another glass of wine. The website was still down, but the Save America website was still being discussed on TV along with the

Senator. One day at a time was all that William and the others could do for now. William continued to be apprehensive about the Save America venture and would probably have another restless night of sleep, if he slept at all. He checked his wallet to see if he had ten dollars to pay Thomas if he quit tomorrow. He needed Jessie to help him sleep.

Chapter 4

The talking head on CNN the next morning told William and the world that the Senator had died of natural causes. The Senator was suffering from congestive heart failure and was being treated by area physicians. One of his physicians made a house call the evening before due to the Senator's chest pains. The physician gave the Senator medication and left him for the evening. The autopsy showed that the Senator had died of a heart failure while he slept. The talking head failed to mention that Save America couldn't be blamed for the Senator's demise.

As William was watching the news, Cal called. "Are you watching the news?"

"I am. Is there anything not being said?"

"The talking head didn't mention the alcohol and cocaine in the Senator's blood. He also didn't mention a young woman in his bed. The Senator's wife was out of town."

"How do you know about the alcohol, the cocaine, and the woman?"

"There was a leak and I found out as the information flowed."

"So the case will be closed quickly to avoid further scandal?"

"I suspect it will. I'll keep in touch." Cal hung up.

Thomas called while William was on the phone with Charlie, so he made it a three way call. They discussed the autopsy results and how they were all relieved.

Before he hung up, William said, "I'll see you tonight."

He started thinking about the two women after talking to Thomas and Charlie. He tried to recall the conversation and remembered them saying that the opportunity came up and they had to take it. William thought of two logical choices. One was that the young woman that spent the night killed the Senator and the second choice was the physician killed the Senator. Since the alleged rapes by the Senator occurred about fifteen years ago, the women would probably be in their thirties. Compared to the Senator, the woman who spent the night could be considered young if she was in her thirties. This seemed more logical than a woman physician in her thirties who was the Senator's heart doctor.

William called Cal. "Did you hear who the woman was that spent the night?"

"No, I didn't."

"Can you find out?"

"If she isn't on the news in a day or two, I can probably find out but it may cost a buck or two."

"How about the Senator's physician who made the house call?"

"I suspect the news folks will find out today and do an interview with the physician."

"You're probably right. I'll wait to see."

"Which woman do you think called you?"

"I don't know. Both could be candidates, assuming the physician is a woman in her thirties. I'll see you at dinner."

William had gotten up early. He wished Jessie was with him so his morning would start out on a good note. He called Jessie instead. He knew she'd be up early with her parents.

"Good morning. What's with the phone call so early?" Jessie was actually up very early tending to her father who was having some discomfort.

"The autopsy for the Senator was released this morning and he died of natural causes." William was in the kitchen pouring a cup of coffee. His stress level had reduced significantly after hearing the good news about the Senator.

Jessie knew all about the Senator and the need to hear about the autopsy. William had kept her abreast of all the concerns with the Senator, including the call from the women yesterday.

"I'm sure you're relieved. I assume you talked to the others this morning." Jessie was sitting with her cup of coffee after the long night tending to her father.

"Yes." William sighed.

"Now what are you going to do?" Jessie asked.

"I don't know exactly. I guess we'll decide tonight when we get together."

"I'll stop by tonight and could be convinced to stay the night. It does depend on my dad's condition."

"That'd be wonderful if you can." He knew Jessie could reduce his stress further.

William really didn't know what he would do now. The past couple of weeks had been hectic. He didn't know what would happen with the FBI. He figured he'd stay busy today with his own business ventures and then go back to Augusta to look at the building again.

When Amy came in, they discussed the Senator's autopsy results and the plans for the Augusta building. William then went over a list of things they could do today for his business ventures. Thomas, Charlie, and Cal had also emailed her some items that they needed help with. William did an internet search to see if he could find out about the mystery woman in the Senator's bed or find anything about the Senator's heart doctor. He didn't find out either from the search but CNN found the doctor for him.

Charlie called and told him to turn on CNN. When he did, a reporter was interviewing a woman that looked to be in her thirties. He kept listening and found out she was the Senator's heart doctor. Her voice sounded familiar and he suspected she was one of the women who called yesterday.

William stayed busy until lunch and then went to Augusta to look at the building again. The Augusta building was unlocked when he got there. Cal's vehicle was parked in front and a security company's truck was parked beside his truck. William walked around the lot and checked the fencing. The fence was an eight foot chain link fence, and it was in good condition. The top of the fence had barbed wire. The lot was a mixture of concrete and gravel with only a couple of trees in a back corner. Two picnic tables were under the trees. The tables had grayed with age and the wood had splits, which was probably the reason the last tenants left the tables.

William paid more attention to the details inside the building. He had been remodeling houses and commercial buildings for a long time and started making a list of things he would recommend. The large open area would need to be divided to set up a call center and car repair area. A new entrance would need to be added for the call center to make it look like a separate leased area. Although the car business had an acceptable entrance, the area needed to have a better separation from the offices the five of them would use.

After making a few sketches and making a list of materials that was needed, he called one of the contractors that he used on his houses. The contractor answered the phone, which was somewhat unusual since he was a busy contractor.

After the contractor said hello to William in his southern drawl, William said, "Hey John. I've got a quick project I need done and wanted to check your schedule." If John was too busy to help, William would go down his list until he hopefully found a contractor who could help.

"One of my jobs just got delayed due to a funding issue so I can help. What's the job?"

"I bought a commercial building and need to modify it to accommodate tenants. All of the work is interior except for a new entrance. I expect you could do it in a week. Can you come and look at it now?"

"I was just going out for lunch so I'll stop by."

William told him the location and John said he'd show up in about twenty minutes. William did a more exact estimate of the materials and made a few marks on the floor where he thought a new wall would go. William had a builder's license in South Carolina but he couldn't use it in Georgia. John would have to use his license if he thought a building permit was needed.

John arrived and William went over the planned changes for the building. The security rep had left so William brought Cal over to listen and to give his opinion. John had a few suggestions and Cal agreed with the changes.

William asked, "When can you start?"

"Tomorrow morning if you can get materials."

"I'll have materials here. Do we need a permit?"

"We're working inside so I don't plan to get a permit."

John didn't exactly answer the question and William didn't pursue it. John left and William went over the list of materials again to ensure he hadn't missed anything. Cal said the security company would start tomorrow as well. It now looked like William's next few days would be spent in Augusta. William took his list to an area building supply store. They priced everything and scheduled it for delivery tomorrow morning.

The Save America venture continued to move at a fast pace. It seemed like yesterday that Thomas and William had made the ten dollar bet and started the website. William was still wondering whether it was such a great idea. One Congressman and one Senator were dead and William still wasn't sure the website was absent of blame. The Congressman's death was ruled an accident and the Senator died of natural causes. William still had the uneasy feeling that they were in over their heads.

William decided on steaks for dinner with vegetables and a salad. He started the grill and had it hot when the other three arrived. He was drinking beer and the others decided on beer as well. He put the steaks on the grill with Montreal steak seasoning sprinkled on top. All wanted their steaks cooked medium rare so William put all the steaks on the grill at the same time. It was still daylight while he was cooking. There were lots of clouds in the sky that were slowly moving. Darker clouds were behind the white clouds. A spring storm appeared to be on the way. The azaleas and dogwoods were blooming in the yard and he mentally reminded himself to turn off the sprinkler so they wouldn't come on in the morning. The wind was starting to pick up as he finished the steaks. A roof on one of the rental houses was repaired today so the rain tonight would be a test of the repair.

While he was outside, the table had been set and they sat down to eat their dinner. They talked about sports for a few minutes while they ate. Charlie changed the TV from CNN to music.

William started the discussion first tonight after he handed out copies of his sketches for the Augusta building.

"I met with a contractor at the building today and he'll start tomorrow. As shown in the sketch, a new entrance will be installed and a divider wall will be added in the large space. A hallway will be added so the bathrooms can be accessed by everyone. Eventually, we can add additional bathrooms but the existing bathrooms will be sufficient for now. Better doors will be added in the back where our offices are located and a hall will be added to the rear exit. A more secure door will be added for the basement for our storage. A dropped ceiling with lighting will be added to the call center area along with additional electrical outlets and wiring for the computers. We already have a full kitchen and the large room will be our conference room. We can have dinners in Augusta instead of here."

They discussed the changes and everyone agreed after a few small modifications. William would revise the sketches tonight and have it ready for John in the morning. John and William had worked together for a long time, and John could work from William's sketches.

William decided to postpone the discussion about the physician until the end, so he asked Cal to give them an update. Cal said the security company would start tomorrow and they should finish in a couple of days. He also said the offer for the building was accepted.

Charlie spoke next and said that he and Amy had worked on the corporations today and had made much progress. He said he picked a name for the for-profit corporation for the purchase of the building.

Thomas told us he had given everyone at the call center their notice. He talked to other call centers in the area and arranged for representatives to interview personnel for their call centers. He said that he finished the contract with the farmed-out call center and training would begin tomorrow. He expected the farmed-out call center could start taking calls by the end of the week. Thomas went on to say that computers and furniture would be delivered to the Augusta building in two days.

William asked, "Are we going to hire anybody to man the call center in the Augusta building?"

"Not to start with. I thought we'd take calls ourselves to make sure the setup works. I figured we would see how the other call center works and then decide how many people to hire in Augusta."

William said, "That sounds like a workable plan. There are two other subjects. One is the Senator's physician and the second is the website. Let's talk about the Senator's physician first."

Cal spoke, "CNN had the Senator's physician on the network this morning and her name is Diana Christopher. I researched her and found out she's thirty four years old and she was an intern for the Senator fifteen years ago. There was another female intern fifteen years ago by the name of Angela Thompson. They were interns for one summer when they were freshmen in college. I couldn't find any complaints that were filed against the Senator as far as I could tell, and they didn't miss any school time. I called Diana's mother and interviewed her. I pretended to be from CNN. The mother stated that she had interned for the Senator and Diana told her she had a great time as an intern for the Senator."

William asked, "What should we do next?"

"I think you should call Angela and Diana."

"What kind of work does Angela do?"

"Both are physicians. Diana is a heart doctor and Angela is a neurosurgeon."

"So both are smart women?" William figured they had to be since they were doctors.

"They were at the top of their class."

"Do you have their phone numbers?" William asked.

Cal slipped William a sheet of paper with the office numbers for both women.

"I'll call tomorrow. Now let's talk about the website and the next Congressman or Senator to be posted."

Thomas spoke, "The next one is Congressman Randolph. I've already created the webpage for him and the reasons he was chosen to the website." He handed out copies of the webpage.

"When should we make the website live again?" William finished his bottle of beer and walked to the fridge for another one.

The opinions varied among the group and a consensus was finally reached that it'd go live again at the end of the week. William and the others now had lots planned for the week. It would be a busy week. This time next week they would have offices in Augusta.

"Anybody have anything else?" William looked around the room at the other three.

No one responded. The week so far had everybody weary.

When Jessie came, William was downstairs in the exercise room working off his week of stress. She had her typical black attire on. Her long black hair was tied in a ponytail showing her smooth complexion.

She walked up to him while he was on the treadmill. "Do you want to spar a little? Maybe that'll help you relieve some tension."

"Sure. Promise to be easy on me."

"I will. I know how to leave bruises where no one can see them."

William kissed her passionately. "Change and I'll be waiting." William now had two ways he knew Jessie could relieve his stress.

Jessie changed in the bathroom. She left clothes at William's house for her workouts. William kept his sweats on.

William had a large area covered in mats for sparring. Jessie came out in her sweats and stretched. William stretched with her.

They started slow with a few easy kicks and punches. She picked up the pace, and William kept up with her and blocked her kicks and punches. He let her take him to the mat and then worked himself back to his feet. She was very quick and she always gave William a good workout. They were sparring for about thirty minutes when

William let her take him down again. This time William flipped her over and kissed her with more passion. She stopped trying to roll him off after he continued kissing her.

They showered together in the exercise room shower and went to the bedroom dressed only in towels. William was still aroused when he went to bed and Jessie aroused him more. He let her pin him to the bed and didn't try to get up or flip her. This night was better than the previous two and he actually slept. He thought having Jessie spend the night was great for him.

When Jessie's mother was in the hospital, William told her mother that Jessie and he would be getting married. It started out as a way to cheer up her mother, and now he thought it needed to happen. Her mother and William had planned for a wedding to occur after Jessie's father was released from the hospital and could attend. Jessie's father was now out of the hospital but still needed assistance to get to physical therapy and to move around.

At breakfast, William told Jessie, "Tell your mother I'll be over soon to finish planning the wedding."

"She asks me several times a week when you're coming over. I told her you were involved with a new business venture. I didn't tell her it was Save America."

William turned on CNN as Jessie was dressing. The Save America website wasn't mentioned and there were no phone calls from the other three. Jessie and William left together as William was going to the Augusta building. He needed to unlock the gate for the delivery of materials and for John and his crew. He also brought his tools in case he wanted to do some work.

John and his crew arrived before the materials and began unloading all their tools and equipment. The materials arrived shortly afterward and were unloaded on the dock. William gave John his sketches and they started laying out the walls and the location of the new entrance. Before long, there was progress being made.

William went back to one of the offices away from the noise and took out the sheet of paper with the phone numbers for Angela and Diana. He called Angela first and got the receptionist for the office.

He left his number with a message that he was returning a call from Angela and Diana. He did the same at Diana's office. He figured they'd understand who he was if both got the same phone message.

William talked to Amy a few times as she was working on his business ventures while also helping the others. She reminded William that a couple of auctions were ending tomorrow, and he needed to sign up and make a deposit today. William had his iPad so he took the time to sign up and make the required deposits. At lunch, he visited the two houses and determined his maximum bid amount. He would set a limit and wouldn't get caught in a bidding war. There'd always be more houses auctioned off and his goal was to make a profit. He also went by a couple of houses being renovated to check on the status. He had been doing a lot of the work himself until Save America was started, and now he was contracting most of the work. So Save America was indirectly costing him money.

There was lots of progress on the Augusta building during the day. The security company showed up and started running wires and installing detectors. By the end of the day, walls and a new entrance were installed. Sheetrock was in place with the first coat of mud. John had brought a bigger crew than William expected. He took pictures and emailed them to his email account. He planned to print them out for the evening meal.

John's crew left at five and William headed home. He started dinner as soon as he got home. At dinner, he showed the others the pictures of the building renovations and told them he'd called the two physicians but hadn't gotten a response.

Cal talked about the status of the security system, Thomas talked about the status of the call center and computers for the Augusta building, and Charlie talked about the corporate documents. All of them had progress to report.

Chapter 5

In Washington, D.C., Angela and Diana were having dinner together at a favorite spot.

Angela said, "I got a call from a Jeremy who said he was returning a call from you and me. I expect it's the Save America guy we talked to."

"I had the same call today. What do you want to do?" said Diana.

Angela sat quietly for a short while and finally said, "I suggest we call him back. He now knows who we are, and he probably researched us."

"Do you think he'll call the FBI?"

"I don't think so. He wouldn't have called us if he planned to call the FBI."

"So what do you suggest?" Diana quizzed.

"I think we should talk to him," Angela responded.

"When?"

"Tonight."

"I agree. The sooner the better and we can see what he wants. What do you think he wants?"

"I don't know. We'll see shortly."

"We'll use your cell phone in case the FBI has mine tapped."

The others had left and William was cleaning the kitchen. His next throw-away cell phone that Thomas had given him to call Diana and

Angela rang. He looked at the number and saw it was a Washington, D.C., area code.

"Hello." William turned off the water to the kitchen sink.

A woman said, "Is this Jeremy who called at the office today?"

"Yes." William could tell they were on a speaker phone so he figured both were listening. "Is Angela there too?"

Diana answered, "We're both here."

"Thanks for calling me back."

Angela said, "You're welcome. How can we help you?"

"Did we talk the other day?"

"I'm quite sure we didn't." Diana and Angela had decided to avoid admitting to the earlier call.

William thought he should select his words carefully and should have prepared for the phone call. William knew they had talked and wondered why he called them. William wondered why he called them too.

"First I wanted to say I'm sorry for what happened to you the summer you were interns. I know it was traumatic and I'm sure it was hard to get over it, especially since you couldn't tell anyone. I'm sure your time as interns left a terrible mark."

William wanted to show them that he knew some of the details so that he could create a conversation. As he was talking, he was thinking and decided the real reason he called them was to reassure them that he wasn't planning to talk about the previous conversation to the authorities.

He continued, "I now understand what you meant when you said the opportunity presented itself. I wanted to let you know that we are very sympathetic and won't discuss our calls with anyone."

Angela asked, "Who's we?"

"There are four of us. Actually, there are five with my administrative assistant. Two of us had this cockamamie idea that we could have an influence on the way things were going in Washington. The main thing we've influenced so far is our sanity. I'm thinking I should just stop this crazy idea."

"You do have a weird business model, but my money says you'll make a difference. You're talked about in my office, and you're starting to let them see how mismanaged our government is," Diana spoke this time.

"Thanks for those thoughts."

Diana continued, "You need to encourage people to call, email, and mail their Congressmen and Senators. America is at the point where there needs to be a civil war against our federal government."

Angela added, "I agree with Diana. If something doesn't change, we'll be another bankrupt country just like Greece and others."

"Thanks for the pep talk. I needed it after the past couple of weeks."

"Thanks for taking the time and effort to understand us and thanks for your efforts to change our government. Maybe after some time goes by, we'd like to meet you," Angela said.

"I'd like to meet you as well. I'll leave another message in a month or two."

Angela said, "Goodbye, Jeremy."

Diana said, "Goodbye and keep at it."

The women hung up and William left the phone to his ear for a few moments. He thought it'd be great to meet them.

After they hung up the phone, Diana looked pensive. "Jeremy seems like a nice guy. I hope he continued his efforts with Save America."

"I hope so but I expect there'll be lots of obstacles along the way." Angela sighed and was now more contented knowing Jeremy wasn't planning to tell anybody about their first call.

"I'd like to call him every week to encourage him. I remember when you called me often fifteen years ago to keep me sane." The conversation with William made her remember the events with the Senator fifteen years ago.

"I called you fifteen years ago to keep me sane."

Angela continued, "I keep wondering whether we should have called Save America in the first place."

"I'm not sure, but it made me feel better to tell someone. We've been planning this for a long time." Diana thought about how it felt not telling anybody about being raped by the Senator.

"Do you think he'll eventually tell the authorities?" Angela asked.

"I don't think so."

"Are you sure? I keep thinking we made a mistake." Angela was a little insecure while Diana was very confident. One of Angela's strengths was her ability to plan. Her insecurity helped because she worried about each detail. For this reason, Diana had confidence in the plan with the Senator.

Angela was the same height as Diana at five feet seven inches tall but had dark brown hair and a darker complexion than Diana. Diana had blonde hair and a fair complexion. Both had bangs and shoulder length hair which was not curled. Both were trim and fit, primarily due to the workouts they did together each week. Both became physicians and lived and worked in Washington, D.C. It was by good fortune that Senator Jones had become Diana's patient. Diana had purposely taken a job with a heart doctor who had the Senator as a patient. When the Senator's heart doctor retired, Diana became his heart doctor. The Senator hadn't recognized Diana and was actually glad to have a woman as his doctor. The Senator even made passes and flirted with Diana, which Diana made jokes about to the Senator. She really knew he was serious.

During a workout session, Diana mentioned to Angela that Senator Jones was now her patient. Angela thought about it during the session and asked Diana to discuss it after the workout when they got home.

When they were home, Angela asked, "Now that our beloved Senator is your patient, when do we get even for the past?"

After a minute to think, Diana responded, "I think it should be soon. His heart is in bad shape, and he may die of natural causes before our revenge."

"He'll probably live longer than us as mean as he is, but the sooner the better. What do you suggest we do?"

"I know of a drug that will make his heart race and will most likely result in a fatal heart attack. That's my first choice. There are other ways but I prefer the drug."

"How do we get him to take it?"

"I don't know that. I can't give it to him in my office and that's the only place I see him."

"Can you get him to invite you to his house?" Angela knew the answer already.

Diana snickered. "He'd invite me if I agreed. It'd probably be his beach house. I certainly don't want to go to his beach house with him."

"Let me think about it to see what I can come up with. Do you want me to get the drug?"

"That would be great, just in case an opportunity presents itself," Diana responded.

Diana and Angela didn't discuss the Senator for a few weeks. Diana hadn't seen the Senator, and he wasn't due back for an office visit for another three weeks. They worked out and had dinner several times when their schedules matched up. They didn't talk about the Senator in public. Neither Diana nor Angela were married and weren't dating. Their careers had taken top priority. They rented a condo together and neither planned to stay in Washington, D.C., for much longer.

At home, after one of their workouts, Angela handed Diana a plain paper bag. "This is the drug for the Senator. I've thought about it and there are extra pills. I was thinking that the extra pills should be left with the Senator so they can be found. He's probably still a drug user."

"Thanks, but I don't know when there's going to be chance to use them."

"Should I figure out a way for the Senator to invite me to a motel?" Angela suggested.

"You wouldn't do that if you had the opportunity. You hate the Senator as much as I do."

"You're right. I wouldn't."

Both Diana and Angela had gone to the Senator's beach house as naive interns expecting a nice weekend with sunning on the beach, swimming in the ocean, and lots of good food. They hadn't expected the Senator to force them to take drugs and demand participation in a nightly orgy. Two other girls Diana and Angela hadn't met before were there as willing drug and orgy participants. Diana and Angela became unwilling participants.

Their cell phones and handbags were taken from them shortly after they arrived and the girls were locked in an upstairs bedroom for five days. At the end of the fifth day, they found the bedroom door unlocked and they found no one in the house except for them. Their cell phones and handbags were on the kitchen counter. Several hundred dollars was in two envelopes next to each handbag. They took a taxi to the bus station and didn't come back to Washington, D.C., until they were physicians. Their summer internship was just about over and the Senator knew they would be leaving soon anyway.

There were probably several other women that took the taxi ride to the bus station. Diana and Angela never told anyone else about their days and nights at the Senator's beach house.

Fifteen years later, the opportunity for revenge did arrive when Diana was called to Senator Jones's house due to the Senator's chest pains. Diana made the house call after going past the TV vans and found the Senator in terrible pain. She gave him medicine, including the drug provided to her by Angela. The Senator was feeling better when she left. The Senator had refused to go to the hospital. Diana was sure the TV vans outside as a result of the Save America website probably influenced the Senator's decision.

Chapter 6

The week went by with the Augusta building modifications completed, the computers and furniture installed, and Cal's Cobra moved into the shop. Cal had also moved tool chests into the shop. Charlie had completed all the legal documents and the call center was now a combination of being farmed out and the Aiken call center. Many of the employees of the Aiken call center had already taken new jobs with other call centers or found other jobs.

Amy was told to report to the Augusta building on Monday morning. This was actually closer to her home so she didn't mind. All of William's rent checks and payments were coming into an Aiken post office box so she would need to get a post office box in Augusta and inform all the renters and others.

William wanted to check out the call center in the Augusta building to see how it worked with the other two call centers. He was sure Thomas had planned it well but he needed to see for himself.

The four of them didn't meet on weekends and the Aiken call center was closed on the weekends. Thomas had set up the farmed-out call center to handle calls on the weekend. It was Sunday night and William was sitting on the patio by the pool with a beer. Jessie was coming soon. The sky was clear and he could see the moon and stars. He made a mental list of things he needed to do on Monday. He prioritized the list since he knew he couldn't get it all done in one day.

Jessie joined William on the patio with a beer. William thought the sky seemed to brighten up when Jessie sat beside him. He also thought the birds seemed to be chirping louder. They sat for a long time talking about the past week. William thought his week obviously trumped her week. Jessie was only staying for a short time so they just talked. William would need to manage sleep without her. Jessie left after a passionate goodbye kiss, which would help keep William awake.

Monday morning came and William went to the Augusta building. He hadn't gone to an office, other than the one in his house, in years. Amy was there already and had started organizing her office. He helped her carry files in from the vehicles. They moved all the files from William's home office.

Cal came in next and started getting his office set up. Thomas and Charlie came in a little later. Thomas helped hook up the computers. He had a network configured so that all could share printers. It took a couple of hours to get set in the offices.

At about ten a.m., Thomas came into William's office and said he was turning on the website with Congressman Randolph as the latest person who was being identified as the most fiscally irresponsible House of Representatives member. They decided to include the two million-dollar offer for any group or individual who helped remove the Congressman from the house. The additional explanation was included to state that it involved only the next election. They didn't need any confusion to lead someone to believe it was a hit fee. William knew about hit money in his past life and he knew two million dollars would be a very tempting hit fee.

Amy had lunch for everyone and they met in the conference room for the first time at noon. Lunch was subs. Amy joined them for lunch and the meeting.

Thomas spoke first, "The network is working fine and I've set up a drive where we can share documents. I've emailed each of you the link. The website is back up with Congressman Randolph as the main character."

Cal spoke next, "The security system was working fine this morning. I'd like to start looking for a mechanic to work on our cars, starting with my Cobra, of course."

"When we get a mechanic, I want to start bringing my vehicles in. All of them need work." William thought a mechanic could be useful.

Charlie was next and he handed out a spreadsheet with last week's contributions and the totals so far.

"As you can see from the spreadsheet, last week was a good week for contributions. The spreadsheet also shows the expenses so far. Cash was loaned to our for-profit corporation to buy this building. The bottom line was that there's about thirty million dollars in our accounts."

William said, "We need to look at ways to use the contributions. There are elections this fall for Congress so one choice is to make contributions to campaigns. Another is to run our own ads. I talked to the physicians in Washington, D.C., and they suggested we encourage folks to call, email, or mail their representative. I'd like to add that option to our website. How hard would it be to add it?"

"There are other websites that already do it like AARP, so I can use their examples. I'll put a few suggestions together," Thomas responded.

Charlie added, "I think that we should ask everyone to call, email, or mail Congressman Randolph. That would put more pressure on one individual at a time and may work better."

"I agree." It was quiet for a minute and William continued, "Let's plan to have lunch meetings this week at noon and not have evening dinner meetings."

No one objected.

Amy asked, "When will you call Congressman Randolph?"

William thought for a minute and then answered, "I think we should wait a few days. If we start a call, email, and mail campaign directed at the Congressman, we may want to wait longer since he'll get more pressure to talk to me."

William left for most of the afternoon checking on the two properties he purchased last week. As he was leaving, he saw Cal working on his Cobra and was jealous. William visited the two new houses and checked on the houses being remodeled. It was four thirty when he got back to the office. Cal was interviewing a mechanic. William didn't know how Cal had an interviewee so quickly and didn't ask. Amy was finishing for the day and getting ready to leave. William went to his office and found several documents on his desk to be reviewed and signed. One was an offer for a few of the lots he owned and others were lease agreements and listing agreements.

Cal came to the office door and said he hired a mechanic and now needed to buy equipment. William told him he'd start bringing his vehicles in tomorrow and get a ride home. Cal also said he'd found a couple of older cars that they should buy and fix up. William told him to bring the details to the noon meeting tomorrow and also the list of equipment the mechanic needed. It looked like they would now need a separate car business meeting and a separate Save America meeting. Save America would need to provide another loan to the car business to get it started. William made a note to have Charlie set up the second loan. Amy would need to start keeping minutes for each business. It was time to add more formality, especially since they were using nonprofit funds for a for-profit business.

William put the signed documents back on Amy's desk, left about six, and got home about six thirty. It was still light outside and warm. He mowed the yard and sprayed weeds. He cleaned out the car he was driving tomorrow so that the mechanic could work on it. The car needed a new clutch and the turbo was acting funny. It appeared to be a wiring problem but William hadn't found time to check it out himself. He didn't have the diagnostic equipment needed for the new cars either. He was sure that was the equipment Cal was talking about.

William didn't go to the office the next morning and stayed home to work out. He called Jessie as she was on her way to work. He caught her up on the Augusta building, the car business, and his houses. She told him about the murder case she was working on. He got to the office about ten and Amy had more work for him.

At eleven, his Save America cell phone rang and it was a call from the Washington, D.C., area code. He answered and it was Diana.

"I just wanted to call and tell you to keep up the good work. You seemed a little depressed last week, and I want you to know that Angela and I support you."

"That's very nice of you. You've made my day."

"I've got to get back to work. I'll call and check on you next week."

William thought about it for a few minutes and couldn't believe Diana took time to call him. He thought that it was very nice. He actually expected never to hear from them again.

At the noon meeting, Amy had salads with grilled chicken. William hoped it wasn't a clue that he needed to lose weight. He told the group that they would have two meetings and the first would be the car business.

Before William started the meeting, Amy said to turn on CNN. There was a TV located in the conference room and Thomas switched it on. Everybody got their salads and watched as a reporter on the TV was interviewing Congressman Randolph on a golf course. They listened to the reporter's interview.

The reporter asked the Congressman, "What are your thoughts about being on Save America as the most fiscally irresponsible House of Representatives member?"

"I'm sure nobody pays attention to it," the Congressman answered.

"Are you aware that two people, Congressman Williams and Senator Jones, who were on the website, are now dead?" asked the reporter.

"I understand Congressman Williams's death was an accident and Senator Jones's death was from natural causes."

"The Save America website has your voting record and it shows that you aren't fiscally responsible. What are your comments about the information on the website?"

"I'm sure the website has their information wrong. I believe in the United States of America and believe the United States of America is the greatest country on earth. All my votes are in support of the United States of America." The Congressman had resorted to his speech lingo so the reporter moved to another subject.

"I understand your trip to Florida was for a tour of a defense contract plant. Why are you on a golf course?" the reporter inquired.

The Congressman hesitated a few moments while he was thinking of an answer. He finally responded, "The golf outing was part of the agenda for the tour of the plant."

The reporter had found out about the other tee times and tennis court times from the starter and tennis pro shop. The reporter said, "I understand you have tee times for the rest of the week and tennis court times scheduled. When were you planning to tour the plant?"

The Congressman responded quickly this time, "I'm sure my staff made a mistake with my schedule."

A Washington, D.C., reporter, Bill Webber, had found out that the Congressman had flown down to Florida on a charter plane charged to the federal government and told the reporter in Florida. The Florida reporter asked, "I understand this trip to Florida was paid for by the taxpayers. How can you justify having the taxpayers pay for your golf and tennis trip?"

The Congressman answered, "I'm in Florida on federal government business. I'm sorry but there'll be no more questions for now."

The last scenes shown from Florida were the Congressman holing out on the fourth hole and doing a fist pump. The Congressman hooked his tee shot on the fifth hole into a water hazard.

The TV switched to Bill Webber who went on to say that Congressman Randolph's golf outing in Florida cost the taxpayers about fifty thousand dollars. He then said that the Congressman had other golf and tennis outings paid for by the taxpayers. Bill also went on to say that the information on the Save America website was correct about the Congressman. The TV switched to another talking head on CNN who said additional information would follow.

They turned off the sound on the TV just in case Congressman Randolph was discussed more.

Thomas spoke first, "I thought we'd have a quiet week but the Congressman has helped to create news for us and him."

William said, "The Congressman certainly supported the information on the website with this trip. He'll now have to answer for all of his trips he's taken."

William continued, "We need to make a loan to the car business to get it started. Cal will be asking for funds in a minute and one of our nonprofits will need to provide the funds. Can we do that?"

Charlie answered, "I'll get the paperwork together after this meeting."

Cal said, "I hired a mechanic today and he'll start full time next week. He'll be part time this week. I have a list of equipment needed. Some of it can be bought used, some can be leased, and some of the software needs to be new." Cal handed out a list of stuff and we all concurred that it could be leased or bought.

Cal continued, "There are a couple of older cars that we can buy and fix up. We should be able to make money on each." The group agreed to buy the cars based on Cal's judgment.

William said, "I brought one of my cars that needs fixed today if someone can give me a ride home. If there's nothing else for the car business, we'll switch to Save America."

Thomas handed out examples for the call, email, and mail effort. They agreed on his recommendations and Thomas said he would add them to the website today. He also said that someone from Congressman Randolph's office had been calling and wanted us to call the Congressman.

Cal said, "My sources said the Congressman has already sent his family out of town and he's added extra security. News trucks are now parked outside his home. If we can flood him with calls and emails, he'll really get excited."

William told them about the call from the physician and how much he appreciated it.

Amy told us how she liked the new offices and thanked us.

William said, "We need to thank you, Amy. The rest of us volunteered but the Save America stuff was added to your plate without volunteering."

"I really like the Save America effort and am glad to help. All of you are doing a great thing."

William split his time doing research about the next Save America leading character and working on his own business ventures. He had the TV on and turned up the sound when Congressman Randolph was discussed. Additional footage was added to the earlier report showing the Congressman at the clubhouse. William assumed it was after the Congressman finished nine holes. The Florida reporter was now joined by other reporters and they were planning to ask the Congressman more questions. The Congressman's golf cart took the Congressman straight to a limousine and he drove away leaving his clubs on the cart. William was sure taxpayers would pay to ship his clubs back to Washington, D.C.

At the end of the day, Thomas gave William a ride home. William checked the website when he was home and the link to email Congressman Randolph, the phone number to call the Congressman, and the mail address of the Congressman was shown. Thomas had built in a counter so that they could determine the number of people who used the website to email the Congressman. There were thousands of emails that had been sent to the Congressman in just a few hours. The website now included a detailed discussion of the Congressman's voting record, bills he had sponsored, and riders to existing bills. Finding the riders added by the Congressman was hard to do. Since the President can't do a line item veto, the riders are a way to spend more funds without sponsoring a bill. Amendments are another method to drive costs up. Congressman Randolph was one of the worst for sponsoring bills and adding riders and amendments to drive the federal government to spend more money. The Congressman had been born into a rich family and never had a real job. He had a trust fund that provided living expenses in addition to his federal salary. He had no real understanding of the real worth of money and what it takes to live on a low income. The

Congressman had gone to Yale and his grades were below average, but he did graduate. William suspected his family donated a lot of money to Yale, which helped him graduate.

Based on the number of emails already, there were probably a lot of phone calls as well, although most people these days opt for a more impersonal approach such as emails or texts. William thought they should probably try to find the Congressman's cell phone number so that people could text him. William made a mental note to mention it to Thomas tomorrow. William expected the Congressman's staff was letting him know about the email traffic.

Chapter 7

In Washington, D.C., the Congressman's staff was aware of the Congressman being on Save America when the website was turned back on at ten a.m. Before the reporter got to the Congressman on the golf course, the staff tried to call the Congressman, who was on a golf outing in Florida with a group of major contributors.

The staffer in Washington couldn't reach the Congressman and called the lead staffer instead. When the lead staffer answered the phone, the staffer in Washington said, "Rodney, we're getting a lot of calls asking about the Congressman's record. They're quoting information provided on the Save America website. We're also getting a lot of calls from the media wanting the Congressman's response to being the target of Save America."

Rodney, the staffer in Florida said, "The Congressman is on the golf course and has his phone off. I have instructions not to bother him."

"When can you talk to him?"

"I'll try when he finishes nine holes and comes back to the club house."

The Washington staffer knew the Congressman had made mistakes in the past when he didn't consult with his staff. He didn't always heed their advice even though they tried to keep him out of trouble.

The Washington staffer told Rodney, "I suggest you and the Congressman return to Washington before the media finds out where you are. We should then schedule a press conference to accuse Save America of having the wrong guy on their website. We should also do a press release showing the fiscally responsible votes the Congressman has made."

Rodney asked, "Has he made any fiscally responsible votes?"

Both staffers knew the Senator wasn't the sharpest knife in the drawer and knew they had to manage the Congressman like a kid most of the time. The Congressman was elected primarily because of his name, his family, and his ability to talk about America without having much substance to his speeches and press conferences.

"Not exactly, but we can manipulate the data to make it look like he was fiscally responsible."

"When should we fly back?"

"I know you're supposed to be there for a few more days but you need to come back today if possible."

"It's a charter flight so we should be able to come back tonight. I'll discuss it with the Congressman when he gets off the course." The Congressman didn't take commercial flights. He didn't want to fly with ordinary people.

The staffer sighed. "Let me know when you're coming back."

The Congressman was supposed to be on a tour of a defense plant in Florida but the staff knew it was a boondoggle since he was taking golf clubs and tennis rackets and had tee times and court times scheduled every day.

The media had started calling at ten a.m. when the Congressman's picture was prominently displayed on the Save America website. The Save America website was now big news with two of the individuals identified now dead.

The Congressman's family and friends had also been calling him. The Congressman would find out his cell phone had a full voice mail and text account when he did access his voice mails and texts.

Unfortunately, the Congressman was on the golf course and had his phone off. Playing golf with major contributors was more important than having his cell phone on. Rodney, one of three staffers with him on the trip, was with him at the golf course in Florida but was told not to bother him on the course. The Congressman was winning money from the other three, was having a great day, and was oblivious to his picture being on Save America. He was also too dense to understand that the contributors were letting him win.

With Save America now being a possible front page news story, all of the media was trying to get in touch with the Congressman. One resourceful reporter, Bill Webber, found out through sources that the Congressman was in Florida touring a defense contractor. After more calls, he found out the Congressman was on the golf course. He called a local affiliate in the Florida area and had them send a reporter and truck over to the golf course. The reporter in Florida took it a step further and took a cameraman and golf cart on the course. The reporter had caddied at the course and the starter told him when the Congressman had teed off.

The reporter looked at the sky and saw a sunny day, which would be great for his cameraman. It was about eleven a.m. and the Congressman should be on the fourth or fifth hole. It was spring and already quite warm in Florida.

The reporter saw the Congressman as he was driving up to the fourth green. He stopped the cart and had the cameraman video the area and zoom into the green. He'd add the words later. He stopped the cart as they were closer to the green and took more video. The cameraman videoed the Congressman making a five foot putt and giving a fist pump.

The reporter let the foursome finish the fourth hole and followed them to the fifth tee box. The foursome stopped at the restrooms between the fourth green and fifth tee box so the reporter waited for them on the fifth tee box.

The Florida reporter called Bill Webber on the way back to the clubhouse. He uploaded the footage and sent it to Bill. Quick editing was done and the footage was aired before the Congressman finished nine holes and made it back to the clubhouse. Bill was pumping his fist in the air when the report was shown on CNN.

The Florida reporter stayed at the clubhouse waiting for the Congressman and only got additional footage of the Congressman getting in a limousine. Additional reporters from the area had joined him after they saw the CNN report at noon. The Florida reporter also found out where the Congressman was staying in Florida and took his cameraman to the resort, which was located on the golf course property. He interviewed the staff at the resort and waited for the Congressman. At about five o'clock, the Congressman and three other people came out of the resort with their luggage and headed to the limousine. The reporter had the cameraman video the group coming to the car and continued while the reporter tried to interview the Congressman.

The reporter asked the Congressman, "Congressman Randolph, have you viewed the Save America website since you left the golf course?"

The Congressman responded, "No comment for now. I've got a plane to catch."

The staffers cringed since they now knew the Florida reporter would follow them to the airport. The Florida reporter called Bill Webber on the way to the airport and told him the latest. The Florida reporter said he'd let him know more when he got to the airport and he'd also send the resort footage.

The Congressman and the others with him went to the private area of the airport. The reporter followed the Congressman into the airport. He had the cameraman video the Congressman loading into a private plane and the plane taking off. Between the two reporters, they found out the plane was a private charter for the Congressman paid for by the taxpayers.

The additional footage was added to the earlier footage and Bill's report was picked up by all the six o'clock news programs. When Bill and the Florida reporter saw their report on lots of stations, they both gave double fist pumps. When the six o'clock news aired, the reporters didn't know that there were thousands of emails and calls to the Congressman as a result of the Save America website.

While the Congressman and staffers were flying back to Washington, the Congressman was informed about the emails and calls that were asking for explanations. The staff recommended that a press conference be held in the morning for damage control. The staffers on the plane emailed their thoughts to staffers in Washington. The contribution by the Congressman was to make sure his press conference included a lot of positives about the United States.

The staffers didn't think that positives were what the media and public wanted to hear, but they included positives. They believed the media and public wanted explanations about the trip to Florida and other trips. They drafted the press release for the Congressman to read at the press conference. The Congressman deleted everything substantial and just left the positives. Nothing was included that explained the trip to Florida, other trips, or the information on the Save America website. The gist of the press release was that the Congressman believed in the United States of America and was doing everything he could to keep the United States of America strong. The Congressman said he wouldn't take any questions at the press conference.

William was up early and had breakfast at home. CNN was still carrying the report about the Congressman. He called Jessie to see how she was this morning. Jessie said she would try to come by the new offices today. She said she would be in North Augusta today and it wasn't too far from the new offices.

William went to the Augusta building after breakfast and met with Amy. They had several property deals working and they went over the details of each one. William took a few go-dos and Amy took the rest. William logged onto the website and saw that the number of emails sent to the Congressman was now in the tens of thousands. The west coast must have been busy overnight. At ten a.m., William went into the conference room and watched the Congressman's press conference. The Congressman didn't explain his trip to Florida or any other trip. He mentioned the Save America website and said the information on the website was full of errors. He didn't elaborate. Most of his press conference involved praising the United States of America. The Congressman didn't take any questions. William wondered, and he was sure lots of others wondered, why he even had a press conference.

Thomas was in the conference room and said, "Why did he have a press conference to explain nothing?"

"I think he believes his rhetoric is enough for the public. He may believe he doesn't have to explain himself."

"I think he'll start getting pressure to explain himself soon."

"I agree."

Amy said, "He needs to be impeached."

Chapter 8

As the week went by, more pressure was placed on Congressman Randolph to explain his trips. None was given by the Congressman. The Congressman's constituents in Virginia had started a petition to recall the Congressman but the Congressman wouldn't legally be bound by the recall. Expulsion was one option Congress did have. Under Article I, Section 5, Clause 2, of the US Constitution, a Senator or Representative may be expelled if there is a formal vote on a resolution agreed to by two-thirds of the members of the Senate or House body who are present. This is typically initiated by an impeachment hearing.

At the Friday noon meeting, William and the other Save America volunteers discussed the plan earlier in the week to call the Congressman at the end of the week. They agreed that it wasn't necessary yet since it appeared that the Congressman was going to be investigated by Congress for his unexplained trips. Several of the Congressman's staffers had left, as they believed they were on a sinking ship. Thomas had added the unexplained trips to the website. The recall petition was sent to Congress and the media by the Virginia constituents but the Congressman hadn't addressed the recall. The Congressman had avoided any questions and had stayed out of the limelight all week.

Thomas said, "If you haven't checked the website today, the number of emails tracked is over a million. I'm sure the number of phone calls to the Congressman is way up there too. I've upgraded the server to handle the additional activity."

Charlie said, "The donations continue to be strong. The call center in Aiken closed today so we're down to just one call center. It's working well enough that we don't need to start up this call center. I'll keep checking on it frequently."

William switched to the car business and said, "Any update on the car business, Cal?"

"I bought the two cars I'd talked about earlier this week. I'll pick them up next week. Your car is just about finished. We had to order a few parts. My Cobra is coming along nicely too, if you're interested."

Thomas said, "I'd like to bring one of my cars in next week."

William reminded Cal, "I'll switch out my car next week and leave another one here."

Amy actually had the oldest car. "My car needs work too but I can't leave it here."

"Give me the keys and we'll check it out today. We'll order any parts we need and finish it while you're here." Cal knew Amy was the one that needed the shop since she was the poorest of the group.

For William, the week was much more relaxed than the previous week with Senator Jones's death. He had concentrated on his business ventures more and hadn't worried as much about Save America. The first week in the Augusta building was smooth. Since they weren't going to start up the Augusta call center, William hadn't started work on the second bathrooms for the building.

The weekend was productive with William completing several projects on his houses. He did play golf on Sunday afternoon and thought of Congressman Randolph during the round. When he putted out on number four hole, he gave a fist pump. The group he was playing with didn't understand why since it was for a bogey. None of the group knew he had started Save America.

After the golf round, he went into the clubhouse for a beer. He didn't have a great round and owed money to the others. While they were having beers, one person brought up Congressman Randolph and the Save America website. William stayed quiet and just listened.

All agreed that the Congressman needed to be impeached and expelled from Congress. None understood why a recall petition couldn't be used on a Congressman. Another person said that he didn't understand why the Congressman was avoiding the media. A couple of people said they used the Save America website to email the Congressman. Several said they'd made contributions to Save America. After William heard that, he didn't feel as bad about losing money to them today. The ones that hadn't made contributions or emailed the Congressman said they were planning to soon. A couple said that they had emailed their South Carolina Congressmen and Senators about Congressman Randolph.

On Monday morning, Congress announced that hearings would start on Wednesday concerning Congressman Randolph. CSPAN would be broadcasting the hearings. Testimony would be given by all of his staff and the results of the investigation would be provided.

At eleven, William received a call from Diana. When he answered she said, "You've been a productive boy the past week."

"The media did all the work for us. We just started the ball rolling."

"I just wanted to let you know that Angela and I still support you. You certainly have an uphill battle but it'll be worth it."

"I'm not sure I'll be alive long enough to make much of a difference. Congressman Randolph's replacement will probably be just like him."

She snickered a bit. "I don't think so. I believe Virginia won't tolerate another person like Randolph."

"I hope not. How are you and Angela doing?"

"We're both extremely busy. Both of us are planning to move to another city."

"I can understand why you would want to. Will you move to the same city?"

"Yes, we plan to stay close. I have to go now. Talk to you next week."

On Monday afternoon, Congressman Randolph held a press conference and announced he was resigning from Congress. A deal must have been worked out since the hearings were cancelled. William guessed Congress didn't want their dirty laundry aired in public.

The official announcement that Congressman Randolph had resigned happened Tuesday. The Congressman was removed from the website when the media showed Mr. Randolph leaving Washington, D.C. The media obtained a copy of the deal with Randolph and he was required to pay the federal government back for all of his boondoggle trips. The funds would probably be taken from his campaign donations rather than his trust funds. The consensus of the talking heads was that he should have been charged with a crime.

The Save America website now showed a blank picture where Randolph was previously located and blanks where the information about Randolph was located. Wednesday's noon meeting would be used to decide on the next person displayed on the website.

At Wednesday's noon meeting, they talked about the car business first.

Cal said, "We finished William's, Thomas's and Amy's cars this week and are ready for more. Progress is being made on the two cars we bought. I'd like to put in a paint booth and will have estimates for you tomorrow if you agree."

William asked, "Why do we need a paint booth?"

"I expect we'll buy a lot of cars that need painted and it would be cheaper for us."

"I'll take your word for it. Unless someone objects, Cal can give us estimates tomorrow."

Thomas asked, "Can I bring another car in tomorrow?"

"Yes," Cal answered.

William switched the conversation to Save America and said, "Let's talk about Save America now. Anything we should discuss before we decide on the next person to display on our website?"

Thomas spoke, "We're getting several suggestions from the people calling into our call center. I had the call center keep a running tally for us."

"Who's their leading candidate?"

Thomas handed out a list showing the candidates and the number of nominations.

"Anything else before we decide?"

Charlie spoke, "Donations and support are still strong. The number of negative calls has slowed down. I'll have the totals on Monday."

They had decided to discuss finances each Monday rather than every day. Charlie would create spreadsheets for them to review on Monday.

Thomas spoke again, "We've also had a few cyber-attacks on our system but our system hasn't let anybody in. I'll be looking for upgrades as they become available."

"Let's discuss the candidates. I've created slides for each candidate." Thomas projected the first candidate on the screen.

Thomas continued, "This is my top candidate and it's also the top candidate from the call center. As you can see, the candidate is Congressman Riley. Congressman Riley is on the armed service committee and has managed to raise our military budget significantly over the past years. Some of the projects shown on the slide are over budget and not needed, if you believe the experts. Congressman Riley needs to be convinced that fewer US military bases are needed throughout the world and our servicemen and servicewomen need to be on bases in the US. This would result in huge savings. Sorry, I know you knew this already. Anyway, this is my first candidate and also my first choice."

Charlie said, "Congressman Riley is my first choice as well."

Cal said, "I think we should go with Congressman Riley."

"Does anyone want to see my second choice?" Thomas asked.

All said no.

Charlie said, "Your second choice will be the next first choice."

It was decided and Thomas would add Congressman Riley to the website tomorrow. The ability to email would be started initially with this Congressman and the phone number to call and the snail mail address would be included. The Save America website had now gotten enough attention that bets could be made on the next person displayed. Congressman Riley was the odds on favorite in the betting. The second choice in the betting wasn't William's second choice so he figured he could win money next time if he wanted to gamble.

William left after lunch. After looking at a couple of houses being auctioned soon, William went home early and walked nine holes of golf. The exercise made him tired but he knew it was good for him. Now that he wasn't having the evening group meetings, he thought he should have more time to exercise. He'd put on a few pounds the past weeks since he tended to eat more when he was stressed. He just finished golf before the rain started. It was a short shower but it was a drenching rain. He fixed dinner and left a plate in the fridge in case Jessie came over. Sometimes she would eat before coming and sometimes not.

It was getting close to tax time so he started putting his tax stuff together. He usually did his own taxes and would probably do them again this year. His brother was a CPA so he leaned on him in the past for questions. This year he could use Charlie too.

Owning businesses was a blessing and a curse when it came to tax time. William was responsible for all of his social security tax since he was his own employer. This was about eight percent more he had to pay the federal government. He wouldn't have minded so much if social security was managed properly. Save America should offer rewards to people who identify social security fraud and abuse. He expected he would run out of reward money quickly with as much fraud and abuse that occurred.

Jessie stopped by late and saved him from his misery of getting his tax stuff ready. He asked her if she wanted him to do her taxes too and she said yes. She didn't eat the plate he left for her and said she would take it to work tomorrow.

Jessie said she couldn't spend the night but wanted her feet massaged. She said she was on her feet a lot today, so he gave her a foot and calf massage. She fell asleep on the couch so he woke her up when he went to bed. She said her father was having some difficulties and she needed to be home tonight.

Chapter 9

On Thursday, William stayed at home in the morning to work on his taxes. He made it to the Augusta office just before noon. Amy had ordered salads again. William guessed she wanted to help him with his weight gain. Amy was a trim and fit twenty five year old. She took time to exercise and ate right. She always wore jeans or pants and typically wore pull over shirts or blouses. Many days the pants and jeans were skin tight and the shirt as well. She was five feet five with dark brown hair. She had a round face with brown eyes. She was also quite intelligent and had common sense too. She didn't wear makeup, just like Jessie. Amy's husband was a lucky guy.

William brought up the website when he got to the office and saw that Congressman Riley was shown in full color. The picture was a recent picture taken at an overseas military base. His voting record was dismal for conserving tax dollars. A long list of riders and amendments were included. It was obvious that the Congressman took every chance he could to add more military spending. Riders were added to every imaginable bill that came through Congress.

Thomas had also included a link that showed the locations of over 600 United States occupied military bases throughout the world and the number of service personnel located outside the United States. Thomas also showed the potential impact with more jobs in the United States and a significant boost to the economy. He showed that it cost a million dollars a year to keep a serviceman or servicewoman overseas. He posed a question. What is the benefit of having overseas troops, especially in places that have their own military and in places we aren't wanted? The answer is none.

While William had the website displayed, the counter for emails was counting up fast. Emails had already started. William thought that most people didn't know there were military personnel at over six hundred bases. The cost associated with these bases was excessive when the United States would benefit substantially from having the military personnel in the United States. William knew that local economies would improve, jobs would be created, and the United States wouldn't be paying other countries to feed and entertain the troops. It was a no brainer for William.

The noon meeting started with the salads.

William asked, "How's the car business?"

Cal responded, "Let's take a tour after the meeting and I'll show you what's going on."

All agreed to have a tour.

"Now for Save America." William filled his glass with unsweetened tea as he spoke.

Thomas said, "If you haven't seen, Congressman Riley is now on the website. I added more information this time for emails, phone calls, and letters."

"I just looked at it and I like it," William concurred.

Charlie said, "I like it too."

"I think we should wait to call Congressman Riley next week. Maybe we'll get lucky like we did with Randolph," William suggested.

Thomas explained, "Congressman Riley has enough contractors paying for his trips so the federal government doesn't have to."

William added, "I'm sure the military budget can pay for his trips. I'm also sure we'll get lots of help looking at his trips. The reporter that put Randolph in the news will probably help us with Riley. If not him, someone else will be looking for the same notoriety."

Thomas said, "I'm sure there's something that can be found."

"There probably is something and I hope it's found. I propose providing funds to the Randolph reporter to help him find any incriminating information." William looked around the room for concurrence.

Charlie finished a bite of salad and then said, "It could be a stretch to spend money investigating someone but it does support our mission. I'd think our donors would also not object. I agree that we should offer."

"Unless anyone disagrees, I'll contact the reporter and offer to hire help for him. He may already be flush with media money and we don't need to help him, but I'd like to talk to him anyway." William nodded his head as he spoke.

Charlie offered, "There are tons of emails already being sent. You can share that with the reporter."

Cal didn't talk during the meeting. He was probably thinking about the tour and how he was going to convince them to buy more equipment or hire another mechanic.

In fact, Cal proposed both as they toured. He wanted to hire a paint and body mechanic and add a frame machine. Thomas and Charlie didn't know what a frame machine was so they asked Cal to explain it. He went on to say that he wanted to start doing a few wrecked cars and a frame machine was needed for that. He convinced everyone when he said there was a used one that was fairly cheap. The group also agreed on a paint and body mechanic since both cars Cal bought now needed paint and body work.

William asked, "Are we starting a car lot too?"

Cal answered, "I've applied for my dealership license so I can buy cars cheaper. I don't think we'll do a lot. If we do, we'll need to set up a separate area away from this building."

William could see he'd already given it some thought. William now thought that the Save America group was now going to be in the car business in a bigger way soon.

William asked where Amy could hear, "Does Amy know she'll be selling cars soon?"

William got a look from Amy and then she said, "I'll sell cars on the weekend if it pays well. I've got a few short skirts and low cut blouses that would work well for test drives and showing customers the engines."

William couldn't believe it. Amy was willing to sell cars.

William shook his head. "Enough already. I'm feeling ill."

"I have high heels too."

"Enough. You can't leave me for a car lot. I've changed my mind. Let's get rid of the car business."

"I'll still work a few hours for you each week."

"Thanks. You're so generous. I'm leaving the tour. I'm starting to get stressed. You're leaving too, Amy."

Amy did a wiggly walk back to her office and grinned at William all the way. William hoped she didn't wear her car selling outfit tomorrow.

When William was in his office, he found a number for the news agency the reporter worked for and placed a call. The message he left was that he was a founding member of Save America and asked the reporter to call him back. He left his Save America phone number. The person he talked with must have relayed the message to the reporter immediately since he received a call back in about five minutes.

William answered, "Hello."

"This is Bill Webber with the UPI. I'm returning your call."

"Thanks for getting back so quickly. First, we wanted to thank you for your reports about Congressman Randolph. It was excellent work. Please tell the reporter from Florida that we thought he did an excellent job too."

"I appreciate that. Your website actually triggered the start of my research, so thank you too."

"We're trying."

"Can I interview you? I'm sure everyone would like to know more about how Save America was started."

"I'm afraid not. It's best to keep us out of the news." William also didn't want everyone to know it started as a ten dollar bet.

"Can I ask you a couple of questions?"

"No. You can't. I do have a proposal for you."

"What?"

William chose his words carefully. "It seems that the efforts you expended with Congressman Randolph were very rewarding to us. We replaced Congressman Randolph with Congressman Riley today. We were wondering whether you were planning to look at Congressman Riley."

"I was."

"Since you're planning to look, we were wondering if you have sufficient support from UPI or have other sources."

"Any additional support would be appreciated. What did you have in mind?"

"We were thinking that funds could be provided to hire additional help for you. Let me know who you need."

"That's a nice offer. I'll let you know who I want." Bill was surprised with the offer.

"Just let me know and don't give this phone number to anyone. I've got to get back to work now." William ended the call.

When the call was ended, Bill went straight to his boss's office.

"You won't believe it but I was just on the phone with one of the founding members of Save America," Bill said to his boss.

"Who was it and did you get an interview?"

"No. He didn't tell me his name and he wouldn't do an interview but he offered to help me conduct an investigation of Congressman Riley."

"What kind of help?"

"They'll hire additional investigators or whoever I need."

"What did you tell them you needed?"

"I'm supposed to get back with him. What should I ask them to fund?" Bill responded.

"I'd ask for a couple of investigators who know about military contracts. Do you know of anyone?"

"I'll ask around the office and call other reporters I know."

After the rounds in the UPI office and a few phone calls to other reporters, Bill settled on two ex-military investigators who were well recommended. They were in business together so they could work with each other. One was located in Washington, D.C., and the other was located in Los Angeles, California. As soon as he decided on the two individuals, he obtained concurrence from his boss and made a call to William.

William answered his cell phone, "Hello."

"This is Bill Webber. I've decided that I'd like you to hire two ex-military investigators. Their names are Daniel Steele and Mark Waldrop. They have an investigation business together."

"Text me their contact information and your contact information. We'll set up contracts with them."

"Thanks. Can I ask at least one question?"

"No. Text me the contact information for the investigators and I'll text you a fact or two that may be interesting to you. I've got to go."

William decided to text him the information about the emails and support Save America were getting. He decided to do it later. He asked Charlie and Thomas to meet him in the conference room. When the three of them were together, he told them about the two ex-military investigators that needed to be hired for Bill Webber. Charlie agreed to create the contracts through one of the corporations. Thomas agreed to check with Daniel and Mark to verify they could use the Tor Network for the email communications. Charlie said that the contract would be ready tomorrow. As they were talking, William received the text from the reporter and forwarded it Charlie and Thomas.

When William was back in his office, he started a search on Daniel Steele and Mark Waldrop. Both were retired military and were now with the same company. The company they worked for had Daniel's and Mark's resumes on the company website. Both resumes were impressive.

William used a different throw away cell phone and called Daniel first. Daniel answered his phone on the first ring and said, "Yep."

"Is this Daniel Steele?"

"It is. Who am I speaking to?"

William didn't answer his question but went on to explain his call.

"We're emailing you a contract tonight or tomorrow to help Bill Webber of UPI with an assignment. Bill is the reporter who did a recent report on Congressman Randolph. We're also sending a contract to Mark Waldrop."

"Who will I be working for?"

"You'll be working for Bill Webber. We're a company that helps reporters. Bill Webber told us he could use help with his research on Congressman Riley and he identified you and Mark as the people he wanted to hire."

William thought his explanation sounded lame. He thought he should've planned the call better. William also couldn't tell him the name of the company employing them because he called Daniel before he found out the company Charlie was going to use. William thought he should have waited, but he decided to try to manage without the company name. William didn't discuss fee because he knew the fees from the website.

"I'll call you back when I see the contract," Daniel said.

"Thanks for your time."

William hung up the phone and went to see Charlie about the company being used for Daniel and Mark. Charlie told him it would be Merion Baker. William thought it sounded like a believable name.

William called Mark next and left a message about a contract. When Mark called back an hour later, he gave him the same spiel but included the company name this time. Mark said he would call back when he received the contract.

By five o'clock, a contract was sent to Daniel and Mark. No one from Congressman Riley's office had called. William went through the garage area and looked at the cars and then went home.

William walked nine holes of golf and then fixed dinner. He birdied the fourth hole and made a real fist pump. Jessie wasn't coming over so he watched the news as he ate. Save America was being shown on the news with Congressman Riley displayed. The talking head was quoting some of the facts from the website. Save America had come a long way from its start a few weeks ago.

Chapter 10

The next morning William went to the office and met with Amy on his real estate transactions. She gave him her researched documents on properties that were coming up for auction. She prioritized them in the dates they would be auctioned. Two of the auctions were coming up this week so William reviewed the documents and planned to visit the houses again before the auction.

About nine, Daniel called and said he signed the contract and emailed it back. William asked him if he included wiring instructions on the contract and he said yes. William told him money would be wired to his account soon. Mark called about fifteen minutes later and William told him that money would be wired soon. William printed out the signed contracts. He then went down to Charlie's office and told him that money could now be wired.

William decided to discuss the first five persons that had been displayed on the website at the noon meeting. For the two that were deceased and the one that resigned, William wanted to talk about the replacements. For the two that agreed to support lower government spending, he thought a review of the progress the two had made was needed. He spent the rest of the morning putting a list of suggestions and questions together for the noon meeting. He also did research on Senator Carlisle and Congressman Freeman.

At the noon meeting, they talked about the car business first. Cal reported that the two cars they bought were making progress. He told the others about a used frame machine that was available and told them the price. He said it would cost more to ship it than to buy it. They agreed and Cal said he would have it shipped tomorrow. Cal passed out photos of two more cars he wanted to buy and they agreed. He also showed them resumes for three candidates he was considering as a second mechanic.

"Now let's discuss Save America. First, the two investigators Bill Webber wanted have been hired. Contracts were signed this morning." William sensed the car discussion had ended.

"I wired funds to both Mark and Daniel a short while ago." Charlie held up the documents showing the funds were wired.

"I'll call Bill and let him know he now has two investigators paid for by us." William knew Bill would be pleased.

Charlie added, "There continues to be lot of donations. I'll have the totals on Monday for the week."

Thomas said, "The call center continues to stay busy with people now making multiple donations. The email tracker shows over a hundred thousand emails to Congressman Riley already. I'm sure there are tens of thousands of phone calls too. I know Congressman Riley must be getting a little pressure."

Cal hadn't spoken out much lately on Save America since the car business started but spoke today. "I know a little about the Congressman and he believes he's above scrutiny so I don't think he feels any pressure. He probably looks at this as positive publicity."

"I've read the same thing about the Congressman," William acknowledged.

William continued, "There's one thing we've been putting off and I'd like to discuss it now."

William handed out the list of the first five people shown on the website that included a list of suggestions and questions for each one.

After everyone had a copy, William said, "The list shows the first five and I need your opinions whether we should take further actions. First is Congressman Williams. The Governor of Pennsylvania hasn't selected a replacement for Congressman Williams yet. We decided earlier not to call the governor to pressure him into selecting a fiscally responsible replacement. What are your thoughts now?"

Thomas answered first, "I still think we shouldn't try to influence the Governor. We could get bad publicity from it."

Charlie responded next, "I agree with Thomas. We should stick to the federal government and not get involved with the states."

Cal replied, "I agree with Thomas and Charlie."

Amy approved, although she hadn't been involved with Save America decisions before, "I agree with them too."

William concluded, "It's unanimous. We won't make suggestions to the Governor. Let's skip to Senator Jones. I assume you have the same opinions about making a suggestion about his replacement."

All shook their heads yes.

William continued, "Now for Senator Carlisle. I've looked into what he's done since being on the website. He's cut his staff and he's crafted a bill to balance the budget. Unfortunately, it's going to take a while to get the bill into committee and up for vote. I'm guessing there won't be sufficient support and it'll probably fail in committee. My suggestion is to do nothing for now. I don't think there's sufficient support yet for a balanced budget bill."

Charlie spoke, "I agree. I don't think asking the Senator to do anything more now is worth it. I knew when we asked Senator Carlisle to craft a bill to balance the budget that it wouldn't get very far, but it certainly made me feel better to ask."

Thomas suggested, "I also think we should wait until we have more support and there's no need to ask the Senator to do anything more now."

Cal and Amy also agreed to nothing now.

William went to the next person on his list. "I assume the same goes for Congressman Freeman."

All said yes.

William continued, "So all we've accomplished so far is to get a Senator and a Congressman to cut their staff in half. We have a long way to go to get a balanced budget."

Thomas surmised, "Even though we haven't accomplished much so far, I think we've made progress."

Charlie added, "I feel good about the progress we've made."

Cal affirmed, "Me too and we now have a car business."

Cal was more excited about the car business than he was about Save America. The car business was a healthy distraction.

"I'm proud of what's being done." Amy injected her opinion.

"I'd like to put a page on the website that relates a real story that describes what's happening in the US. I'll have it tomorrow," Thomas suggested. He had thought of the idea while reviewing other websites.

"That'll be good. Anybody have anything else?" Nobody did so William adjourned the meeting.

William expected the group would decide to do nothing when it came to the Congressman, the Senator, and the Governors. William knew Save America really didn't have much clout yet but maybe it would one day. William also knew the decision to ask Senator Carlisle and Congressman Freeman for anything more at this time wouldn't be fruitful.

William took a couple of hours in the afternoon to look at the two houses being auctioned off later in the week. He also stopped by to visit Jessie at the police station. He'd called ahead to make sure she'd be there. She was surprised and happy although she didn't greet him with a passionate kiss or a hug. He knew Jessie didn't like to display affection in public.

Daniel and Mark began working for Bill only a few hours a day while they finished other work. Both men were in their mid-forties and in great physical shape. Daniel was about six feet tall and was an inch taller than Mark. Both were about two hundred pounds of muscle. They actually competed against each other to see who was the fittest. Daniel and Mark had started their investigation business after retiring from the military where they were in the same investigation unit. They were licensed and bonded and still had a lot of contacts in the military. They created offices in both Washington, D.C., and Los Angeles to generate more business. Their business had grown and they had staff in both offices.

Daniel called Mark as soon as he had the funds in the company account. "Hey Mark. Did your contract get finalized?"

"I just checked and the funds are in the bank account."

"Do you want to do the work yourself or let one of our staff do the work?" Daniel asked.

"I want to do it myself. I'll give my work to the staff. This gig could get us more work and it could get us publicity."

"I agree. I'm going to assign my other work to someone else too."

Daniel asked, "How do you want to divide up the work?"

"I'll start snooping here in Washington, D.C., and you can start looking at the government contracts and the Congressman's travels."

"Let's touch base in a couple of days."

"Great," Mark agreed.

Mark called his contacts and had recent financial information for the Congressman. The financial information showed his salary each year from Congress, income from a savings account, and income from a blind trust. Mark knew blind trusts were used to avoid a conflict of interest with public owned companies.

Mark had other contacts in the Congressional travel section and obtained information on all of the trips the Congressman had taken in the past three years. The information showed several trips a year overseas to military installations or to US military bases. Nothing seemed unusual except that it was costly to the taxpayers.

Mark's next plan was to find a disgruntled person on the Congressman's staff. Based on the personality of the Congressman, there had to be someone who'd talk to him.

Daniel called his contacts in the military and obtained information about the Congressman's travels. The Congressman had visited several overseas sites the past year and Daniel didn't see any obvious wrongdoings. However, Daniel did find out a few strange facts about the Congressman. When he talked to hotel staff about the Congressman, the hotel staff remembered a few details. It seemed that the Congressman had a list of requirements that had to be provided in his room before he arrived. This included a room facing the rising sun, Egyptian cotton sheets with at least a 400 thread count, a bowl of Reese's Pieces, six bottles of vitamin water, and his bed turned down with chocolate on the pillow. The Congressman had taken his wife with him on a couple of overseas trips but the Congressman had personally paid for her expenses.

Daniel talked to contractors that had gotten military contracts while the Congressman was head of the Armed Forces Committee. All of the contractors had spoken highly of the Congressman and thought he was a great Congressman.

After two days, Daniel called Mark to talk about their progress. Daniel asked, "What are you finding out?"

"Nothing much yet. I'm going to go further back to look at his finances and his trips since I haven't found anything unusual from recent years." Mark was disappointed he hadn't found some dirt.

"I did find out the Congressman has a few strange requests at hotels but it appears there's nothing else obviously wrong. I'm continuing to look," Daniel said.

"I'm going to find a disgruntled member of his staff that will hopefully tell me the dark secrets."

Mark was positive he could find someone in the Congressman's office that would tell him the scoop on the Congressman. There was always someone who felt like they needed to talk. From his investigations, he had developed contacts in Washington. Some of them were clients who appreciated the work he'd done for them and were happy to help. The clients knew Mark would discount their next offer. The relationships he'd developed with clients resulted in repeat business and additional work.

Within a day, Mark had the names of all the staffers for the Congressman with photos of each. The hard part now was to find the one that would talk. There was always one or more but he only needed to find one. Congress was out of session and the Congressman was on a trip and had taken several staffers. He called the Congressman's office and made an appointment knowing that a staffer would be talking to him. He was lucky with the staffer he got to talk to. The staffer's name was Howard Crisp. He was about twenty five with red hair and fair skin. He was about Mark's height but not as fit. Mark made people feel at ease and could have been a psychologist if he wanted. Mark told the staffer that he was a Senator's staffer when he was young. The staffer eventually told Mark he was unhappy that he didn't get to go on trips and the Congressman played favorites. He told Mark of the Congressman's strange requests when he went on a trip and that one of the staffers had to take care of them. He told Mark that the Congressman liked to eat at nice restaurants and had moved his office several times to get a better office. He told Mark that the Congressman played golf sometimes when he should have been in the office. Mark asked if the Congressman used alcohol excessively and was told no. Mark asked if the Congressman used drugs and was told no. At the end of the conversation, Mark didn't have any new information of substance. The Congressman had some flaws but not enough to be a concern and no dark secrets.

Mark called Daniel to update him.

When Daniel answered, Mark said, "I had no luck with a staffer for the Congressman. The staffer was unhappy and talkative but there wasn't anything worth following up on. You have any suggestions?"

"I suggest we go further back into his financials and his relationships with past contractors. Maybe he was evil and changed his ways."

Mark agreed, "I'll start looking at his financials for more years back."

After hanging up the phone, Daniel had one of his employees start making a list of military contractors that the Congressman may have dealt with in the past. While this was getting prepared, Daniel did work for other clients.

Mark made calls to his contacts and asked for financials for more years for the Congressman. After being promised that the information would be delivered tomorrow, Mark also did work for other clients.

William called Bill Webber and asked him how everything was going.

Bill said after the greetings, "The investigators are looking but haven't found anything of significance. I'm talking with them tomorrow to see if there's anything new. I'll call you if they have any news."

"I'm glad they're helping." William hung up before Bill could ask any questions about Save America.

Bill was doing his own research through the news agencies and his sources. So far his research had identified some of the same items that Mark and Daniel had found but nothing worth pursuing. Everybody he talked to and the documents he'd read showed the Congressman to be a little eccentric but not anything criminal.

The Congressman had made a few enemies along the way during the Congressman's thirty years in the House but none of them said anything negative about the Congressman except for political rhetoric. Bill interviewed staffers that had worked with the Congressman but none had anything significantly negative to say except for his eccentricities.

Bill had used the hook that he was writing an article about the long serving members of the House and Senate. Nobody placed him as the one who was involved with Congressman Randolph. To Bill's dismay, there wasn't any obvious serious faults that he could determine.

Chapter 11

For William, the next Monday came around quickly as the weekend was filled with home chores and work on houses. At Monday's noon meeting, Thomas handed out his proposed page on the website. He had loaded the linked webpage and William read it.

The linked webpage had the picture of a young couple about thirty. Behind the couple were two new luxury cars, a large boat, and a large house. The words under the picture were the following:

We wanted to live just like the federal government by borrowing lots of money. We bought a large house with a large mortgage. We bought two new cars, which we financed. We bought a nice boat that was financed. We dined in nice restaurants each week and enjoyed good wine. We travelled frequently for vacations.

Our income was only enough to pay for our dining and travels so we lived off of credit cards. Credit cards were used to pay our house, car, and boat payments. At first, credit cards were easy to get. Our credit scores went down as our credit card balances increased. The interest rates increased and it became impossible to get credit cards.

After our credit card balances were maxed out, we didn't have a source of funds to pay for our loans and credit cards. Our only option was bankruptcy. We lost our house, cars, and boat and no longer dined out or took vacations.

The United States of America is living just like we did and is also headed for bankruptcy.

On Tuesday, William went to work early so Amy could help him plan the week. He had a couple of houses ready for sale or rent so they needed to start advertising them. Another house was scheduled to close this week and the inspection identified a couple of minor items that the buyers wanted. There was also a house being auctioned off this week and they needed to research the property.

Amy was in her office when William arrived. He heard the clank of metal and hammering in the garage area. Cars were being worked on and a paint room was being built. Funds were going out but there wasn't any money coming in yet, unless the repair of the cars counted.

William spent the morning on his business ventures and went into the conference room at noon. Amy had ordered salads again. William had lost a few pounds in the past week since his stress level had decreased. He tended to eat more when he was stressed and it was usually not healthy food. The first order of business was the car business.

Cal started the discussion, "The paint booth is being installed and should be ready in a day or two. Both of the cars I bought are ready for paint. The two salvage cars I bought are being worked on. The second mechanic we hired is helping out a lot."

Charlie handed out a spreadsheet. "These are the totals for the car business. We have a goodly amount of funds obligated so far with no income."

Thomas spoke next, "I've created a website for the car business. We'll start listing the cars on eBay and will create an eBay store. We can use eBay to generate traffic for our website when we get more cars ready."

William said, "We talked about a car lot in the corner of our lot at the street. I have a contractor coming out this afternoon to give me an estimate for changing the fence and for a building. I'm leaning towards a prefab building but I'll get an estimate for a stick built one anyway."

Amy smiled. "I have my outfit ready when the car lot is ready. I can show off my tramp stamp."

Everyone laughed but William thought Amy was serious. No one asked to see the tramp stamp.

They switched to Save America next.

William said, "The investigators we hired haven't found anything of substance yet. Neither has Bill Webber."

Charlie asked, "How long do we need to fund the investigators?"

"I think a week or two more but we may want to keep them on retainer in case Bill finds a lead and also to help Bill again."

No one else spoke about the investigation. Noticing the pause, Charlie handed out a spreadsheet showing the totals and the donation for the past week. The total donations through last week were fifty five million dollars and last week was twelve million.

Thomas was next. "The call center is going well and handling all of the traffic. It wouldn't hurt for us to take a few calls this week. I plan to use our call center to take some. I loaded the webpage about the bankrupt couple and put a link on our website. Response this morning is good. Charlie and I have also starting generating numbers to show the impact of bringing overseas military back to the US. The impact is astounding with additional people employed, people off of self-employment benefits, and people off of welfare and food stamps. The numbers cascade even more as the money left in the US rather than overseas generates more taxes, investments, and more jobs."

William said, "I look forward to seeing the numbers."

Thomas continued, "Our website keeps getting attacked by hackers so I'm putting more safeguards in place. I'm also getting more prepaid phones for us to use. I'll have a list of the new numbers tomorrow."

"I'll need to call Bill Webber with the new phone so he'll have it," William said.

Thomas continued, "The email counter for Congressman Riley is now over a hundred thousand and growing. I've also created an email link on our webpage so that people can now email the President. I haven't made it active yet until we discussed it."

The consensus was to make the link hot today.

When the time came to meet the contractor for the car lot, William drove his vehicle out of the car lot and parked it on the street near the fence where the car lot would be located. He didn't want the contractor to know he had an office in the building.

The contractor showed up and gave William an estimate for the fence and the building. The price for the fence was acceptable and the contractor agreed to start tomorrow morning. William knew he needed to be scarce while the fence was being built. At least two days was needed to install the fence since the posts would be concreted into the ground. The fence would be a metal fence that matched the existing fence around the property. William decided to buy the prefab building rather than construct a building.

William checked before he left for the day and the email counter to the President was spinning. He hoped the President would notice but was sure there were many other email links to the President.

The car lot fence was started the next day so William made himself scarce. He left when the crew was at lunch and didn't return until Amy told him the crew had left for the day. He stopped to check on the progress and all of the fence posts had been concreted in the ground. He'd ordered a ten foot gate and it was to be delivered tomorrow morning. He didn't want it to be left outside overnight. Since the security was compromised, Cal stayed in the building during the night.

Daniel called Mark and said, when Mark answered, "How's it going?"

"Not great. I did notice that the Congressman has done well with his blind trust so I'll work on that tomorrow. The stock market has done well lately so there's probably nothing there."

"I've checked with contractors from twenty years ago and can't find anything. Everybody likes the Congressman and there doesn't seem to be any impropriety. I have some of the staff looking at actual contracts to see if there's any inconsistency."

"This looks like a dead end. It's a shame since I'd like to have more business from Webber."

"I'll talk to you in a day or two."

One of Mark's employees at the Washington, D.C., office had obtained records for the Congressman's blind trust. When asked, the employee told Mark that it cost five thousand dollars to get the information. The employee's specialty was in accounts and finances and he had looked at the information before showing the information to Mark.

The employee said over his thick glasses, "I think a few things look strange."

Mark asked with a puzzled look, since he wasn't a numbers person, "What do you mean?"

The employee responded, "First, the trustee for the blind trust is the Congressman's brother-in-law which is a little unusual. The second strange item is that large deposits were made into the blind trust that doesn't match the Congressman's income. The third thing is a number of stocks were purchased in companies that have military contracts. All this together looks fishy to me."

"What do you recommend?"

The employee responded with a furled brow that had creases from being furled thousands of times, "I'd like to create a spreadsheet with all the deposits and stock purchases laid out. I can understand it more when it's on one spreadsheet."

"Let me know when you're done."

It was late the same day when the employee called Mark. The spreadsheet went back to the creation of the blind trust thirty years ago. The brother-in-law was a broker and had been assigned as trustee. The blind trust contained only about twenty thousand dollars when it was created. The blind trust was worth forty million now.

The employee said facetiously, "I think I want the brother-in-law to manage my money. He must be good."

"It sounds like more than smart investing."

The employee asked, "What's next boss?"

"If possible, I'd like to find out where the deposits came from and I'd like to see if the purchases of stocks match military contracts that were let."

The employee said, "Right on it, but it may take a day or two and more paid help."

Mark knew what more paid help meant as information sometimes costs a lot of money.

The fence was finished the next day and the building arrived early. The building turned out to be in stock. Since it was a legitimate business, Amy arranged for a real phone line, internet, and cable. The lot was left as a gravel lot for now. The building was a prefab ten foot by twenty foot building with one small office at one end. The power company ran a separate feed to the building. They were in business, except that there weren't any cars to sell yet.

Amy ordered two signs. One was for the fence and one was for the building. They decided the car business would be called Cal's Cars since Cal had the idea.

The noon meeting didn't involve any new business. Thomas told them about the email traffic. He told them that he and Charlie were still working on the data for the overseas troops being brought home.

William worked on the real estate deals and visited the house being auctioned off. He left early, walked nine holes of golf, and prepared dinner for himself and hopefully Jessie. Jessie's visits depended on how her parents were doing. He'd offered to pay for full time help for her parents but Jessie refused. He was asleep on the couch when she came. She got on the couch with him and they snuggled. She stayed about an hour and then left.

The next day for William was a routine day with real estate work, the noon meeting, and metal banging in the shop. The paint booth was finished so William went to the garage for a tour. It was a metal enclosed room with two doors big enough for a car to be driven in. Hoses were on the wall for spraying. Enclosed lights were in the ceiling and Cal reminded William they were explosion proof lights. The frame machine was also installed and looked pretty much like a metal platform. Cal assured William that it worked.

The employee called Mark in the afternoon after he'd been putting data together all day. When he met with Mark he said, "The information we bought was worth the money, there are multiple things that show problems."

"Explain."

"I compared the stock purchases of the military companies to the release of military contracts. In all cases, the stock purchases match."

"I'm sure you don't think the Congressman was letting the brother-in-law know about the contracts."

"I'd bet the Congressman was the one, although it could be his wife or a staffer. My money would be on the Congressman. Do you want to make a side bet?"

"No. I'd be betting on the Congressman too. What else is there?"

"About twenty five years ago, deposits started in the account that didn't match the Congressman's income. A long trail shows that the first money came from a contractor who just happened to be getting a government contract. The best I can tell is that it was a loan that was paid back later."

"So without a detailed look, the loan looked legitimate?"

The employee answered, "Yes, at first glance it looked legitimate."

"How many loans were shown?"

"About twenty from different contractors but the loans stopped about ten years ago. It appeared the Congressman and brother-in-law had sufficient funds in the account to sell stocks and purchase new stocks just prior to the release of military contracts."

Mark didn't think there was any more but asked, "Anything else?"

"One more detail. Some of the stocks that were purchased were for small disadvantaged companies and their stock prices increased significantly. That was a good return for the blind trust."

"Put all of this information into an understandable package and we'll meet with Bill Webber tomorrow. I'll shoot for early afternoon so you'll have plenty of time."

Mark called Daniel as soon as the employee left the office.

Mark said, "The Congressman was quietly amassing millions through his blind trust with no one the wiser." He explained the whole scheme to Daniel and that he was setting up a meeting with Bill Webber tomorrow afternoon.

"I'm flying tonight so I can be at the meeting. I'd like to meet Bill Webber and I'd like to see his face when we show him the information."

Mark called Bill Webber next and set up a meeting for one o'clock the next day. Bill wanted to know the reason but Mark told him to wait until tomorrow.

Bill called William and asked if he wanted to come up for the meeting and meet Mark and Daniel. William declined.

Chapter 12

William was busy the next day with his business ventures and also went to the call center. The system was set up so he could take calls anytime he wanted. Most people wanted to make donations while some just wanted to show their support. Others wanted to state their disapproval. Many said they emailed the Congressman and the President.

The noon meeting involved a tour of the car shop. A car was in the paint shop, a car was on the frame machine, and three cars looked like they were finished, including the Cobra. Cal told them that two cars would be ready to sell in a day or two. Amy told them she had ordered forms, displays, and other materials for the car lot.

Back in the conference room, Thomas said he and Charlie were still validating the information he was working on. He told them that the information would be scrutinized and the data needed to be conservative.

William told them he didn't have any new information from Bell Webber and didn't expect any results that would help. He told them that Mark and Daniel were meeting with Bill this afternoon but didn't know the purpose.

At one o'clock, Mark, Daniel, Bill Webber, and the employee met in the conference room at Mark's offices. The employee had time to create a presentation that was displayed on the wall screen using his laptop.

The employee showed the blind trust information with the brother-in-law as the trustee. The employee then went through the details of the loans and the purchase of stock for military contractors.

After the last slide, Bill asked, "Are you sure this is accurate? This is very damning."

The employee answered, "I double checked all the information and called my source again to confirm the information was accurate."

Mark said, "I believe the information is reliable."

Bill asked, "Was the information obtained legally?"

Mark answered, "Not exactly. Some money changed hands to obtain it."

Bill thought for a few minutes and then said, "Maybe if we just use the general information rather than the specifics I can still run a story. I'd better review this with our legal group and my boss first."

Mark said, "We've made a copy of everything for you on a thumb drive and also have a hard copy."

Daniel said, "Can you obtain the same information through the press?"

"I can't."

Mark asked, "What else do you need us to do?"

"Unfortunately, I can't tell anyone where I got the data so I can't let you help me now."

Daniel said, "We understand."

Bill didn't call William because he didn't know how to manage the story. He called his boss and the boss agreed to meet with him at four thirty. Bill asked him to have someone from legal present.

At four thirty, Bill, his boss, and a representative from legal met, and Bill reviewed the information.

The lawyer asked, "Was the information obtained legally?"

"No."

The lawyer asked, "Can we get it legally?"

Bill answered, "I don't think so."

The lawyer then stated, "I'm afraid the information can't be used."

Bill asked, "What can I say?"

The lawyer thought for a minute, brushed his hands through his hair and said, "You can probably state that the information was from an anonymous source but we may still get into a legal battle."

The boss said, "At the least, you need to interview the brother-in-law and the Congressman to get their statements."

Bill was thinking that the information could be placed on the Save America website but decided against it quickly since he wanted to be the one to release it. He had started making a name for himself with Congressman Randolph and now wanted the additional recognition for Congressman Riley.

Bill asked, "What exactly can I say if I don't get any collaboration from the brother-in-law and the Congressman? The reason I ask is that I'm sure the brother-in-law and the Congressman won't answer my questions. The brother-in-law knows it's wrong, but I'm not sure the Congressman believes he did anything wrong. He probably thinks he deserves the extra money."

"Footage with the interviews will add airtime and airtime is what we want." The boss said reminding everyone that money is made when reports are picked up by the networks and cable news.

"My problem is that we can't say unconfirmed or reports from anonymous sources. No one would put that on the air. We could release the information to the other news agencies and cause a stir but I'm sure you don't want to do that," the lawyer said.

Everybody was quiet as they thought about what to do. The dilemma was that Bill wanted to be the one reporting the information, the boss wanted UPI to make money from the report, and the lawyer didn't want a lawsuit.

The boss finally said, "Interview the brother-in-law and the Congressman and then let's reconvene. I'd suggest the Congressman first."

"I'll try to do the Congressman first if I can," Bill said wanting a better approach.

"As soon as you do your interviews, call me so we can decide the next step," the boss said.

After the meeting, Bill checked and found out the Congressman had just returned from visits to military bases and was holding a press conference in the morning. Bill decided that he could question the Congressman at the press conference. Bill called the brokerage firm that the brother-in-law worked at and set up a meeting with the brother-in-law in the afternoon. He was pretending to be an investor with millions in another firm and was referred to the brother-in-law.

The next morning Bill went early to the press conference and selected a location so that his two cameramen could capture both the Congressman and him. The press conference started on time with the Congressman making statements about the health of the military, the need to maintain a strong military, and the need for funding to replace aging equipment.

The other reporters who came to the press conference were probably there because they were told they had to come. Everyone knew it would be another lame press conference. A few obligatory questions were asked by the reporters. This was a press conference that never made it on the news. The atmosphere changed when Bill started asking questions.

Bill stood up so the cameras could catch him and the Congressman and asked, "Do you have a blind trust managed by your brother-in-law?"

The Congressman stammered for a few seconds and then responded, "Yes. I do." It was a direct question so the Congressman didn't pass on it.

All of the other reporters had asked their obligatory questions and were putting away their pads so Bill had the floor.

Bill asked, choosing his words carefully, "Have you been involved with the decisions made with your blind trust?"

Another direct question which the Congressman elected to answer by talking down to Bill, "No, I haven't. That's the purpose of a blind trust."

The Congressman's staff didn't think they needed to usher the Congressman away since they didn't know anything about the blind trust. They would if they sensed controversy.

Bill asked another question, knowing it was probably the last since three questions in a row was frowned on, "Did you take money from military contractors to fund your blind trust?"

The Congressman didn't need to be ushered away as he ended the press conference himself by saying, "I have a busy schedule so I'll need to end the press conference. Thank you."

The other reporters came over to Bill and asked him what was going on. Bill told them that there were rumors he was trying to confirm and it appeared there was nothing to them.

The meeting with the brother-in-law was cancelled as Bill was told that the brother-in-law had to leave town unexpectedly. As soon as Bill found out, he called Mark and Daniel and asked for help. Using their contacts, Mark and Daniel found out the brother-in-law had a flight out of Dulles early the next morning for Singapore. Mark and Daniel knew that Singapore allowed secret bank accounts.

Mark and Daniel dressed in black suits and visited the brother-in-law that evening at his house. The brother-in-law's wife was leaving the house as Mark and Daniel arrived, which was fortuitous. The brother-in-law was so befuddled that he didn't notice the documents that Mark and Daniel presented weren't federal documents.

Mark told the brother-in-law, "You'll need to come with us downtown to answer a few questions. You'll be back in about an hour."

The brother-in-law said, "What's this about?"

Mark answered, "Just routine. Nothing to worry about."

The brother-in-law asked, "Do I need a lawyer?"

Daniel responded, "No."

They took the brother-in-law to their offices in DC. Bill had set up hidden cameras in the conference room. Water was on the table with food so the room didn't look like an interview room.

When the brother-in-law was brought into the room, Mark and Daniel joked with Bill about wasting their time and could Bill get this over quickly. Bill said he was supposed to be at his kid's recital so he wasn't happy either. With all the joking and complaining, Bill didn't have to show the brother-in-law any credentials. The brother-in-law obviously didn't know who Bill was. Bill wanted to change that.

Bill started the conversation. "Thanks for talking to us. I only have couple of questions."

The brother-in-law asked, "Do I need a lawyer?" The brother-in-law knew he wasn't Mirandized and didn't ask to be. He was thinking that he could use that later if needed.

Bill answered, "No."

Bill thought he would edit that out if he used the interview.

Bill then said, "There was a reporter asking questions about Congressman Riley's blind trust and inferring that contractors were supplying money to fund the blind trust and the Congressman could be involved in the blind trust decisions. We need to confirm there isn't a problem."

The brother-in-law was starting to get nervous and was perspiring. Bill decided to slow things down a bit.

Bill continued, "I haven't eaten since this morning. Do you mind if I take a minute to eat. Help yourself if you want something."

Mark and Daniel sensed the same thing and joined in for the food. While they were eating, they joked about the waste of an evening and how they weren't getting paid. The brother-in-law didn't relax much.

Bill then said, "Tell us about the blind trust so we can all go home."

The brother-in-law said, "There's not much to tell. It's a blind trust."

Bill asked, "How much is the blind trust worth?"

The brother-in-law said, "That's confidential."

Bill asked, "Did the Congressman fund the blind trust with money from military contractors?"

The brother-in-law said without answering the question, "Anything about the blind trust is confidential."

Bill expected these answers from the brother-in-law so he was prepared. Bill turned on the projector that showed the blind trust information. The brother-in-law watched as Bill flipped through slide after slide showing the money from the contractors and the stock purchases that correlated with the letting of military contracts.

The brother-in-law was wringing his hands, sweating, and breathing heavy.

Bill said, "We haven't been exactly straightforward with you. We actually already know everything about the blind trust. We know the Congressman took funds from contractors and had you buy stock just prior to contracts being let. I'm sure you know that this is very serious."

The brother-in-law said, "It was all Riley's idea. He assured me that blind trusts never get reviewed."

Bill didn't have what he needed yet. He needed the brother-in-law to state details.

"We believe that the Congressman is the only one that needs to be accountable. I'll tell you what I'll do. There'll be no charges against you if you provide a statement. Here's a signed document from the federal prosecutor that he's signed. Please review it and sign it."

Bill had created a document for the brother-in-law to sign that guaranteed no prosecution. Bill figured that would be the case anyway since the Congressman was a bigger fish. The brother-in-law signed the document and breathed a sigh of relief. He took drink of water, released tension, and eased down in his chair.

Bill said, "Tell us about the blind trust."

The brother-in-law was very talkative this time and gave a detailed description of the loans, the purchase of stock, and the growth of the blind trust from thousands to millions. The brother-in-law remembered specific details as he discussed the history of the trust. After the brother-in-law was finished, Bill didn't have any questions.

Bill said, "Thanks very much. Mark and Daniel will take you back to your house."

The brother-in-law asked with surprise in his voice, "I'm free to leave?"

Bill said with a casual tone, "Yes. There may be a little follow-up but that's all."

The brother-in-law was relieved and left with Mark and Daniel. He didn't call the Congressman.

When the brother-in-law left, Bill called the boss and told him that they should meet in the morning. Bill and the cameraman he brought with him removed the cameras and loaded the digital recording on the laptop. They showed the recordings on the projector and made notes where the editing would occur. It turned out to be limited since the brother-in-law explained the events in detail. As they finished watching both recordings, Mark and Daniel came back. All high fived and fist pumped. Bill was still stoked when he left and didn't sleep well during the night.

Bill's meeting with the boss and the lawyer was at ten the next morning. Bill told them about the press conference and the statement from the brother-in-law.

The lawyer asked, "How did you convince the brother-in-law to talk to you?"

Bill told them whole story about the meeting with the brother-in-law.

The lawyer asked, "Did you give him a copy of the agreement?"

"No. He didn't ask and I didn't offer," Bill said.

"And you didn't tell him you were with any government organization?" the lawyer asked.

"No."

The boss was still skeptical. "Let's watch the footage and see if it's okay while we think about the interview."

Bill told them the footage was edited so that it showed only the brother-in-law talking about the blind trust, the loans, and the stock purchases. He told them that it was the footage he wanted to use in his report. When the footage was done, everyone paused.

The boss finally said, "I'm thinking that the footage needs to be shorter. When the report gets picked up, we can offer the full footage."

The lawyer said, "I'm concerned about the method in which the interview was obtained. The plus is that I don't think it will matter when the real investigation starts. The bottom line is you should use the interview but don't discuss any of the details of the interview."

The boss said, "Let's meet in two hours to review your report. Can you be ready in two hours?"

"Yes."

In two hours, Bill had combined the interview, the Congressman's press conference, and added his intro and discussion around the interview and press conference. He thought the end product was very good.

When he met with the boss and lawyer in two hours, they agreed. They decided to put in on the wire immediately and add live discussion by Bill later.

The report was shown on CNN at four o'clock. The other cable news and networks picked up the report and it was on all the six o'clock news. Bill didn't have time to call William as he was wanted for interviews on all the cable news shows and networks. Bill finally took a break after the eleven o'clock news.

Chapter 13

Amy monitored CNN throughout the day in case Save America was mentioned. While she was monitoring CNN at four o'clock, she heard Congressman Riley's name mentioned so she paid closer attention.

She knew the reporter, Bill Webber, was the same reporter who found the problems with Congressman Randolph. A continuous recording for CNN was set up by Thomas, so she knew it was being recorded. After she heard the report, she found the others. All five assembled in the conference room and Thomas replayed Bill Webber's report on the wall screen.

Thomas asked, "Did you know that Bill had this information?"

William answered, "No. He didn't call me."

Thomas asked, "Did our investigators find it or did Bill find it?"

"I don't know but I'll check on it."

Charlie asked, "Should we link the report to the website?"

"Not yet. Let me talk to Bill first."

Thomas suggested, "It looks like we'll need a new face for our website soon."

William left the conference room and tried calling Bill but had to leave a voice mail. He then called Mark and did get an answer.

When Mark answered he asked, "I just heard Bill's report on CNN. Where did this information come from?"

"I'm putting you on speaker since Daniel is here too."

"Hey, Daniel."

Daniel said, "Hello. What do you think of the news about the Congressman?"

"I hadn't talked to Bill so I was surprised. Who found the information?"

Mark and Daniel said in unison, "We did."

"Any details you can share with me?"

Mark answered, "Not really. It's best you don't know."

"I understand. When did you find out?"

Daniel responded, "Last night. That's probably why Bill didn't call you. He's had a busy night."

"Thanks for your help." William wondered why Bill didn't call to tell him since Save America was footing the cost for Mark and Daniel.

"Glad to be of service. Call us if you need anything else," Mark said.

The mood was somber in Congressman Riley's office. His staff had also watched replays of the report and asked the Congressman about it. The Congressman had assured the staff and other Congressmen that there was nothing to the report.

At the same time, the Congressman was desperately trying to contact his brother-in-law. The brother-in-law didn't answer his cell phone and the brokerage office said he wasn't in the office. The brother-in-law's wife said she didn't know where he was.

The brother-in-law was actually at home. After the meeting the night before, he cancelled the flight to Singapore. He told his wife everything and told her he'd be immune from prosecution as long as he testified against the Congressman. He did warn her that he'd made a lot of money from the blind trust and he may have to pay some of it back.

The press was trying to contact both the Congressman and the brother-in-law. Trucks with reporters and cameras were waiting outside the Congressman's house, the Congressman's office, the brother-in-law's house, and the brokerage firm. It was a light day for news, so trucks were sent to all the locations.

One of the Congressman's staff registered in a hotel in the staffer's name and they stuck the Congressman in the hotel. There wasn't time for Egyptian sheets, Reese's Pieces, and vitamin water. Not to be deterred, the Congressman did ask for his sheets, Reese's Pieces, and vitamin water for the next day.

Unfortunately, the next day wasn't a good day for the Congressman. A federal prosecutor was assigned to the case and subpoenas were issued for the blind trust records. A swarm of agents showed up at the brother-in-law's brokerage firm and collected records, the brother-in-law's computer, and all of the files from the brother-in-law's office.

Agents were sent to the brother-in-law's house and he was taken downtown for questioning. The Miranda was read to him this time. The agents were confused when the brother-in-law said he had signed an immunity letter. When the brother-in-law continued to rant about the immunity letter, the agents thought they had a crazy person on their hands.

When the brother-in-law continued on and on about immunity, the prosecutor was brought in and talked to the brother-in-law. The prosecutor knew it would be easier to charge the Congressman if the brother-in-law cooperated. The brother-in-law's cooperation would also expedite the case, which would make the prosecutor look better. The prosecutor had political aspirations and bringing down a Congressman would help. As Bill, Mark, and Daniel predicted, the brother-in-law was offered an actual deal replacing the fake deal from the night before. The prosecutor agreed to give the brother-in-law immunity but there could be financial consequences. The brother-in-law agreed. This time it was real.

The brother-in-law was very cooperative after the prosecutor left. He told the same story as he told the night before. A warrant for the Congressman's arrest was issued later that day. Since he was a Congressman, a courtesy call was placed to the Congressman's office to let the Congressman know about the warrant. The caller to the Congressman's office also said that arrangements could be made to have the Congressman out on bail today if a meeting could be set up. A ten o'clock meeting was arranged with a judge, and the Congressman was out on bail.

The news trucks were still parked outside the Congressman's house, the Congressman's office, the brother-in-law's house, and the brokerage office. The Congressman hadn't issued a statement, scheduled a press conference, or gone to his office all day. After he was out on bail, the Congressman scheduled a press conference for the next morning at ten.

The next morning, Bill found time to call William.

When William answered, Bill said, "I guess you've seen the report on the Congressman."

"I did. I also talked to Mark and Daniel and they said it was best if I didn't know the details."

"They're right. They did a great job finding the …. Let's just say they did a great job."

"I understand. Let me know if you need more help."

"I will. The Congressman's having a press conference at ten. You may want to watch since I'll be there too."

William let everyone know about the press conference at ten. They would watch it in the conference room.

Bill went to the press conference early and had the cameras arranged as before. Bill saved his seat by placing his backpack in the seat.

The press conference was packed this time with reporters and cameras. Reporters volunteered to come to this press conference, unlike before. The Congressman arrived at ten and started with a statement. He stated that there was a misunderstanding that would be cleared up in a day or two. He went on to talk about the important work he was doing in the House of Representatives and this distraction wouldn't prevent him from forging ahead with essential legislation.

When the press conference was opened for questions, Bill was the first one to ask a question. In deference to Bill, no one else raised their hand or stood up. The Congressman was forced to take Bill's question. Bill knew he may have only one so he choose it wisely and asked a question that only the Congressman and he would know.

"Before the major contract was awarded to AeroVironment, how much stock did you buy and how much money did you make on the stock?"

The Congressman answered quickly, "I have a blind trust which manages stock purchases."

Nobody else stood up or raised their hand so Bill asked a second question.

"Before JRC Systems was awarded a contract that doubled their business, did you buy twenty five percent of JRC stock and make three million dollars on the stock?"

The Congressman was slower with his answer this time, "I have a blind trust which manages stock purchases."

The other reporters sensed that the press conference would end if Bill asked another question so others stood up and raised their hands. The Congressman selectively chose the reporters for questions based on past experience. Unfortunately, all the reporters selected asked questions about the blind trust. The Congressman gave his standard answer about the blind trust and then gave up and ended the press conference.

The other reporters came over to Bill after the press conference ended and wanted to know more details. He told them more details would be included in his report today.

The Save America conference room had all five people in attendance during the press conference. All were elated with the leading questions asked by Bill and the questions by other reporters. None of the questions were the typical softball questions normally asked at press conferences.

After the press conference, William said, "As you can tell, Bill knows more than he told in his report yesterday. I'm guessing he'll divulge more details today. Let me know when he broadcasts today, Amy."

Thomas was thinking ahead. "We need to decide on the next honoree. I need to make sure all the information on the website is accurate."

William thought for a few seconds. "My choice is Congressman Swindell. He was my second choice last time. Everyone should bring their choice to the noon meeting and we'll decide."

"The betting in Vegas doesn't have Congressman Swindell as the odds on favorite so we could make a little money in Vegas. I'll volunteer to fly out," Charlie offered.

William grinned. "We can't place a bet. No. That would be insider trading."

Everyone laughed as they left the conference room.

Bill heard that the brother-in-law had been taken in for questioning and assumed the brother-in-law had spilled the beans. Based on that, Bill decided to provide more details in his follow-up report today. Bill called his boss to arrange a meeting with the boss and the lawyer. The boss and lawyer agreed to meet as soon as Bill returned.

The boss and the lawyer were waiting on Bill when he returned. Bill didn't have to tell them about the press conference since it was broadcast live this time. Bill explained that he'd like to include more specifics in his follow-up report today.

The lawyer warned, "That could be risky. If the brother-in-law hasn't discussed the same details, you could be brought in for questioning. You were already taking a chance at the press conference."

"We know that the blind trust records were obtained this morning so the prosecutor has the information. They'll most likely assume it was a leak but I don't think they'll care. The prosecutor has his eye on a political seat. In fact, we should highlight the prosecutor on the follow-up, show a picture of him, and talk about his history on other cases."

The boss and lawyer agreed to take the risk with the other details and to highlight the prosecutor in the follow-up. Bill tried to get an interview with the prosecutor but was unsuccessful.

Bill's follow-up report later that day was picked up by everyone. Bill went into more detail about the Congressman's stock purchases that correlated with contracts being awarded and the amount of the money taken from contractors. Bill didn't call them loans since taking money sounded harsher. He stated that the blind trust was now worth forty million and it started with twenty thousand. Bill ended with a picture of the prosecutor, the efforts he did so far with the Congressman's case, and what great work the prosecutor had done in the past.

Bill or the UPI didn't get any calls from the prosecutor or from the prosecutor's office. The prosecutor was elated about the favorable remarks, that he had an open and shut case, and didn't want negative publicity from questioning the ethics of Bill or UPI.

At the noon meeting of Save America, a short discussion was held before deciding on Congressman Swindell as the next person for the website.

Thomas offered, "I'll do more research on Congressman Swindell and validate it. You're welcome to research the Congressman as well."

Thomas continued, "Also, the number of emails soared after the news about Congressman Riley's blind trust issues. The amount of donations also increased yesterday and today too."

William sighed. "I'd hoped that Congressman Riley would resign but he seems to be a stubborn guy."

Charlie asked, "Should we go ahead and replace Congressman Riley on the webpage?"

Thomas answered, "I think we should leave him. The donations are pouring in so we should take advantage of it."

William responded, "Let's leave Congressman Riley on for now. Let's talk about cars now."

Cal said, with a slight bit of enthusiasm in his voice, "I'd like to buy three more cars. The first two we fixed have already sold, thanks to Amy, so we don't have any for our lot. I'm certainly not going to put my Cobra on the lot."

Cal had finished the Cobra and was driving it every day. He bought a leather hat and jacket so he looked like a Cobra owner. A large picture of the Cobra was in his office. He wanted to put the same picture in the conference room but was outvoted.

William said, with an envious tone in his voice, "I'd like to have a Cobra too. Can you find one for me? I have a little extra spending money this month."

William had sold four houses this month and made a tidy sum on each. William thought he could buy another house but a nice car would be better. He figured he was still young and had the rest of his life to work on retirement. William wasn't sure he'd retire anyway since he liked working on houses and didn't see why he needed to stop even when he was old.

Cal asked, "Do you want automatic or manual?"

"I prefer manual."

"What size engine?"

"A 302 would be preferred. I don't want the 427."

"I'll have some choices tomorrow. Anybody else want a car?"

Amy answered quickly, "I'd like a Cobra too."

William said, "Do we need to work out payments?"

"I'm willing to go up to twenty dollars a week."

Cal said, "I'll see what I can find for that amount."

William asked, "Can we buy cars that don't need work?"

Cal responded, "We can, but the profit isn't as good. Maybe we should if we keep selling cars as soon as we fix them."

No one else had anything else to say so the meeting was adjourned.

It wasn't Monday but William received a call from Diana in the afternoon.

Diana said, "I see you've been a busy boy."

"Just doing my job, ma'am."

"It seems you're conducting a little moonlighting activity," Diana mused.

"I'm sure you're confusing us with another service organization like AARP."

"Congratulations on your latest coup."

"It was nothing. I hope the next one turns out as well."

"Who's the next one?"

"Congressman Swindell."

"Do you have any dirt yet?"

"Not yet. We'll wait on Bill Webber, the reporter, to get on board first."

"So you did help Bill Webber?" she quizzed.

"Probably. But no to anyone else."

"I've got to go. Talk to you later. Angela said hi," she said as she cut off the call.

Chapter 14

Bill was invited back on the networks and cable news programs throughout the day. He tried to accept different ones from the previous day. Bill was enticed to tell more details but repeated only the ones that were public.

At the end of the evening, he had only a little time to relax and prepare for the next day. He decided to try again to interview the prosecutor, although a number of other reporters had already tried. He hoped that since he was the one that broke the story that he would get access. Bill also wanted to have another follow-up story with additional details and he needed to meet with the boss and the lawyer to get concurrence.

Bill called the prosecutor the next morning to set up an interview and was told to come over at nine thirty to talk to the prosecutor. He stopped by to see his boss and the lawyer came over. They decided that more information could be released today depending on the flavor of the meeting with the prosecutor.

Bill called William as he was going to meet the prosecutor.

William answered, "Hello Bill. How's life treating you?"

"I'm on my way to meet the prosecutor. If I'm not arrested, I'll have another report later today with more details."

"Is the Congressman standing fast that it's a misunderstanding?"

"I believe so."

"We've picked the next person for our website."

"Who is it?"

"Congressman Swindell," William answered.

"When will you put him up?"

"We're waiting until Congressman Riley resigns. Donations are too good to take Congressman Riley off."

"I see. You're just capitalist bastards. You know Riley is history."

"The publicity is also good for our cause. Do you want Mark and Daniel to help with Congressman Swindell?"

"That would be great. Can they start now?"

"I'll check. I'll have them call you if they can."

"I've got to go since I'm at the prosecutor's office." Bill hung up.

Bill was invited to the prosecutor's conference room where there were others already sitting. Two were from the Securities and Trade Commission. They were introduced to Bill and all appeared to know Bill already. They'd watched Bill's reports as part of the case against the Congressman.

The prosecutor was the first to speak. "Thanks for stopping by. Since you wanted an interview, I thought we could ask each other a few questions if it's okay."

"I'm agreeable to that."

The prosecutor asked, "How did you find out about the Congressman's involvement with his blind trust?"

"I'm not at liberty to tell."

"I thought that would be your answer so I have orders from a judge to place you in jail until you divulge your source."

Bill responded with a gaping mouth, "Really."

The prosecutor smiled. "No. I just wanted to see your reaction."

The group, other than Bill, laughed.

Bill spoke as the rest were still laughing, "I'd heard you had a sense of humor but wasn't expecting it today."

"Today's a good day for humor. I've got an open and shut case against the Congressman even though these SEC boys want to take the case from me."

"Are you letting them?"

"I'm trying not to. So what can you tell me about the Congressman and the blind trust?"

"I can't tell you any more than you heard from the brother-in-law."

"I have the feeling you heard the same story based on the brother-in-law's claim about immunity."

"I don't know what you're talking about."

"Are you adding more details today to your report?"

"I think so but nothing you don't know."

"Will you include this discussion?"

"I will and I'll make sure I speak highly of you," Bill answered.

"You'd make a good politician. I'll keep you in mind when I need a press secretary."

"I'd be open to a press secretary job when you become Governor. What's your plan now?"

The prosecutor and hopeful future Governor responded, "We're waiting on the Congressman's attorney to offer a plea. Most of these cases are settled without a trial. The publicity is a bitch."

"Have you talked to the Congressman's attorney?"

"We have. The problem is the Congressman wants to keep the forty million."

"And you don't think he should."

"I don't and the SEC fellows don't either. I'm sure the press would have an issue with the Congressman keeping the forty million."

"How much do you want him to keep?"

"We're thinking in the thousands."

"Millions to thousands is quite a difference."

"That's exactly the problem. I suspect there could be a trial because of the difference."

"It'd be good publicity for you."

"That's only if the SEC boys let me try it." The prosecutor smirked at the two SEC boys.

The SEC boys grinned.

"Have you heard anything from the Office of Congressional Ethics?" Bill asked.

"I have, and the OCE Board is meeting today to decide about an investigation into the Congressman's activities."

"It shouldn't take very long for a decision."

The prosecutor responded, "Protocol has to be followed."

"Have you frozen the money in the blind trust?" Bill was sure he knew the answer already.

"We have."

"Why did you want to meet me today?"

"There wasn't a real reason. I just wanted to meet you."

"I appreciate the opportunity to meet you as well. I was being truthful in my reports about you doing a good job."

"I'll take that for what it's worth since you're from the press."

One of SEC boys asked, "Do you have any information related to this case in your possession?"

"I don't have anything more than you have."

The same SEC boy challenged Bill and said, "We can make you give us your information."

The second SEC boy said, "You better provide the information to us or suffer the consequences."

The prosecutor said, "Stop the threats. Bill doesn't have anything I don't have and it'd be a waste of time for you."

"Thanks."

"I think it's time for Bill to go while the rest of us have a conversation."

After Bill left, he assumed the conversation was to explain to the SEC boys some unwritten rules. Bill was glad he gave the prosecutor kudos in yesterday's report. Including praise in today's report should be helpful too.

Bill called his boss and told him about the meeting. The boss said he'd talk to the lawyer but was sure Bill could add additional details today. When he returned to the office, Bill created a new report for today with reduced footage of the Congressman's press conference and more discussion of the details from the blind trust including the actual money received from contractors and the actual money made from the stock purchases. The last part included the interview of the prosecutor and a general discussion of the prosecutor's plans. He would praise the prosecutor as part of the report, which should maintain an amiable relationship with the prosecutor.

The report was picked up again by all networks and cable news. Bill was again invited to discuss the report on all the networks and cable news stations. With both the Congressman Randolph and Congressman Riley scandals identified by Bill, he was now a celebrity.

While Bill was meeting with the prosecutor, William called Mark and Daniel.

When Mark answered, William said, "Hey, Mark. We need more help."

Mark said he was putting me on speaker again since Daniel was still in town. Mark then said, "It's just Daniel and me here so tell us what you need."

"I've talked to Bill Webber and he's agreed to look into our next person that'll be on our website."

Mark asked, "Who will it be?"

"Congressman Swindell. We aren't planning to put him up on the website until Congressman Riley resigns."

Mark said, "Will you provide us another contract?"

"We can amend the existing contract or issue a new one."

Mark and Daniel talked for a few moments and then Daniel said, "You can amend the existing contract. Just increase the limit. I don't think we spent the total from the last contract."

Mark asked, "When should we start?"

"Right away. We'll send you the background we have on Congressman Swindell along with the amended contract. We'll also send the information to Bill. Contact Bill to tell him you're helping him with Congressman Swindell. Let us know when additional funds need wired."

Mark said, "Thanks for more business. We'll do our best."

William ended the call and sat quietly for a few minutes. He thought about the past weeks. There were two dead and two who have or will be out of Congress. It had been a strange few weeks. Maybe he just needed to go back to flipping houses and his other ventures. It would be simpler and definitely more peaceful. After

Congressman Swindell is added to the Save America alumni, there would be seven honorees. When this was started, William thought he just wanted to change a few people's minds about the way the federal government was run. It was farthest from his mind that he'd be hiring investigators to find dirt on Congressmen. He thought he needed a day off to work with his tools on his houses and forget about Save America for a day. William could see why Cal was so contented with the car business. After all of his thinking, he remembered it was Friday and he had tomorrow off anyway.

Amy and William were working on his business ventures when Amy expressed her displeasure that she didn't get to sell the two cars in the car lot. William assured her there would be many more. William didn't know why he said many more but he guessed his subconscious must be thinking they'd be around for a while.

While Amy was working at her desk, she saw Bill Webber on CNN. They assembled again in the conference room, except for Cal who was busy in the shop. Thomas played the footage and they listened to Bill talking about more details of the Congressman's exploits.

Thomas said, "I'll bet he's gone by Monday."

William said, "I don't think so but maybe by next Friday."

Charlie said, "The longer he holds out the more donations we'll get."

"How are we doing on Congressman Swindell?" William asked.

Thomas answered, "I'm ready as soon as we remove Congressman Riley."

"I'm sure it'll be next week. If he doesn't resign, he'll probably be expulsed."

William finished the day planning the next week with Amy. He did have to show a couple of houses this weekend. He always tried to sell the house himself before listing the house. He could save the buyer a goodly amount of money. He'd usually price the house at least six percent below what he'd ask when he listed it with a realtor. The realtor would charge a six percent commission and the buyer paid for it through a higher house price.

In his life before Save America, William enjoyed the work week and didn't cherish the weekends as much. With Save America, he was now looking forward to each weekend. As he was getting ready to leave for the day and week, Cal came into his office. He spread a bunch of photos of different Cobras on William's desk. William's eyes widened and he became short of breath as he looked at each one. Who would have thought a poor boy from the Appalachians would be driving a Cobra, even if it was a Cobra kit car. Most of his friends from his youth were working in coal mines or at least, in the coal mine industry.

Cal said, "I've numbered them in the order I believe they should be from best value to least value. My number one is still a project that wasn't completed so it's reasonably priced. The seller says he has all the parts but that may not be completely true."

"What about the engine and transmission?" William knew that some project cars didn't always include the drive train.

"The engine and transmission have been rebuilt. The engine is a 302 and the transmission is manual like you want."

"When can we get the car?"

"I've made an offer already and should hear back tonight."

"So why did you want to ask me about my choice?"

"I knew you would agree with me, so I went ahead and made an offer." He grinned as he answered.

"Let me know tonight if we get it. Where's the car?"

"It's in Virginia. Do you want to take a road trip this weekend?"

"I may. I'd need to postpone a couple of house showings but it would be for a good cause, which is my sanity."

"I'll let you know."

Now William felt better. He now knew he could be getting a Cobra this weekend and could be taking a road trip to get it. His slight depression was cured temporarily.

Chapter 15

William stopped at the credit union and withdrew enough cash to pay for the car. He then went home and cooked dinner. Cal gave him the picture of the Cobra so he taped it over the stove hood. He'd move it to the TV before Jessie came over since she wouldn't notice it on the stove hood. He prepared grilled chicken with mixed vegetables for dinner. He was on his third glass of wine when Jessie walked in. They were small glasses. Before her mother and father were released from the hospital, Jessie was a regular overnight guest so he gave her a set of keys. She didn't have access to his guns that he used in his previous life. William was sure she wouldn't have approved of his life as a contract killer. His life of crime did subsidize his business ventures, which kept him on the straight and narrow with only an exception or two now and then.

She kissed him and massaged his neck as she said, "You've been busy based on Bill Webber's reporting today. How long is the Congressman going to last?"

"We don't know. I expect next week will be his last."

"Who's next?"

"Congressman Swindell."

"What's your beef with him?"

"I don't personally have a beef with him but the taxpayers, including you, should. He's sponsored a lot of bills for entitlements that has cost the taxpayers a lot of money."

"That's a good reason. My feet hurt and they need massaged."

"Do you want dinner?"

"Not right now. Massage my feet first and then I'll have a bite. Be sure to pop my toes."

"Here's the remote. Lay down and I'll rub."

She took the remote and looked at the TV and said, "What's that?"

"It's a car."

"Why is *it* on the TV?"

"I may buy it."

"It's in pieces."

"It makes for a better price."

"Are you buying it by the piece?"

"Would you like your feet rubbed or would you like to keep insulting my car?"

"Start rubbing my feet," she said.

William got up and took the picture off of the TV. He brought it over and laid it on her tummy. He sat down and started rubbing and popped all but one of her toes. It was a difficult toe. As he was rubbing, he said, "I may take a road trip to Virginia to get the car."

"You mean the pieces of a car."

"I may take a road trip to get the pieces of a car."

"When?"

"When Cal calls. He made an offer and we're waiting to see if the offer is accepted."

"How much is it per piece? Sorry. Ignore that remark. I forgot I'm getting my feet rubbed."

William rubbed for a long time while thinking about the car. The body wasn't painted so he had to pick a color. He thought about what the car would look like and what he would look like driving the car. He heard snoring from the other side of the couch. He then heard his cell phone ring. The call was from Cal.

"The offer was accepted so can you make a road trip tomorrow."

"Yes."

"Meet me at the shop in the morning at five. We'll take the trailer and get you a Cobra."

"See you in the morning."

Jessie was still snoring so William didn't wake her to tell her the good news. She would probably have a snide remark anyway.

William slept well even though it was going to be an early morning. He met Cal at five and they headed out in his truck pulling the trailer. William brought along his iPad since he knew Cal wasn't a talker. He also brought magazines and newspapers to read. Cal's plan was to go up and back the same day. It'd be a long day but worth it. William called the Saturday prospective buyers that were going to look at the house today and put them off until Sunday after his other showing.

When they arrived, the seller had everything crated up. This was good for them to load but they couldn't tell if all the parts were included. It took a couple of hours to load everything and they were back on the road. It was late when they got back to Augusta so they decided to wait until Monday to unload. They uncoupled the trailer and left it behind the building.

It was one o'clock a.m. when William got home. It was a long day but worth it. He took pictures of the car as they were loading them expecting to show Jessie the next time she visited.

William was up early the next morning since his car kept him from sleeping. He read the news but didn't see anything different about the Congressman. The attorney for the Congressman did release a statement saying that he was representing the Congressman. The attorney announced that he would talk to the press at nine o'clock Monday.

William couldn't help himself so he sent the pictures of the car to Jessie. He knew he was a big boy and could handle her criticism.

She must have been looking at her email and responded. "It's very lovely but I can't tell it's a car."

William emailed her back, "You'll be surprised when it's done."

"When will that be?" Jessie emailed.

"It'll be a month or so."

"I really am glad you got a Cobra," she emailed.

"Thanks," William emailed.

William worked in the yard, had left-over grilled chicken and mixed vegetables for lunch, and went out for his two house showings. He took contracts with him just in case. The first showing was for a nice ranch house he had just finished. It was a four bedroom home with a large living area and a large kitchen. He had remodeled the kitchen and that helped make the sale. The couple signed a contract to buy the house. He would finance the house for up to three years and then the couple would need bank financing. Since William's rates were higher than a bank, he suggested they try to get bank financing sooner.

The second showing was with an older couple who were downsizing. The house he was showing them was a single story house with three bedrooms. The couple had a two story home with the master bedroom upstairs and the steps were getting more difficult for them each year. The house he was showing had a new roof, new HVAC system, new appliances, new flooring, new paint, and remodeled bathrooms and kitchen. From overhearing their discussions, it was exactly what they wanted, but they wanted a day to talk about it. Older couples always wanted a day or two to talk so he wasn't surprised. He told them he'd call them if someone else wanted to make an offer.

It was a good day with one sale and a good prospect. He left the contract in the car so he could give it to Amy Monday morning. He relaxed when he was home while he enjoyed a glass of wine. He was asleep on the couch when Jessie stopped by. He woke up briefly but was back asleep when she rubbed his feet. She kissed him as she left to go back to her parents' home. He woke up a couple of hours later and went to bed. He needed to catch up on sleep from the past two nights.

Monday morning came and William couldn't wait until he went to the office. Cal was already there and had the trailer backed up to the loading dock. William had on his work clothes and helped unload the trailer. A space was available in the shop and they laid all the crates beside the car shell and frame. They looked in every crate and made mental notes about the contents. The crates appeared to have all the parts. The seller had provided a computer printout listing the parts so he must have been somewhat organized.

After giving Amy the contract to the house, William stayed in the shop working on the car the rest of the morning. He could see why Cal was happy in the shop. Fixing a car was just like working on a house. It was rewarding to see a car or a house being restored.

Just before the noon meeting, Diana called again.

Diana said, "How's everything with you?"

"It's a good day. I bought a Cobra this weekend. I mean I bought the parts for a Cobra. I've been working on the car this morning so it has been a good day."

"Boys and their cars."

"Just a phase I'm going through. I'm sure I'll get over it in a few years."

"I don't have much time but wanted to tell you that you're doing a good job."

"Thanks. I can send you pictures of the car."

"I've got to go," she said before agreeing to have the pictures of the car sent.

At the noon meeting, William didn't need to show pictures of his car since he made everyone come out to the shop to look earlier. Cal told them he had bought the other cars and they would arrive this week. When they switched to Save America, Charlie went over the week's totals. Last week was the best week yet for donations. He said that emails were now being sent to the President in record numbers. Few emails were being sent to Congressman Riley. William guessed everyone thought the effort was fruitless since the Congressman was on his way out. Charlie told them that the contracts with Mark and Daniel had been amended and funds would be wired when needed. William told them that Mark and Daniel had agreed to start working on Congressman Swindell immediately. William told them Diana was still calling at least each week to tell all of them that they were doing a good job. The last thing they did was watch the Congressman's attorney make a statement. Any had recorded it for the meeting. The statement was the typical statement declaring his client innocent and stating that it was a travesty of justice.

As the meeting was ending, Charlie said, "I'm taking off until Friday. I need a break and my wife wants to take a short vacation. She reminded me that retirement was supposed to include vacations, so I told her we would leave tomorrow. We're meeting my two older brothers and their wives."

William was thinking his next vacation was overdue. "That's good. Vacations are good."

Thomas added, "I'm planning the same thing. My wife is frustrated that my retirement doesn't include vacations. I'll be leaving tomorrow too and be back Friday."

"That's great. I hope to do the same soon after I finish my car."

Cal said, "I won't be leaving. I've got more cars coming in this week."

Cal wasn't getting stressed and William could see why after working in the shop during the morning. William split his time between his car, his business ventures, and talking to Thomas and Charlie to get turnover on anything they were working on. It turned out the stuff they were working on was stuff William couldn't do or it could wait until they returned. The only item that may need to be done was loading Congressman Swindell on the website. They decided that it could wait.

Amy reminded William about an auction ending Wednesday and that he should go look at the house. She told him she already registered him for the auction. She also reminded him to check on work being done on a couple of houses. William decided to look at the house being auctioned off this week and check on the houses being worked on before coming to the office tomorrow. He stayed late at the shop working on his car. He picked up a sub sandwich on the way home to eat for dinner. Jessie didn't come over.

Tuesday came and Congressman Riley was still in office. Bill Webber was still making his rounds and was on the morning and evening talk shows. The Congressman hadn't scheduled any press conferences and was still living in the hotel. The brother-in-law had left town and was living in a rental home a town away. The news trucks had left the brokerage office and the brother-in-law's house. The news trucks were still at the Congressman's house and at his office. The Congressman was no longer front page news.

William checked out the house that was being auctioned off and the houses being worked on. The house needed as much work as his car so he decided on a low maximum bid. The older couple that looked at the house Sunday called to say they were buying the house. He arranged to meet them at eleven to sign the contract.

William cancelled the noon meeting and the three of them went to lunch. He invited Jessie but she was busy. There was a great seafood place not far from the office. William had catfish. He spent the afternoon working on the car. He sanded the body so that it could be painted soon. The seller had already done a lot of work on the body so he just needed to finish a few areas. He then started installing the brakes. The seller had new disc brakes for all four wheels. He worked late again on the car and got another sub sandwich on the way home.

William was at the shop early Wednesday working on the car. The auction ended at one so he had the morning to work on the car. Bill Webber called about nine. He must have been between news shows.

"Hello Bill."

"The prosecutor called me this morning and said that a reasonable plea had been offered by the Congressman's attorney and they may take it."

William knew that the last plea he heard about wasn't reasonable.

"When will the prosecutor decide?"

"He said today."

"That would be great. By the way, have you heard from Mark and Daniel?"

"I have and they're investigating Congressman Swindell."

"How do you like being on all the news shows?"

"It's what a reporter waits for. I hope it continues. If the Congressman does cop a plea today, I'll be in demand even more."

"I hope the plea happens today, although having Congressman Riley on our website has been very rewarding."

"I've got to go. Thanks for your help."

"Our pleasure."

William worked on the car until the noon meeting. Amy had ordered salads for lunch. He told them about the call from Bill and the plea that may happen today. Cal told us a car would be delivered today and another one tomorrow. He decided to have the car delivered rather than take off a day to pick it up. William could understand now that he'd worked in the shop for a few days. The auction was at one and William was the high bidder. Amy completed the paperwork that needed to be faxed to the auction company. Closing would be within thirty days.

Bill called again around three and spoke quickly. He said that a plea bargain was reached and the prosecutor would be making an announcement at four. He said the prosecutor told him he could report on the plea bargain early so he would be on the news soon. William told Amy and Cal.

Amy was monitoring CNN and watched Bill report that a plea bargain had been reached between Congressman Riley, the OCE, and the prosecutor. Bill stated that the Congressman would serve ten years in a federal prison camp in Pensacola, Florida, and the confinement would start immediately. The Congressman would have to pay back all the money he gained illegally. Bill also said a couple of positive things about the prosecutor.

Amy came to the shop and told them about Bill's report. William went to his office at four and watched the prosecutor make his announcement about the plea bargain and then watched Bill's earlier report. It looked like Bill became a friend of the prosecutor.

Chapter 16

William worked late on the car and met Jessie for dinner at a Mexican restaurant on his way home to Aiken. He had a big beer and a burrito. Jessie had chicken soup. He showed her pictures of the car but she didn't appreciate his efforts. He told her about the Congressman's plea bargain. She had been busy and hadn't heard about it yet.

She asked, "Has the congressman been removed from the website?"

"Not yet. Thomas is on vacation and won't be back until Friday."

"What's a vacation? I don't remember."

"I'm not sure. I'll look it up tomorrow."

"Does the Congressman get to serve his time in a white-collar pen?"

"I'm afraid so. He'll be in jail in Pensacola, Florida, away from all the real criminals. I looked it up today and there's unlimited visitation on Friday, Saturday, and Sunday. It's more like a hotel on weekends."

"What about the millions he gained from his endeavors?"

"I'm sure the government will take it from him and use it carelessly. I'm sure they won't consider returning it to the taxpayers."

She shook her head in agreement. "It was nice to have dinner together."

William wanted to say that they could do it more after he finished his car but didn't think it sounded too romantic.

Instead William said, "We should do it more."

Thomas called while they were eating and said he heard the news about the Congressman. He confirmed he would be back on Friday and would take Congressman Riley off the website.

Daniel had gone back to Los Angeles and Mark stayed in Washington, D.C. Congressman Swindell had been in the House of Representatives for a long time and had been on or chaired several committees. The Congressman was presently the chairman of the Ways and Means Committee which writes the rules that govern taxation, tariffs, child support, Social Security, and Medicare, among other programs.

The main purview of the committee is the general raising of revenue, including all individual and corporate income taxes, excise taxes, estate taxes, gift taxes, and other miscellaneous taxes. The second purview is the bonded debt, which includes the authority to borrow money. The committee also oversees national social programs, including Social Security, Medicare, Supplemental Security Income, Temporary Assistance for Needy Families, child support enforcement, child welfare, foster care and adoption assistance, unemployment compensation programs, and social services determined by each state. The last purview area is trade and tariff legislation, including NAFTA.

Mark and Daniel divided up the work again. Mark would start on the financials and Daniel would start on the relationships with lobbyists and the Congressman's travels. Mark called his contacts again and started collecting the financial statements completed by the Congressman and began looking for a way to get the information about a blind trust. Daniel started talking to lobbyists about the Congressman and checking on the Congressman's travels.

On Thursday morning, William went to the shop early and worked on his car. Today was paint day for the car body. He was finishing up the brakes and would start working on the engine and transmission. They would drop the engine into the car before the body was placed on the frame.

While William was in the shop, Amy came out to say it was official about the Congressman. An announcement was made by the Congressman's office that he had resigned. William figured the Congressman wouldn't make his own announcement. He probably still thought what he did was legal.

William helped Cal unload another car. It was a 2012 Audi S8 that had a crushed rear end. The car would need much work to get it back into shape, but it should end up being a nice car.

The mechanics had starting taking apart the car that was delivered earlier in the week. The car was a 2013 Camaro ZL1 with a 6.2 liter engine. William wasn't sure he'd be in enough of a hurry to drive the car, but he'd try when it was finished.

William called Bill and said when he answered, "Hey Bill. Are you still the talk of the town?"

"I think the Congressman took over that title. I'm still making the circuit though."

"Did you find out what the final deal was with Congressman Riley?"

"I don't know if you heard but Riley is no longer a Congressman."

"I did hear."

"The prosecutor called me this morning and said that the deal resulted in Riley losing almost all of the forty million and had to pay penalties."

"I had hoped that was the case. We'll have Congressman Swindell on the website tomorrow."

"The President just announced he's having a press conference at three this afternoon. It'll be televised if you want to watch. I'll be going."

"What's it about?"

"I'm guessing it's about Riley and Randolph and their unethical behavior."

"We'll see together."

Amy ordered pizza for lunch. She must have thought William had lost weight, which he had. Working on the car gave him exercise. Cal and William talked about the cars and the schedule for completing them. Cal said he found another good buy if he wins the auction. William told them about the former Congressman and the deal. He paused to wait for some sympathy but didn't hear any. He told them about the President's press conference at three and asked Amy to have it playing in the conference room. Thomas would be back tomorrow.

At three, William went to the conference room with a large glass of ice water. Working in the shop made him thirsty. The President started the press conference with the usual statements. He went on to talk about the former Congressman Riley and former Congressman Randolph. He stated that elected officials are in Washington to represent the people and not to violate the trust of the people that elected them. He said that he was ashamed of elected officials who believed they deserved to profit from their public service.

He then said that he too was elected to serve the people. He said he had received over five million emails, phone calls, and letters in the past weeks asking him to help reduce military spending in foreign countries. He said the emails started making sense to him when he thought about the drone effort and the ability to deploy military personnel from anywhere in the world quickly. He said that he decided that military personnel could be deployed from the United States as well as another country and that the military personnel could be closer to their families and jobs would be created in the United States. For this reason, he said he appointed a committee to determine the best approach for bringing military personnel home to the United States.

The President had to stop talking because the crowd, which was mostly press, was applauding.

The President said that the applause and cheers were unexpected. He then said that the United States still needs a strong military and bringing troops home wouldn't make the military weaker. He said that, in fact, it may make the military stronger because troops may stay in the service longer and provide a more experienced military. He said that he asked the committee to provide initial recommendations to him in two weeks.

He then said that there's a website which has helped open his eyes about having troops overseas and has resulted in the millions of emails, phone calls, and letters. He looked in the camera and said that people with the Save America website should please call him before posting his picture on the website.

He then said thank you and God bless America.

Cal and Amy had joined William in the conference room and they were speechless. The President actually talked about the Save America website. In a few weeks, they went from nobody to national notoriety. William hoped it wasn't their fifteen minutes of fame.

Amy finally said, "I'm impressed. The President spoke about us."

William said, with concern in his voice, "I hope we can still stay anonymous. When Thomas and Charlie come back tomorrow, we need to discuss more precautions."

Cal thought for a while and said, "We may have more nutcases trying to find us now."

"We'll meet in the morning after Thomas and Charlie come back to figure out what else to do."

William figured he could think about it while he worked on his car. His stress level was actually very low before the President talked about Save America. It was what they wanted when they started the website, but he was not sure he was happy about it now. He worked on the car all afternoon.

William stayed late again and worked on the car. The body would stay in the paint booth to get several clear coats so he needed to get the frame ready for the body. He still needed to do wiring and install the gas tank. He called Jessie after working for a couple of hours and asked her to meet him for dinner. She said her father was having some difficulties so she needed to stay with them. William decided to work another hour on the car.

On Friday morning, William left early for the office and worked on the car for about an hour. Cal, Charlie, and Thomas came in about eight. William told them they would meet at nine since Amy didn't arrive until eight thirty. The mechanics also came in at eight thirty.

William spoke first when they met in the conference room, "I wanted to meet early to talk about our security. As each of you have heard, the President mentioned us in his press conference yesterday.

My concern is that more whackos will be trying to attack our website and try to find us. What do we need to do to protect ourselves?"

Thomas answered, "The website is well protected. I can add more layers if you want. I can also talk to the phone center and let them know there'll probably be more negative calls."

"I'd like more security," William confirmed.

Cal offered, "The hackers are getting more sophisticated every day."

"I'll start looking for improvements today," Thomas responded.

Charlie suggested, "I'd like you to check and see if more security is needed for the money transactions."

"I'll look at that too," Thomas responded.

It seemed that everyone was getting more paranoid the longer they kept Save America around. William knew he was getting more paranoid but it appeared all of them were. It was nice to have Thomas and Charlie back.

"When will you put Congressman Swindell on our website?" William asked.

"I made him hot just before the meeting."

"That'll be number seven," William said.

"Only about five hundred and thirty to go," Charlie added.

"Just like eating an elephant. One bite at a time," Cal said.

Amy asked, "Does anyone eat elephants?"

"Yes, there are people who eat elephants. Parts of the elephants are in high demand. The tusks sell for a lot of money and the male's privates also sell for a lot," William said.

"Yuck. Who'd want to eat that?"

"Some people think it will increase their sexual prowess," William said as he smiled.

Amy shook her head and grimaced. The rest of them grinned.

William said, "Let's stop with the elephants. I haven't heard anything from our two investigators about Congressman Swindell. I'll call Bill Webber to see if he's heard anything."

"Our luck has to run out soon. There has to be at least one honest representative in Washington," Thomas said.

"I'm sure there's one or two. I wasn't planning to call Congressman Swindell yet. I figured I'd wait a week or so."

"Maybe he'll just resign after he sees his picture on our website," Charlie suggested.

"Any of *them* that have been in Washington for very long become arrogant so I don't expect our website will give him much discomfort." Thomas emphasized them when he said it.

"Maybe he will after he starts getting emails and calls," Charlie offered.

William said, "I imagine the emails and calls will make him worry a little but his staff probably takes care of them."

"What else do we need to talk about this morning? We'll talk about cars at noon." William looked at Cal while he was talking.

For the noon meeting, Amy had ordered barbecue. It was a real treat and included potato salad, cole slaw, and hash.

Cal told us he was buying another car since another one would be ready to sell soon. He said the two mechanics were doing great and he didn't think another mechanic was needed yet.

Charlie asked, "What's with the yet? We aren't making money so far."

Cal answered, "We'll start making money soon. The cars will sell as fast as we fix them."

"I hope so," Charlie added.

"I agree with Cal. The cars look great and should sell quickly," William said.

Amy said, "I hope not so quickly, so I can run the car lot."

An image of Amy in her car selling outfit came into William's head. He blinked his eyes to get rid of the image.

William asked, knowing Cal's answer, "Are you sure we don't want to buy cars just for the lot?"

"No. We can do better by fixing cars."

Charlie said, "I'll go over all the car business financials on Monday."

"Let's talk about Save America. Is there anything new since this morning?" William asked.

Everyone shook their head no so William said, "Let's adjourn then."

Daniel called Mark on Friday afternoon and said when Mark answered, "Tell me some good news. Have you found anything about Swindell?"

"Nothing yet. So far he's a model citizen. What have you found?"

"I haven't found anything either. I'm sure we will if we keep looking. Remember, he's a politician."

"I'll call you Monday."

This meant Mark was taking the weekend off.

Chapter 17

William worked on the car the rest of Friday. The other four had left. Amy gave William a few things to do over the weekend. One was collecting rent from a tenant.

William called Jessie to see if she was available for dinner and she was. She suggested they meet at a Mexican restaurant. William didn't object even though he knew that Mexican food on top of the barbecue lunch would wreak havoc. A large Mexican beer probably wouldn't help either but it was a requirement to have a large beer or a margarita at a Mexican restaurant.

William decided on a quesadilla and didn't spice it up. Jessie had the chicken taco salad, and she also ate a lot of chips and salsa. He ate a few chips with salsa.

Jessie said, "I saw where you have a new contestant on your website." She must have not been too busy at work, so she viewed the website.

"Thomas came back today and loaded him on the site."

"Has he called to say he's resigning yet?"

"I expect he will by Monday."

"Who's next on your list?"

"I don't know. We've got a lot of possibilities. How was your day?" He drank a big gulp of his beer and hoped he'd changed the subject.

"I didn't shoot anybody today but we've got a few good leads that we're tracking. How was your day?"

William decided to only talk about the car business and not Save America. "I made progress on my car today. Maybe I can have it finished in a week or two. A couple of clear coats are still needed on the body and I've made progress on everything else. Maybe we can drive it to the beach after it's done."

"That'd be nice. Are you working on the car this weekend?"

"I don't think so. I need to work on houses instead. Cal's taking the weekend off too."

They chatted about their friends and family for the rest of the meal. Jessie said her parents were improving each day. He wanted to ask her when she was going back to Chicago but didn't want to know the answer. He believed she had made a mild conversion to the south. William had told Jessie's mother and father that Jessie and he would be getting married and the idea sounded better every day.

They left the restaurant and they raced to William's home. In a week or two, she wouldn't stand a chance in the race against the Cobra, even with her policed up Impala.

She agreed to stay for a short while before going to her parents' house. He convinced her with little effort to go in the bedroom and relieve his tension. William thought she did an outstanding job. She showered before going back to her parents' house.

William spent the weekend working on houses and enjoying time with Jessie. He visited her parents on Sunday and had lunch. Jessie's mom insisted on finalizing the wedding plans since Jessie's father should be able to walk Jessie down the aisle in a few months. William agreed to help soon.

Monday came too quickly. Monday was a rainy and gloomy day. Dark clouds were in the sky as far as William could see. He turned the sprinklers off so he didn't duplicate the rain. He went to the office early since his car had been pining for him all weekend. He was sure the car was lonely. He'd also collected rent and needed to give the money to Amy to deposit.

William picked up on the car where he left off on Friday. He worked on the wiring until Amy arrived. He gave her the rent check and they discussed the activities for the week. There was one closing during the week, a renter that was moving out, an online auction ending on Thursday, and work was being done on three houses. She politely reminded him that he needed to spend time on his properties this week and less time on the Cobra. William reluctantly agreed.

She stared William in his eyes and asked, "Can you spend time this week helping me?"

William gave his most childish look, "I guess so."

William really wanted to spend all week finishing the car but the business paid for Amy and his new project car.

"When you're out checking on the houses today and looking at the house being auctioned off, you can make the bank deposit." She looked William in the eyes again probably knowing he was thinking of the car.

William said shyly, "I'll be glad to. I'll do it after lunch."

When he got back to the car, his Save America phone rang. He thought it was Amy reminding him again that he needed to help today. It wasn't Amy. It was Diana.

Diana said, "I see you have another Congressman on the website."

"Yes. We have. He's just as bad as the others we posted. How are you and Angela doing?"

"We're doing fine. We've had tentative offers from a few hospitals but they want to interview us first. We may be going for interviews this weekend."

"That's great. Where are the hospitals?"

"They're in LA, Chicago, Denver, and Augusta, Georgia."

"Where's Augusta on your list?"

"I don't think we'll take jobs in Augusta but we may come for interviews. We're leaning towards Chicago since we both have family there. We plan to take jobs in the same city and still live together."

"If you come to Augusta for interviews, I'd like to meet you."

"So you live in Augusta?"

"No, but I live close to Augusta. I'd be delighted to meet you if you come for interviews."

"Angela and I would like to meet you too. I've got to go for now. I'll call you later."

"I talked to Bill Webber and he didn't have any news about Congressman Swindell. Apparently, the investigators haven't found anything of substance yet," William said.

William had mixed emotions about Congressman Swindell. He certainly wasn't looking forward to dealing with him if it was left to that option. He'd have to put on his big boy pants and let the Congressman know Save America would keep his picture, email address, mailing address, and phone numbers on the website for as long as it took. He was almost sure the Congressman wouldn't agree to their requests based on his research.

Charlie said, "There's no rush with the investigators. They can take as long as they need."

Charlie was saying the same thing William was thinking. There wasn't any need to rush. It took years to create the financial mess in Washington and a few days wouldn't make a difference. William wasn't sure they were going to make a difference anyway. Eventually they'd probably be shut down or disregarded.

William said, "I agree with being patient. There's no need to be impetuous."

Thomas reminded everyone, "Just in case the Congressman is removed from the website after he agrees to our requests, you need to pick the next representative to honor our website."

Charlie grinned. "I've narrowed it down to about five hundred and thirty."

Thomas questioned, "I assume you don't believe any of our representatives are in Washington for our benefit."

Charlie chuckled. "Maybe when they were there for the first month before they were tainted by the other hundreds. I do actually have my top ten and will narrow it down to one or two."

William said, "I still have my initial list and will make my next first choice."

The meeting was adjourned and William met with Amy separately about his business ventures. She had to leave the office to file for a tenant eviction in North Augusta. The tenant was notified by the court after the filing and this was sometimes all that was needed.

The tenant would either pay their rent or move out voluntarily. The eviction hearing would be cancelled in these cases. For the tenant who refused to pay their rent and refused to move out, a court hearing was used to evict the tenant. This required more time since the court scheduled several hearings back to back with no definite schedule. The tenant would then be given one or two days to move out. If the eviction request went to a hearing, William could lose at least a month's rent. Amy usually handled all of the evictions. William preferred this since he tended to be more soft-hearted than Amy. Now that the offices were in Augusta, William agreed that he'd file for the Aiken County evictions if they were in Aiken. Amy would still handle the North Augusta evictions.

While she was gone, William spent time in his office reviewing documents and looking at auction websites. Amy would also check the sites for auctions but William enjoyed it, so he did it too. He checked the Master-in-Equity website and looked for foreclosures by local banks. He knew the people from the local banks that handled their foreclosures and had bought properties directly from the bank after the Master-in-Equity auction. He'd make a low offer with an attached letter explaining the expenses the bank would need to do before selling the property, such as real estate commissions and repairs. Sometimes his offer was taken and sometimes there were counteroffers. He didn't always get the property, but he did get many.

After Amy came back, William reviewed documents with her that he had questions on. He then left the office and checked on houses and properties that were being auctioned. He returned to the office about four o'clock.

William spent the rest of the day working on the car. Thomas and Charlie came out to see his progress and decided they wanted to fix up a car in the near future. William told them to start looking and decide what they wanted. Both of them left while he stayed to work on the car. He was still working on the wiring and it was taking longer than he planned. Another clear coat was put on the car that day so the painting of the car was nearly done. It looked like he'd be the holdup for placing the body on the frame. His backup plan was to have one of the mechanics help him. So far he'd done the work himself except for the painting. Painting seemed to be more of an art than a skill.

Daniel called Mark late on Monday to check on the status. Daniel asked, "Have you any good news?" In this case, good news would be bad news for the Congressman.

"Nothing worth talking about. The Congressman had a few traffic violations when he was younger and reportedly smoked pot but neither is a concern these days. How about you?"

"Nothing as well. There were a couple of interns that quit after a short stay but both were accepted into summer classes for law school. He was divorced once but it appeared to be an uncontested divorce. The ex-wife got most of the properties and monies along with child support and alimony. The Congressman hasn't remarried since the divorce. I also can't find anyone that he has dated regularly since the divorce. I can't get access to the divorce papers."

Mark said, "I'll keep digging."

"Me too. I'll call in a couple of days."

Chapter 18

As the week went by, William worked on the car and Cal worked in the shop. He found some time to help Amy, check on his houses, and bid on a couple of houses. Another car that Cal bought showed up and two cars were finished. Amy and Cal listed the cars on eBay and Craigslist and the eBay bidding looked like a healthy profit. The listing was for ten days on eBay so the final sale wouldn't happen until next week. The cars weren't put on the car lot. Amy was driving them until they were sold, which made her happy. They decided to wait until they had several cars for sale before putting them on the lot.

Several local buyers and a couple of distance buyers wanted to see the cars, so they left the car being looked at in the car lot. They didn't want visitors in the shop and office area. They left the gate open at the car lot with a phone number on the car. A few people called the number and Cal met them at the car. One of the cars sold locally so Amy removed the listing from eBay and Craigslist. It was a 1966 GTO. Cal painted it fire engine red and installed fancy chrome wheels on the car. Cal rebuilt the 389 Tri-Power motor and the four speed transmission. The interior was redone and it was a very nice car. William would've preferred a convertible but the GTO was a two door coupe. The second car was a 1970 Chevelle SS with the 396 motor. This car was a convertible. Cal painted it fire engine red as well. The black interior was redone and the convertible top was replaced. Cal put chrome rims and new tires on the car. It was a fast muscle car.

They met each day during the week and decided to avoid calling the Congressman for now. Donations kept coming in and emails and phone calls continued to the Congressman. Working on the car allowed William to lose weight so Amy didn't have salads for lunch during the week. Charlie took time off since he had relatives visiting and was traveling with his brothers. Charlie was taking more time off lately. All were volunteers except for Amy and the mechanics. Charlie was supposed to be retired. Thomas spent time in the call center during the week so he could get a feel for how things were going.

William finally solicited help from one of the mechanics late in the week to help him get ready for placing the body on the car. The body was painted and staring at him while he worked on the car. William believed Cal deliberately placed the body next to the frame so he had to look at it each day. This provided additional pressure to get the car ready for the body. It looked like early next week the body could be attached to the frame.

During the week, they received a little press about Save America but the news trailed off. They were relinquished to only a mention occasionally. Congressman Swindell didn't mention them at all. Bill Webber must have been busy with his book about the scandals, and William didn't hear from him all week. Bill was on a few talking head shows but his air time had diminished.

While Thomas was taking calls in the call center on Friday, a call was transferred to him from the remote call center. When Thomas answered a male voice asked, "Do you have the website with Congressman Swindell displayed?"

Thomas answered, "Yes. We have the Save America website with Congressman Swindell on it."

The man said, "I told the first person I talked to that I had important information about Congressman Swindell."

"That's what I was told before the call was transferred."

The man continued, "When I was a young boy, I was a friend of the Congressman's son and daughter. We lived in the same neighborhood and I went over to their house occasionally."

The man paused and took deep breaths before continuing. Thomas didn't rush him. "One day I went over and the Congressman told me his son was in the basement. The Congressman went with me to the basement and took me to a room in the back corner of the basement. The lights were out when we went in and the Congressman closed the door before turning the lights on. I remember later that it was a deadbolt with a key on the inside."

The man took more deep breaths and said, "Just a minute." After more deep breaths he said, "I don't think I can talk about it. I've never mentioned it to anyone before."

"Take your time."

The man was still taking deep breaths when he spoke, "This isn't easy. I debated for days whether to call. I truly believe in what you're trying to do so that convinced me to call."

"We're trying to make a difference and I think we will."

"If I didn't think you would, I wouldn't be calling."

"Thank you for calling. Take your time."

The man sighed and took more deep breaths. His voice kept getting shakier. "Where was I? Yeah. When the Congressman turned the lights on, his son was tied to a bed with his face down. I didn't know what to do. When the Congressman's son saw me, he yelled at me. He told me to run. It was too late as the Congressman took my wrists and tied them together. It was like a dream as he tied me to the end of the bed."

The man stopped talking and Thomas could hear him crying and taking deep breaths. Thomas didn't encourage him or discourage him from talking. "I know it's difficult."

Neither Thomas nor the man said anything for a couple of minutes until the man spoke. "I can't talk about it anymore. It was awful."

The man stopped talking again and Thomas heard deep breaths and crying. Thomas didn't say anything and waited for the man to start talking again. After a minute or two, the man said, "Are you still there?"

The man started crying more and then said, "After the Congressman had sex with me and I finally calmed down, my friend told me that I shouldn't tell anyone. He told me that his father would hurt his mother, his sister, and him if he told anyone. He told me he'd probably do the same to my family. After about two hours, the door was unlocked. I ran home and never went over to my friend's house again. I didn't tell anyone. I was only nine years old and believed the Congressman would harm my family."

Thomas said with empathy in his voice, "I'm so sorry."

The man was still crying when he said, "I've never really got over it and it was tough calling you."

Thomas wanted to ask him questions about the Congressman's son and whether the son had other friends like him but didn't.

The man said after a pause, "I can't talk about it anymore now."

After the man didn't say anything for a couple of minutes, Thomas asked, "Can we contact you?" Thomas was thinking that Mark or Daniel could visit him.

The man answered, "Maybe. I'm not sure."

"How do we get in touch?"

The man answered quickly, "My name is Jim ….." The voice trailed off. The man continued, "My wife's here so I can't talk any longer."

The phone call ended and Thomas sat for a few seconds before going to get William. Thomas asked him to come to the conference room and Thomas closed the door.

"I just took a call from a man who said he was molested by the Congressman."

"Do you think he was truthful?"

"I'm not sure but he was believable. He also said the Congressman was molesting his own son, who was his friend."

"How old was the man when it happened?"

"He said he was nine."

Thomas told William the rest of the story and they decided to call Daniel and Mark.

William called Mark and put him on the speaker phone. Mark added Daniel. William added Bill Webber. Thomas went through the call again with them.

Mark asked, "Could you guess what he was going to say for a last name?"

"He stopped talking right after saying Jim. I was sure he was going to tell me his name and give me a phone number."

Daniel asked, "Do you think he'll call back?"

"I'm not sure."

Mark asked, "What are your thoughts about contacting him?"

"He appeared to be willing to talk more so you should try to contact him."

Mark said, "We will. What about the son?"

William said, "I think you should try to talk to him."

"I'd like to be with you when you talk to Jim and the son," Bill added.

Daniel said, "That's okay with us. We'll find out who Jim is and where the son is located and let you know. Do you want to talk to the ex-wife as well?"

"I would."

Daniel said, "We'll keep you posted."

William said, "Let us know also."

They ended the call and both Thomas and William sunk down in their chairs. William shuddered when he thought of the Congressman and his son. He shuddered more when he thought it could be the Congressman's daughter too.

Daniel and Mark stayed on the phone and talked after the call ended.

Mark said, "I'll start checking to see who went to school with the Congressman's son and is named Jim. You can find out where the ex-wife, son, and daughter live. After that, we'll figure out the next step."

"I'll call you tomorrow and let you know what I've found. I was also thinking of having someone follow the Congressman. My guess is that he hasn't stopped. What do you think?"

"I agree. I'll assign a few folks from here to follow him," Mark said.

The Congressman met with his staff Friday afternoon to let them know his schedule for the next week. He would be on a trip to visit military bases in the United States.

One of the staffers asked, "What do we do if we hear from the Save America folks?"

"Nothing."

The same staffer asked, "What about all of the emails and phone calls?"

"Ignore them. The emails and phone calls will eventually stop."

William called Jessie and asked her about her evening plans. She agreed to meet for dinner. He took pictures of his car to show her. He'd invited her to the shop to see the car but she'd been too busy to stop by. They decided to meet at a steak restaurant since he was in the mood for a steak.

At dinner, William gave her a general overview of the day. He didn't go into details about the Congressman since they were in public. He'd give her the details later, assuming she had time to visit or stay the night. She told him about her day and a general overview of her cases without telling him the names. The steak was great and William thought it was nice to have dinner with Jessie. He did think about the car at dinner and about Jim and the Congressman's son. He also thought what his life would be without Save America. He wouldn't have known about the representatives' unethical activities and would have probably been happier. As many have said, ignorance is bliss.

They went to William's home after dinner and he had a beer while he told Jessie the rest of the story about Congressman Swindell. She was appalled.

"Were there other kids that were molested by the Congressman?" she asked.

"I don't know but I suspect there probably were."

William showed her the pictures of the car before they went to bed.

She said, "It's still in pieces."

He sneered at her, "Only for a day or two."

She grinned. "Show me a picture when it's a car."

William grimaced and said, "I'm not putting a seat belt on your side."

"I'm still not sure it's going to be a car."

William figured she would keep saying something about the car so he didn't respond. He knew she would think differently when she got to ride in it. He figured the best way to avoid her criticism was to kiss her and get her in bed, which he did. She left after a couple of hours to go back to her parents' house.

William spent the weekend working on his properties and didn't work on the car. His discussions with Amy this week reminded him of the need to pay attention to his properties. The tenant that Amy filed an eviction on decided to move voluntarily, so he went to the house to check it out. A few repairs were needed so he hired some help and worked on the house. Hopefully Amy would have it rented again soon.

William went by the house he won at auction on Thursday and changed the locks. The house already had enough damage and he didn't need more things to fix. The house was sold as-is so it was his responsibility to fix everything. There was a combination box on the door which he left inside the house. He'd return it to the realtor if they called. The realtor should have removed the lock before the auction but they rarely did.

Chapter 19

William thought about his car all weekend and went to the shop early Monday morning. The car hadn't changed since Friday. He worked on the final items before dropping the body on the car. The body was made of fiberglass so they could put it on the car without a hoist. If he kept working on the car today, he figured the body could be on the frame tomorrow.

At noon, they met in the conference room. Thomas told them the details of the Friday phone call from Jim.

When Thomas finished, Charlie asked, "Did Jim say whether there were other boys?"

"He didn't say and I didn't ask. He was pretty emotional as he was talking so I didn't ask questions. My guess is that there were more."

Charlie asked, "Have the investigators starting looking for Jim?"

"We told them about Jim on Friday so I hope they've already started."

Thomas said, "Jim lived in the same neighborhood so he shouldn't be too hard to find. The question is whether he'll talk to Bill Webber. It was easier to talk to me over the phone and keep his anonymity. He may not talk about it in person."

Amy asked, "Do you think the Congressman's son will talk?"

Thomas answered, "That's a good question."

William said, "It depends. The son may still think he's protecting his mother and sister so he won't talk."

Cal made an oomph sound and said, "I'd like to have a few minutes with the Congressman alone."

Cal's background was in special ops and all of them knew he could make the Congressman be very chatty. Maybe that was an option, but probably not.

William said, "I'm sure you could make him talk but I'm sure that's not the most legal approach."

"His actions weren't legal."

"A good point," William admitted.

Charlie changed the topic. "Let's talk about financials." He handed out spreadsheets for the car business and Save America.

Charlie continued, "The car business looks much better now that another car sold last week. I didn't think the older cars would bring in that much money. When the second car sells this week, the car business will look even better. I've filed the monthly payroll forms and made the deposits for taxes."

Cal sat up straighter in his chair and puffed out his chest, "I told you the car business would make money."

"I'm starting to become a believer. For Save America, the donations continue to come in and I've created a new nonprofit corporation. I'll have a list of possible ways to use the funds next week. We can start now or wait until election time. My preference is to wait until election time and buy ads. We'll probably also get donations from the ads."

William said, "I'd prefer to wait and run ads. By election time, we should have more clout."

Thomas said, "I also prefer to wait until election time."

Cal said, "I prefer to hire someone to take one representative out at a time. Some of my old military buddies would love to have the job. They'd work cheap knowing it was for a good cause."

Charlie said, "I'd have to revise my nonprofit paperwork I filed to allow us to hire hit men."

Cal asked, "When can you start?"

William said, "I don't think we should be hiring hit men, at least for now."

Cal said, "Just a suggestion and I think we can afford it. I've got a few weapons in my office and shop they can use."

Amy said, "I have a skin tight leather outfit I could wear to help the hit men."

William said, "I believe they work alone but we'll keep you in mind. I mean, we'll consider it."

Everyone laughed at the faux pas. William did have a picture of Amy in a skin tight leather outfit in his mind. Amy was a shapely woman with the right curves to fill a skin tight leather outfit. He even pictured her with a leather mask and leather boots. Others must have done the same thing since they were smiling after they stopped laughing. He hoped Amy wasn't offended and didn't take it out on them at lunch tomorrow.

William adjourned the meeting and went back to work on his car.

The day went by without any calls from Bill Webber or the investigators. William worked late and had a to-go dinner at a fast food restaurant. It was grilled and would have been healthy except for the French fries. He did have a diet drink to counterbalance the grease in the fries. Jessie called earlier to say that she'd be stopping by later. William didn't put the body on the car so he didn't bring pictures home to show Jessie.

When she came in the door, she said, "I expected you to have your new car in the driveway tonight."

William rolled his eyes and grumbled, "It'll be there soon."

"Soon as in this month or this year," she said as she was grinning.

"You shouldn't laugh at a poor man's dream."

"I'll stop laughing after you put the pieces together."

"It'll happen soon."

"Looks like later."

"It's my bedtime." William went into the master bath and starting brushing his teeth.

She came into the bathroom and pulled his shirt out of his pants. She put her cold hands on his chest. After almost gagging on the toothpaste, William turned and put his hands up her blouse and rubbed her back. He kissed her and guided her to the bed. They tumbled into bed without hurting anything and became passionate quickly. They maneuvered for position until they both were spent. William fell asleep after completing his conquest. Poor man's sleeping medicine worked well and he slept all night. Jessie left while he was sleeping.

The next couple of days went by without hearing anything from Bill. William did hear from Diana on Tuesday morning.

After the greetings, she said, "We decided to come to Augusta for an interview with University Hospital. We'll be in Augusta next week."

"That's great. Let me know when you're coming and I'll meet you for dinner. It'll be nice to meet you."

William had a fleeting thought that they were coming to Augusta to get rid of everyone that knew about their involvement in Senator Jones's demise and everyone included him. The fleeting thought went away quickly. They were respected physicians.

"How's everything going with Save America?"

William started to tell her about Congressman Swindell but decided he shouldn't. He'd better wait until it was confirmed by the investigators.

"Going fine. We're waiting on Congressman Swindell to give in to our charm and good looks." William laughed after he said it.

"I can't wait to enjoy your charm and good looks."

"Are you and Angela ready to get out of Washington?"

"We are. It'll be wonderful to live somewhere else. I've got to go. I'll let you know when we're coming to Augusta."

Chapter 20

The people Mark assigned to tail Congressman Swindell didn't have anything to report so far. The Congressman had spent the weekend in his house in Georgetown and left Monday morning for Columbia, South Carolina, to visit Fort Jackson. Mark called a local private investigator in Columbia to tail him until his people drove down from Washington. When they got to Columbia, the Congressman was still at Fort Jackson so they didn't miss anything. They tailed the Congressman to a hotel in downtown Columbia.

Mark didn't have any luck finding a Jim that went to elementary school with the Congressman's son. Mark had found out that the Congressman's son was named Jefferson Andrew Swindell. The daughter's name was Abigail Elizabeth Swindell and she was two years younger than Jefferson. The Congressman's children had gone to a private school in Milwaukee, Wisconsin. Mark went on the web and searched for any information about Jefferson or Abigail. He found a few references to Jefferson and Abigail when they were older but nothing when Jefferson was about nine. Mark decided to go to Milwaukee.

Daniel had better luck finding the location of the Congressman's ex-wife and the location of Jefferson and Abigail. The ex-wife still lived in Milwaukee while Jefferson lived in Chicago and Abigail lived in Milwaukee. The ex-wife had gone back to her maiden name of Tracy. Her full name was Caroline Rose Tracy. Caroline worked at the local high school as a math teacher. Jefferson was a lawyer and Abigail was a physician. Daniel decided he needed to go to Milwaukee.

Daniel called Mark, "I'm going to Milwaukee. Both the ex-wife and the Congressman's daughter Abigail live in Milwaukee."

Mark said, "I need to go to Milwaukee too. I'll meet you there tomorrow. I'll call Bill to see if he wants to go."

Bill said, when he was called by Mark, "I'd like to come to Milwaukee but I need to check with my boss. I'll call you back in a little while."

Bill checked with his boss, told him what was happening with Congressman Swindell, and told him he wanted to go to Milwaukee. Bill hadn't told his boss about Congressman Swindell until now since he wasn't sure anything would come from the investigation. Bill told his boss it may be a fruitless trip and the call to Save America could be a prank.

The boss listened to Bill and said, "You've had two money making reports on a Senator and a Congressmen so I think a trip to Milwaukee is okay even if you don't find anything. You're probably already in the running for a Pulitzer and you'll be a shoo-in if you find out Congressman Swindell has skeletons in his closet."

"I'll be back as soon as I can."

Bill had other possible news stories he was working on in Washington and didn't want them assigned to someone else.

The boss asked, "Can you work on your book while you travel?"

"I can and will. I'd like to get a draft completed this month, if possible."

"Do you want me to assign some of your work to others?" the boss asked knowing that Bill was a workaholic and wouldn't agree.

"I'd like to keep all my assignments. If the Swindell thing pans out, I may take you up on the offer." Bill was hoping the Swindell thing did work out. He would then add Congressman Swindell to his book and sales would increase.

Bill called Mark back. "I'll catch a plane to Milwaukee tomorrow morning and will call you when I land."

"We've got rooms at the Holiday Inn at the airport."

"I'll book a room there too. I suppose you'll have a rental car."

"Yes. Daniel will be there first and will get a car. We may need a second car but we can determine that when we get there. There's a shuttle from the airport to the Holiday Inn."

"I'll see you tomorrow." Bill ended the call.

Daniel arrived first, Mark second, and then Bill. They met for dinner to decide on their strategy. Each had a cold beer and didn't order appetizers. When the server came back with the beers, Mark and Daniel ordered burgers and fries and Bill ordered a grilled chicken sandwich with a salad.

Mark spoke first, "I don't know if we can work with someone who doesn't eat burgers and fries."

Bill smiled and said, "I had a burger and fries for lunch in the airport and wanted a change."

Daniel said, "Take a picture next time so we know you're one of the boys."

"You may see me eat one tomorrow."

Mark got a serious look on his face and said, "What approach would you like to take?" Mark was looking at Bill.

"I'm not sure. Whoever we approach first will tell the rest, so we need to pick wisely."

"I'd like to talk to Jim first but I haven't located him yet. I thought we'd start researching tomorrow in the Congressman's old neighborhood and in the schools. I was thinking you could pretend to be doing a story on the Congressman and his family and get a look at old school yearbooks. Daniel could do research at the library," Mark said.

Bill thought for a few seconds and said, "I'd like to go to the major newspapers first. The newspaper may have old photos or articles."

"It sounds like we each need another car. I'll go online and reserve them and we can pick them up in the morning," Daniel said.

Mark said, "Let's plan to meet for lunch at noon if possible. If we've made progress, we can adjust our plan."

Daniel said, "I'll pick a place to eat and let you know."

"I'm tired and I still have other work to do so I'll see you in the morning. Let's meet for breakfast at seven." Bill got up from the table.

After Bill left, Mark said, "Call me if you find anything at the library that'll help me while I'm in the Congressman's old neighborhood. I think finding Jim is the most important thing right now."

"I agree. I don't think the family will talk unless we find Jim."

Mark suggested, "I'll see if Bill will call Save America in the morning. Maybe they've heard from Jim again which would save us some trouble. I think I'll call it a night too. Traveling is tiring. I'll be working out at five in the morning."

"I'll see you at five. I checked the hotel gym and it's functional."

Both Mark and Daniel got up from their chairs. A bystander would've thought they were Bill's bodyguards.

At breakfast, Bill said, "I plan to start with the biggest newspaper from twenty years ago and then try the other papers if I can't find anything."

Bill was dressed casually since he was meeting with his counterparts in the news business. He was wearing khaki pants, loafers, and a long sleeve dress shirt with a button down collar.

Daniel said, "I'll be in the libraries. I'll call if I find anything."

Daniel was also dressed casually with khaki pants, a mock turtle neck shirt, and a thin jacket.

"I'll be going door to door asking questions. Anybody want to trade?" Mark offered.

Mark was dressed in a dark blue suit with a white shirt and red tie. He had found out that people were more willing to open a door for someone in a suit.

Both Bill and Daniel shook their heads no.

Mark added, while he was looking at Bill, "We thought we should call Save America this morning to see if Jim called again."

"Good idea. I'll call now."

William answered the phone when Bill called.

"We just wanted to check to see if you've heard from Jim again."

"No. We haven't. I'd hoped he'd call back."

"If he does, call me right away. Mark, Daniel, and I are in Milwaukee trying to track him down."

"When did you go to Milwaukee?"

"We flew in yesterday."

"Good luck. I'll call if Jim calls."

After getting the other rental cars, they went separate ways.

Daniel headed to the local library near the Congressman's neighborhood. The library wasn't busy so one of the librarians helped Daniel.

Daniel told the librarian, "I'm looking for old newspapers or articles about Congressman Swindell and his family from about twenty years ago."

Daniel introduced himself and the librarian introduced herself as Michelle.

Michelle was about Daniel's age and took a good look at Daniel. She liked what she saw and didn't have librarian type thoughts in her head. She had been divorced for about a year and her friends had been encouraging her to date. Michelle thought Daniel would be a good start.

Daniel returned the survey. Michelle was about five feet eight inches tall with fair skin and large black glasses. Her black hair was in a bun on top of her head with a pen stuck in it. She was wearing a loose fitting dress that had a high collar. Daniel's first impression was great when he imagined what was underneath the loose dress.

Michelle let her mind return to the question and said, "We were using both digital storage and microfiche twenty years ago so I'll show you how to look at both."

Daniel followed the librarian to a rear room where there were several viewers for microfiche and monitors for digital storage. The librarian told Daniel to sit at a viewer.

The librarian took a file from a drawer next to the viewer and leaned against Daniel as she placed it in the viewer. Daniel knew how to use a viewer but didn't stop the librarian. She had a fresh smell with a slight hint of lavender. Daniel closed his eyes for a moment enjoying Michelle's touch and smell.

Michelle looked from the viewer at Daniel and Daniel was looking at her instead of the viewer.

Michelle asked, "Are you listening?"

"I am, but I'm confused."

She moved away from Daniel and said, "Should I stay and give you more instructions?"

Daniel was thinking of the instructions that Michelle could give him but didn't and said instead, "If you'd be so kind, I'd truly appreciate it."

Michelle pulled up a chair and moved next to Daniel. She was thinking she could sit on his lap but her thoughts had her straddling Daniel in the wrong direction to see the viewer. She did put her leg against Daniel's as she moved close to the viewer.

She asked, "What are you looking for?"

Daniel was breathing through his mouth, closed it, took a deep breath through his nose and answered, "Someone about five feet eight inches tall with intelligent eyes and works as a librarian. Sorry. I'm looking for information about Congressman Swindell about twenty years ago."

Michelle turned her head slowly towards Daniel with her lips pursed and asked, "And what would you do with this librarian if you found her?"

"I'd wine and dine her, take her on nice trips, and then marry her."

Michelle wasn't expecting that and asked, "Is that a proposal?"

"Are you in the market for a proposal?"

Daniel wasn't sure she was playing with him or what.

Michelle wasn't sure about Daniel but kept playing along. Michelle took off her glasses, thought for a few seconds, and said, "I need a couple of facts first like your marital status, where you live, and whether you are gainfully employed."

Daniel didn't see any harm in answering. "I'm single, I live in Los Angeles, and I'm gainfully employed. What about you?"

"I'm single, live in a suburb of Milwaukee, and am employed. What's your gainful employment?"

"I own a private investigation business. Let's go ahead and set a date."

"Are you asking me to go on a date?"

"No. I'm asking you to set a date for the wedding."

"I'm a little old fashioned. Let's get to know each other a bit first."

"How about a date tonight?"

Michelle thought for a few minutes and said, "Okay, but I'll meet you somewhere."

"That's fine. We'll pick a place before I leave."

Michelle changed the subject since she thought Daniel was just playing with her. "Let me show you more about the viewer and the microfiche."

"I know about viewers and microfiche."

"I figured that but I'm staying anyway. We'll count this as our getting to know each other. Move over and I'll run the machine."

Chapter 21

Bill arrived at the newspaper office and introduced himself. The guy who was assigned to help him was Ralph.

Ralph said, "I've researched you and you've made a name for yourself lately."

"I was just doing my job."

"Your job has made you a celebrity in the news business. I saw where you're writing a book too."

"It's just my fifteen minutes of fame. The book was someone else's idea."

Bill thought that a little white lie didn't hurt. The book was actually his idea.

Ralph asked, "How can we help you?"

"I'm doing research on Congressman Swindell and wanted to look at any information from about twenty years ago."

"Isn't he the Congressman on the Save America website now?"

"He is."

"Are you doing a story about Congressman Swindell like the other two?"

"No. I'm just doing some research."

Ralph didn't believe Bill since he knew Bill wouldn't come to Milwaukee just for research. Ralph thought he may be able to get a story so he decided to work closely with Bill.

Ralph looked like a small town newspaperman rather than a city newspaperman. He had on a flannel shirt, cargo pants, and hiking shoes. The red in his flannel shirt matched his red hair. Ralph was wearing horn rimmed glasses.

Ralph said, "All the newspapers from twenty years ago are now stored digitally. There's an office that's not being used that you can work in."

Bill followed Ralph to an office on one of the side hallways. Ralph didn't introduce him to anybody along the way since everybody looked busy. Ralph showed him where the bathroom and the coffee pot were located. When they got to the office, there was today's newspaper on the desk. There were typed instructions on the desk for accessing the computer.

When Bill sat down at the desk, Ralph said, "The sheet should get you into the system and tell you how to search. I'll check on you to see if there's anything more you need. There'll be a few people coming in to meet you. They all know you're here."

"I look forward to meeting everyone. I'd also like to meet anyone that worked here twenty years ago."

Bill really didn't want to meet just anyone and get interrupted but it was the polite thing to do. The visitors may know more than the information in the newspapers so he could ask questions about the Congressman. There could have been rumors that didn't get published. Ralph was too young so Bill didn't ask him anything.

Bill logged into the computer and started reviewing newspapers from twenty years ago.

Mark started at the house that the Congressman lived in twenty years ago. He knocked on the door and an older lady answered the door. Mark introduced himself and said he was assisting with research about Congressman Swindell. The lady introduced herself as Marge.

"Can I come in and ask a few questions about Congressman Swindell?"

Marge thought a minute and figured it was okay. She had her medical alert around her neck in case there was any trouble. Since her husband died a year ago, she did like having someone to talk too.

Marge opened the door, invited Mark in. "Can I get you something to drink?"

"No. Thank you." Mark sat down in a chair in the living area. Mark noticed the room was full of pictures on the walls and the tables.

"Are these your children and grandchildren?" Mark figured it was an easy guess.

"I have five kids and ten grandchildren. They're spread out all over the US. It's different than when I was young."

"You still look pretty young."

"I like you already. How can I help you?"

"As I said, I'm doing research about Congressman Swindell and this was his house at one time. What do you remember about Congressman Swindell?"

"I don't know much about the Congressman. We bought this house from the Congressman and his wife about twenty years ago. My late husband got a promotion at work and we decided to buy a bigger house. We had our fifth child and had outgrown our other house. The Congressman and his wife were getting a divorce and the house was being sold. We made an offer and it was accepted."

"Do you know why the Congressman was divorcing?"

"I really don't. I was too busy with my children to even watch the news."

"Did any of the neighbors talk about the Congressman when you moved here?"

"I didn't talk to the neighbors except to say hello. Raising my children was more than a full time job."

"Did any of your neighbors live here twenty years ago?"

"There's a neighbor two doors down who lived here then. They are John and Sandy Combs."

"Did you meet the Congressman's children?"

"No. The house was vacant when the real estate agent took us through and I didn't meet them. Neither the Congressman nor his wife came to the closing."

"Have you heard any rumors about the Congressman?"

"I did hear someone say he may be gay since he never married again but that was all. I think he's still not married."

"Do you know where his wife or children live now?"

"I don't. I'm sorry."

"Did you meet any of the children that lived in the neighborhood when you bought the house?"

"My kids played with a lot of kids in the neighborhood. The neighborhood is filled with old people now but there were lots of kids twenty years ago."

"Do you remember any of their names?"

Marge thought for a few minutes. "I remember a Cathy, a Johnny, a Tim, a Sandra, a Karen, a Jackie, a Mikey, a Ron, a Peter, and that's all. I know there were more but I can't remember their names right now. The ones I mentioned were the ones my kids played with the most."

"What about a Jim?"

"I don't remember a Jim." Marge thought before answering.

"He would've been about nine or ten years old when you moved here."

"No. I don't remember a Jim."

Mark decided to change the subject and asked, "What condition was the house in when you bought it?"

"It was great. There wasn't anything we needed to do to the house when we moved in. I've updated some things in the past twenty years but it's still a great house. It's too big for me now and I don't like having to climb the stairs to my bedroom and to the basement to do laundry."

"How many rooms are in the basement?"

"It's mostly open. The kids could play down there in the winter and when it was raining."

"Are there any separate rooms downstairs?" Mark needed to verify part of Jim's story so he kept probing.

"There were two separate rooms downstairs. One is the laundry room and the second one is in a back corner."

"Was there anything in the back corner room when you saw the house for the first time?"

"No. The room was empty."

"What kind of locks were on the room?" Mark kept probing.

"It was strange. There was a deadbolt on the door that could be locked from both sides. We removed that right away since we thought our kids would lock another kid in the room."

"Would you mind if I looked at the room?"

"Not at all. Let's go now."

Mark followed Marge down the basement stairs. Mark saw the room in the back corner. It was storage now but he could imagine it with a bed. Mark was thinking that he had a little validation of Jim's story. He couldn't think of any more questions to ask while he followed Marge back upstairs.

Mark didn't sit back down. "Thank you very much Marge. It was very gracious of you to talk to me."

"You're a nice gentleman and it was a pleasure."

Marge showed Mark where the Combs lived when they stepped outside.

Daniel and Michelle were busy looking at old newspapers from twenty years ago. The microfiche didn't allow a search so it was tedious work. Having Michelle beside him made the job less tedious.

Michelle asked, "Exactly what are we looking for?"

"Anything about the Congressman."

"That's very broad. Can you narrow it down some?"

"I just want to see what was written about him twenty years ago and about his divorce."

After about an hour, Michelle said, "I'm going to leave you for a while if you think you'll be okay."

"I don't know if I will be. Will you come back often?"

"I will. Since you're going to be my future husband, I don't want you to sneak out the door."

"You're the person I've been looking for my whole life so I'm not leaving."

"I bet you tell all librarians that."

"I've only told one and that's you." Daniel smiled.

Michelle went back to the front desk and was rethinking her bantering with Daniel. She thought it was fun but now didn't think anything would come of it.

Daniel kept looking through the newspapers on the microfiche. He was looking at all the newspapers published twenty years ago. He knew that several were probably no longer published due to the move to digital news. He was finding lots of articles about the Congressman. It was a reelection year so that added to the articles. The Congressman was back in his home district to politic.

There were articles about the Congressman's divorce but there weren't many details. The articles said the divorce was mutual but didn't include anything about the divorce agreement. There was one article that said the Congressman's wife had full custody of the two children.

It was getting to be about ten so Daniel took a break from the microfiche. He walked by the front desk and motioned for Michelle to walk outside with him. He didn't expect she would but she showed up outside a few minutes later. He was standing watching traffic go by when she walked up beside him. He could smell her before she arrived. She had her library shoes on so there wasn't much noise from her shoes.

Michelle asked, "Are you counting cars?"

"I'm giving my eyes a break from the microfiche viewer."

"Have you found what you are looking for?"

"Not in the microfiche, but I have in you."

Michelle decided to be more specific and said, "What exactly are you looking for about the Congressman?"

Daniel thought about telling her since she was his future wife but thought better and said, "Just general information."

"That's available on the web."

"Let's talk about us rather than business. Would you be willing to move to Los Angeles?"

"You mean today or tomorrow?"

161

"By the end of the month would be good."

"I may if the offer is good enough."

"How does a lifetime full of happiness sound?"

"I had that promise before and I was shortchanged."

"How long were you married?"

"Twenty years. I stayed married until the kids turned eighteen."

"How many kids do you have?"

"I have two wonderful kids. How about you?"

"I have two kids too. Where do your kids live?" Daniel asked.

"One is in Los Angeles and one is in San Diego."

"Perfect. You'll be closer to your kids when you move to LA."

"I'd like that but it's expensive to live in Los Angeles or San Diego."

Daniel put his arm around Michelle and she didn't move away. He turned as he pulled her around to face him. He then kissed her and she didn't stop him or push him away. He continued to kiss her until a horn beeped on the street next to the library. He stopped kissing her but didn't release her from the embrace. She had her arms around Daniel and didn't release her arms.

She finally said, "That was nice. It's been a while and that was very nice."

"Have I asked you to marry me yet?"

She grinned as she looked up into Daniel's face. "I believe you have and I still need time to get to know you."

"Do you know there are people watching us from the library windows?"

Michelle pushed Daniel away. "I'd better go back inside."

Daniel returned with her and grinned at the other librarians as he went back to the microfiche viewer. He was sure Michelle would be asked lots of questions about the stranger. The other librarians would certainly make fun of Michelle if she told them she had just met Daniel.

Bill was looking at some of the same newspapers as Daniel. He was finding the same articles as Daniel. The difference was that Bill could look faster since the information was digital and he could do searches. The slow part was the interruptions. During the morning, people kept coming in to meet the celebrity. This included reporters, administrative assistants, and editors. He questioned them all about Congressman Swindell but wasn't learning anything helpful. The editor-in-chief of the newspaper came in and talked for about thirty minutes. The editor-in-chief was only in his job for ten years and didn't know any details about the Congressman from twenty years ago. Bill spent more time talking to everyone than he did researching.

The editor-in-chief asked, when he was visiting, "How did you find out about Senator Jones and Congressman Riley?"

"I had a source tell me about them."

The editor-in-chief must have thought about it before coming in and asked, "Was Save America the source?"

Bill could answer honestly since Mark and Daniel had actually given him the information on Congressman Riley. "No. They weren't."

"It was quite a surprise that you found information about them that no one else did."

"I was just lucky." Bill was getting a little annoyed.

"I wish my reporters had your luck. One story is lucky but you had two in a row."

"I'm sure you have great reporters. Your paper has maintained its circulation while others haven't." Bill tried to change the subject.

"I'm not sure it'll last but the paper is doing well. Our reporters could learn from you though. What's your secret?"

Bill was feeling edgy from being bantered about his recent reports. "I was lucky and had some good information."

"I know there's luck always involved but you have to make your own luck in this business. Would you mind having a session with some of our reporters? When they heard you were coming, all of them wanted to talk to you."

Bill turned his head towards an office wall, rolled his eyes where the editor-in-chief couldn't see them, and answered, "I'd be glad too.

This afternoon would be fine or tomorrow morning." Bill thought that a scheduled discussion may keep the traffic away from the office.

"That'd be great. I'll see what works best for us and we'll set up a time. I'll let you know."

"Just let me know when and where."

"I've got a meeting and have to go. I look forward to your discussion with our reporters."

Bill turned back to his terminal knowing he'd be interrupted again soon. He wished he could close the door but he was a guest and didn't want to be rude.

Chapter 22

Mark walked down to the Combs' house. It was another two story house much like the Congressman's house. There was a large porch with white columns and a garage attached to the house. There were two massive front doors that were about nine feet tall. Mark climbed the steps and rang the doorbell. He could hear the chimes in the house. They were extremely loud. He thought the doorbell must have been adjusted as the Combs got older. He waited a minute and then rang the doorbell again. No one came to the door. He rang the bell a third time and still no one came to the door. Mark took out a business card, wrote a note on it to call him, and slid it between the door and the door frame near the door knob. He figured the Combs would see it when they went through the door.

Mark left the Combs' house and walked to one of the immediate neighbor's houses beside the Congressman's house. He went through the same routine and then left his card. He walked to the opposite neighbor and climbed the steps to the big doors. He thought the builder must have gotten a good deal on these doors since they were in all the houses.

He rang the bell on the third house and an older lady came to the door. Mark introduced himself and the lady introduced herself as April.

"I'm doing research on Congressman Swindell and would like to ask you a few questions."

"I don't know anything about the Congressman."

"Did you live here at the same time as the Congressman?"

"No. My husband and I moved here about ten years ago." She stood at the door and didn't invite Mark in the house.

"Have any of your neighbors talked about the Congressman since you lived here?"

"Marge and her husband mentioned that the Congressman used to live in their house but nothing more."

Mark could see that April was getting a little annoyed so he only asked one more question.

"Do you recall a boy named Jim that lived in the neighborhood?"

April did take a little time to think instead of brushing Mark off. "No. I can't recall a boy named Jim."

Mark figured he was about to be told to leave so he made a graceful exit. "Thanks for your time. It was a pleasure meeting you."

Mark went to the house across the street facing the Congressman's house. A lady named Connie told him the same story as April, except they had moved into the neighborhood six years ago. Mark tried two more houses with similar results. Mark decided to take a lunch break and try the Combs house after lunch. Mark called Daniel to see how he was doing and see if he wanted a lunch break.

When Daniel answered, Mark asked, "Do you have time for lunch?"

"Yes. I do. I need a break from the microfiche viewer."

"Where should we meet?"

"There's a deli restaurant across from the library on First Street."

"I'll meet you there in about twenty minutes."

Mark called Bill next and told him that Daniel was meeting him for lunch at the restaurant across from the library in twenty minutes. Bill said he'd be there too.

Daniel closed his eyes so he could focus enough to walk and went to the front desk. Michelle wasn't at the front desk and another librarian looked up from a desk.

The librarian asked, "Can I help you?"

"Yes. Will you be a bridesmaid at Michelle's and my wedding?"

"I guess so. When's the wedding?"

Daniel picked a date out of the air. "June 12."

"I'm sure I can make it. Where will the wedding be?"

As she was answering, Michelle walked up.

Daniel said, "We're thinking of having the wedding here in Milwaukee. Where do you recommend?"

Michelle asked, "What wedding are we discussing?"

The librarian answered, "Your wedding of course. This nice gentleman invited me to be in your wedding."

Michelle glared at Daniel. "I believe I'm supposed to do the inviting."

The librarian was a frail woman who looked like she could break into tears easily. "Does that mean I'm not going to be in the wedding? I think of you as my daughter."

Michelle was careful in picking her words since she knew the librarian would break into tears if she said the wrong thing. "It's just that I wanted to personally invite you. Of course I want you in the wedding."

The librarian got up and hugged Michelle. "I'm so happy for you. I could tell you loved each other when I saw you kissing."

Michelle looked at Daniel. "Outside."

"I think you meant to say, let's take it outside."

Michelle raised her brow and pursed her mouth as she was trying not to grin. Daniel followed her out the door.

When they were outside she said, "Why are you causing trouble?"

"I thought I was helping."

"I don't need that kind of help."

"Fine. You can plan the wedding, but I'm a great planner."

"Why were you aggravating her?"

"I came up front to invite you to lunch and she asked me if she could help."

"I brought my lunch."

"I'm meeting my friends across the street at the deli in about twenty minutes. Can you join us?"

"I'll think about it."

"How long will it take?"

Michelle thought for only a few seconds. "I've decided to go. I'll be ready in about ten minutes." Michelle thought it couldn't do any harm to have lunch and she could save her lunch she brought until tomorrow.

"I'll be outside waiting. Should we ask your bridesmaid to go as well?"

Michelle didn't answer and walked back inside.

Daniel stayed outside and away from his nemesis, the microfiche viewer. Michelle came out in about ten minutes. Daniel took her hand and they walked across the street to the restaurant. They got a table for four and ordered their drinks. Both ordered tea.

In about five minutes, Mark showed up and found the table. Daniel introduced Mark, "This is Mark, my business partner. Mark manages our office in Washington, D.C. This is Michelle, my future life partner and wife."

"Congratulations to both of you. It doesn't appear that you've been working since you've had time to get engaged this morning."

"It only took a few minutes to know I'd found my true love. Isn't that right, sweetie pie?"

Michelle thought of what approach to take and then decided. "That's right, my honeybun." She leaned over and kissed him on the cheek and pinched his other cheek.

"I'm leaving and coming back in again. I'm sure I'm in the wrong restaurant. Did Daniel put you up to this as a prank?"

Michelle answered, "I helped Daniel this morning and he invited me to lunch."

"That's better. I was concerned for a minute."

Michelle decided to take another tack. "What do you mean? Do you think I'm not good enough for Daniel?"

"That's not what I mean. I'm just…"

Michelle interrupted, "You're just being mean. I'm going back to work and eat my leftovers." Michelle looked at Daniel and winked.

Daniel said, "Please stay honey. I'm sure Mark will promise to stop being rude."

Mark became defensive, "I'm not being mean. I was just saying…."

Michelle interrupted again, "You were saying Daniel shouldn't be with someone like me."

Mark opened his mouth to talk and Michelle said, "Just kidding Mark. Give me five Daniel."

Michelle raised her hand for a high five and Daniel pulled her over and kissed her. Since Mark was watching, Michelle gave it extra effort and made it last longer. When they separated, Mark had his mouth agape.

Bill came in at the same time and saw the kissing. He said, "Am I at the right place?"

Mark said, "That's what I said when I came in."

Bill asked, "Is this one of your undercover investigators."

Daniel responded, "Not quite. This is Michelle the librarian. That is Bill Webber, the famous reporter."

Michelle's mouth went agape this time before she said, "You're the Bill Webber. The one I've seen on the news talking about Senator Jones and Congressman Riley."

People at the adjoining tables looked over and then whispered about Bill Webber being in the restaurant.

"Yes."

Michelle looked at Daniel. "You didn't tell me you were working with Bill Webber."

Daniel asked, "Could I have gotten better help if you knew I was working with Bill Webber?"

"Of course you would."

"I'm offended."

"Take it any way you want."

Daniel said, "I forgot to mention that this is my future wife, Bill."

"I didn't know your fiancé lived in Milwaukee. Congratulations."

"We just met this morning."

As a good reporter Bill knew when to change the subject. "I see. Have you ordered lunch?"

"Not yet. Here comes the server now."

All four ordered sandwiches. Bill and Mark ordered tea.

Daniel said, "Please don't repeat anything you hear, Michelle."

"I'm a librarian and I'm paid to be quiet."

Daniel was first to speak. "I'll begin. I've looked at microfiche all morning and haven't found anything we didn't know. I'm planning to do more research this afternoon. That's been my morning."

Bill went next. "Most of my morning has been talking to everyone from the editor-in-chief to the janitor at the newspaper. Everybody wanted to meet me and talk to me. The little time I had to do research I didn't find anything new."

Mark was next. "I talked to several neighbors with most moving into the neighborhood after the Congressman moved out. I did talk to the lady who bought the Congressman's house twenty years ago but she didn't meet the Congressman, his wife, or the kids. The house was vacant when she saw the house. She also couldn't remember a Jim that lived in the neighborhood. I did see the room in the back corner of the basement. The owner said the room had a deadbolt when they moved in."

Michelle asked, "Have you looked in the census records?"

Daniel answered, "Not yet. I was planning to put it on my list."

Michelle said, "I can do it. Does Jim have a last name?"

Daniel responded, "No." He looked at the other two and asked, "Is it okay for her to help?"

Bill responded, "If you two are going to be together anyway, she might as well help."

"Good. Can she come to dinner too?"

"Dinner too, but she needs to go to the powder room if it gets touchy," Bill answered.

"I'll bring plenty of powder." She was thinking that she was now working with Bill Webber, star reporter. Working with Daniel was nice but now she was working with Bill.

The three guys laughed. They didn't discuss why the basement room was important since it was only a part of the story.

Mark sat his glass down after a drink. "I'm going back into the neighborhood to talk to more neighbors after lunch, unless Daniel would like to switch."

"I'm not switching. I'm counting today as a first date with Michelle." He raised his eyebrows as he talked.

Michelle replied, "You should switch with Mark if you think it's a first date."

Bill sighed. "I'll be back at the newspaper. It was so much easier when I was an unknown. I may have a session with the newspaper staff this afternoon so there may not be much progress from me today."

Mark said, "I was hoping to find out where Jim lived today so we could make our plans at dinner. Maybe we'll be lucky this afternoon."

Mark paid for lunch and everybody left. Daniel held Michelle's hand as they walked back across the street. The other librarians looked up at them when they strolled into the library.

Daniel asked, "Will you show me where the census records are located?"

"Let me check in first and I'll come back to your viewer in a few minutes."

Daniel turned his viewer back on and picked up where he left off. He had gone through six months of newspapers and had years to go before he finished, unless he found the information he needed. In a few minutes, Michelle came back to the viewer and he followed her to a terminal. Michelle logged into the terminal and stepped through several screens before a screen came up for the census. She went to the 2000 census and entered search data for Milwaukee and for the street. Daniel watched her hands as she worked the keyboard and thought she had the loveliest hands. He thought her hands moved like she was playing a piano. He was startled when Michelle poked him in the ribs.

Michelle pointed at the screen. "This is the census data for the street the Congressman lived on. Help me look to see if there's a Jim or James."

Daniel moved close to Michelle to watch the terminal screen as she scrolled though the information. They didn't see a Jim or James on the street so Michelle moved to the other streets nearby. After an exhaustive look, they found two named Jim and three named James. For the five, the ages were too young or too old.

Michelle offered, "Jim's parents could have moved to the neighborhood after the census."

"Can we look at the 2010 census?"

"Sure." Michelle closed out the 2000 census and opened up the 2010 census. She went through several screens and found the street where the Congressman lived.

Daniel moved close and looked for a Jim or James as Michelle scrolled. Michelle then changed to the nearby streets and they looked together again. After this look, there were six who were named Jim or James and none were the right age.

Michelle suggested, "We could look at property tax records to see if there was a Jim or James that bought property after the 2000 census."

"Sounds good. Can you do that too?"

"Yes. I'll pull up the county records."

Michelle pulled up the county website on her terminal and started searching. It was difficult since the county searches were typically by last name and not by first name. When she searched using James and Jim, the searches came up as too many properties to display. The next searches she did were by street. She could type the street name and all the property owners from that street would be displayed. When she used the Congressman's street, a long list of present and past property owners were displayed. She printed two copies of the list and gave a copy to Daniel. Daniel scanned the list and highlighted all names with a Jim or James that were located within a few blocks from the Congressman. While Daniel was scanning the list, Michelle searched using adjacent streets and printed out lists of present and past property owners.

After the lists were printed, Michelle said, "I need to go back to the front for a while. I'll check on you later."

"I'm not sure I can manage without you."

"You can come and get me if you get too overwhelmed."

"I will."

Daniel poured through the lists and highlighted any possible Jim or James that owned property within a few blocks of the Congressman. The next step was to conduct a search of the county's database to see when the property was owned by the Jim or James. The lists that were printed by Michelle didn't show when the property was owned. Daniel thought he could do the searches but thought Michelle could expedite the effort. He went to the front desk and waited for Michelle while she was talking to another librarian.

When he got her attention, he said, "Can I get a little more help please?"

"I'll be back in a few minutes."

"I'm going outside for a few minutes."

"Check with me when you come back in."

Daniel stood watching the traffic while he rolled his neck and his arms and flexed his hands. He stretched his legs on a bench and massaged his neck. He thought about Michelle as he took his break. He hoped she didn't think he was hitting on her just to get her help. He also hoped that a more lasting relationship developed.

As he was thinking of Michelle, she walked up beside him. "What do you need help with?"

"I was just thinking of you."

"Good thoughts I hope."

"They were, and I wanted to get back in the county database to see when the properties were owned."

Daniel took her hand as they went back into the library. She didn't object. Michelle showed him how to get into the database and showed him how to search each property record. Daniel had done this in other states and counties and there were nuances to each. Michelle stayed while he did the first property search. The first property search showed the property being sold by the Jim prior to 2000. Daniel continued to search and found two possible properties owned by a James and none owned by a Jim. From his two possible candidates, he cross referenced them to the census records and found that neither had a child named Jim or James. This effort took several hours to complete and Daniel decided to take another break. He went outside.

Chapter 23

After lunch, Bill scoured through newspapers when he wasn't being interrupted. The editor-in-chief had set up sessions for him to talk to part of the staff at two p.m. and another part of the staff at nine a.m. tomorrow. He thought he had agreed to only one session but didn't object. With the time he had to review the old newspapers, he identified a couple items he wanted to follow-up on. The main one was the divorce. The newspapers didn't have very much information about the divorce. He would have thought a Congressman getting divorced would have generated more detailed news.

Just before two, the editor-in-chief came in and took Bill to a large conference room. There were already lots of people in the room and more came in with Bill and the editor-in-chief. After the room was full, the editor-in-chief introduced Bill. Bill had decided to give a quick overview of the Senator's story and the Congressman's story. After the overview, the editor-in-chief asked if anyone had questions. There were plenty. Most were centered on the source of the initial information. Bill did tell them that his newspaper had access to investigators as he was sure they did in Milwaukee.

One person asked, "Have you had any contact with the Save America people?"

Bill wasn't sure whether to answer truthfully or not but decided that it wouldn't hurt. "I have."

This got everybody's attention. Many hands went up to ask a follow-up question. Bill acknowledged the individual who asked about Save America.

"Have you interviewed anyone with Save America and will you include the interview in your book?"

"I haven't interviewed anyone."

The same person asked, "What did you discuss with them?"

Bill was now regretting answering truthfully about Save America. "They actually called me to thank me for my reports about the Senator and the Congressman. I tried to interview them but they refused. They made it clear that they didn't want to be interviewed and wanted their privacy."

More hands went up and Bill acknowledged another person. "Did they give you a phone number and will you call them?"

Bill decided a little prevarication was needed this time and said he didn't have a way to contact them. The mood changed in the room and only a few hands went up this time.

Another person asked, "Did Save America provide any help to you?"

"No. They just called to thank me." Another lie didn't hurt.

Another question. "When will your book be published?"

"In about three or four months, if I can find time to finish it."

Another question. "Why did you come to Milwaukee?"

Bill decided to lie again and responded, "I needed a break from Washington and volunteered."

A few more questions were asked and answered. The editor-in-chief finished the session by asking everyone to give Bill applause. Bill now needed to remember to give the same answers in the morning.

Bill went back to the newspaper searches but didn't get any clear answers about the divorce and didn't find any connection between a Jim or James and the Congressman's children.

Mark went door to door in the Congressman's old neighborhood. About half of the neighbors were home and all knew the Congressman lived in the neighborhood but didn't know him personally. Several neighbors knew the Congressman had two children and knew the Congressman was divorced. None knew any details about the divorce. Almost all of the neighbors had moved into the neighborhood after the Congressman had moved out. Mark decided to stop for the day about five o'clock but decided to stop by the Combs' house before he left the neighborhood. He looked at the front door and his card was still in the door jam. Mark called Bill and Daniel and told them he would meet them back at the hotel. Bill told Mark that the newspaper closed at five so he'd be on his way.

Daniel asked, when Mark called, "Where are we having dinner?"

Mark answered, "I don't know. We'll pick a place after we get to the hotel."

"I wanted to let Michelle know where to meet us."

"Have her meet us at the hotel."

"I don't know if she will but I'll try."

Daniel found Michelle at the front desk. He asked, "Can you meet us at the hotel since Mark doesn't know where we're having dinner?"

"Let's go outside," Michelle said while she shook her head.

When they were outside she said, "I've thought about it and I can't have dinner with you tonight."

"Do you have plans?"

"No, I don't but that would be like a date."

"Let's just call it a social gathering with Bill, Mark, you, and me."

"Bill will be at dinner." Michelle thought they were pulling her leg at lunch.

"Yes."

"What time?"

"Can you be at the Holiday Inn on Third Street at six thirty?"

"I can be there at six thirty."

"Is there a nice restaurant nearby?"

"There's a great Italian restaurant almost next door."

"Sound good. See you at six thirty." Bill kissed her lightly and squeezed her. She was trim and fit underneath the loose dress.

Daniel called Mark and Bill and told them to meet him in the lobby of the hotel at six thirty. Daniel stopped by the Italian restaurant and made reservations for four at six thirty.

After freshening up, all three met in the lobby at six thirty. Michelle was waiting on them.

Bill said to Michelle, "I'm glad you could join us for dinner. Daniel would be heartbroken if you couldn't."

"I came mainly because of you. I wanted to learn more how a great reporter works."

"Daniel and Mark are the ones who make me a great reporter."

Mark asked, "Where's dinner?"

"We're going to an Italian restaurant within walking distance. I made reservations at six thirty."

The Italian restaurant was a small local restaurant owned by a couple. The wife met them at the door and sat them at a table in a corner. Bill ordered a bottle of Chianti and all four decided to imbibe. Four large stemmed wine glasses were already on the table. The server filled water glasses and told them about the specials. Bill and Michelle ordered the seafood pasta special and Mark and Daniel ordered the three cheese lasagna special. All four had mixed green salads with Italian dressing.

After placing the orders, Bill said, "I didn't find anything new this afternoon. The editor-in-chief scheduled a group grope with the staff that took an hour and I was interrupted a lot. I still have questions about the divorce and didn't find anything about Jim."

Daniel went next, "Michelle and I went through the 2000 and 2010 census and through the county property records. We found lots of individuals named Jim or James but none that was the right age. We were hoping that a Jim or James who owned a property had a son named Jim or James but that didn't happen either."

Michelle added, "We searched all the streets next to the Congressman's house."

Mark was next, "I'm afraid I didn't find anything more either. I talked to a lot of neighbors and they didn't know anything helpful. Most had moved to the neighborhood after the Congressman moved out." Mark didn't mention the Combs since he figured they probably wouldn't know anything either.

Bill looked to Daniel. "Can you go to the courthouse tomorrow morning and see if you can find any documents on the Congressman's divorce? The editor-in-chief scheduled another session with the staff in the morning so I can't go."

Daniel answered, "I can. I'll go first thing."

Bill said, "Call me and let me know what you find."

"I'm going back to the neighborhood tomorrow. There has to be someone who knows something."

Michelle asked, "Why are we looking for Jim?"

Daniel answered, "He's just someone who may be able to provide important information about the Congressman. It would be nice to chat with him."

"I'm sure there's more to it but it's probably none of my business."

The server brought bread and none of the three said anything to explain. Daniel wanted to say that he'd explain it at breakfast but thought better of it. He did think he would try to get Michelle to stay with him tonight. It was the second date, if lunch was counted. He was thinking he would stay in Milwaukee a few extra days if needed to woo Michelle. He was convinced she could be the soul mate he had been looking for all of his life. Bread was passed around with all taking some.

Bill was buttering his bread. "Let's hope we find something soon. I need to get back to Washington before all my other assignments are divvied out to other reporters."

Mark asked, "Do you want to interview the Congressman's wife before we leave?"

"I still want to talk to Jim first if possible." Bill thought about saying he would call Save America but he didn't want to say it in front of Michelle. He was glad Michelle was helping so he didn't mind limiting his discussion.

As Bill was talking, Mark's phone rang. He looked at the phone number and saw that it was a local call. He pointed at the phone as he left the table.

He said, "Hello."

The person on the other end said, "This is Sandy Combs. We just saw your card a few minutes ago when John went to get the mail. I hope it's not too late to call."

"Not at all. I'm glad you called. I was hoping to stop by and ask a few questions about Congressman Swindell."

"Can you come by in the morning? John has a doctor's appointment in the afternoon."

"Is nine o'clock okay?"

"It is. See you at nine." Sandy ended the call.

Mark went back to the table and the server was placing the salads on the table. He waited until the server had left. "The call was from a neighbor who lived close to the Congressman and knew the Congressman. I'm meeting with them in the morning at nine."

Bill said, "Let me know if you find out anything."

"I will."

The four ate their salads and didn't talk. All were thinking about the next day or the evening. Daniel was thinking about both.

Finally Michelle spoke, "Thanks for allowing me to be part of your merry group for a short while. It's been fun."

Bill said the right thing, "You're welcome to continue as long as we're in Milwaukee."

"That'd be great. I'll try to help when I can."

Daniel knew that Bill was the main reason she wanted to help but hoped he was part of the reason.

She said as she looked at Bill, "I know a few people at the courthouse if you want me to go with Daniel."

Daniel was saying yes in his head and hoped Bill said yes verbally, and he did.

The server brought the main course. He offered parmesan and all four had the server grind the cheese on their dish. The server emptied the wine bottle in the glasses and Bill ordered another bottle of Chianti. A quiet came over the table as everyone dug in.

Bill spoke first, "This is great and an excellent choice, Michelle."

Michelle smiled and said thanks.

"I could eat here tomorrow night too if it's okay with everyone," Bill suggested.

All agreed, including Michelle, that they would return tomorrow night.

The server offered dessert but there were no takers. The entrees were large and filling. They stayed to finish the wine. Michelle talked about Milwaukee. Bill and Mark talked about Washington. Daniel talked about Los Angeles.

All four walked back to the hotel together. Mark and Bill went to their rooms while Daniel stayed outside with Michelle.

Daniel asked, "Would you like to come in for a while?"

"I don't think so. I'd better get home."

"Can we sit in the lobby and talk?"

"No. I need to go. When would you like to go to the courthouse?"

"I'll meet you at the library at nine," Daniel responded.

She put her arms around Daniel and kissed him firmly on the lips. "See you at nine."

"Are you sure you don't want to share a few more kisses."

"Maybe tomorrow."

Daniel showed his best puppy dog look. "I won't be able to sleep."

She waved goodbye as she went to her car.

Daniel stood with his mouth agape.

The next morning they met for breakfast at seven. Daniel did sleep some.

Bill had a worried look on his face. "Let me know if you find something. I'll be paying my dues at the newspaper this morning with another group gathering. I then hope I have time to search more old newspapers."

"I'll call you after my nine o'clock," Mark said.

Daniel said, "I'll call after going to the courthouse."

Bill said, "I'll check with Save America after breakfast."

Bill called William after breakfast but Jim hadn't called again.

Daniel went into the library at nine and saw Michelle behind the counter. "Hey, sweetie pie."

Save America

Michelle answered, "Hi there, handsome."

The library staff at the front desk all looked up at Daniel and saw him with a big smile. Daniel was thinking this was going to be a good day. The courthouse was nearby so they walked. One of the people Michelle knew was in records. She was Amber.

Michelle asked Amber, "How have you been?"

Amber hugged Michelle and answered, "Fine. And you?"

"Doing okay."

"Who's the hunk?"

"This is Daniel. I'm helping him with some research."

"How can I help?" Amber asked.

"We'd like to see the files for Congressman Swindell's divorce."

Amber asked, "When was the divorce?"

"About twenty years ago."

"Those files should have been scanned. I should be able to access them."

Michelle and Daniel watched her work the keys on her computer and saw her looking at her two screens. She punched more keys and stared at the screens more.

She finally looked up. "The files are sealed."

Michelle asked, not knowing the right way to ask the question, "How can we get the documents unsealed?"

"You'd have to file a petition and have a very good reason."

"Can you tell me who the lawyers were for the divorce?"

Daniel was planning to ask the same thing but Michelle was doing okay without him. He had noted both lawyers from the library search so it'd be good if the court records agreed.

Amber's eyes moved on her screens as she pushed on more keys. She finally said, "The wife's lawyer was Catherine Womack and the husband's lawyer was Alfred Tompkins."

Michelle asked, "Is there anything else?"

"That's all there is. The lawyers' names are shown on the files but I can't get into the files."

"Thanks Amber. Take care."

"You too."

181

As they were walking back to the library, Daniel said, "Can you find the lawyers' addresses? Maybe I could convince them to show me their files."

"Would you be planning a little strong arming?"

"No. Not me. I'll just use my charm."

"I'll look when I get back to the library."

While Michelle looked, Daniel left a message on Bill's phone. He figured Bill was still in his group gathering. Michelle had printed out two MapQuest pages with the addresses and directions. Both were within walking distance. Lawyers tended to have offices near the courthouse.

They walked to Catherine Womack's office and asked to speak to Catherine. Catherine was available and emphatically told Daniel and Michelle that they couldn't see the files.

Daniel said, as they walked to Alfred Tompkins' office, "It's a nice day for a walk even with the ill temper of that woman."

"She wasn't very nice."

"I'm certain Alfred will be nicer."

They arrived at Alfred's office and it was no longer Alfred's office. The front door was open so they walked in. There were drop cloths on the floor and paint cans scattered about. They walked into a rear office and there more drop cloths and paint cans. There wasn't any furniture. The offices were bare.

They saw a guy in white coveralls and asked, "Is this Alfred Tompkins' office?"

"Nope. It's gonna be a real estate office when we finish," the painter answered.

Daniel asked, "Do you know where Mr. Tompkins moved to?"

"Nope."

They walked in another room and saw another painter. The other painter gave the same answers.

They walked next door to a deli and asked about Mr. Tompkins. They were told that Mr. Tompkins died at his desk a month ago and his law office was now closed. They were told that he didn't have a partner and his wife cleaned out the offices. She's renting the building to a real estate firm.

Michelle asked, "Do you know where the wife lives?"

The lady at the deli answered, "I don't."

Michelle said, "Thanks."

Daniel held Michelle's hand as they walked back to the library.

Michelle said as they walked, "I'll look up her address when we get back to the library."

"I'd like to see if she still has the files. Even if she does, she probably won't give them to us."

"Maybe we can convince her we're opening a law office and would like to buy the law books and everything else that was left."

"Do you have a suit?" Michelle asked.

"I don't have one with me."

"You'll need one to wear when you go see the wife."

Daniel grinned, "Then you'll need a lawyer's wife dress."

"And what would that be?"

"I was thinking about a short black cocktail dress with an open back, low cut front, and a slit up the side."

"What kind of lawyer are you?"

"I'm a tart lawyer."

"You mean a tort lawyer."

"Maybe so, but you'd look great in the tart lawyer dress."

"If you turn out to be a keeper, I'll wear a dress like you described."

Daniel looked at her and undressed her. Then he dressed her in the black dress with red heels.

"What are you thinking?"

"I was imagining you in the black dress with red heels."

"Get those thoughts out of your mind. We're back at the library."

Michelle looked up the lawyer's address and phone number in the local phone directory. The phone number was in the lawyer's name. She wrote them down and gave them to Daniel.

Daniel called the number and a woman answered.

Daniel said in his formal voice, "Hello. This is Daniel Wingate. I'm a new attorney who's looking for law books and office furnishings.

I understand you may have both and wondered if you would be interested in selling them."

The lawyer's wife was Abigail. "I do have law books and some office items and would like to sell them."

"When can we meet to discuss them?"

"I'm available this morning. The items are in a storage unit on Walnut Street. Can you meet me in about an hour?"

Daniel thought about the suit that Michelle had suggested. "Will an hour and a half be okay?" He thought that would give him enough time to get a suit.

"An hour and a half would be fine. Just a minute and I'll find the address." Abigail laid the phone down and then picked it up when she found the address. "It's 2605 Walnut Street."

"See you there," Daniel said and ended the call.

Michelle was standing next to Daniel and Daniel repeated the address. "Where do I get a suit?"

"I'll show you. I'll tell the others inside I'll be gone for a while."

Michelle directed Daniel to a mall and to a chain store that sold suits. She picked out a nice reasonably priced suit, a dress shirt, and a tie. She then picked out shoes and socks. No one had picked out clothes for him in a long time. Daniel paid and took them into a dressing room to change. The suit was gray, the shirt white, and the tie was red.

Michelle was impressed with Daniel and said, "You look very handsome in your new duds."

"Thanks. That's the nicest thing you ever said to me. Should we buy your black dress now?"

"I don't believe there's enough time. Maybe later today."

"Are you going with me to the storage unit?"

"Abigail may recognize me so you're on your own."

Daniel kissed Michelle as he dropped her off her at the library. "Can you do lunch?"

"I think so. Stop back by and we can go across the street again. You'll have to wear your suit."

"I'll stop and get your dress on the way back."

Daniel arrived at the storage unit about ten minutes early. The gate was locked so he waited for Abigail. About five minutes later, Abigail drove up in a new black Mercedes, keyed in the code for the gate, and motioned Daniel to follow her. She drove to a unit in the middle and parked. Daniel parked behind her in his rental car.

Daniel walked up to her in his new suit and said, "Hello. I'm Daniel Wingate."

Abigail looked at him and was impressed. She looked at his fingers when they shook hands and didn't see a wedding ring. She thought a month was long enough and she wouldn't mind being Daniel's cougar. She made the handshake last a bit longer.

Abigail said in a sultry voice, "It's nice to meet you, Daniel."

"It's nice to meet you too. You have a very nice car." Daniel decided to compliment her car rather than her.

"I just bought it this week. I always drove hand-me-downs from my husband so I treated myself."

"You have good taste."

"Let me show you the storage unit." She took a key from her purse and unlocked the unit.

Daniel reached down with one arm and lifted the rollup door. The unit was filled with file boxes, lamps, chairs, pictures, and desks. It was a large unit.

"This is it. Somewhere in there are the law books. I hired a couple of guys to pack it up and move it here."

Daniel saw boxes of files in the storage unit and figured Abigail moved the whole office here including the divorce file for the Congressman. "Would you be willing to sell everything in the storage unit? I can probably use it all."

Abigail didn't show her pleasure at finding a buyer for everything. "I would if the price is right." She thought she would probably give it to him for nothing but didn't want to look too disingenuous about her husband's items. She also thought she would like to barter with Daniel. Daniel could come to her house this afternoon and complete the transaction.

"What price are you thinking of?"

"I was thinking of two thousand."

Daniel didn't want to lose the deal but wanted to appear like a lawyer just starting out. "How about one thousand?"

Abigail had just received the life insurance money and had found out her late husband's frugality had resulted in a large amount of investments so a few hundred dollars didn't seem important. She also didn't want to keep paying for a storage unit. The main reason to save her husband's items in the first place was for the appearance of being a concerned widow.

"Let's split the difference and say fifteen hundred."

"It's a deal." Daniel said. He had stopped on the way and made a withdrawal from an ATM.

"Let's go inside and transfer the storage unit to you and find a piece of paper to give you a receipt."

They went inside. Daniel paid her the fifteen hundred dollars, and the storage unit manager put the unit in Daniel's name and gave him a code to the gate. Abigail had paid for two months when she rented the unit so no rent was due. She also put the security deposit in Daniel's name.

Chapter 24

Mark went to the Combs house at nine and rang the doorbell. He had forgotten how loud it was from the day before.

Sandy answered the door and Mark introduced himself.

Sandy said, "Come on in. John is in the back."

Sandy led Daniel into the back of the house to a sunroom. John was sitting in a chair reading a newspaper.

"This is my husband John. This is Mark."

Mark shook his hand. "Glad to meet you."

Sandy had left her hair grey, short, and straight. A small amount of brown hair was mixed in. She was a petite woman with blue eyes and was in her late fifties. She wasn't wearing any makeup and had a glow to her skin. She had a jogging outfit on and had just got in from a long walk. John was the same age and had a little paunch. He also had short grey hair with a little black left. He had brown eyes and wore black reading glasses on the middle of his nose. He was wearing khaki pants, a golf shirt, and no shoes.

The sunroom had large windows on three walls and furniture with yellow and green flowers. Two tables were located between the chairs and sofa. A ceiling fan was turning slowly.

John said, "Have a seat. Sandy made a pitcher of lemonade. Want some?"

"I think I will. Lemonade sounds great." Mark didn't just accept the drink to be polite but liked lemonade.

"Sandy mentioned you wanted to ask us questions about Congressman Swindell."

"I did. Thanks for taking time to meet with me."

"Not a problem. This'll be a nice distraction."

Sandy came back with a pitcher of lemonade and a glass of lemonade that she gave to Mark. She filled John's glass with the pitcher.

When Sandy sat down, Mark said, "One of the neighbors said you were living here at the same time Congressman Swindell lived here."

John said, "We were. The Congressman lived here about twenty years ago."

"Did you know the Congressman's family very well?"

"We did. We spent a lot of time with his wife Karen and a good amount of time with Paul," John answered.

"So you knew their children?"

"Yes. Their children were younger than ours but we knew their children."

Sandy added, "They were nice children too."

"Did your children visit the Congressman's house?"

"They did when they went with us for a visit," Sandy answered.

"Tell me about the divorce."

Sandy answered, "We don't know much about it. It appeared to be fairly sudden. One day Karen and Paul were in the neighborhood and then they were gone. At first we thought they were on vacation and then a moving crew showed up. The house was then put up for sale. Both of them left without talking to us. We heard about the divorce through the newspapers. Both of them didn't talk to us after they moved."

"Do you know why they got a divorce?"

Sandy answered again, "No. As I said, we didn't talk to them after they moved and there was nothing in the newspapers that said why they were divorcing."

"Did you hear any rumors about the divorce?"

John answered, "No. We only knew what we read in the newspapers."

"Have you talked to the children since they moved?"

"No. I haven't even seen the children since they left," Sandy responded.

"I'm sure I saw the son in town a couple of times but we didn't speak," John added.

"Do you know who got custody of the kids?"

"We don't really know," Sandy responded.

Mark thought that it didn't appear like the Combs knew anything helpful about the divorce or the reason for the divorce. He had hoped they would have told him the Congressman was a pervert and abused his kids and that was the reason for the divorce, but no such luck. Mark decided to switch to the Jim.

"Was there a young boy named Jim that lived in the neighborhood when Karen and Paul moved?"

Sandy answered, "I believe there was a kid named Jim. Do you remember the red headed kid?"

John got a thoughtful look on his face. "I do remember. Unfortunately, I'm starting to remember things from twenty years ago better than things from yesterday."

Sandy was looking at John. "He was only in the neighborhood for a short time. His mother was recently divorced and was renting the house a few doors down. Is that right John?"

"That's correct, from what I remember. I believe they moved shortly after Karen and Paul moved. It was strange that they only lived here for a few months."

Mark asked, "Do you remember Jim's last name?"

Sandy thought for a minute. "I think it was something like Gilbert but I'm not sure."

John added, "It was Gibson. Little Jim Gibson. He had the reddest hair and freckles. He had a bicycle that he rode past our house. I believe he played with Karen's son Jeff. Paul always called him Jefferson while the rest of us called him Jeff."

"I'm sure you're right. I believe it was Jim Gibson. His mother was Amanda Gibson. She was such a quiet lady. Rumor was that she had just gone through a nasty divorce before moving here."

John said, "You're a witness that Sandy said I was right."

Sandy grinned. "You're right sometimes, honey."

"Do you know where Amanda Gibson moved to?"

Sandy answered, "No. She was gone as quick as Karen and Paul. One day she was here and next day she was gone."

Mark decided he probably couldn't find out anything else and said, "Thanks for taking time to talk to me. You're a very nice couple."

Sandy said, "It was no bother. It was nice to talk to you."

Mark left the Combs house and got in his rental car. He drove a few blocks and pulled over. He called Bill and Daniel and had to leave messages for both. He decided to go back to the hotel and start trying to find an Amanda and Jim Gibson.

Bill went to the newspaper in time for the other session with the newspaper staff. He went through the same spiel as the day before and asked for questions. The questions were similar to the day before. There were a few follow-up questions from the day before. Some of the staff must have discussed yesterday's session.

When he was through with the session, he went back to the office he was using. When he checked his cell phone, one of the calls was from Mark. He called.

Mark answered the call. "I found out from the interview with the neighbors that called last night that Jim is Jim Gibson. They only lived in the neighborhood for a short time while his mother, Amanda, rented a house. Amanda and Jim moved out of the neighborhood about the same time that the Congressman moved."

"Did the neighbors know where Amanda Gibson moved to?"

"No. They didn't. I'm back at the hotel searching for Amanda and Jim Gibson now."

"I'll do a search here. Have you heard from Daniel?"

"No. Not yet."

"We'll figure out our next steps at lunch." Bill ended the call.

Bill did a search in the newspaper's database for Amanda and Jim Gibson. He found a reference to Amanda Gibson's divorce from George Gibson about twenty years ago but didn't find anything else about an Amanda Gibson of the right age. He didn't find any information about a George Gibson. His search found lots of information about a Jim Gibson and James Gibson. He printed all the articles that could be found about the Jim Gibson they were looking for.

At about eleven thirty, Bill got a call from Daniel.

Daniel said, "Can you meet for lunch at noon?"

"Yes. Where at?"

"The same place we had lunch yesterday."

Bill asked, "Did you find anything this morning?"

"I did. I'll tell you at lunch."

Daniel called Mark and told him about lunch at noon.

Daniel went back to the library to get Michelle for lunch. Michelle brought him inside to show him off to the other librarians. Daniel still had his suit on. Michelle held Daniel's hand as they walked across the street to the deli. They got a table for four in a corner and ordered their drinks.

Mark and Bill arrived at about the same time and came in together. They were both shocked to see Daniel in a suit.

Mark asked, "What's with the suit, dude?"

"Michelle and I got married this morning."

"Congratulations. I'm disappointed I wasn't the best man."

"One of the librarians was the best man."

Bill looked puzzled and asked, "You're supposed to be working. What's this about getting married?"

Michelle piped in, "We didn't get married, although Daniel is quite striking in his suit. Daniel met with the divorce lawyer's wife this morning and a suit seemed more appropriate for the occasion."

"And what was the occasion?" Bill asked.

"We found out that the Congressman's divorce lawyer died about a month ago and the wife moved the office furnishings and law books to a storage unit. Since the divorce filing was sealed, we decided to try to buy the dead lawyer's stuff hoping to get the sealed file. I called and said I was a new lawyer and needed law books and office stuff. The wife agreed to meet me at the storage unit. Michelle thought it would be better if I showed up in a suit."

"So what happened at the storage unit and what was in the storage unit?" Bill asked.

"The storage unit was full of files, law books, lamps, desks, and pictures. I'm guessing that the lawyer's legal documents are in the storage unit too. The wife appeared to be glad the lawyer had died. She was driving a new Mercedes and was dressed nice. She gave me a good looking over like she was on the prowl. It turns out she would sell the whole storage unit, so I bought it for fifteen hundred dollars. I'm going back after lunch to search the files."

Mark said, "Do you need help?"

"I could use some help moving stuff. The storage unit is full and the files we need are probably in the back of the unit."

Michelle said, "I'm going to help."

Daniel looked at Michelle. "That would be wonderful. I'll be digging in a storage unit with my future wife."

Mark said, "It'll be a compatibility test. If Michelle's helping, I'll finish looking for Jim Gibson."

"Jim Gibson. That's the Jim we're looking for?" Daniel asked.

"It is. The neighbors I interviewed this morning knew little Jim. He was a red headed and freckle faced boy. His mother was Amanda Gibson."

Bill said, "I searched the newspapers and found several possibilities. Mark and I will compare what we found so far."

Michelle asked, "Do Jim and Amanda still live in Milwaukee?"

"The neighbors didn't know and I couldn't tell from my looking."

"Would you like me to search library cards to see if one was issued to Amanda or Jim Gibson?"

Bill responded, "We would. Can you do it before going to the storage unit?"

"Yes."

Bill looked at Mark. "I'll come back to the hotel and we can compare what we found."

The waiter came and they ordered lunch. Bill and Michelle had turkey and provolone on wheat. Mark had ham and Swiss cheese on rye. Daniel ordered a six inch Italian sub. All ordered chips.

Bill asked, "What's the likelihood that the storage unit has the lawyer's legal files?"

"We talked to someone at the restaurant next door and it sounded like the wife just wanted the stuff out of the building as soon as possible. The wife has already rented the building to a real estate company," Daniel answered.

"Call us when you find out if the files are in the unit," Bill said.

Mark asked, "Are you taking the suit back?"

"No. This'll be my wedding suit. If Michelle will agree, I'll use it before leaving Milwaukee."

Michelle said, "The store we bought it from is on the way back to the storage unit."

Mark said, "I guess she told you."

"I'm keeping it. I think I can still persuade her."

Bill said, "If you find something helpful in the storage unit, I'll help persuade her."

The sandwiches came and all ate heartily. Mark and Bill went back to the hotel and Daniel and Michelle walked back across the street to the library. They held hands again. Michelle was getting comfortable being with Daniel and she liked Bill and Mark. Daniel took a seat in the periodical section while Michelle looked for Amanda and Jim Gibson in the library database.

Daniel was reading the local newspaper and had it spread out across a table. He started with the sports section.

In a few minutes, Michelle came over and sat down at the table. "I think I've found them."

Daniel looked up from his paper. "That's great."

"I traced their address back to the Congressman's street so I know it's the right Gibson. There's a woman at the same address as Jim so I'm guessing he's married. They have a couple of children shown too." Michelle handed Daniel a printout of the information.

Daniel looked at the information. "I've got to go back to the hotel to change so I'll give it to Bill and Mark. Would you like to go with me while I change?"

"I want to remember you in the suit."

Daniel looked disappointed. "You're not going to the storage unit with me?"

"You thought I was dumping you?"

"The thought did occur to me. I hope you're kidding."

"I was. I'm going home to change and I'll meet you at the storage unit."

"You scared me. I was serious about us. I wasn't just using you for library help."

Michelle snickered. "See you in a little while." She leaned down and kissed him on the top of the head.

Daniel went to the hotel and found Bill and Mark in the lobby. He waved the sheets of paper as he walked in.

Daniel said, "Michelle found Amanda and Jim Gibson in the library database. Both of them still live in Milwaukee. We think Jim is married and has a couple of kids. I'm changing and going to the storage unit."

Bill said, "Now that we have his address, we can find out everything about him. Mark and I will scope out his house. We may come by the storage unit later. What's the address?"

"It's 2605 Walnut Street. Knock before you come in, just in case."

"Michelle doesn't look like someone who would succumb to your advances in a storage unit," Mark said.

"I believe there's a sofa and you know how women can't resist me when I'm hot and sweaty."

Bill said, "You're joking. Aren't you?"

Mark answered, "He is."

Daniel changed into cargo shorts and a tee shirt with Nirvana on the front. At the storage unit, Daniel waited for Michelle at the main gate. She arrived about ten minutes after him. He keyed the gate and Michelle followed him to the storage unit. She was wearing tight fitting shorts and tight shirt. Daniel pulled her to him and kissed her for a long time. She didn't resist.

When the kiss stopped, Michelle asked, "What brought that on?"

"I figured I'd kiss and hug you before I was sweaty."

"I may like you sweaty."

"Don't hesitate to show it. I'm available for hugs and kisses."

"Where should we start?"

"I was thinking we'd move enough stuff to clear a path to the file boxes. We could set up a table and chairs outside for us to go through the files. Hopefully they're identified on the outside of the box but I doubt it since the wife was so hasty in moving the stuff."

"Sounds like a plan. Let's get started."

Michelle was as fit as she looked and carried stuff along with Daniel out of the storage unit to make a path. They found chairs and a table and set them outside the unit. After about an hour, they had a path to the file boxes which were in the rear of the unit. There were also file cabinets in the rear of the unit. Each brought a box out to the table and each opened their box.

Michelle said, "They're the lawyer's files. I'd guess the old files are in the boxes and the newer ones are in the file cabinets."

Daniel found legal files in his box too. "I think so too. We'll start with boxes."

Both looked through their box and didn't find files for the Congressman. Daniel went back and got two more file boxes. Each searched their box and there was nothing about the Congressman. The boxes accumulated outside the storage unit as they continued.

Daniel said, "Let's take a break, get something to drink, and go to the bathroom."

He had seen a convenience store nearby as he came from the hotel and drove them to it. After using the bathroom, Daniel splurged and got each of them each a seventy nine cent thirty two ounce drink.

When they got back to the storage unit, Bill and Mark were at the front gate. Mark had just taken out his cell phone when Daniel drove up.

Daniel said, "Can I help you gentlemen?"

Mark said, "I thought you'd be inside."

"Michelle couldn't resist me when I got sweaty so we rented a motel for the afternoon."

Michelle said, "I can hardly walk now."

Bill was shaking his head.

"The truth?" Mark demanded.

"We went to get a drink. We haven't found the Congressman's file yet. Follow me in and I'll show you what we own."

Bill and Mark followed Daniel back to the unit and saw the large stack of file boxes outside the storage unit along with the furnishings.

Bill said, "That's a lot of boxes."

"There are more inside."

Daniel asked, "What did you find out?"

Bill answered, "We researched Jim and he's married with two children. One is a boy that's ten years old. I'm guessing that could be a reason he called Save America. Jim works as an accountant and his wife is a school teacher. We drove by Jim's house and Amanda's house. We have phone numbers for his home and where he works. I think we should call him at work but I was hoping the divorce papers could provide some information for our first contact with him."

Daniel said, "I'll bring out a couple more chairs and we can all go through the boxes."

All four continued to go through the boxes and didn't find anything about the Congressman.

After the boxes were done, Michelle said, "Maybe he kept the sealed files locked up in a file cabinet."

Bill said, "He probably did. Can we get to the file cabinets?"

"We can now that all the boxes are moved out," Daniel answered.

"Did you find keys?" Mark asked.

"I haven't, but I haven't been looking for keys. We can check the desk drawers for keys. It may involve moving more stuff."

Daniel and Michelle went into the unit and checked the drawers that they could get to. Michelle held up a ring of keys after looking in the second set of drawers.

Daniel came over to her and kissed her. "You're the best."

He took the keys and tried them on the file cabinets. All of them were now unlocked. It was dark in the unit so Daniel pulled out a drawer and carried it out to the table. He brought other drawers out and set another one on the table and the rest of them beside the table. There were twenty file cabinets and they found information on the Congressman in the tenth cabinet. It was a thick file with a large red tab on top saying the file was sealed. Bill took the file and starting going through it while Daniel, Mark, and Michelle carried the drawers and file boxes back into the storage unit. Bill didn't say anything as he was reading the documents in the file.

After being about half done with the return of the items to the storage unit, Daniel, Mark, and Michelle took a break and sat down at the table.

Mark said, "I could use a drink and a restroom break."

"Me too," Daniel said.

"Me three," Michelle said.

"Me four," Bill said as he looked up from the documents.

All four got in Daniel's car and they returned to the convenience store. Bill brought the file with him. After the restroom break and drinks, they returned to the storage unit. All four sat at the table with their drinks enjoying the short rest.

Bill finally said, "There's some interesting information in the file."

"Can you tell us?" Mark asked.

"I'm not sure. Let me finish reading the file first."

Daniel, Mark, and Michelle went back to their manual labor while Bill read.

Mark asked, "Since we own the unit, what are we going to do with it?"

Daniel answered, "When I bought the unit, I thought I'd not pay the monthly rent and let it end up in a storage auction. I don't think that's such a good idea now since all of the files are in the unit."

Michelle said, "I can have the local Habitat store pick up all the furnishings. They have a truck and volunteers. There are companies that handle shredding and I can find out if they can come out and shred the files."

Daniel said, "That would be great. You're a special lady."

Mark added, "I think so too."

"I'll call Habitat in the morning and also find a shredder."

Mark smiled. "We should be paying you."

"You've bought me lunch and dinner."

"Don't forget the convenience store drinks?" Daniel added.

"Yes. Those too."

Everything was put back in the unit except for the table and chairs. All were now sitting at the table. Bill was shaking his head and staring at the file. He had his forefinger and thumb of his left hand on his chin. He thought about talking in front of Michelle but figured it wasn't best. Daniel and Mark had signed contracts but Michelle didn't.

Bill finally said, "I can't tell you anything until I read the files more. I'm ready for dinner."

Mark suggested, "Let's put the table and chairs in the unit and get dinner."

Daniel looked at Michelle. "Can you do dinner?"

"I need to change. Are we eating at the Italian restaurant?"

"Yes," Bill responded.

Chapter 25

Daniel didn't change back into his suit, which disappointed Michelle when she saw him at the restaurant. Michelle had changed into a dress. It wasn't a little black dress but it was white summer dress that showed cleavage. Her shoulders were tan and she was wearing a multi-colored stone necklace.

Daniel said, "You look lovely."

"Thanks. It's not black."

Daniel leaned over and kissed her on the cheek when she sat down.

Mark agreed, "You do look nice."

Bill still had a studious look on his face and didn't speak even when he sat down. He had his left palm over his mouth and his other arm across his chest. Daniel or Mark didn't interrupt his pondering.

Mark ordered the same Chianti as the night before when the server came over. The server talked about the specials but Bill didn't hear her. Bill did change his position with his hands clasped and he was rubbing his chin on his hands.

He came out of his trance and said, "Did you order wine?"

Mark answered, "I did."

"Did the specials sound good?"

Daniel responded, "They were the same as last night."

All looked at their menus and then closed them. The server came back with the bread and Michelle ordered the veal parmigiana.

Daniel decided to order the same. Bill ordered the lasagna. Mark ordered spaghetti with large meatballs. All had salads.

Bill finally spoke, "I'll be talking to my boss tomorrow morning about the files. Our lawyer will also be in the discussion. I just don't know the legality of me having these files. I could be in hot water if I discuss them with anybody so I'm not going to tell you the content of the files."

None of the three commented since they understood. Michelle understood less than the others.

Bill went on. "Before I talk to Jim, I need to find out where I stand from my boss and the lawyer. I'm scheduled to talk to them in the morning at eight so I should know by nine. Let's plan to meet in the lobby at nine tomorrow."

Michelle said, "I'll call Habitat when I get to the library in the morning and find a shredder."

Bill looked puzzled since he didn't hear the conversation earlier so Michelle explained. "You own the storage unit contents so I'm helping you dispose of them."

"Oh. I must have missed that discussion earlier."

Mark asked, "What do you need Daniel and me to do in the morning?"

"I think we've got everything for now. You can give some thought to our approach with the divorce file and our approach without the divorce file."

Mark looked at Daniel. "I'll meet you for breakfast at eight."

The rest of the dinner involved discussion of the efforts to get the information, the work on the storage unit, and compliments to Michelle for finding Amanda and Jim Gibson in the library database. The server offered dessert but all refused. Mark paid for the meal and left. Bill was right behind him. Daniel and Michelle stayed behind.

Michelle asked, "Is this your last night here?"

"I don't know. It could be depending on what Bill wants us to do."

"How long have you worked for Bill?"

"This is our second contract with Bill. Bill will let us know when we are done with this contract."

"Were you kidding or do you think we can keep seeing each other?" Michelle eyes were a little teary as she spoke.

Daniel pulled her to him and hugged her. "I haven't been kidding. I'd like to have the rest of my life with you."

Michelle's teary eyes went to full tears and she put her head on Daniel's shoulder. "I have enjoyed being with you the past couple of days."

"Would you like to come up to my room?"

"I would. I'll drive my car down since I have my overnight bag in the car."

Both had taken a shower after perspiring at the storage unit so Michelle slipped under the cover with only her negligee after brushing her teeth and removing her makeup. Daniel was waiting in his birthday suit. He figured it was almost as good as his other suit he was wearing today.

Daniel and Michelle kissed and moved their hands over each other's body. After just a few minutes, Michelle rolled on top of Daniel and started using his manhood. Daniel tried to get on top but Michelle was reluctant. She rolled off only after completing her mission. Both were still tired from the storage unit and fell asleep.

Daniel woke her up at two a.m. when he rolled on top of her. He kissed her and convinced her with little effort to do round two.

Daniel and Michelle met Mark for breakfast at eight.

Mark said, "I see you had a good night."

Daniel said, "Tell Michelle what a great guy I am. I want her to move in with me in LA."

"He's a great guy."

"More than that," Daniel said.

"Okay. Daniel is my best friend and business partner. He's smart and we make a great team. He's kind, thoughtful, and funny. You won't go wrong with Daniel."

"That's better. Will you come to LA?"

Michelle thought for a few minutes about being closer to her children and how great it was to be with Daniel. "I will, but not right away."

"That's wonderful. Let's celebrate with breakfast."

Michelle had them make her breakfast to go. "I need to go in early since I was out yesterday. Call me, Daniel." She kissed Daniel on the lips before leaving.

After Michelle left, Mark said, "She's a special lady and a keeper. What's her story?"

"I checked her out after the first day and she told me some of her history. Her marriage wasn't the best and she seems afraid to try it again. She has two children, one in San Diego and the other one in LA."

"So she'll be closer to her kids."

"She will and I'll be happier."

"The two of you certainly look good together."

"Depending on what Bill needs, I might stay here an extra day. I do need to take care of the storage unit."

"The storage unit is important."

After breakfast, Mark and Daniel moved to the lobby and talked about their business. Each called their office in Washington and Los Angeles to catch up. They had hired great people and everything was going well at both offices. Michelle called Daniel just before nine and told him the Habitat truck would be at the storage unit at two and a shredder company would pick up the documents at four.

Daniel said, "I need to go to the storage unit to get the stuff ready. The Habitat truck will be coming at two and a shredder company will be coming at four. I'll need to buy some heavy duty garbage bags for the file cabinet documents."

"We could make money off of the other sealed files."

"We could end up in jail too. I think I'll have them shredded."

Bill came down from his room a little after nine. Mark asked if he had breakfast and he said he had room service.

Bill said, "I had a long conversation with my boss and the lawyer. The lawyer said that I can't use or quote documents in the file but he said I could use the general information."

Bill looked around before continuing. "As you might expect, the Congressman's wife initiated the divorce based on the Congressman's molestation of their son, Jim Gibson and Vernon Wright. The Congressman didn't contest the divorce and agreed to all of the financial terms and full custody of the kids by the wife. The Congressman did require the file to be sealed and that the wife wasn't allowed to discuss the details. The Congressman's lawyer also arranged settlements with Amanda Gibson and the Wright family for one hundred thousand each with an agreement to maintain their silence."

"That's sick," Mark said.

Bill continued, "You're right. The documents include details that made me feel ill. Jefferson must have told his mother specifics and they were included."

Bill paused for a minute and then handed Mark and Daniel a sheet of paper each with handwritten notes. "This is the information about Vernon Wright and his parents in the file. I'd like for you to find him and his parents. Vernon's and Jim's parents signed a confidentiality agreement but Vernon and Jim didn't."

Mark said, "Daniel has to meet Habitat and a shredder company at the storage unit this afternoon but we'll hopefully find him this morning."

Bill said, "I'll plan to call Jim Gibson about ten or so."

Both had brought their computers down at breakfast so they set them up in the lobby and started looking for Vernon Wright and his parents.

Daniel called Michelle after turning on his computer.

Michelle answered her cell phone on the first ring and said, "Hello, Daniel." Daniel was impressed she had his number in her phone.

Daniel said, "Hi there, sweetheart. We need a little more help."

"Anything for you."

"Could you look up Vernon Wright? He was another kid that lived near the Congressman and should be about the same age as the Congressman's son. His parents' names are Carol and Matthew Wright. Would you see if they are in your database too?"

"I'll call you back shortly."

Mark and Daniel searched property records and police records and found a few Vernon Wrights. Michelle called Daniel back in about twenty minutes.

Michelle said, "I've found him and his parents. Got a pen?"

"Go ahead."

Daniel wrote down the addresses of Vernon Wright and his parents.

"Thanks sweetie. I owe you dinner."

"I hope I get the same dessert as last night. See you later."

Mark and Daniel found out the rest of the information about Vernon Wright. He worked at one of the breweries, was married, and had three kids. They found his phone number and the phone number of the brewery. Daniel called Bill and told him they had the information about Vernon. Bill came down to the lobby and retrieved it.

Bill said, "I've put my notes and thoughts together and I'm ready to call Jim. I'm going to call him from my room so he won't hear any other voices."

Bill went to his room and called. When the accountant office answered the phone, Bill asked to speak to Jim Gibson.

When Jim answered, Bill said, "Hello Jim. My name is Bill Webber and I'm with UPI news. I'd like to meet you and ask a few questions."

Jim said in a hushed voice, "I wondered when someone would track me down. When would you like to meet?"

"I can meet you for lunch."

"Okay. Meet me across the street from our office at noon. It's a coffee shop but they serve food. I'll be outside."

Bill went back downstairs and told Mark and Daniel he was meeting Jim at noon.

"What can we do now?" Mark asked.

"Nothing for now. I may need help after the noon meeting with Jim."

Mark said, "Daniel and I will go the storage unit. Call us after the noon meeting."

Mark and Daniel changed into working clothes and left for the storage unit. At the unit, they started taking out furnishings and lining them up outside the unit. They figured it'd be easier to load on a truck. At about eleven thirty, Daniel called Michelle and told her they were working on the storage unit. Michelle offered to bring them lunch and they agreed. Daniel told her the gate code. At noon, Michelle showed up with sandwiches, chips, and drinks. She had ordered the sandwiches from the deli.

Daniel said, "You impress me more each day. What's the bill for lunch? We can include it in our bill to …well … to our client."

Michelle caught the hesitation. "It's twenty eight dollars. I included my lunch since I helped this morning."

Mark said, "We could use someone like you in our offices."

"That's what I was thinking about today. Could Daniel use me in the LA office?"

"I'm sure I could. You certainly would be an asset," Daniel agreed.

"When can you start?" Mark asked.

"Soon. I just need a few days here."

"You know you'll be working for your husband." Daniel raised his eyebrows.

"I think I can handle him. He's a pushover."

Daniel and Mark had set up the table and chairs and they sat down for lunch.

Daniel said, "I changed my mind about the furnishings. I think I'm having them shipped to my house in Los Angeles. I'd like to try industrial décor."

Michelle smiled. "You can choose between the furnishings and me. I'm not going to live in a house with these."

"Let me think. I've decided on you."

"Good choice. I've also decided to visit you in Los Angeles this weekend to see what furniture I need to ship down and what you need to get rid of."

"I'm very attached to my furniture and especially my art," Daniel said, although he didn't mean it. He really didn't care about the décor as long as it was functional.

Mark snickered. "His art is framed prints of sports figures and his furniture needs replacing."

"Some of them are signed prints and my furniture is broken in. I do have a nice bed mattress," Daniel retorted.

Michelle said, "We'll see when I check it out."

"You mean the mattress?"

"The mattress too."

Daniel and Michelle embraced and kissed before she went back to work.

Mark said, "This has been quite a trip to Milwaukee. We have a new employee, you have a future wife, and you get new furnishings in your house. I'll come out after the house is redone."

"Hopefully you can come out for a wedding soon. You'll be my best man."

They went back to work moving stuff out of the storage unit and moved boxes to get to the file cabinets. They took a drawer at a time outside and emptied it into heavy trash bags.

Bill called at about a quarter to one. "I'm coming over to the storage unit."

Daniel told him the code to the gate.

They returned to their work with the file cabinets. Daniel was glad that Mark came to help. After a file cabinet was emptied, they brought it outside, replaced the drawers, and put a key in the lock. They were finishing the last file cabinet when Bill arrived. They were happy to sit down.

When he sat down, Bill said, "Jim and I had a long conversation. He's willing to tell the authorities about the Congressman but would prefer it be confidential. He said his son is ten and he'd been thinking a lot about the Congressman. That seems to be the reason he called

Save America. He said he was nervous about calling Save America a second time but was glad I found him. I asked him if he knew about the settlement his mother had made and he did. I asked him about Vernon Wright and he said he didn't know about Vernon. He said Vernon was a kid in his neighborhood and was in his class in school. He said they moved shortly after the incident and he hadn't seen Vernon since moving. He said he hadn't spoken to Jeff since the incident. I called my boss and lawyer and they're figuring out the logistics for Jim. I'm going to call Vernon after I leave here and try to talk to him."

Mark asked, "Is there anything we can help with?"

"No. I'll stop back later."

It was now about one thirty and Daniel and Mark decided to make a bathroom and drink run. Michelle called Daniel while they were at the convenience store and told them the truck was on the way. They waited for the truck at the main gate.

The truck showed up with an old volunteer as the driver and the passenger that was even older. Daniel and Mark were concerned when the two old guys hobbled out of the truck. All introduced themselves and the old guys lowered the lift gate on the truck. They raised it to get in the enclosed bed and brought dollies down with them. Daniel and Mark watched the old guys use the dollies to load items on the truck while Daniel and Mark carried items on the truck. The old guys were slow but knew how to move stuff without a lot of effort. It took almost an hour to load everything and lash them inside the truck. The driver gave Daniel a donation receipt and Mark a donation receipt. Both had the Habitat logo with the address on top of the receipt and the driver's signature on the bottom. The list of donated items was blank. After the Habitat truck left, all that remained were the file boxes and trash bags full of files. Daniel and Mark arranged the boxes so they could sit down. Michelle called at two thirty and said the shredder truck was coming. They went to the gate to meet the truck.

The driver of the shredder truck was young as well as the passenger. These were obviously not volunteers. The truck also had a lift gate and the young guys brought dollies and a scale down from the truck. Each box and bag was weighed and a tally was kept by the driver. All were loaded and Daniel was presented a bill for the shredding. He used his credit card to pay the bill.

Daniel and Mark went to the office and borrowed a broom and dust pan. They still had a few trash bags left for the sweepings. They cleaned out the unit and returned the broom and dust pan. Daniel told the manager that the unit was cleaned out. The manager took his golf cart back to the unit to check. After the manager checked, Daniel was given the deposit that had been made by the lawyer's wife for the unit.

They hadn't heard anything from Bill so they went back to the hotel to clean up. Mark called Bill and left a message on his cell phone. Daniel called Michelle and told her they would be having dinner later but didn't know the time yet. Michelle said she would come to the hotel when she left work.

Daniel and Mark went to their rooms and cleaned up. Michelle showed up about six and knocked on Daniel's door. He greeted her at the door with only a towel around his waist and wet hair. He had just shaved. She loosened the towel and it fell to the floor. He started unbuttoning her blouse when the phone rang. Daniel answered it reluctantly and Mark told him Bill wanted to meet at the Italian restaurant at seven.

Daniel said, "We're having dinner at seven at the Italian restaurant."

"Do we have time for a quickie?"

"I believe we do," he answered as he took off her blouse.

Michelle had already unbuttoned and unzipped her pants. They tumbled on the bed and didn't waste time getting entwined. Daniel watched the clock beside the bed and told Michelle they had to get ready to go to dinner. There wasn't enough time for a shower so they dressed and left for the restaurant. They walked in a little after seven. Bill and Mark were already at the table. They rose out of their chairs until Michelle sat down.

Bill said, "Mark said you got the storage unit cleaned out."

Daniel responded, "We did."

"Thanks Michelle for getting the addresses we needed," Bill added.

"You're very welcome. It's been a pleasure working with you."

"Mark says you'll be working for them soon."

"I hope so."

The waiter came and Bill ordered a bottle of Chianti. Michelle looked at the wine list and it was the most expensive one on the list. Celebration, she thought.

Bill said, "I talked to Vernon Wright at five thirty. He met me after he got off from work."

Bill wanted to be cryptic since they were in public. "Vernon is willing to take the same approach as Jim. I left a message for my boss and the lawyer to call me in the morning at eight. Depending on the results of the conference call, I may end up calling Jeff. I don't think I'm going to talk to the Congressman's ex-wife or the parents of the other two."

The waiter came back with the wine, the bread, and filled the glasses with water. He asked if they were ready to order and all said yes. Daniel ordered veal marsala. Bill ordered shrimp fra diavolo. Mark ordered chicken saltimbocca. Michelle ordered linguine with clams.

Mark asked, "Do you need us to stay around tomorrow?"

Bill answered, "Let's meet in the morning at nine. I'll decide then."

Bill was in a great mood tonight and didn't look stressed like the night before. He talked about his other assignments and how he needed to get back to Washington. They talked about Michelle working for Daniel and Mark and the move to Los Angeles. The meal was great and they finished a second bottle of Chianti. The four walked back to the hotel together. Michelle and Daniel went to his room and picked up where they left off before dinner. Morning came after they repeated the entwinement several times. They met Mark for breakfast at eight. Michelle left for work and Daniel and Mark moved to the lobby. At about nine, Bill joined them.

"Good morning," Mark said.

"Good morning to you. How was breakfast?"

"Good," Mark responded.

"I just got off the call with my boss and our lawyer. They don't want me to contact Jeff or anyone else now. They want the authorities to get statements from Jim and Vernon first. Both are scheduled for early next week," Bill said.

"So we're leaving town?" Mark asked.

"We are. We're done in Milwaukee for now."

"I guess we'll check out this morning," Mark said.

"You should check about a flight first."

Both Daniel and Mark had their computers on and started checking for flights. Both could get on flights in a couple of hours. Bill used his cell phone and reserved the same flight as Mark.

Mark asked Daniel, "Are you staying an extra day to be with Michelle."

"No. It's over."

"I thought you were getting along well," Bill said.

Mark grinned. "He's kidding again."

"Sorry Bill. Michelle's coming to Los Angeles this weekend so I'll leave today."

All three checked out of the hotel. Bill called William on the way to the airport and gave him a quick synopsis of the events in Milwaukee and said he'd call from his office in the morning. Daniel called Michelle and told her he was stopping by but couldn't stay long.

When he got to the library, Michelle was waiting outside and got in the car with him. They kissed and hugged.

Daniel said, "Here's a credit card. Make your reservation for Los Angeles this morning. Let me know your schedule and I'll pick you up at the airport."

Michelle was excited. "I can't wait. I'll see you shortly."

Daniel went to the airport in time to catch his plane. Bill and Mark were already on their flight back to Washington.

Chapter 26

The week dragged by for William with work on his car, activities on his business ventures, helping Amy, and Save America plugging along. He made it to work early knowing Bill was going to call. He didn't tell the others since he didn't have the whole story. At eight, Bill called.

William answered.

"I'm sorry for such a short overview of Milwaukee. I figured I'd have more time this morning to give you details."

"I understand. Thanks for letting me know what's going on."

"Let me start from the beginning. Daniel, Mark, and I went to Milwaukee to look for Jim and the Congressman's family. After a lot of effort, we found Jim and I talked to him. Jim has a young boy about the same age as he was when the Congressman molested him, so that's what made him call Save America. He'll be giving a confidential statement to the authorities early next week. During our search, we found out that another boy was molested at the same time and I talked to him. He'll also be giving a confidential statement early next week. My boss, our lawyer, and I decided not to talk to the Congressman's family until after the statements are taken next week. The Congressman paid the families of both of the boys twenty years ago and we aren't sure what the Congressman would do if he found out the two were giving statements. I'm waiting to see what the authorities do before my next step. I'll call you next week."

Bill didn't talk about the divorce file since he didn't want to publicize that he had it. He would show it to his boss and their lawyer.

William said, "I'll talk to you next week."

The group met at lunch and Amy had subs for lunch. Potato salad and cole slaw were sides for the day.

William started the meeting. "Let's start with Save America first today. I just talked to Bill Webber. He's been in Milwaukee with Mark and Daniel. They found the Jim that called in last week and also found another person that the Congressman molested. Bill talked to both of them and they'll be making confidential statements to the authorities early next week. I expect the Congressman has a limited stay on our website."

Thomas asked, "Did he talk to the wife or the son?"

"Not yet. He wanted to wait until Jim and the other guy made their statements."

Cal asked, "Who are the guys making statements too?"

"Bill didn't say."

Thomas asked, "How did he find out about the second guy?"

"He didn't say."

More questions were asked that William didn't know the answer.

Thomas said, "I don't know if you've been watching but the number of emails to the Congressman has stayed high. I expect they'll go through the roof if the news of his molestations hits next week."

William asked, "When the news does break, do we want to use our website to implore other guys to call in if the Congressman has molested them?"

"It'll probably lead to a lot of crank calls," Thomas responded.

"We can use Mark and Daniel to check out the callers," William said.

"I think we should. It'll put pressure on the Congressman and we may find more victims," Cal pointed out.

"I agree. There could be crank calls but it should be worth it," William said.

Charlie changed the subject. "Donations continue to come in. I'll probably need to start another charitable corporation soon."

William sensed the discussion about Save America had waned so he changed to the car business.

"Let's switch to cars."

Cal smiled. "We sold another car today, thanks to Amy. We have a couple more about to be finished."

Charlie said, "It looks like this month will actually be profitable for our car business, if you don't include the startup costs."

William said, "My car will be done this week if anyone is interested."

Thomas asked, "Can we sell your car?"

William answered, "Maybe later after I've driven it some."

Cal said, "I'm picking up two cars tomorrow if anyone wants to take a road trip."

Amy said, "I'd like to go."

William thought for a few seconds and said, "If you really want to go, you can. The business will survive for one day. You'll need to transfer the office calls to your cell phone."

"Where's the road trip?" Amy asked Cal.

"Atlanta."

"I think I'll pass on Atlanta."

"When do you think we'll have cars for the lot?" William asked.

"Amy keeps selling them as fast as we finish them so it could be a while. I didn't plan to buy cars just for the lot but that plan may need to change."

They finished lunch and William went into the shop to put the finishing touches on the car. He was installing the seats today. He did stop to take a call from Diana. Their interviews were now scheduled for Wednesday. He told Amy to make reservations at a nice restaurant. He would tell the rest of the group about the dinner plans.

Wednesday came and Diana let William know they were in flight to Augusta. William told them about the reservations for dinner and there would be several of them from Save America. The hospital had also made arrangements for dinner but Diana and Angela turned them down. Amy, Thomas, Charlie, Cal, and William were at the restaurant when Diana and Angela arrived. Amy had made the reservations at a restaurant where they had a separate room. All stood when the women came in.

William was planning to shake their hands but both hugged him. The women also hugged everybody as all were introduced.

William said, "Welcome to Augusta."

Diana said, "It's a lovely town."

Angela added, "What we've seen is very nice."

Both were wearing dresses that weren't very revealing. Diana's dress was beige and Angela's dress was a light green. Their actual color probably had a more sophisticated name like fawn and mantis. They probably didn't want to look too sexy for their interviews.

William asked, "How was your flight?"

"Uneventful," Diana answered.

The server was filling the water glasses and taking the drink orders. William suggested a couple bottles of wine and all agreed.

When the server left the room, Diana asked, "Are all of you involved with Save America?"

"Yes. Thomas is our computer guru. He keeps us isolated from the hackers and the rest of the world. Charlie is our CPA. He keeps track of our donations and keeps them in our charitable corporations. Cal is our security specialist. He ensures our facility is protected and also has many contacts in government. Amy is the most important. She manages our office and has helped me with my business ventures for several years. She has also become very proficient at selling cars lately as we've gotten into a car business."

Angela asked, "What's your role?"

"I'm just a figurehead for the group. Thomas and I were actually the first two involved and we brought in everybody else as it evolved."

Angela asked, "How did you get started?"

"It started as a bet between Thomas and me, which he has never paid. He bet me that we couldn't influence the way the government was being run. Even with what we've done, we still haven't had much influence."

Thomas said, "He hasn't won the bet yet. I'll be glad to pay him the ten dollars if we do make a difference."

Diana said, "This started as a ten dollar bet."

"It was more than ten dollars. My manliness was challenged," William said as he grinned.

The waiter came back with bread and all agreed on their order. The waiter topped off the wine glasses even though it wasn't needed. He was working on a good tip.

After the waiter was gone, Diana asked, "I see that Congressman Swindell is your latest addition. Has he been cooperative?"

"I haven't talked to him but we may not have to."

"Why not?" Diana asked.

"I'm sorry, but I can't say since the news story hasn't broken yet. Watch the news the next few days and you'll see."

"Were you involved with the reports about Senator Jones and Congressman Riley?" Angela asked.

"We were somewhat involved with the Congressman Riley story."

"I applaud your efforts so far. I donated before we talked to you," Angela said.

"Thanks. We don't have the opportunity for face to face appreciation with the donors. We do get lots of calls supporting us."

Thomas added, "We also get lots of calls from folks who don't support us."

Diana remarked, "There'll always be naysayers."

"The call center gets to hear them and not us, unless we're taking calls," Thomas said.

"Have you raised much money?" Angela asked.

Charlie said, "We've received quite a few million."

"What's your plan for the funds?" Angela inquired.

Charlie replied, "We'll most likely use the funds during the elections by running ads."

"That sounds like a good use," Angela commented.

It was obvious that Angela was the thinker since she asked more probing questions.

The waiter came back in and brought the salads. Fresh pepper was offered with most accepting the offer. Wine glasses were topped off again. The waiter probably also wanted to sell more wine.

After the waiter left, Angela asked another question, "Why did you get into the car business?"

Cal answered, "We bought a building in Augusta that was large enough for a shop to fix cars. I had a Cobra kit car that I brought to the shop to finish. We decided to hire a couple of mechanics, bought a paint booth and frame machine, and started fixing wrecked cars."

"That sounds like a fun business," Diana remarked.

"It's been lots of fun and two of our cars are in the parking lot," Cal answered.

"You probably parked your Cobra close to mine," William said.

"I did. That's why I knew where your car was," Cal answered.

"Are you involved in other businesses?" Angela inquired.

"Thomas, Charlie, and Cal were retired before they were suckered into helping. I'm primarily involved in real estate now with Amy running it for me."

"What kind of real estate?" Angela asked.

Amy responded, "Mostly foreclosures now. We buy and then sell or rent properties."

"Are there still a lot of foreclosures?" Angela inquired.

"There are. We'll buy quite a few each year," Amy answered.

The waiter came back and collected salad plates. Angela and William hadn't finished their salads so the plates were left. The wine glasses weren't topped off.

William asked, "How are the interviews going?"

Diana answered, "This is our last interview. We've already decided to take positions in Chicago. We came here just to meet you."

"I'm glad you did. It's nice to put a face to the voice. When will you move to Chicago?"

"We'll move in about a month. We plan to rent a house together in the beginning. We're looking at pictures of properties every day as our real estate agent sends them," Diana responded.

"Do you have family in Chicago?" Amy asked.

"We do. We're both from Chicago and our families are happy to see us move back," Diana answered.

The waiter, along with a second waiter, brought the entrees. They served the women first and then the men. As usual, the food looked great. The waiter topped off the wine and William handed his salad plate to the waiter although he hadn't finished it. Angela did the same. Everybody was quiet for a few minutes while they worked on their food.

Before anyone spoke again, the owner of the restaurant came in. "Hello William. How's dinner tonight?"

William looked at Diana and Angela and they looked puzzled.

William got up from the table and shook the owner's hand, "It's great as usual, John. Thanks for letting us use the room."

"Our pleasure. How's your golf game? I haven't seen you on the course."

"I've been building a Cobra. I just finished it this week."

"Did you drive it tonight?"

"I did. It's parked outside."

"Holler at me when you leave. I'd like to see the car."

"Let me introduce you to my friends. This is Diana and Angela. They're physicians from Washington, D.C., who interviewed at the hospital today. This is Amy, who runs my property business. This is Thomas, Charlie, and Cal, who are my friends."

John said, "Good to meet you and I hope you have a nice dinner. You should make William pay since he's skinned me on the golf course too many times."

John left the room and Diana and Angela still looked puzzled.

Finally Angela asked, "Why did he call you William?"

"That's my real name. I use Jeremy just for Save America and Thomas, Charlie, and Cal aren't their real names. Amy's real name is Amy."

"That's strange but I guess it makes sense," Angela said.

"All of us are known in the community and we needed to keep our involvement with Save America confidential," William said.

Amy asked, "When are you going back to Washington?"

"Early tomorrow morning. I think it's the first flight out. Both of us have to work tomorrow," Diana answered.

Angela asked more questions and Diana commented. All had a great evening and all thought it was nice to meet Diana and Angela. William showed John his Cobra when he left. He got home late but he didn't need to be at work early now that the Cobra was finished. Amy had several errands that she assigned to him to check on properties and renovations. He decided that he'd get back into house renovations next week now that the car was done.

William was still home on Thursday morning when Bill called. He said he was going to issue a report on the Congressman tomorrow. He said he had arranged for a Milwaukee UPI reporter to be available to interview the Congressman's son when he made his live report. He said that another Milwaukee UPI reporter would be available to interview the ex-wife. Bill said he would make his report from the Congressman's house and William should watch CNN at eight p.m.

William asked, "Why are you doing it at such an odd hour?"

"We're hoping that the son and ex-wife are home and the reporters can talk to them."

"You've done another great job," William commented.

William told the rest of the group about the report when they had lunch. Amy bought salads again. William guessed she figured he'd put on weight since he wasn't working on the Cobra and wasn't working on houses. They decided to watch Bill's report at their homes since it would be on Friday night. It sounded like a good opportunity to snuggle on the couch. It's probably not the best snuggling plan. More questions were asked that William didn't know the answer.

Charlie asked another question that William didn't know, "Are Mark and Daniel still working for Bill?"

"I don't know. I'll call them today."

Thomas said, "I've created the change to the website to request other victims to call in. The phone number will be a separate number in our call center. I didn't want the contracted call center to take these calls. I'll have an appropriate message in case we can't answer the call."

"That's smart. Victims calling the regular call center number would probably be annoyed with the script used by the contractors. When will you go hot?"

"I was thinking Monday morning. I wanted to start it while we were in the office in case we get calls right away."

William called Mark after the meeting. When Mark answered, William said, "Bill said you were successful in Milwaukee."

"It was a good trip. I believe Bill has all the information he needs for now."

"Are you planning to help more with Congressman Swindell?"

"Bill said we should be available just in case."

"We're placing a phone number on our website for victims or anyone knowledgeable of the molestations to call. We need help screening the calls to determine the legitimate calls."

"We'll be glad to help. I believe there's still funding in our contract."

"I'll let you know or Bill will."

Chapter 27

John had reminded William that he hadn't played golf lately so he took off for the afternoon and played Palmetto Golf Course, which was his home course and the course Amy pays dues to every month. A couple of fellow golfers were arriving the same time as William. They looked at William's car and liked the Cobra. They invited William to join them. The golf course was built in 1892 just for golf and tee times weren't required. They were walking so William walked. Amy would be pleased. William's game was rusty since he was distracted with building the car. John could have won some of his money back today. Amy called while William was on the course. Amy heard the playing partners yell that William was away so he was caught. Amy just needed William to call someone working on one of the houses to answer a question, so golf continued. William called while he was walking down the next fairway.

William was relaxed on the couch at eight Friday night. He had just eaten half of a pizza. He thought he deserved it since he walked the golf course Thursday. He also justified having more than one beer.

CNN had been announcing all evening that a live special report would be aired about Congressman Swindell at eight. The report ended up being on after eight since CNN added a couple of commercials before the report started.

Bill came on the screen standing in front of the Congressman's house. William knew this since Bill said he was standing in front of the Congressman's house.

Bill was stoic as he reported, "I'm located in front of Congressman Swindell's house. Two people, who were young boys twenty years ago, have come forward accusing Congressman Swindell of molestation. The names of the young boys remain a secret. An anonymous source has also told us that Congressman Swindell's ex-wife divorced him because of this possible molestation. A reporter is live at the ex-wife's house to talk to the ex-wife."

The picture on the screen switched to a reporter at a house in Milwaukee. The reporter was at the front door of a house ringing the doorbell. The Congressman's ex-wife came to the door. The reporter asked, "I'm Joe Block with CNN news. Two gentlemen have come forward accusing Congressman Swindell of molestation. Do you have any comments?"

The ex-wife responded, "I don't." She closed the door.

The picture on the screen went back to Bill. He said, "We also understand that the Congressman's son may have knowledge of these molestations."

Another reporter showed up on the screen. He was shown ringing a doorbell at another house. The reporter said, "This is Ralph Peabody. I'm located at the house of the son of Congressman Swindell. We observed Jeff, the son of Congressman Swindell, arriving at his house a short while ago but he's not answering the door."

Bill was back on the screen. "More information will be forthcoming on these serious accusations against Congressman Swindell. If you have any information about these accusations, call CNN at the number below. This is Bill Webber with CNN."

A talking head came on the screen and asked, "Do you think the Congressman's son was molested?"

The screen went back to Bill, "There's no evidence to support it."

The talking head, "When will formal charges be filed against Congressman Swindell?"

Bill replied, "I understand the Congressman has been contacted about these charges. The Wisconsin authorities are also looking at the statute of limitations."

The talking head asked, "So the Congressman may not be charged because of the statute of limitations?"

Bill responded, "That may be the case."

The screen went back to the talking head, "Thanks Bill. CNN will have more information as it develops."

William thought the report was well choreographed with the reporters at the Milwaukee houses and the leading questions from the talking head.

William's Save America cell phone rang and it was Thomas. "I think I'm going to add the phone number to our website in the morning. I'll forward the calls to my cell phone. I'd hate to see the Congressman skate because of the statute of limitations."

"I would too. Mark and Daniel will research each caller so keep a record of each one."

"I've created a list of questions with answer blocks for us to document each call."

The Congressman's staff had notified the Congressman that Bill Webber was making a special report about him at eight. The Congressman didn't expect the report to be in front of his house so he invited his two staff members that he relied on the most to come to his house to watch.

After the broadcast, the Congressman said, "Schedule a press conference for Monday so we can clear up this situation."

One staffer said, "The report said that you had been contacted. Who contacted you?"

"It was a special prosecutor from Wisconsin. I know him personally and he notified me as a courtesy."

"Will they press charges against you?" the staffer asked.

"The prosecutor said that the statute of limitations was exceeded even if the accusations had merit."

The Congressman was hoping that the two boys from twenty years ago were the only ones that came forward. The Congressman had asked the prosecutor who made the statements but the prosecutor said their identities were being maintained confidential. Their friendship was suggested as a means to get the information but the prosecutor didn't relinquish. The Congressman thought of the others he had molested and the boys he had paid. Many had occurred in his house where they were talking about the situation.

"Do you want us to call CNN to ask them to retract the report?" the other staffer asked.

"I'll mention that in the press conference. Both of you should start writing a statement for the press conference. Get a draft to me tomorrow so we can fine tune it."

The staffers left and the Congressman poured a stiff whiskey. He thought about the repercussions if additional accusations were made. He thought of his strained relationship with his son and daughter. He thought of molesting his son twenty years ago, finished his drink, and put his face in his hands.

Bill spent the rest of the evening on various news shows. The next morning he was on morning news shows discussing the Congressman. He did get to pitch his book. When asked whether he would add Congressman Swindell to the book, he said he wasn't sure, although he really was sure Congressman Swindell would be added. Bill spent all day on the news shows. He couldn't talk about the divorce documents although he would have liked to. Sunday repeated Saturday with Bill being on more news shows. Bill was now more of a celebrity.

Thomas added a message to the website asking for calls about possible molestations by the Congressman. The phone number shown was forwarded to Thomas's Save America cell phone.

Thomas received ten calls on Saturday. He logged all of them and filled out his question sheet for each one. He could tell that nine of them were probably phony while one was probably legit. On Sunday, he received eight calls with two that could be legit.

On Monday morning, William went to the office early. Amy had left paperwork on his desk that needed to be reviewed. Thomas was already at the office when he arrived.

William asked, "How did the weekend go?"

"I had eighteen calls this weekend from the phone number we added. I think there are three calls that could be legitimate but all of them should be checked out."

"How many left their names?"

"All gave me names. I'd like to send the list to Mark and Daniel for them to start working on."

"I'll call them this morning."

"Did you see the increase in email traffic to the Congressman?"

"No. I just got here."

"It's the highest we've ever seen so far."

"Has the Congressman made any announcements this morning?"

"He's scheduled a press conference at ten this morning."

"I'm certainly curious as to what he'll say."

"I'm sure it'll be a complete denial," Thomas said.

William called Mark after leaving Thomas's office.

"We have eighteen names so far that called the phone number on our website. Can you have someone start screening them?" William said to Mark.

"We can. Email them to me and we'll get started today."

Mark waited a couple of hours before calling Daniel in Los Angeles. He pulled up the Save America website to see the added phone number and message.

Daniel answered and said, "I see that Bill's report included a phone number for other victims to call. Has Bill called needing more help?"

"No. It's our other client that needs help. They added a phone number on their website for people to call that were victims or had information. They had eighteen calls this weekend and want us to check them out. I thought it would be a good assignment for Michelle on her first day."

"I'm sure she would be glad to take it on."

"How is she? Did she get moved okay?"

"She's doing great and I'm doing great now that she's moved."

"Tell her I'm glad she's part of our family," Mark said.

"She wants a wedding in a month or two so you'll be hearing from her."

"She's a special woman and the two of you were meant for each other."

"I keep telling her that every day. Her daughter came over this weekend and her son will be coming up from San Diego next weekend. Her daughter was very nice."

"I'll email you the information and I'll call Bill to see if he needs anything else."

Mark called Bill and said, "That was quite a performance on Friday Bill."

"I thought it was very effective."

"I just wanted to let you know that Save America listed their own number and we're checking out the eighteen calls they received so far."

"Let me know what you find. CNN has their own staff to check out the calls they're getting."

"Are you going back to Milwaukee?"

"The reporters in Milwaukee are trying to set up interviews with the son and ex-wife. If they do, I'll be going to Milwaukee."

"Let us know if we can help. I haven't told you that Michelle moved to Los Angeles and started working for us today."

"Tell her I certainly enjoyed working with her in Milwaukee."

"I will."

William and the others went into the conference room to listen to the Congressman's press conference. The Congressman stated that a terrible injustice was being done and that the truth would be revealed. He blamed the opposition party for targeting him. He was appalled at the insinuations made against him.

Questions were taken from the press.

A reporter asked, "What was the reason for your divorce?"

"My ex-wife and I had a no fault divorce based on incompatibility. My ex-wife and I had grown apart after I was elected to Congress."

Bill stood up and raised his hand and all the other reporters lowered their hands. The Congressman had to point to him. Bill asked, "Did you know that a judge is ruling today about unsealing your divorce file?"

The Congressman stammered and responded, "A judge can't do that. The file was sealed."

Bill followed, "Don't you think there are extenuating circumstances now that two people have given sworn statements about your molestation of them?"

The Congressman didn't respond and said the press conference was over.

As soon as he got away from the microphones, he told a staffer to find out which judge is ruling on his divorce file as quick as he could. The Congressman rushed back to his office, poured himself a stiff drink, and called the prosecutor in Wisconsin.

The prosecutor took his call. The Congressman talked with his best Wisconsin accent and said to the prosecutor, "I understand a judge is ruling today about unsealing my divorce file. Is there something that you can do to stop it?"

"There's an allegation that your divorce resulted from possible molestation. We're doing our best to confirm whether it is true based on the statements we took from two persons."

"Can I talk to the judge about the file?" the Congressman asked.

"The judge is reviewing the file and will make the decision."

"We go back a long time to our youth. Can't you intervene with the judge? My ex-wife would be heartbroken if the file was unsealed."

"We spoke to your ex-wife and she didn't object. I've got to go now. I can call you after the judge makes a decision."

"That'd be nice."

The Congressman left his door closed and poured another stiff drink. His secretary buzzed and then called him when he didn't respond.

He finally answered, "Yes, Carlie."

"Two of your staff are out here waiting to see if you need anything."

"I'm fine for now, Carlie. I don't want to see anyone for a while. I'll open the door shortly."

The Congressman poured a third drink and sat in his chair. He didn't have anyone that he could confide in about his predicament. He thought that he could resign immediately if the divorce file was unsealed. Maybe that would save a lot of embarrassment. After the fourth drink, he decided that the judge wouldn't unseal the file since the statute of limitations has passed for the information in the divorce file. He decided to stay behind his office door for a bit longer and maybe a drink or two longer. The Congressman finally decided to have someone drive him home.

Daniel came into Michelle's office and closed the door. They had sex all weekend after she arrived on Friday evening. Daniel had taped Bill's report and played it for her on Sunday. He told her the rest of the story about Milwaukee and Save America.

Daniel said, "I've got your first assignment."

"Does it involve me submitting to my boss?"

"That'll happen again tonight," Daniel made his eyebrows raise and lower.

"So what can I do for you, big boy," she said in a sultry voice.

"It's really a work assignment."

"You mean I have to work. I'm the boss's concubine," she said inquisitively.

"Yes, you do, even though you're my concubine. I need you to research these eighteen names. The Save America folks created a phone number for victims or someone who has information to call.

They want us to research the callers from the weekend." Daniel gave her the eighteen sheets of paper.

"I love you, Daniel."

"Where did that come from?"

"From my heart."

He pulled her up out of her chair and kissed her. "You make me very happy and I love you too."

Daniel finally left her after a long embrace.

Michelle set up a spreadsheet with the eighteen names and started with the first one.

Judge Bingham read all of the divorce papers for Congressman Swindell during the past week. CNN had petitioned the court to unseal the divorce papers and the special prosecutor had also requested that the divorce papers be unsealed. Judge Bingham was also a friend of the Congressman just like the special prosecutor. He wasn't aware of the reasons for the divorce. The Congressman had told him it was a no-fault divorce due to incompatibility. Now that he read the divorce documents and thought about the two boys who made statements last week and his own son, the Judge decided to unseal the divorce documents. He called his clerk in to draft the document for him to sign.

CNN had a reporter at the courthouse waiting for the decision. His instructions were to notify his boss at CNN and then Bill Webber about the decision. At one o'clock in the afternoon Milwaukee time, the Judge made a decision to unseal the divorce documents. The Judge still had all of the documents in his office so no one could have looked at them yet. The clerk would return the documents to archives later today.

Bill was prepared for the decision and CNN was ready. Bill was going to use his copies of the documents to make a live report. He would be way ahead of any other reporter. The talking head on CNN interrupted the program to announce a live broadcast concerning Congressman Swindell. Bill had been waiting in front of the Congressman's house along with a dozen other network trucks.

Amy notified William and the others that Bill was coming on. William was still in the office and went into the conference room. The others were already there.

Bill came on the screen standing in front of Congressman Swindell's house. "We have just learned that Judge Bingham has unsealed the divorce documents for Congressman Swindell. The divorce proceedings began when the Congressman's ex-wife filed for divorce because Congressman Swindell had molested their son and two other young boys. The other two young boys referenced in the divorce documents were the two individuals who gave sworn statements last week stating that the Congressman had molested them. Congressman Swindell denied these allegations this morning in his press conference but the divorce documents confirm these allegations."

Bill paused for a few seconds and then continued. "Cash settlements were made with the two young boys' families to maintain their silence. The settlement with the Congressman's ex-wife also required her to maintain her silence. It appears that Congressman Swindell won't be charged for these heinous crimes due to the statute of limitations. Call the number below if you are a victim or have information about a victim of Congressman Swindell."

The talking head on CNN asked, "Has Congressman Swindell released any statement since this morning's press conference?"

"No. He hasn't. Congressman Swindell was seen returning to his home shortly after the press conference. It's my understanding that he's inside the home behind me now."

The talking head asked, "What'll happen to Congressman Swindell now?"

"Since he won't be charged for a crime, he can continue as a Congressman unless the house elects to exercise the expulsion option. Normally expulsion is only used for disloyalty to the United States or abuse of their official position."

The talking head asked, "So unless a more recent victim comes forward, Congressman Swindell will continue as a member of the House of Representatives."

"That's correct."

The talking head said, "Thank you, Bill Webber."

It was another well-choreographed script.

William said, "It seems a shame that the Congressman won't be charged."

Thomas said, "I'm hoping that recent victims do come forward. I received six more calls so far today of potential victims. I've already forwarded the information to Daniel. It's been handled out of the Los Angeles office."

Charlie asked, "What can we do?"

"Wait and hope."

They dispersed and William left to take his golf clubs for a walk on the golf course. He had planned to get back to helping with house renovations but hadn't. He thought he'd start tomorrow.

Chapter 28

Michelle spent the first day eliminating the people she knew made crank calls. The information provided to Thomas was obviously made up for most of the calls. Many were women, which were ruled out in the first whittling. She had whittled the eighteen down to three. She hadn't started on the six other names sent her today. She decided to call the three names and have a second discussion.

She made the first call to a Jonathan Brooks. Jonathan provided a cell phone number. Jonathan answered on the third ring.

Michelle said, "I understand you called Save America about Congressman Swindell."

"I did."

"Based on the discussion you had with Thomas this weekend, your parents are friends of Congressman Swindell."

"Yes."

"And you spent some time with Congressman Swindell while your parents were out of town?"

"Yes."

"Your parents are Taylor and Ann Brooks and they live at 2234 Jones Street in Milwaukee?"

"Yes."

Michelle had found out the parents' names and address since they weren't on the question sheet.

"And this happened when you were thirteen?"

"Yes."

Jonathan had told Thomas the details so Michelle didn't ask him to repeat them. She didn't really want to hear them anyway.

"And you're twenty two now?"

"Yes."

"Would you be willing to talk to the special prosecutor?"

"Yes. I've thought a lot about it during the past weekend after I heard about the other two boys. I thought it was my fault, since I'm gay."

"Do you now understand that it wasn't your fault?"

"I do, partially, but I'm sure it wasn't the two ten year old boys' fault either."

"Can I have the special prosecutor call you today?"

"I'd prefer today before I change my mind."

"I'll try to have him call today. Thanks for being brave."

Before she called the next person, she went to see Daniel in his office. She walked into the office and said, "I think you should wear a suit to work."

"The next suit I'll wear will be to our wedding."

"I just called the person that was the most believable of all of the eighteen. I think he was molested by the Congressman. He's agreed to talk to the special prosecutor in Milwaukee and would like to talk to him today. He blames himself because he's gay."

"Let's call Bill now."

Daniel had watched Bill's report a little after ten a.m. pacific time and knew he was probably available to talk. He called Bill's cell phone.

Bill answered the call, "Hey, Daniel. How are you?"

"I'm fine. I'm switching to speaker phone and putting Michelle on."

In a few seconds Michelle said, "Hello Bill."

"Hey, Michelle. Did you make your move to Los Angeles?"

"I did and I starting working for Daniel today."

Daniel said, "This is actually a business call. Michelle started sorting out the first eighteen people that called Save America this weekend. She just talked to one she believes was molested by the Congressman and has agreed to talk to the special prosecutor."

Bill was concerned it would be another situation that exceeded the statute of limitations so he asked, "How old is the person?"

Michelle answered, "He's twenty two and the molestations happened when he was thirteen."

Bill stated, "That's within the statute of limitations."

Michelle thought it was a question and replied, "I don't know but I can find out."

Bill said, "That was a fact and not a question."

Daniel asked, "Do you want me to call the special prosecutor or do you want to?"

"I'd like to. I want to ask him a few questions as well."

"Michelle added some notes to the original question sheet so we'll send it to you."

"Thanks again for helping, especially you, Michelle."

Michelle said, "Will you come to our wedding?"

"I wouldn't miss it."

"Michelle will continue working on the list and we were sent six more names today."

"Let me know if you have more that want to talk to the prosecutor."

Michelle kissed Daniel on the head and went back to continue her calls.

As soon as he received the question sheet, Bill called the special prosecutor. The special prosecutor had told his office to screen out all reporters but he wanted to talk to Bill. He wanted to know how Bill knew the information in the divorce documents so quickly.

Bill's call was routed to the special prosecutor and the prosecutor answered, "Hello."

"This is Bill Webber."

"My assistant said you were on the line but I was skeptical. I've had a lot of reporters trying to talk to me today."

"I'm glad you took my call."

"You were the only one I told my assistant to let through."

"The first thing I need is an email address to send you the name of another boy who was molested."

The special prosecutor had been getting lots of people calling his office with names of boys who were molested by the Congressman and he had turned the names over to the police.

"You should just send the information to the police. That's where I'll send it when I get it."

"This is different. We've already screened this one and it's legitimate. All of the facts were verified and the victim is willing to talk to you today. The guy is twenty two now and he was thirteen when he was molested."

The special prosecutor was more interested now since he could charge the Congressman if it checked out. "Maybe I will call this person. Send the information to my assistant's email address." The prosecutor gave him the email address.

"Call him soon. He may change his mind. Can I ask you a few questions?"

"Only if I can ask you some first."

Bill said, "Go ahead."

"How did you get the information in the divorce file before everyone else?"

"I had my sources."

"Did you get the information legally?"

Bill didn't hesitate since the purchase of the storage unit was legal. Daniel had a receipt. "It was legal."

"Would you be willing to tell me how you got the documents?"

"It's an interesting story. I'll tell you off the record the next time I'm in Milwaukee."

"Were you in Milwaukee recently?"

"I was and it's a great city."

"Did you talk to anyone associated with the Congressman Swindell case while you were here?"

"I did. I talked to both of the guys that made sworn statements to you last week."

"Any others?"

"No." Bill could answer truthfully.

"I have a feeling that you knew a lot about this case before you came to Milwaukee."

"I may have but you had to make the case official."

"So you used me to get the information out about Congressman Swindell?"

"I wouldn't put it exactly like that."

"Do you have any information I don't have?" the prosecutor asked.

"No. I believe you have the same information I have."

"When will you be back in Milwaukee?"

"Maybe in a few days. Would you like to have an informal talk when I'm there?"

"Yes. I would. Call me when you're in town."

"Can I ask a couple of questions now?" Bill asked.

"You can but you probably already know the answers."

"Is it official that you won't charge Congressman Swindell with molestation based on the two victims so far?"

"With the evidence I have now, I can't charge him and make it stick since the statute of limitations has passed."

"Will you continue to investigate the case?"

"I will. The case will stay open until we've exhausted all avenues."

Bill thought it sounded like a political answer.

"Will your friendship with Congressman Swindell have any influence on the case?"

"My friendship with the Congressman won't influence my decisions." The prosecutor thought it might before he read the divorce documents. The prosecutor had two sons that were around the Congressman as they grew up.

"Will you let me know when you decide to press charges?"

"I may have my assistant call you."

"Thanks for talking to me. Please call the guy on the email that has already been sent to your assistant."

"I will."

The prosecutor checked with his assistant and read the question list with added notes. He knew Jonathan Brooks and knew the parents. He knew that Jonathan was gay. He decided to call.

Jonathan answered the call, "Hello."

The special prosecutor said, "This is Jerry Wilcox and I'm the special prosecutor for Milwaukee."

"Yes sir. I know you."

"I know you too and I know your parents. How are they doing?"

"They're fine. I visited them this past weekend."

"I received information that you may have been molested by Congressman Swindell."

"I was. It happened when I was thirteen."

"Would you be willing to make a sworn statement?"

"I would."

"Can you come in today?"

"What time?"

"Anytime is fine."

"I wasn't able to work today after actually telling someone about the Congressman so I'll come in now. What's the address?"

Jerry gave him the address.

After the call, Jerry arranged to have a room set up for the statement. He hoped the statement was believable enough to file charges. In about thirty minutes, Jonathan showed up and was escorted to the special prosecutor's office. Jonathan was wearing jeans and a tee shirt with Milwaukee's Best on the front. He was wearing tennis shoes. His hair was dark brown and was cut short. He was slightly underweight but muscular.

The special prosecutor said when Jonathan came into his office, "Hello, Jonathan. Thanks for coming in so soon."

"Hello, Mr. Wilcox."

"We're going to interview you in the conference room down the hall. Can I get you something to drink?"

"I'd like a Coke please."

They went to the conference room and settled in. The special prosecutor decided to take the statement himself since he knew Jonathan.

Jerry asked, "Is it alright if we record this conversation."

"Yes."

"We need you to take an oath before the statement."

"I understand."

Jonathan took an oath to tell the truth.

"Do you want this to be confidential?"

"It doesn't matter. I'm actually willing to testify publicly."

"Tell us in your own words the occasions when Congressman Swindell molested you. Take as much time as you need." Jerry didn't want to pressure Jonathan.

"My parents went out of town on a weekend trip and left me and my older sister at home. My older sister is… was … very mature. Congressman Swindell called the house and asked if I'd like to go to a Milwaukee Brewers baseball game. I asked my sister and she thought it'd be okay."

Jonathan took a drink of Coke and then continued. "The Congressman picked me up at our house. I thought his son would be with him but he wasn't. We had a great time at the game. The Congressman bought me hotdogs, pretzels, and drinks. The Brewers won."

Jonathan breathed deeply and continued. Jerry didn't interrupt. "When the game was over, the Congressman took me to his house rather than mine. He said he needed to stop at his house for a few minutes and I didn't think anything about it. When we went in, he offered me a beer. I said sure. I'd already tried beer with my friends. He then lit a joint and asked me if I wanted to try it. I said sure. He poured a shot of whiskey and I drank that too. I think I drank several shots of whiskey. I was feeling good after a short time. I tried to get up to go to the bathroom and stumbled."

Jonathan then told how the Congressman had molested him. Jonathan stopped talking and took another drink of Coke. He took more deep breaths and sighed.

Jerry asked, "Do you remember the date?"

"No. I don't. It was in April and the Brewers were playing Oakland and it was a Friday night."

"Have you told this to anyone else?"

"I told it to the guy that answered my phone call this weekend and a little bit to the lady that called me."

"What guy and lady?" Jerry asked.

"The Save America guy. They posted a phone number to call. I think his name was Thomas. The lady called this morning. I thought she worked for the police. Her name was Michelle. She said she'd have you call."

Jerry was taking notes even though it was being recorded.

Jerry asked more questions to get the details and Jonathan gave as many details as he could remember.

Jerry was curious and asked, "Why did you call the Save America number and not the CNN number?"

"I did call the CNN number but it was a recording to leave a number. When I called the Save America number, there was someone who talked to me. I liked that better."

Jerry made a note to call the number to see who answered.

"I apologize for this question too. Did your impairment with the alcohol and the joint affect how you remembered what happened that night?"

"No. I still remember it. I was a little out of sorts but not enough to forget what the Congressman did."

Jerry asked a few more questions and others in the room asked questions. Some were identical questions that were framed differently. Jerry took Jonathan to his office and talked about his work, his hobbies, and his family while the statement was being typed. The statement was given to Jonathan and he signed it after reading it. Jerry thanked him for coming in and he was escorted to the exit. Jerry had his assistant assemble his staff in the conference room to discuss the interview with Jonathan.

Jerry asked, "What are your thoughts about Jonathan?"

One of his staff lawyers answered, "I believe his story and think it'll hold up in court."

Jerry said, as he was being the devil's advocate, "He was impaired."

Another staffer said, "The Congressman was the one that got him impaired."

Jerry said, "Jonathan is gay."

The first staffer said, "He was thirteen."

Jerry said, "Does anyone think we shouldn't proceed?"

No one objected.

Jerry looked at the first staffer, "Draw up the paperwork and we'll file a criminal complaint tomorrow. You need to figure out the exact date based on the baseball game. I'm sure we'll have a little leniency on the date since Jonathan was a minor at the time."

On the way back to his office, Jerry told his admin assistant to call Bill Webber and let him know that a criminal complaint would be filed for the sexual assault of a minor tomorrow.

The admin assistant called and Bill answered, "This is Jerry Wilcox's administrative assistant. Mr. Wilcox asked me to call and tell you he's filing a criminal complaint for sexual assault tomorrow."

"Thanks for calling," Bill said.

Bill called his boss and told him about the criminal complaint being filed tomorrow. They decided that Bill should prepare a short report today rather than wait until tomorrow. Bill went to his office to write the script. It would be short. Bill called CNN to arrange for a time for the report. They agreed to do it in about an hour. Bill drove down to the CNN truck at the Congressman's home.

The talking head on CNN announced that a special report would be coming from Bill Webber shortly about Congressman Swindell. This continued periodically for the hour preceding Bill actually giving his report.

The talking head finally said that they were going on location in Washington, D.C., with Bill Webber.

Bill said, "I'm here at Congressman Swindell's home in Washington, D.C. A new victim has come forward accusing Congressman Swindell of molestation. The new victim has provided

Milwaukee's special prosecutor with a sworn statement. The date that this new victim was molested is within the statute of limitations and a criminal complaint for sexual abuse will be filed tomorrow in Milwaukee."

Bill was guessing, but was pretty sure a sworn statement was made since a complaint was being filed. He was also guessing, but certain, that the new accusation was within the statute of limitations.

The talking head asked, "When will Congressman Swindell be notified of the criminal complaint?"

"I'm sure the special prosecutor will notify Congressman Swindell tomorrow."

The talking head said, "Thank you, Bill Webber."

Bill spent the rest of the day on the news programs. He was asked about knowing the content of the divorce papers so quickly but didn't disclose his source was the storage unit.

Chapter 29

The next person Michelle called was Ralph Lowrie. Ralph lived in Chicago, based on the information on the question sheet. He had been molested by the Congressman in Milwaukee when he was twelve. The Congressman had picked him up on the street and offered him money to pretend he was his son. Ralph agreed and went to the Congressman's house where the Congressman molested him. Michelle called Ralph and went over the facts on the question sheet. Ralph was now twenty six. Michelle had researched Wisconsin's statute of limitations and believed Ralph's molestation was within the window.

Michelle had verified Ralph's residency in Milwaukee fourteen years ago and his mother was a resident of Milwaukee fourteen years ago. Ralph's mother was a single mother who worked, so Ralph was not supervised much when he was twelve. Michelle talked to Ralph and verified that Ralph was most likely telling the truth. After she confirmed that he was willing to give a sworn statement, Michelle went to see Daniel.

"Do you want to close the door and get your performance evaluation?"

Michelle said, "You can give it to me later tonight."

"A promise?"

"A guarantee. I plan to reward myself after my first day of work in Los Angeles."

"And I'm your reward?"

"You are. Are you agreeable?" she raised her eyebrows.

"Agreeable and willing."

Michelle changed the subject before they decided to start early. "I've identified another guy who was most likely molested by the Congressman. He was twelve fourteen years ago when it happened." Michelle handed Daniel a copy of the question list with her added notes.

Daniel said, "Let's call Bill."

Daniel called Bill's cell and had to leave a message. His message was that Michelle had identified another guy that was probably molested and he was emailing the question sheet.

Daniel said, after ending the call, "Thanks. You're going to fit in well here."

"So far it's been good."

Michelle kissed him on the head again, went back to her office and started on the third guy from the first eighteen.

After Bill finished with another talk show he checked his messages and emails. He listened to the message from Daniel and opened the email with the information about Ralph Lowrie.

Bill called the special prosecutor and ended up talking to the admin assistant.

The admin assistant said, "Mr. Wilcox is in a meeting and I don't have direction to connect you this time."

Bill said, "Am I off the Christmas list too?"

The admin assistant asked, "What Christmas list?"

"Never mind. I'm emailing you information about another potential molestation victim of Congressman Swindell. Would you give it to Jerry soon?"

"I'll give it to him when he comes out of the meeting."

"Tell him to call me if he needs more details."

Bill had reviewed the question sheet for Ralph and knew it contained enough details for Jerry.

Michelle called the third guy from the first eighteen and thought he wasn't very believable. His story was different than the story from the question sheet. He asked several times whether he would be paid for testifying. She decided not to discuss this person with Daniel.

Michelle started on the six additional names that were provided by Save America. For the six names, one appeared to be a legitimate call. She started her research on Billy James. From the question sheet, Billy was molested in Washington, D.C., by the Congressman. He was thirteen when he was convinced to go to the Congressman's house with an older friend. The older friend was nineteen and was being paid by the Congressman to have sex. Billy was told he could play video games while he waited since the Congressman had a great setup. The older friend told him that he'd have money for food and a movie after the Congressman paid him. Michelle was having a little trouble reading the rest of Thomas' notes so she decided to call Billy. Billy was twenty now and still lived in D.C.

Michelle called and Billy answered. "This is Michelle and I'm following up on a phone call you made to Save America this past weekend. Do you have time to talk?"

"Sure do."

"From the notes I read, you ended up at the Congressman's house with an older friend."

"That's right. My friend saw the Congressman often and I went along one time. My friend said I could play video games on the Congressman's killer system. We were going to get some grub and a movie after the Congressman paid him. Turns out my friend passed out shortly after we got there. He was already high as a kite. Since my friend was passed out, the Congressman had sex with me instead and paid me. After that, the Congressman paid me many more times."

"Why did you decide to call?"

"I saw where he molested ten year old boys and he was probably still doing it. He told me he liked young boys. Someone like him needs to be stopped."

"Would you be willing to give a sworn statement to the authorities about the Congressman?"

"I would."

"When could you give this statement?"

"Anytime. I'm between jobs right now."

"Would your older friend that was with you that night be willing to give a statement?"

"My friend's dead."

Michelle thought she had enough information to pass on. She believed Billy but wasn't sure the authorities in Washington, D.C., would contact him.

Michelle said, "Thanks for talking to me. Someone will be calling you soon to get your sworn statement."

Michelle went to Daniel's office to discuss Billy with him. Daniel had people in his office and raised his finger to show her he'd be with her shortly. She walked outside to get fresh air and stretch. She was watching the Los Angeles traffic and wondering when her furniture would arrive. She was renting in Milwaukee with a month to month lease so she didn't have to break a lease. She had cleaned up the apartment so she got her security deposit back. Daniel agreed to pay for moving her furniture as part of her employment package. She was thinking about the furniture in Daniel's house that needed to be discarded.

Daniel walked up beside her. "Are you counting traffic?"

"It'd be lots more difficult here than in Milwaukee."

"We do have a lot of vehicles in Los Angeles."

Daniel put his arm around her, pulled her to him, and kissed her. He kept kissing her and she rubbed her leg up the inside of his thigh. A horn blew and they stopped.

"Just like Milwaukee, except I know what's going to happen tonight."

"You're confident."

"I had a guarantee earlier and I'm holding you to it."

"Business first. I talked to Billy James in Washington, D.C."

Daniel interrupted, "The Congressman is active in Washington, D.C., too."

"He is but the situation with Billy James is a little strange. The short version is that Billy went with an older friend to the Congressman's house. The older friend was being paid by the Congressman. The older friend was on drugs and passed out before earning his money. The Congressman molested Billy instead and then paid him. The Congressman then paid him to come back more times."

Daniel interrupted again, "That does sound strange."

Daniel thought a minute and asked, "Can the older friend make a statement?"

"He's dead, according to Billy."

"The Congressman could be charged with soliciting for prostitution with a minor. That probably has a serious penalty."

"It does. It's up to twenty thousand dollars and up to twenty years." Michelle had looked it up.

"Wow, wow, wow," Daniel said.

"Let's email the question sheet to Bill and let him decide. I expect he'll forward the information to the right Washington, D.C., authorities. We'll call him after I email it."

Daniel scanned the question sheet with Michelle's added notes and sent it to Bill. In a couple of minutes, they called Bill. Bill must have been between his talk show appearances and he answered, "Hello Daniel."

"It's Daniel and Michelle. We just emailed you a strange one."

"Just a minute and I'll read it." Bill could read fast. His years of reporting had taught him to read quickly.

In a few minutes, Bill said, "It's strange. I think I'm going to send it to a Washington, D.C., prosecutor I know and ask him his opinion. I see your notes that he could be charged with soliciting a minor for prostitution. That could be the more logical option. We'll see after the prosecutor reviews it."

Daniel said, "We'll be reviewing more as we get them from Save America."

"I sent the last one to the special prosecutor in Milwaukee but haven't heard anything about it since. Thanks for your good work."

After the call ended, Michelle said, "I'm done with the names from Save America. Should I call them to get more?"

"Let me call them and I'll introduce you. You can call them the next time," Daniel said.

Daniel called Thomas on a speaker phone and introduced Michelle. He gave Thomas Michelle's email address. Thomas said he had five more sheets that he could mail.

Daniel said, "Based on Michelle's further research, there were three names we forwarded to Bill. One of the names you sent us led to the criminal complaint against the Congressman in Milwaukee."

"I'm glad we decided to add the phone number to our website," Thomas said this more for himself than Daniel and Michelle.

"Nice to meet you Michelle," Thomas said as he was ending the call.

The Congressman didn't go to the office and stayed home. The special prosecutor called the Congressman's office and was given his cell number.

"Congressman, this is special prosecutor Jerry Wilcox," Jerry said when the Congressman answered.

"I know who you are, Jerry."

"I'd like you to come to Milwaukee so that we can work out your bail with the judge. We presented our information to the grand jury today and they agreed that we should proceed with a criminal case. I can arrange a private hearing without the press."

"I'm not sure what I want to do yet. Can I call you back later today or tomorrow?" the Congressman asked.

"I'll expect a call tomorrow or I'll start getting pressure to issue a warrant for your arrest."

"I'm sure I'll be coming in a day or two but I need to work out a few details here first."

"This is serious, Paul. Don't do anything stupid."

They said their goodbyes.

The prosecutor in Washington, D.C., read the question sheet sent him by Bill Webber. He had the same concerns that Michelle, Daniel, and Bill had. He decided to have a couple of his deputy prosecutors read it. After a lot of discussion, the prosecutor decided to call Billy James and have him come in to give a sworn statement. A deputy prosecutor called Billy and arrangements were made to have Billy picked up and brought in within the hour.

Billy told the prosecutor the same story he told Michelle. The prosecutor asked for additional details that occurred prior to going to the Congressman's house and after they left. He asked for more details about the sexual act. Additional details were requested about the older friend.

After the sworn statement was taken, the prosecutor decided that he would file a criminal complaint for the sexual assault of a minor and a criminal complaint for soliciting a minor for prostitution. He thought he could sell it to the grand jury. He also thought he would be criticized if he didn't do something with all the recent publicity about Congressman Swindell. He didn't know the Congressman so he didn't feel an obligation to call him. A deputy prosecutor was assigned to draw up the complaints.

The prosecutor called Bill after the decision was made.

"We've made a decision about Billy James. We're going to file a criminal complaint for the sexual assault of a minor and a criminal complaint for soliciting a minor for prostitution."

Bill asked, "Would it be okay if I reported that the complaints are being filed?"

"I think so. You'll owe me dinner for letting you know."

"You can bring your wife and girlfriend too," Bill teased him.

"I'll decide which one to bring. What's it feel like being a celebrity? It's a long way from our misspent youth."

"You're still jealous because I got all the girls," Bill jabbed.

"I got the one that counted."

"You did. Tell Jill hello for me and we'll do dinner soon."

Bill called his boss and told him about Billy James and the complaints being filed. His boss agreed he should call CNN to get on the air.

Bill called and was scheduled to be on the air in an hour. He left for the Congressman's house and thought of his words as he drove. The talking head on CNN periodically said that Bill Webber would be making another live report.

The talking head announced, "We're now going live with Bill Webber."

Bill began as he displayed a stoic reporter facial expression, "This is Bill Webber live from Congressman Swindell's home. We've learned that criminal complaints will be filed against Congressman Swindell in Washington, D.C. A criminal complaint will be filed for the sexual assault of a minor and a criminal complaint will be filed for soliciting a minor for prostitution."

Bill paused as he heard a gunshot from inside the house.

Bill looked towards the house. "We've just heard a gunshot from inside Congressman Swindell's home. We'll stay live. Two police officers assigned to the house have gone to the front door."

The CNN camera focused on the police officers going to the door. The police officers rang the doorbell and no one answered. They knocked hard on the door and still no one answered. Sirens were heard in the distance.

Bill kept reporting the events live.

The officers went back to their police car and took out a battering ram. Another police car showed up and two more officers joined the first two. They took the battering ram and knocked the front door open. They went inside and found Congressman Swindell sitting in a living room chair with CNN on the TV. A handgun was in his lap and blood was pouring out of his mouth.

Bill was still reporting live.

More police officers arrived, along with two ambulances. Paramedics went into the house. The coroner arrived and pronounced the Congressman dead.

Bill continued reporting.

A spokesperson for the police department came on the steps of the house and announced it appeared that Congressman Swindell had died of a self-inflicted gunshot.

The spokesperson took questions about the location of the Congressman, whether there was a suicide note, whether there was anyone else in the house, and more details.

Bill stayed and reported live until the Congressman was taken away in an ambulance.

Chapter 30

William checked on the houses being renovated and used his tools for a change. He showed up at the office at noon in his work clothes. He was in his truck and not in the Cobra.

Amy had chicken salad and tuna salad sandwiches for lunch. She brought in a toaster to have toasted bread sandwiches. She served bread and butter pickles and iced tea. William's plate came without chips and Amy gave him unsweetened tea. William gave her a glare.

William sighed before starting the meeting. "I'm sure everyone has heard about the demise of Congressman Swindell."

Thomas was shaking his head. "I'm actually surprised he committed suicide."

Cal was the last to arrive and sat down with his lunch. "There was a lot of information coming out about him in a short time so I'm not surprised he offed himself."

"I've taken him off the website and we need to decide on our next participant. Tell me your first choice and we can see if we can reach a consensus." Thomas placed chips on his plate.

"I nominate Congressman Murphy," William suggested.

"I like Congressman Murphy too," Charlie said.

"Congressman Murphy was my second choice, so I'm okay with him," Cal said.

"I'm alright with Congressman Murphy. I'll start assembling the facts about him for the website. I should be ready to display him tomorrow."

Amy hadn't wanted to participate in the selection of the Congressmen and Senators so she didn't suggest anyone.

"I called Michelle this morning and let her know we didn't need her to research any more names. She said she stopped the research as soon as she heard about the Congressman killing himself," Thomas said.

"Who's Michelle?" two asked at the same time.

"She works for Daniel in the Los Angeles office. She researched the two men that gave sworn statements in Milwaukee and the one in Washington, D.C.," Thomas answered.

"Speaking of Milwaukee, I received expense reports from Mark and Daniel just before the meeting and there are some strange expenses, including an expense of fifteen hundred for buying a storage unit. Does anyone know about a storage unit in Milwaukee? There's also several lunches and dinners for four. I thought that only Mark, Daniel, and Bill were in Milwaukee," Charlie said.

"Let's get Mark on the phone and ask. I'd like to thank him for the efforts with Congressman Swindell." They called from the conference room phone. William didn't use the speaker phone at first. Mark answered on the second ring.

After he answered, William said, "Hello Mark. I'm going to put the whole group on the speaker phone."

"Can I try to patch Daniel in too?"

"Sure."

William put the Save America end on the speaker phone and after several beeps they heard Daniel say he was on the line.

Daniel said, "I'll be on a speaker phone too. I have Michelle here."

"This is Thomas. You did a great job Michelle."

"Thanks."

William said, "First of all, I wanted to thank you for your efforts with Congressman Swindell. It certainly wasn't the ending I expected but he was an evil man."

Mark said, "You're welcome. We're glad to help."

Daniel said, "Same here."

"We've decided on the next candidate for our website. It's Congressman Murphy. Bill will probably call you to help him with Congressman Murphy."

"We'll be glad to help. We sent you our expenses through last week this morning."

"This is Charlie. I received the expense reports a little while ago and had a few questions. The first one is about the storage unit."

Daniel said, "I'll explain that since I bought the unit. The Congressman's divorce lawyer died about a month ago and the wife cleaned out his offices quickly and put everything, except for a few things she sold, in a storage unit. The wife was anxious to sell so I bought the whole unit. After much sweat, we found the sealed divorce documents for the Congressman."

William said, "That explains why Bill knew the contents of the divorce documents before anyone else."

"It does, but he couldn't talk about the contents until the judge unsealed the documents," Mark added.

"What about the expense for shredding documents?"

"We thought it was best to shred all of the lawyer's files after we owned them," Daniel said.

"What about the hundred and twenty dollar credit?"

"That would be the security deposit refund for the storage unit."

"The expense report has meals for four people rather than three."

"Michelle joined us for meals."

"I don't see any travel expenses for her," Charlie said.

"She lived in Milwaukee."

"She did?" Charlie asked.

"She now lives with me in Los Angeles and works for us. She's also going to be my wife."

There was silence for a few beats.

Michelle finally said, "All of you are invited to our wedding when I pick a date."

William said, "I'm confused, but that's normal."

Michelle said, "I was a librarian in Milwaukee when Daniel came in looking like a lost puppy so I adopted him and moved to Los Angeles to take care of him. I also fell in love with him."

William said, "That's very touching."

"This is Amy. I'll be glad to help with the wedding even though I'm in Georgia. Maybe the guys will let me come to Los Angeles early."

Daniel said, "I've got extra rooms if they let you come."

"I'll make their lives miserable if they don't."

"Spoken like a real woman," Michelle said.

Daniel said, "I didn't charge you for the suit Michelle made me buy to meet the lawyer's wife. I'm going to wear it at the wedding."

"Thanks," Charlie said. Charlie thought of the Save America money as his own. In fact, Charlie was thinking more about taking some of the money. His two older brothers had retired as a physician and a lawyer and had much more money than him. They were always asking him to go on expensive fishing and hunting trips and vacations. Charlie had to make excuses since he couldn't afford the trips. He had divorced late in life and gave up half of his savings. His two older brothers hadn't gotten divorces. The benefit of his divorce was his second wife was wonderful and made him happy.

Daniel said, "I did donate a lot of items from the storage unit to Habitat and we kept the receipts, if that's okay."

"It is and that's all the expense report questions I have," Charlie replied.

William said, "I'll call Bill and let him know Congressman Murphy will be next. Let Charlie know what's needed to amend the contract and add funds. Thanks again for your efforts."

Michelle said, "Thank you for bringing Daniel to me."

William ended the call and said, "We'll discuss the wedding when she decides on a date. Let's talk cars."

Cal said, "Amy sold another car today and we should have another car ready for sale in a couple of days. We've started on the cars I bought in Atlanta. It looks like easy fixes. Everyone is welcome to help in their spare time."

Charlie said, "I was skeptical at first but Cal has made a believer out of me. The car business will definitely be profitable."

William said, "I'm still getting lots of compliments on the Cobra. There are several unfinished Cobras on eBay routinely. Should we buy them and finish the projects?"

Cal answered, "I'd rather stick to the salvage and wrecked cars now. I know they're profitable. There's also a lot of Cobras for sale on eBay for less than it cost to build them. We'd be competing with those prices."

"You're right. It's not cheap to build one and I agree we couldn't compete with the prices. There was a nice one on eBay that sold yesterday for twenty six thousand."

Charlie said, "I'd like a fifty five Chevy, a fifty five Thunderbird, or maybe a sixty six GTO."

Cal said, "I'll try to find a classic car to fix. We can leave it here for all of us to drive. Charlie can decide whether he wants to keep it or Amy can sell it."

Amy said, "It can be my lunch and errand car."

"Anything else?"

Charlie said, "I'm taking off the rest of the week. I'll have my computer with me and I'll have an amendment to Mark and Daniel's contract done today." Charlie was taking more time off than everyone else but he was still managing the Save America affairs fine.

Thomas said, "I'm going to take some time off soon. My wife is itching to travel."

Cal said, "I'll take some time off next month. I do need to make sure someone is managing the shop when I'm gone." Cal looked at William. Since William was the only one with some knowledge of cars, William knew he would need to be here when Cal was gone.

Amy gave William a couple of errands to do during the afternoon. There was an auction coming up next week so William thought he'd go by and look at the house to determine if he should register for the auction. It was on his way. After going to the bank and dropping a signed contract off at a realtor's office, he checked out the house. It was a single story ranch house with light blue vinyl siding. The roof looked fine but the HVAC unit outside the house was missing. It was vacant, which was good. The banks were now selling occupied homes since they didn't want to do the evictions. The homeowners already disliked the bank for foreclosing and would dislike them more if they evicted them, so the banks let the winning bidder at the auction do the evictions. The lot for the house needed work, although the bank had kept the grass mowed. The house had a concrete driveway and carport. He decided he'd tell Amy to register him for the auction.

William had forgotten to call Bill while he was at the office so he called him from the house being auctioned. Bill didn't answer so he left a message.

While William was looking at the house to be auctioned, a realtor texted to make a counteroffer on two tax sale properties her client had acquired through a tax sale. He had made an offer a couple of weeks ago knowing that the two years wasn't up and he would still need to do an action to clear title. The properties were near the house he was looking at so he decided to take another look. The houses were being sold as-is, which is how he bought all of his houses.

He walked around the first one. It was a brick house that was built in the seventies. The roof needed to be replaced and the yard was a mess. The HVAC was still in place but it was an older unit that needed to be replaced. The second house was built in the fifties. It looked like asbestos siding. The house had windows broken out but the roof and HVAC unit looked fine. Both houses were locked so he didn't get the inside tour.

William finally made it to his house that was being worked on. He helped with new trim that was being installed. Painting would be next after the trim was installed. At the end of the day, all the trim was installed. He would help with the painting tomorrow.

William was tired when he got home and fell asleep on the couch watching ESPN. Jessie wasn't coming over tonight. He didn't need to watch CNN tonight. The phone woke him up and it was Bill.

William must have sounded groggy and Bill asked, "Were you sleeping?"

"I was. You weren't on CNN keeping me awake."

"I was on several other networks and cable shows today and tonight. You could have watched me on those."

"I chose ESPN tonight. We've created enough news lately. I called to let you know the next person on our website will be Congressman Murphy. We're amending Mark's and Daniel's contracts to add funds if you want to use them."

"I'll keep using them. I'll call them tomorrow."

"We conference called them today and Michelle was on the line. It sounds like Daniel found himself a nice woman in Milwaukee."

"He did. I like her a lot and she's smart."

"We called them because we were confused about the storage unit included on their expense report."

"Did they explain it?"

"They did and it cleared up how you knew what was in the divorce file."

"Mark and Daniel can be resourceful and we were lucky."

"Did the Congressman's ex-wife or son grant you an interview? It'd be interesting to hear their side of the story."

"No. They didn't. I'm a little disappointed."

"Are you going to delay the book and add Congressman Swindell?"

"I think I am. Thanks again for supporting me with Mark and Daniel."

"And Michelle," William added.

"Especially her."

William made it to the office early the next morning. He had his truck again as he was planning to help with painting in the afternoon. He checked the website and Congressman Murphy wasn't on the website yet. He checked the email counter and the number of emails that was sent to Congressman Swindell was huge. Thomas would need to reset the counter.

William went into the shop and toured the cars being repaired. There was a Chevy Cruze that he wasn't sure about the year. There were two Chevy Camaros that were newer models. There was a newer Dodge Challenger. The last car was a newer Ford Mustang. He didn't know the years of the cars so he checked the files in the shop office. He figured he could impress Cal when he knew the years, except Cal caught him looking in the files.

Cal said, "You didn't know the years of the cars."

"I didn't but I was planning to impress you with my knowledge acquired from the files."

"Sorry to interfere with your plan."

"It's okay. You can just tell me."

They walked through the shop and Cal told William each car's year and what was being done to the cars. He told William he was looking at a sixty six GTO that had been wrecked and he was planning to bid on it. William promised not to tell Charlie.

When Amy came in, William asked her to register him for the auction next week. The auction company had changed the rules lately, requiring a detailed registration for each house showing the availability of funds for cash sales. A phone interview was also required for some houses. William imagined it was a result of people failing to complete the transaction even when they were the high bidder. The deposit is typically a credit card deposit so it could be disputed and not paid.

William checked with Thomas and he was still putting the facts together for Congressman Murphy. He checked his emails and Charlie had copied him on the contract amendments for Mark and Daniel. Amy was instructed to file the amendments when they were returned from Mark and Daniel. The email said there should be enough funds for a week or two but Charlie could transfer funds on his laptop if needed.

William read the rest of his emails and thought about buying a couple of the Groupon offers. He bought some in the past and failed to use them. He was sure that's what Groupon counted on and that's why he was still on the email list.

William read the text from the realtor again and decided to make a counteroffer. He split the difference between his first offer and their counteroffer. He reminded the realtor in the text about the risk he was taking and the cost to get a clear title. He sent it expecting that it'd be accepted. Amy would admonish him since he already had too many houses that needed to be worked on and this would be two more.

William wore his work clothes to work and left to help paint. Painting was not his favorite task but it certainly improved the look of a house. He used a light brown or beige paint on the interior walls of all the houses. After he was through painting a house, he could use the left over paint as part of the mix for the next house. This allowed him to buy discounted paint and leftover paint from the Habitat store or a home supply store. The Habitat store also provided him with doors, light fixtures, plumbing fixtures, and other miscellaneous items.

Amy had salads for lunch using the chicken and tuna salad from yesterday. She bought a couple of bag-o-salads and some fresh tomatoes and cucumbers to add. William thought it was actually pretty good.

Since Charlie wasn't there, Cal passed around a picture of the sixty six GTO he was going to bid on.

Amy said, "It'll be perfect for me. Can we leave it red?"

"I think we can. I like red too," Cal replied.

Cal said, "A Camaro will be finished tomorrow so Amy can sell it."

"Can I drive it until it's sold? I'll put a for sale sign in the window," Amy asked.

"It's okay with me," Cal said. He knew that Amy had become invaluable for the car business so a little perk was okay.

"When will you know whether you have the GTO?" I asked.

"The auction is in the morning in Savannah."

Amy said, "I'll go with you to Savannah if we get it."

Thomas passed out the screen shots that he planned for Congressman Murphy. Congressman Murphy was chairman of the Transportation and Infrastructure Committee and his voting record was fiscally irresponsible.

The jurisdiction of the Committee on Transportation and Infrastructure includes the Coast Guard, federal management of emergencies and natural disasters, flood control and improvement of rivers and harbors, inland waterways, registering and licensing of vessels and small boats, the Capitol Building, the Senate and House Office Buildings, construction or maintenance of roads, construction or reconstruction, maintenance, and care of buildings and grounds of the Botanic Garden, the Library of Congress, and the Smithsonian Institution, merchant marine, purchase of sites and construction of post offices, customhouses, Federal courthouses, and Government buildings within the District of Columbia, marine affairs, public buildings and occupied or improved grounds of the United States generally, public works for the benefit of the benefit of navigation, including bridges and dams, roads and the safety thereof, transportation, including civil aviation, railroads, water transportation, transportation infrastructure, transportation labor, and railroad retirement and unemployment, and water power.

The screen shot showed his voting record and tallied up the amount of deficit the Congressman had created as a result of his votes. They all agreed with the screen shot and Thomas said he would make it live after lunch. William had looked at the Vegas odds for Congressman Murphy being next and it was ten to one. He thought he should have placed a wager.

William said, "I talked to Bill last night and he wants to continue to use Mark and Daniel, as well as Michelle. I think Michelle impressed him when she helped them in Milwaukee."

William continued, "Charlie amended the contracts with Mark and Daniel and they were sent to both of them."

William didn't talk about the funds for Mark and Daniel and no one asked. Amy was checking the timecards for the two mechanics and writing their weekly checks. She was writing her check too but William had to sign it since Charlie was off.

William left after the meeting and went to paint. He was assigned to paint the trim he had installed. He hadn't heard back about his counteroffer and didn't expect to so soon. The responses were normally slow since the owners were in Atlanta.

At the end of the day, the painting was almost done. They would be hanging doors, installing lighting, and doing the last little items tomorrow. He'd bring a for-sale sign tomorrow and place it on the street. Amy would list it on Craigslist. If William couldn't sell it himself in a couple of weeks, he'd either put it up for rent or let a realtor sell it.

The next house he was having these guys move to was nearby so he figured he'd move all the tools, paint, and leftovers tomorrow morning. The next house needed a lot of work but he didn't pay a lot for the house. The first step was to tear out all the old carpet and padding. The tack strips would be taken up in the living area where engineered flooring would be installed. The cabinet doors would be taken off since new ones would be installed. They would work on one bathroom at a time so they could remove the commode and vanity for a new tile floor. The lighting fixtures would be removed and temporary lights installed. New light fixtures would be installed after painting. All of the switch and outlet covers would be removed. The switches and outlets would normally be replaced since they were usually painted or discolored.

William checked the website when he got home from painting and Congressman Murphy was shown with his voting record and total amount of deficit he had created. The email address, mail address, and phone number of the Congressman was shown with a request to send him an email, letter, or call him.

Chapter 31

The next morning William went straight to the house that was painted and loaded up his truck with the tools and supplies he would move to the next house. Two guys had stayed and completed the final touches, which were installing the switch and outlet plates and cleaning.

William made it to the office about eleven thirty and talked to Amy about a couple of houses and the upcoming auction. She said she had registered him but didn't like the new process.

At noon, they talked about the car business first since William wanted to know about the GTO. Amy didn't mention it so she must not know either. Lunch was pizza.

"We'll talk about cars first."

Cal said, "I know you want to know about the GTO. Well, we got it. I'll pick it up tomorrow."

Amy said, "I'm going with you if it's alright with you." She looked at William with a droopy face.

"Sure. You can go. Transfer the phone to your cell and call me if I need to address anything quickly tomorrow."

Cal said, "Amy has several people interested in the Camaro. I expect we'll sell it quickly."

"Send me pictures of the GTO when you get there tomorrow."

William continued, "Let's talk about Save America."

Thomas said, "As you've probably already seen, Congressman Murphy is on our website. I also identified a possible problem this morning. I was searching the web as usual looking for possible threats and saw a copycat website. It looks like it was started today. I'll show you."

Thomas had his laptop already connected into the conference room projector and a website was displayed when he turned on the projector. The website had Save Our America displayed. The page was red, white, and blue with a flag waving in the background. Across the bottom of the page were words that offered a five million dollar reward for the death of Senator Callahan.

Thomas said, "We also started getting calls in our call center about eleven this morning asking how to collect the five million dollars."

"Could you find out who started the other website?" William asked.

"I didn't in the short time I looked. I'll look more after lunch."

"This could get serious. What do you suggest?"

"I'd suggest taking our website down until the Save Our America website gets shut down. I would expect the government would get involved quickly. We could also be implicated if anything happens to Senator Callahan."

"We could edit our webpage to state that we have nothing to do with Save Our America, but that may lead to confusion. I agree that we should shut our website down. How fast can you do it?"

"Just a second. It's done."

"That was fast. What about the call center?"

"I had them stop taking calls this morning."

"Let me know what you find out about the other website. We can get help if you need it."

"I'll keep you informed on what I find. I don't know if I need help."

William adjourned the meeting so Thomas could get started. He didn't know enough to help him. The other website bothered him a lot. He hadn't considered that there'd be a copycat website that would be extreme. He did think that there'd be copycats that tried to do the same thing they were trying to do. A bounty on a Senator's head was extreme. Whoever started the website may not have five million dollars but it didn't matter if someone decided to act first and then ask for the five million. William was sure the website would be shut down soon but not soon enough. He decided to stay in the office for a bit longer to see if Thomas found out anything. He was nervous so he went and talked to Amy. They talked about the status of all the houses being rented and renovated. They talked about the upcoming auction and he brought up the counteroffer on the tax sale properties.

Amy said, "Are you sure you want to buy tax sale properties? We'll have to hold them until we get a clear title."

"I think it's worth the risk."

"I'm not sure it is, but you *usually* make sound decisions," Amy said as she grimaced.

"I get the message. Maybe they won't take my offer. I won't go higher."

William was still nervous so he went into the shop. His mood improved as soon as saw the cars being worked on. Much like when he saw a house being renovated. The front end was off the other Camaro including fenders, hood, and grill. The Camaro had a front end accident so parts were going to be replaced. He looked closely and it appeared that there wasn't frame damage or motor damage. It could be an easy fix with parts being replaced and a paint job. William was sure Cal did a more thorough inspection than him and probably had it on the lift to do it.

Cal came over while William was looking at the Camaro and said, "What do you think?"

"It looks like an easy fix but I didn't look underneath."

"It'll be easy. We'll make money on it. The Cruze won't be as easy."

William turned and saw the front end off of the Cruze and walked over. The frame was damaged and the radiator pushed into the motor.

"The hood wouldn't come up so the auction didn't have pictures of the engine compartment. There was a little more damage than

I thought but the price was cheap. I'll use the frame machine to straighten it out."

"Have you decided when you'll be taking off?"

"Not yet."

William left the shop and went back to his office. He thought of his former life where he was paid to make people go away. For five million, he was sure he could figure out a way to get to Senator Callahan. William was paid well to end lives but never five million. His Save America cell phone rang and it was Bill.

"Someone just showed me a website that's similar to your website. Did you create it?"

"We didn't. Someone is copying our website. We took our website down as soon as we found out about the other site."

"Do you have any idea who started it?"

"Thomas is looking but he hasn't found out yet."

"Do you have any idea why Senator Callahan is shown? Do you know there's no Senator Callahan."

"I don't and didn't."

"Let me know if you determine who started the website. Our nerds are also looking."

They skirted the legal concerns on the Save America website since they didn't threaten to eliminate any elected officials. At one o'clock, the copycat website was shut down. William turned on the news and the news programs were discussing the website but no one had come forward to take credit for shutting down the website.

Thomas came in William's office and said, "I didn't make much progress with the website. It was strange since I could download the code."

"Why were you allowed to download the code, assuming that can't normally happen?"

"I don't know but I'll look at the code to see if I figure it out. I thought it may be a virus but our system didn't detect anything."

"Keep me posted."

William left the office and went to work on the house. A lot of the destruction was done yesterday but he did get to help some. He then helped install backer board for the tile in the bathrooms and kitchen. Next was a trip to his storage unit to get the leftover wood flooring. He'd go tonight and buy more. It was late when he got home and he hadn't heard from Thomas. Jessie didn't come over again tonight. Her father was having problems.

The next morning William called Thomas and he hadn't noticed anything unusual about the code from the website. William told him he'd be in the office at lunch.

William helped with the flooring for a couple of hours. He checked on the workers in the shop and they were doing okay. Cal had explained what he wanted them to do today. As soon as he got to his office, Thomas found him and said there was another website with a Senator Mulberry, who also didn't exist. He said he downloaded the code for that site too and the website was a CNN clone.

William asked, "Is it a computer game?"

"It could be but I don't know how to tell."

"Bill said they had nerds working on it. Let's call him."

When Bill answered, William said, "I think it could be a computer game. What do your nerds think?"

"They believe it could be a game as well."

Thomas said, "I downloaded the code thinking that would tell me something."

"Our nerds downloaded the code too and got nothing from the code."

William said, "I'm going to call Mark and Daniel to see if they know of a gamer that can help."

When Mark answered, William said, "Thomas and I have a question. There're copycat websites that started yesterday. They appeared to be a sham at first but we think it could be a computer game. Do you have anyone that might know?"

"We have a small cyber group that may know. Unfortunately, they always come in late in the day and work late into the night. I'll call you back as soon as they come in," Mark responded.

"Thanks." William ended the call.

It was an hour later that Mark called back.

"I talked to our cyber group and they know about the game. The game's been advertised on most of the gamer sites and our guys were trying to figure it out today. Evidently there are clues in every webpage and a location where there's five hundred thousand dollars. There was a ten dollar entry fee."

William asked, "Do they know who's running the game?"

"They don't."

"Do they know why our site was cloned?"

"No. They didn't know."

"How long does it last?"

"They said ten days. There'll be a different copycat website each day."

"Do they know where the money went?"

"No. They don't."

"Can you find out?" William asked.

"I asked my cyber guys if they could help locate the persons who created the game and they didn't want to help. They thought they'd be disqualified. They're also very busy on our accounts. One of our cyber employees left for another job last week leaving us short."

"Great. Does Daniel have someone that could help?"

"His guys are playing the game too and also working on our cyber contracts."

"I'll check with Bill and see if he knows someone who can help."

William called Bill and said, when he answered, "I just talked to Mark and the copycat websites turn out to be a game. Mark's cyber group is playing the game. I asked if they could help find the persons running the game and they're too busy to help."

Bill said, "We found the same thing."

"Do you know that it runs ten days?"

"We found out that too."

"Do you need any funds to help find the persons running the game?" William asked.

"No. We've put several of our resources on it."

"Let me know if you do," William said as he ended the call.

At the lunchtime meeting, which was just Thomas and William, William told Thomas what he'd heard from Mark and Bill. Cal and Amy were picking up the GTO in Savannah. Amy had left subs in the fridge for the lunch meal.

Thomas said, "We'll need to leave our site down for the next ten days and maybe a few days longer. I think we should start our call center back up and give them a script about the game being run."

"I agree. There'll be less traffic with our site down and we could ensure callers know we're not associated with the game. Will you put the script together?"

"I will."

Amy sent William pictures of the GTO and he pulled them up on his phone for Thomas to see.

Cal and Amy showed up with the GTO at four. Thomas and William went out to meet them. The car was red but had damage all over the car.

William asked, "What happened to the car?"

"The auctioneer said the driver ran off the road in a storm and drove it through brush and trees. I'm concerned about the undercarriage so I'll put it on the rack to check."

"Is that hail damage too?"

"It is."

Amy said with a cheery voice, "It's going to be a great car."

Amy was optimistic while William was thinking of all of the work that needed to be done to the car.

"I had a wonderful time going to Savannah. We had lunch at a boarding house restaurant. I had a shrimp salad sandwich and Cal had seafood gumbo. I had peachy green beans and Cal had peach pie. I want to go again on the next road trip."

Cal said, "I enjoyed having her along, except for all the calls she made for you."

"I'm sure it wasn't too many."

"I enjoyed my day," Amy hugged Cal.

William helped Cal unload the car. The car started and ran so Cal drove it into the shop onto the lift. Amazingly, there wasn't much damage underneath the car. The body would still need lots of work.

"When will you start on this car?"

"In a few days, we'll try to finish another car or two first."

"How are the guys in the shop doing?"

"They seem to be happy and like working here."

William went to talk to Amy about properties. She said she had taken calls all day and didn't need any help. He left the office and went back to the house they were working on. The flooring was coming along fine and the tile was going in a bathroom and kitchen. He helped with the flooring until the work crew left. He walked around and made a list of all the materials needed. He'd go round up materials tonight.

William spent most of the next few days working on properties and less time at the office. The owner of the tax sale properties took his offer so he now owned two more properties. This wouldn't make Amy happy.

William made it to the lunch time meeting Monday since Charlie was back and Amy needed to give him instructions for the week. Cal had covered the GTO so they could show it to Charlie after the meeting. Cal hadn't found time to work on it yet.

Amy had tuna and chicken salad sandwiches again. William's work on the houses had resulted in a little weight loss so Amy wasn't feeding him tossed salads. Charlie had spent the morning tallying up the donations from last week and the car business expenses. Thomas had told him about the website being down before William arrived.

Charlie said, as he handed out spreadsheets, "Donations were down last week but we still had a fair amount of money donated. The spreadsheets show the funds in our accounts. I'll file tax forms this afternoon."

Everybody was familiar with the spreadsheets after seeing them many times and no one had comments or questions.

Thomas was next. "The website is still down. I'll turn it back on tomorrow since the attention has turned to the other copycat websites."

William added, "I've talked to Bill and they haven't found who's running the game. The webpages should stop this week. Bill did a good job of reporting that it was a game and not affiliated with us."

"The websites were only a copycat of our website the first day, which helped a lot," Thomas explained.

Thomas had sent William links to the copycat websites and the websites were copycats of news networks and government websites. This helped plenty to get pressure off of Save America.

William changed the topic. "Let's talk about the car business."

Amy spoke first, "I sold the Camaro this weekend. The buyer was approved for his car loan this morning so we'll meet him at a branch of his credit union this afternoon."

Charlie said, "That'll raise the profit for the month. You're quite the salesperson."

"Thanks. I'll miss the Camaro. My husband liked riding in it."

Cal teased Amy. "The Cruze is ready so you can drive it."

"That's not quite the same," Amy sneered.

Charlie handed out a spreadsheet. "These are the totals for the car business. We're doing better than I thought we would."

Charlie was now seeing money being made in the car business and envying all the donations for Save America. His two brothers had invited him to go on a Patagonia expedition cruise fly fishing trip, which included cabins aboard a yacht and a Bell 407 helicopter to fly fish in remote areas. McKenzie boats and jet-skiffs were placed in strategic spots among the Patagonian fjords to fish in the deeper territories. The trip went to Puerto Montt, Auchemo Island Bay, Tic Toc Bay, Ventisquero Sound, Guaitecas Archipelago, and Leptepu Fjord. Charlie couldn't afford to take expensive trips with his older brothers and kept making other excuses why he couldn't go. His brothers would send him photos while they were on their trips.

Cal said, "I'm bidding on two cars in the morning so we could add them to our inventory."

Amy asked, "Where are they?"

"Atlanta."

"Shoot. I don't want to go to Atlanta. I'll give you list of places I'll go so you can buy cars from those places."

"I've also scheduled the two mechanics in training for all day Friday. We're planning to lease new diagnostic equipment that is much better than the unit we have. The vendor will be doing training at another shop in town so our two mechanics will attend."

"What's the cost of the new equipment?"

"Only fifty dollars more a month." Cal paused for more questions and then said, "There's one thing we need to discuss and we need to go in the shop to discuss it."

Charlie looked confused since he was never consulted on anything in the shop but he went along. They arrived at the GTO with the cover on it and Cal pulled the cover off.

Charlie said, "You found a GTO."

Cal said, "Amy and I went and got it while you were gone last week."

Amy said with a happy tone, "It's going to be pretty car."

Charlie saw the damage. "It's going to be a lot to work."

"It's just cosmetic. The engine sounds perfect. I think it was rebuilt by the previous owner." Cal threw Charlie the keys.

Charlie grinned as he opened the driver's door, got in, and started the engine. He revved it a couple of times and then shut it off.

As he got out, Charlie said, "It does sound good. When can you work on it?" Charlie thought briefly that he could wait until his car was done before moving forward. Then he thought about his two older brothers' fishing trip.

Cal offered, "I thought we would start today."

Charlie still had the keys. "I'll help where I can. I don't know much about cars."

Charlie had already taken initiatives to pillage Save America. He now knew he would have more money than his older brothers after the Save America funds were his. Now that he knew the mechanics would be off on Friday, he would confirm and execute his plan on Friday.

Mark called Daniel late on Monday to see if any progress had been made.

Daniel said, "Michelle is researching the Congressman. I had to help with other work this week."

"I had to work on other stuff too. Tell Michelle we're counting on her."

Chapter 32

William worked on his houses as much as he could during the week. He did make it to the office for the noon meetings. Congressman Murphy hadn't called him and he hadn't heard from Bill, Daniel, or Mark during the week. Bill's presence on the talk shows had diminished. Charlie was nervous all week so he caught him after the Thursday meeting.

William asked, "Are you feeling okay?"

Charlie fabricated a quick story. "I have a doctor's appointment tomorrow and am a little anxious."

"Anything serious?"

"I don't think so. The doctor ran tests last week and the results are in."

"I hope everything is fine. Call me and let me know."

Charlie thought that William should worry about his own health since the prognosis wasn't good for tomorrow.

William went to work on houses on Friday morning and made it to the office for the noon meeting. Lunch was subs. Charlie was off so just the four of them met. Cal was talking about the car business for a few minutes when his phone, William's phone, and Thomas's phone rang a warbling tone.

Cal said, "It's the alarm system. I'm going to my office and check."

Thomas and William followed him and saw a John Deere Gator and five guys at the back fence. They were dressed in camouflage.

William uttered quickly, "Thomas, take Amy to the basement. Lock the door and don't come out unless we call you. Cal and I should be able to handle it so don't call the police."

Thomas looked at William like he was crazy but he took Amy to the basement.

Cal asked, "How do you want to handle it?"

"Get your guns and I'll get mine. When they come through the fence we'll defend ourselves."

Cal knew he could use a gun but didn't know about William. He figured he would be the one defending the fort. Cal went to the shop and got his guns. He had two Glock 22s with lots of rounds. He was standing at the back door looking through the window when he saw William's sniper rifle with a silencer and tripod. He also had a Glock 22 with a silencer. Cal didn't say anything since they were in a hurry.

William said, "Hold the door open enough for me to sight through."

William got on the floor with the gun propped on the tripod. He sighted the gun at the fence where the five guys were located. The fence had been cut and they were separating the fence so the Gator could drive through. He let the Gator get about thirty feet from the fence and shot the driver in the head. The Gator was still rolling when he shot the passenger in the head. The passenger slumped and he shot someone behind him in the head. One got out of the driver's side and he shot him in the head. A fifth one got out and he shot him in the leg. William thought he needed to talk to one of them. The five shots took less than ten seconds.

William threw Cal his truck keys and went out the back door watching the fifth guy with binoculars. The last one he shot had dropped the handgun and was trying to get back through the fence with much difficulty. Cal pulled the truck up to the fence as the attacker was just getting through the fence. There was a Hummer with a trailer about two hundred feet away behind the building in the rear of the Save America building. The building had been vacant since Save America moved in. William got out of the truck at the fence and yelled for the attacker to stop and lay face down. He did.

Cal checked the four others at the Gator and was satisfied they wouldn't be any more trouble to anyone again. William walked through the fence and saw that it was a woman. Cal joined him shortly.

Cal suggested, "You should put a tourniquet on your leg. Take your shirt off and wrap it around your leg."

She turned over and took off her shirt to make a tourniquet. She took a knife and cut the shirt so she could tie it around her leg.

William asked, "Would you care to tell us who you are and why you're here today?"

"I wouldn't."

William already had his Glock out and shot her in the other leg. She didn't scream but panic went across her face.

Cal didn't seem surprised that William shot the other leg and said calmly, "You should use the rest of your shirt for a tourniquet on the other leg."

She took the rest of her shirt and tied a tourniquet around the other leg.

William asked again, "Would you care to tell us who you are and why you're here today."

She was breathing hard and clenching her teeth as she spoke, "We were hired to take all the people in that building hostage."

William wasn't sure whether to believe her.

Cal asked, "Who hired you?"

"It was a man named John. That's probably not his real name." She was laboring with her breathing now.

"How did he find you?"

"We have a training camp in upstate New York. He showed up at camp one day and offered to hire us."

"Are there more of you involved?"

"No. Just five of us."

"What does John look like?"

"He's about five feet eight inches tall, bald on the top of his head, slightly overweight, clean shaven, and wears glasses." She described Charlie.

"How did you know to come today?"

"He called me and told me."

William didn't ask for her phone since he knew he would have it soon.

"How much did he pay you?"

"He gave us two hundred thousand up front with another two hundred thousand after the job was done."

"Where's the money now?"

"It's in the Hummer. I was afraid some of my group would back out so I kept the money. I told them I'd give it to them later today on the trip back to New York."

"Who knows you're in Georgia?"

"Nobody. We're supposed to be on weekend training trip."

William pointed the Glock at her right arm and said, "I don't believe you."

"It's true. I planned it and didn't even tell the others where we were going."

William thought she actually sounded truthful and she made sense. He wouldn't have told the others either and would have kept the money until afterward too.

"So you scouted us out?"

"Yes. I came down last weekend."

"And you thought it would be easy."

"I did. John gave us the details of the building and descriptions of the four people. John told us you wouldn't get the police involved."

"What were you going to do with us?"

"We were supposed to take you to our camp in New York and then call John."

So she wasn't going to kill everyone. Charlie had a heart.

"How long were you going to keep us?"

"John said he would let us know."

It sounded like Charlie was going to empty the Save America accounts and disappear. William wondered if his wife knew he was departing.

William looked at Cal, "What's next?"

"Hospital?"

"Agree. Let's carry her to the trailer. We don't want to get blood in the Hummer."

They both put on gloves and William grabbed her underneath the arms. Cal grabbed her feet. She was in pain but didn't show it. They put her in the back of the trailer. William shot her in the head with his Glock. Cal didn't flinch.

Cal and William went to the Gator and loaded three of them in the Gator's bed. William pushed the driver over, drove the Gator into the trailer, placed his rifle and Glock in the trailer, closed the door, and secured the padlock. Cal walked up to the Hummer and saw that the keys were still in the vehicle. He drove the Hummer to the side of the building where it couldn't be seen from the Save America building. Cal took the keys and locked it. They walked to the fence and pulled it together as best as they could. Cal drove William's truck back to the Save America building.

Cal said while he was driving, "I'm glad you're on my side."

"Thanks."

"What's next?"

"We'll fix the fence first, go see Charlie, and then we get rid of the Hummer and trailer tonight."

"Let me know what I can do."

Cal put his guns back in the shop and he called Thomas. It was over in less than thirty minutes.

"You can come back up."

William heard the door unlock and Amy and Thomas came upstairs. Amy was very upset.

Amy asked, "What's going on?"

William answered, "It looked like there were some thieves who wanted to break in. Cal and I scared them off."

William winked at Thomas. He'd tell him the real story later but he didn't want to get Amy excited and the real story would do that.

Cal added, "They must have thought the building was vacant. After they saw us, they ran."

"We went back to the building behind us and watched them drive off. They must have cut the lock on that gate," William said.

"Copper prices have thieves stealing from every vacant building," Cal said.

"You should take the rest of the day off Amy. Is there anything that has to be done today?"

"No. It can wait until Monday."

"Let me shut down my computer and get my purse."

"Turn on the answering machine to take the calls. We'll be leaving soon after I line up someone to fix the fence."

"I need to put up the tools in the shop before I go," Cal said. "I also need to make sure the security system is reset."

After Amy left, Thomas asked, "What's the real story?"

Cal showed up as Thomas was asking the question.

William answered, "We believe Charlie was planning a run on the Save America funds. He hired some folks to take us hostage. We'll find out when we talk to Charlie. I'm assuming he would disappear after he had the funds."

"What happened to the guys that were hired?"

"Cal and I went outside with our guns and scared them off. We shot a few rounds close to them and they got the message. I don't think they'll be coming back."

Cal took William's lead again. "They looked like young punks so I don't think they'll be coming back."

"Why do you think it was Charlie behind this?"

"Charlie's been acting a little strange lately and he's not here. I know it's not you since you still want to win the ten dollar bet."

"Charlie *has* acted a little strange. I'd better check the accounts to see if all the funds are still there," Thomas said.

"Can you change the passwords?"

"I can and I'll put a hold on all of the funds. Are you going to see Charlie?"

"Cal and I will later after we fix the fence." William didn't see a need to hurry to see Charlie, assuming he hadn't already left with the Save America funds.

"Can you tell if all the recent donations were deposited?"

"I can. I get the totals for the donations just like Charlie and I can compare them. It'll take a day or two."

"Put it on your list of things to do."

Cal and William already had work clothes on and they went to the fence. Cal brought tools from the shop and William had tools in his truck. They checked the vacant building behind them. The back door was unlocked, probably due to the scouting by the female attacker. They found a small roll of chain link fence fabric. They went to the front gate of the vacant building and put a new padlock on it. The padlock that had been cut off was on the ground next to the gate.

William had a come-along in his truck and they pulled the fence tight enough to lace the new section into the fence. William also had aluminum ties to attach the fence to the posts and rail. They were through in a couple of hours.

They went back into the building and Thomas was still in his office working.

William interrupted him. "We're through with the fence and planning to go see Charlie."

"I'm still checking the accounts. I checked the past few weeks and it looks like the numbers match. I'm guessing Charlie didn't want to raise any suspicion before he absconded with all the funds. I'll stay for a little longer."

"Fine. We're on our way to see Charlie. I'm sure Charlie already noticed that the funds were locked and he didn't have access any longer. He'll be expecting us," William said.

Cal drove his Cobra and they went by the Hummer and collected the two hundred thousand. It was locked in one of the storage compartments. The female attacker was truthful about the money so William was hoping she was truthful about everything else. He'd hate to see a large group of disgruntled members of their camp showing up. They probably couldn't surprise them.

On the way to Aiken, Cal asked, "Where did you learn to shoot like that?"

"Squirrel hunting growing up."

"Just like Sergeant York."

"Exactly."

"I believe there's more than squirrel hunting involved, especially since you have a sniper rifle with a silencer."

"If you want more than one squirrel, you have to be quiet."

Cal drove without speaking and then asked, "Can the rifle be traced to you?"

"No."

Cal drove a ways further while thinking about William putting the rifle and pistol in the trailer, "Should I ask why?"

"No."

"Are we going to leave your rifle and handgun in the trailer?"

"Maybe. I've been thinking about that."

More driving and more thinking and Cal said, "You're quite a mystery. Should I check you out further?"

"I'd appreciate it if you didn't."

"I won't."

"What do you want to do with the Hummer and trailer?" Cal asked.

"I think we should take it back up north. What do you think?"

"I agree," Cal answered without any additional thoughts.

When they got to Charlie's house, his wife Emily answered the door.

William questioned, "Is Charlie home? We need to chat with him for a few minutes."

Emily responded, "He's in the sunroom. Can I get you something to drink?"

"I'll have a beer." William was still thirsty from working on the fence.

Cal said, "I'll have a beer too."

William had been to Charlie's house before and walked to the sunroom. Charlie was in one of the chairs and didn't get up. William understood why after hearing him speak.

With a very slurred speech, Charlie asked, "What brings you to my dwelling?" He had lots of trouble saying dwelling.

Emily came in and handed them beers and closed the door as she left. She rolled her eyes and shook her head. Emily had stayed out of the Save America venture, although she approved of it.

William said, "Some of your friends stopped by today and left something for you."

"And what would that be?"

William stuck his hand in the expansion folder and saw Charlie cringe. He pulled out the large envelope and handed it to Charlie.

"What is it?" He slurred all the words. His eyes were about half closed.

"It's a refund on the services you hired. The people you hired changed their minds."

Charlie wrestled with the envelope and finally opened it. He saw the money and said, with his head tilted and drool coming out his mouth, "Who's this from again?"

"Consider it a retirement gift. You've been replaced at Save America."

William wasn't sure whether he was too drunk to understand or was playing with them.

"What do you mean? That's it."

Charlie must have expected them to beat the crap out of him but William didn't see the need.

Cal didn't either and said, "It was nice working with you Charlie. Do you have your keys to the building?"

They both saw keys on a coaster next to his chair. He must have taken them off his key ring for them. He finally managed to grab them and handed them to Cal.

William drank the rest of his beer and so did Cal. They didn't say any more and left the house. Emily wasn't around so they didn't say goodbye to her.

Cal and William got in the car and Cal asked, "When do you want to take the Hummer and trailer north?"

"I'd like to leave soon. I'd rather not be driving the Hummer and trailer in the middle of the night. I left other clothes at the office that I can take."

"I have other clothes at the office too so let's get started."

William called Thomas when they were in the car and told him about Charlie. Thomas asked about Charlie's response and William told him about Charlie being very drunk. Thomas said he checked a lot of the deposits and they matched. He said he would finish next week and was leaving now. William told him they were on the way back to get his truck.

Cal drove for a while and finally said, "I'm glad we didn't do anything to Charlie. I thought about all the things I could do to him."

"I hope we don't regret it. Charlie should have enough sense not to try anything else."

"I think he will. We should have taken pictures of his hired hands and showed him. That would have convinced him," Cal offered.

Cal drove for a while and then asked, "Where are we taking the Hummer and trailer?"

"I was thinking New York. That's a long way from Georgia."

"I agree. Do we need to get rid of the guns on the way?"

"No. They're fine in the trailer," William responded.

"Are you sure?"

"I'm sure."

"Are you absolutely sure? I don't want any of this coming back on me," Cal said with concern in his voice.

"If it makes you feel better, we can do something else with them."

"It'd make me feel much better. Let me think about it." Cal sighed.

"I'll drive the Hummer and you can follow in the Cobra. We'll stop about ten at a motel. I have enough cash to pay for the motel, food, and gas."

"I'll fill up the Cobra before we leave. I think I want to leave the rifle and handgun in the shop and I'll cut them up on Sunday."

"Bring something to wrap them in and you can drive them back around in the Cobra." William preferred leaving them in the trailer. They were given to him for a job but he used other means so he knew they were untraceable. He didn't like depending on other people to do disposal so he'd come in on Sunday to help with the guns and that'd make him feel better. William knew it was going to be a long weekend.

They picked up their clothes and two new tarps at the Save America building. They retrieved William's guns in the trailer and Cal wrapped them in one of the tarps. They attached the ratchet straps to the Gator so it was secured inside the trailer. They didn't want it to roll around. They placed the other tarp inside the Hummer across the front seat. William checked out the Hummer and the Hummer had a Garmin in the passenger seat and he turned it on. He pushed home on the Garmin and the destination was upstate New York. The woman had been truthful about their location. He checked the registration and it also showed a location in upstate New York. The vehicle was registered in St. Lawrence County with an address in Potsdam. William wasn't sure he wanted to go all the way to Potsdam and the residents would recognize the Hummer and trailer since it was a small town. William thought he would figure out where to leave it while he was driving the fifteen or sixteen hours. Binghamton may be a better choice since it was barely in New York and would save hours of driving. He checked the Hummer and it was full of gas. He guessed they didn't want to stop after they had the four hostages in the trailer.

Cal and William hit the road about five thirty. William called Jessie as soon as he left. They didn't have plans tonight so he didn't have to break any plans.

William said, "Hello, love of my life."

"Who is this?"

"It's the yard man. I wanted to know if you wanted your bush trimmed tonight."

"What time are you thinking about?"

"I'm actually on the road to pick up a couple of cars Cal bought. We'll be back tomorrow." William figured he could use a story about

Cal's truck having mechanical problems or the car trailer having problems to cover the late return tomorrow.

"I need to stay with my parents tonight anyway. Dad has taken a turn for the worse, and I'll need to take him to see the doctor tomorrow."

"Tell him I'm thinking of him. I'll call you in the morning."

The Hummer had a satellite radio and William tuned in to a talk show to catch the news. He'd switch to music later. He called Cal and told him they'd stop in Petersburg, Virginia. William had stopped there before and there were several truck stops. He parked the Hummer and trailer next to a cattle trailer. He figured the smell wouldn't be as noticeable. It was about eleven thirty and they ate in the truck stop. William bought a sticky roller and a towel to clean the Hummer. They rented a room with double beds in the Motel 6. They decided to leave at five the next morning. Cal parked his Cobra at the truck stop and they walked to the motel. William put a Ford Mustang as the car they were driving on the registration.

They both filled up with gas and left about five a.m. William still hadn't decided where to leave the Hummer and trailer. William didn't want to stop until they made it to New York. He finally decided to leave it at a truck stop at the intersection of Interstate 81 and Interstate 86. If possible, he thought he would leave it parked with the trucks. He also thought it probably wouldn't be noticed for a few days if they were lucky.

William found a truck stop with a fairly remote parking area and pulled it into a space. He wiped the truck down although he had worn gloves for the whole trip. He pulled the tarp out and would put it in the Cobra. He used a sticky roller to clean the seat and carpet. He locked the Hummer and took the keys and the Garmin. The attackers didn't use the Hummer navigation to get to Georgia and had used the Garmin instead. William had worn his nylon hoodie while he was driving and used it while he looked for Cal. He was at the side of the lot and he got in. He had the top on the Cobra so they had some invisibility. They headed back to Aiken and didn't stop for a couple of hours for food and gas. They decided to drive without stopping with each taking a nap as needed. They made it back to Aiken at three a.m. William had called Jessie on the way to tell her they had trouble with the trailer. She was still busy with her father so she didn't question him. Cal said he wanted to go to the shop at one.

Cal and William met at the shop and cut the guns up into little pieces. William would take them to the dump tomorrow along with other metal scrap. The dumps weren't open on Sunday. The pieces weren't recognizable as guns.

William called Jessie on the way home and she was still tied up with her father. He asked her if she needed any help and she said no. He went home and fell asleep on the couch.

Chapter 33

Monday morning seemed like a normal Monday, until William remembered the events of the last three days. He went to the office first so that he could talk to Cal and Thomas. They wanted to decide if they needed another accountant.

Cal was in the shop so he asked him how he was doing and he said fine. Cal told William that he worried about him since he wasn't used to combat. William asked him to come to Thomas's office. They closed the door and sat down.

Thomas said, "I haven't finished looking at the accounts. So far I haven't found any problems but I still have lots to look at."

"I wanted to talk about a replacement for Charlie. I can do the tax filings and handle the accounts but I'll need help if I need to create another corporation or file the taxes for the corporations," William said.

Cal said, "You lost me when you talked about tax filings."

"I think we'll need someone later but we should be able to handle it for now. I can handle all the deposits and we can keep adding to the existing accounts," Thomas said.

"Do we have potential volunteers that are accountants? I think we should have someone that is retired, although Charlie was retired and that didn't work out," William said.

"The call center maintains a list of people who want to volunteer so I'll check it today," Thomas answered.

"We can take someone from Augusta this time. Maybe we should interview them first," William added.

William left Thomas and went into Amy's office. She had just arrived. William asked, "How was the weekend?"

"It was nice having a longer weekend. Maybe I could do that more."

"We can probably work it out."

"Would I get paid?"

"I'll pay you for the past Friday but not normally."

"That's too bad. I liked having a short Friday."

"Work extra hours during the week and you can take part of Friday off."

"I may. Has anything more happened with the break-in attempt?"

"No. Cal and I fixed the fence and the security system didn't show anybody else trying to get in this weekend. Cal and I did replace the padlock on the gate they came through."

"Maybe we need to install a neon open sign so everyone knows the building is occupied."

"I'll look into it." William figured Amy was kidding since she knew they needed to be as inconspicuous as possible.

William went to his office and checked the newspapers and TV and radio station websites near Kingswood, New York. None had anything about five people being killed. William was sure it'd be news in a few days.

William went to see Amy and asked, "Is there anything I need to follow-up on today?"

"No. I don't need you today but there are a couple of assignments for tomorrow."

"I'll be ready."

William left to check on the houses being worked on. He dropped the boxes of scrap metal including the gun pieces at an Aiken County recycling drop-off center which was on the way. It was painting time again so he grabbed a brush and helped. He made it back to the building at noon. Amy had grilled cheese sandwiches and tomato soup for lunch.

Cal spoke first, "It looks like another car will be ready tomorrow. Can you help sell it?" Cal was looking at Amy.

"Which one is it?"

"It's another Camaro."

"Good. I'll drive it until it sells. I'll be our quality assurance person."

"I'm bidding on two more cars tomorrow so I may be taking a road trip on Wednesday."

"Where?"

"Savannah."

"I'm going if you get the cars. I'll start looking for another restaurant today." Amy was looking at me when she was talking.

William nodded his head yes and mouthed okay.

They didn't have spreadsheets to review since Charlie was no longer involved.

Amy asked, "Where's Charlie?"

"He's decided to be a full time retiree," William said. Since Charlie had taken a lot of time off lately, Amy didn't ask any more questions.

Thomas asked, "Have you heard from Bill, Mark, or Daniel?"

"No. I'll check with them today."

William called Mark after the meeting and Mark said they hadn't found anything.

Michelle had worked on Congressman Murphy for a week. She had compiled a listing of all the places the Congressman had lived and where his children and step-children lived. The Congressman had been divorced twice and was married for the third time. Michelle found the addresses of each ex-wife and found the county where the Congressman's divorces had occurred. She couldn't access the divorce papers online. She printed a copy of the Congressman's Financial Disclosure Form. The Stop Trading on Congressional Knowledge Act or Stock Act was voted in last year and required senators and congressmen to file Financial Disclosure Forms. Michelle therefore only had the past year of information. The Congressman had been in the House of Representatives for thirty years so she listed the committees he had been on and the ones he chaired. He had been a member of or was the chair of the Transportation and Infrastructure Committee for the past twenty five years.

With Daniel's okay, she travelled to the counties where the Congressman was divorced and copied the Congressman's divorce papers. When she reviewed the papers, there didn't appear to be any concern with the divorces. The grounds for the divorces in both cases were irreconcilable differences, which was a no-fault divorce in both cases. After she reviewed the divorce papers, she went to see Daniel.

"Both divorces by the Congressman were irreconcilable differences. Should I talk to each ex-wife to see the real reason? The real reason could be something else."

"Have you found anything that suggests the Congressman had serious marital problems?"

"Not yet. The Congressman married his first wife after high school. They were both nineteen. The ex-wife decided to go away to college and on to medical school. The Congressman wanted to stay home with the family building supply business. The decisions led to the divorce."

"What about the second marriage?"

"The Congressman married his second wife six months later. She was also from his high school. The second wife decided to become a nun, which led to the divorce."

"Who was his third wife?"

"The Congressman didn't marry his third wife until he was twenty six. She was the daughter of a builder who was the most successful builder in the area. The builder was probably a customer of the building supply business. The Congressman and his third wife have been together for forty years. They had three children who are grown now and there are six grandchildren."

"Based on what you found, I don't think we need to talk to either ex-wife. Did the blind trust look fine?"

"The Congressman didn't have a blind trust. The Congressman has managed his own investments which are primarily real estate.

I'm putting a spreadsheet together on the properties listed on the Financial Disclosure Form."

"Keep at it."

"I will."

"Anything you need help with?"

"I could use advice on real estate investments."

"Call Jeremy at Save America. I believe he dabbled in real estate."

"I will."

"Anything else?"

"I have a craving for a man in a suit. Can we get dressed up tonight?"

"I will if you wear a black dress."

"I'll go buy one."

She walked behind the desk and gave Daniel a long wet kiss. She straddled him while she was giving him the kiss. She squirmed on his lap and felt him getting excited. He finally had to push her away. "Slow down. We're in the office and the door's open."

"I'll close the door," Michelle said softly.

"Let's wait until we get home."

"Promise you'll let me straddle you at home."

"Wear the little black dress without any undies and you can straddle me."

"Deal."

Michelle continued on her spreadsheet when she got back to her office. Daniel's excitement had gotten her excited.

She called Jeremy, not knowing he was really William.

William answered, "Hello."

"This is Michelle. I need your help."

"I'm not sure I can but what do you need?"

"Congressman Murphy invested primarily in real estate. Daniel suggested I call you for advice. I've started a spreadsheet on the Congressman's properties but I'd like you to look at it and help me look for any problems."

"I'll look at it and give you my opinion."

"Great. I'll email it to you."

William received the email and it was two pages of information. He didn't know where to start. The spreadsheet was formatted similarly to his Scottrade statement with each purchase, each sale, and real estate still being held. It looked organized and could be easily used to file tax returns. Nothing seemed unusual to him.

William made a copy and gave it to Amy.

William said to her, "This is a list of real estate for Congressman Murphy. Can you take a look at it to see if there's anything unusual. We'll compare notes after I look too."

"What are we looking for?"

"I don't know. Maybe nothing."

William went back to his office and started adding columns to the spreadsheet for information he'd like to see. This forced him to review each purchase or sale individually. He made notes on the spreadsheet until it was five o'clock. It was Tuesday and Jessie had promised to come over tonight. William was planning a special dinner with candles with Jessie being the dessert. He hoped she could stay long enough for a second helping of dessert.

The dinner William planned was going to be oysters casino, a tossed salad, baked lobster tails, and baked asparagus. He figured the garlic and onion in the oysters casino would be okay since both would be eating it. He put two bottles of a nice Sauvignon Blanc in the fridge this morning to share at dinner.

William thought of Jessie all the time he was fixing dinner. She was the first woman he had even considered marrying. He thought about her going back to Chicago and it depressed him. If he did ask her to marry him for real, he may want to tell her about his past and how he earned his initial money for the real estate ventures. Being with the police, William thought she may not think too kindly of his illegal activities or even the semi-legal ones this past week. He refreshed his wine glass and decided to stop thinking tonight and enjoy his time with Jessie.

Jessie came at six forty five. The oysters casino was in one oven staying warm and the lobster tails and asparagus were in the other oven. He took the oysters out of the oven when he heard the front door open.

"What smells so good?"

"I took a bath just for you."

She came up to him and wrapped her arms around him and kissed him. She fondled his manhood and the twins, which surprised him.

As he was catching his breath, William said, "You're the dessert. Not the appetizer."

"Too bad. I'm ready now and I see you're almost ready."

"Dinner will spoil if we don't eat. I slaved all day over the stove." William's voice was high pitched.

"We wouldn't want that to happen but let's eat quickly."

"I'll serve all three courses together."

She freed the twins from her grasp and he took the lobster and asparagus out of the oven. She placed it on the table while he poured her a glass of wine. The meal looked wonderful but his appetite for food had waned. Jessie took her holster and gun off and placed them on the table. William thought a woman who could handle a gun was sexy. They each ate an oyster casino, a couple of bites of salad, one spear of asparagus, and a bite or two of lobster tail.

William said, "I'll put the food away while you prepare the bed."

"I was just eating to be polite. I wanted to have dessert first tonight."

"I'll join you in a few minutes. It'll take a little while for the oysters to work."

William stored all the food and rushed to the bedroom. Jessie had thrown the bedspread and sheet off the bed and was lying naked. He was taking his clothes off as he was entering the room. He tripped on his pants as he was taking them off but made it to the bed uninjured and naked. The oysters must have worked since he was ready for engagement when he got in bed. They engaged and continued for an hour. After both were exhausted, they fell apart.

She said, "I'm thirsty now."

"Me too. The wine is in the kitchen."

"I need water first to replace the fluids I just lost."

"I could use some water before the next round."

"There'll be no more rounds. I have to go soon."

"What about my needs?" William used his little boy voice.

"I think you got plenty. Maybe we'll repeat it tomorrow night."

William went to the office on Wednesday morning and forgot Amy had gone to Savannah with Cal. She left him a list of things that needed to be done today. He had a few items on his own list so he didn't work on the Congressman's real estate list. It was just Thomas and William so they went out to lunch. William checked on the mechanics and they had plenty of work to do. Cal had given them specific instructions. William was sure he didn't want them asking him questions, although he was somewhat knowledgeable of cars. William knew Thomas wasn't. William had his Cobra so they drove to a seafood restaurant. William had a grouper sandwich and Thomas had fish and chips. William paid for lunch. Amy would need to reimburse him.

About an hour after they returned from lunch, Thomas gave William a list of possible replacements for Charlie. William decided to put off some of his work and review the list. He narrowed it down to two people that he thought would work out. One was female and one was male. Both were retired and lived in the Augusta area. He looked them up in the county records and both lived in nice neighborhoods. Charlie had also lived in a nice neighborhood but wanted to live in a distant neighborhood with all of the Save America funds. William decided to talk to both and see what his first impressions were.

He called the lady first. Her name was Inez Wright. She answered when he called.

"Hello," she said.

"This is Jeremy from Save America. I understand you called and offered to volunteer to help."

"Yes. I did."

"Tell me why you want to volunteer."

"I believe you're trying to make America better. As an accountant, I am appalled at the way the federal budget is handled. I was also a certified financial planner and would never advise my clients to keep going deeper in debt each year."

"What's your availability of time to help with Save America?"

"It depends where you're located. I'm retired and I'm not going to leave my husband to travel very far or for very long. I'd like to work remotely."

"I understand. If there wasn't any traveling, when could you start volunteering?"

"I can start right away. I've been retired for two years and need something to keep me occupied. My husband keeps suggesting that I should start a hobby."

"Thanks for your time, Mrs. Wright. I'll get back with you today or tomorrow."

"Can I ask a few questions about Save America?"

"You can when I call you back. Thanks again."

Inez sounded like a good prospect. William's first impression was very good. William decided to call the man and get his first impression of him. His name was Alfred Jenkins.

"Hello," Alfred said.

"This is Jeremy with Save America. I understand you volunteered to help."

"I did."

"Why did you want to volunteer?"

"I support the efforts you're doing and believe it'll make a difference."

"What's your availability to help?"

"Not very much right now. I'm helping my daughter remodel her house in Atlanta and won't be done for about three months."

"I'll make a note to call you in three months. Thanks for your time."

William's two choices went to one choice. William went to see Thomas and told him he'd like to meet with Inez Wright. He told him about the conversation and his first impression. Thomas agreed. William asked Thomas if he wanted to go meet her tonight and

Thomas said he was busy tonight. William called Cal on his Save America phone and asked him if he agreed.

Cal said, "I'll trust your judgment, although the last accountant you selected wasn't the best."

"Thanks for your support. If Mrs. Wright can meet me tonight, do you want to join us?"

"No. I'm going to be tired when I get to Augusta."

"How are the cars and Amy?"

"Both are great. I'm glad you let Amy come along again."

"What time will you get back?"

"About five but I'm not unloading the cars tonight."

"See you at five."

William called Inez back. She sounded like she would be a good fit from his first impression. William thought he'd know more after he met her and chatted with her more.

She answered again after the first ring.

William said, "This is Jeremy with Save America again. I'd like to sit down with you and let you ask me some questions before you volunteer."

"When do you want to meet?"

"Later today. Can I stop by your home?"

"How far away are you?" William could hear the puzzlement in her voice.

"Not far. Can you meet at six?"

"I can. My address is 2480 Muirfield Drive in Martinez. I'll call you in the gate." They lived in a gated golf course community that William was familiar with.

"Tell them Jeremy Walter is visiting. See you at six."

William was sure he confused Inez but she'd understand when he saw her and explained. William actually had identification as Jeremy Walter since it was one of his aliases in his other life.

Cal and Amy arrived back at five with a wrecked Mustang and a wrecked Charger. Both looked like they needed quite a bit of work but William trusted Cal with his purchases. Amy was cheery and all smiles when she got out of the truck.

She said, "I had the best time. We had lunch at an Oyster Bar on River Street. We could watch the boats while we ate. I need to get home. I'll tell you the rest tomorrow."

She hugged Cal and went to her car.

William told Thomas about meeting Inez before he left for the day and told Cal as he was unhooking his truck from the trailer. William told Cal he'd lock up.

Chapter 34

William drove his Cobra to see Inez. The guard gave him a pass to put on his rearview mirror. He arrived at their house at about six. Inez already had the front door open when he parked in the driveway. She was a short woman that was trim. She had short salt and pepper hair that framed a round face. She was wearing a jogging outfit. The house was a large two story older brick home with white shutters and a wooden double front door.

William introduced himself as Jeremy Walter. He thought he would tell her his real name only after she volunteered.

She introduced herself and asked William to come in. Her husband was just inside the door and they shook hands. She introduced him to Gerald.

She said, "Please sit down. Can I get you something to drink?"

"A glass of water would be nice."

Gerald questioned, "So you're with Save America?"

"Yes."

Inez brought William the water and sat down. William took a drink and placed the water on a coaster. The room was furnished with practical furniture that wasn't pretentious.

Gerald asked, "How long have you been involved with Save America?"

"Since it started. Another gentleman and I started it this year."

Inez asked, "How did you get here so fast? Were you in Augusta on business?"

"Our offices are in Augusta."

"You're kidding me. I thought you'd be from a big city," Inez said with a surprised tone in her voice.

"I thought the same thing," Gerald added.

"Did you call me because I lived in Augusta?"

"That's one reason. We also need an accountant to help us."

"Where are you located?"

"I'd rather not tell you until you're sure you want to volunteer." William had already decided that she would be acceptable but wanted to make sure she was satisfied with a decision to volunteer. It's one thing to tell someone on the phone that you'll volunteer but another thing to make the actual commitment.

"When could I start?"

"Tomorrow, if you want." William probably sounded desperate without intending to.

"Are there other people involved?"

"Yes. There are three others."

"Where are they located?"

"All of us are in Augusta."

"How much time do I need to help each week?"

"About twenty hours a week or maybe less." William didn't want to ask for forty hours a week since it may scare her off.

"What'll I be doing?"

"We're getting donations every day and we have several nonprofit corporations set up. You'll be managing our finances, filing all of our tax documents, and keeping us out of trouble. We also have a for-profit business with a couple of employees."

"Anything else?"

"We have contracted services with a call center and others."

"What others?"

"I'd rather not say until you agree to help."

Gerald clarified, "If I understand correctly. You want Inez to agree to volunteer without knowing where your offices are and everything you're involved in."

"Don't forget she doesn't know who she'll be working with."

"That too. That's quite a sales pitch you have," Gerald offered.

Inez said, "Even with your awful sales pitch, I'd like to be involved. I do want the option to change my mind after a week or so."

"That's agreeable. Can you come to the offices to meet the rest of us tomorrow?"

"I can. What time?"

"Is nine okay?"

"Yes. Where are your offices?"

William gave her the address and his Save America phone number.

"I'll meet you at the front gate. We keep it locked. You can bring Gerald if he wants to come. It's important that both of you know our office location should be kept a secret. We do have people who would prefer we didn't exist. It's also important that no one knows you're affiliated with Save America for your personal safety." William made it sound very serious for a reason. William knew his personal safety was also at stake as he saw last week.

"I understand and I'm sure Gerald does too. I'll see you in the morning."

William called Jessie after he left the Wright's house and she was busy tending to her parents. He stopped for a fast food dinner. He thought an occasional burger and fries didn't hurt.

William got to the office about eight thirty the next morning. Everyone else was already there. William told them Inez and Gerald would arrive at nine. William met them at the gate and told them to park in back. He walked around to meet them.

William explained, "We park in back so no one thinks the business is open." William told her part of the truth.

Cal was outside with the two mechanics unloading the wrecked cars. William took Inez and Gerald over and introduced them.

After introducing them, William said, "The car business is our for-profit business. I'll tell you more about it inside."

William introduced them to Amy and Thomas next.

"Amy manages my personal real estate ventures for me and helps with Save America as well. Thomas is the brains behind the website and all of the other computer and data stuff. These are our offices back here. Up front is the car business."

William walked into the shop and they followed him.

"Cal buys wrecked cars and restores them. Amy sells them and Cal buys more cars."

"Why did you get into wrecked cars?" Gerald asked.

"We bought the building planning to have our call center in Augusta. Thomas decided to farm it out so we started working on our cars and it grew to wrecked cars. It's actually a good business."

William showed them the small call center and led them into the conference room. Thomas joined them. William handed out spreadsheets for Save America. He figured Inez would tell Gerald anyway so William included him in the discussion.

"The first spreadsheet is for the car business and the second one is for Save America. The car business is becoming profitable and Save America has lots of funds. Our plan is to use the funds to buy campaign ads during the election this fall."

Inez looked at the totals for Save America. "My, my. That's a lot of money and several nonprofit corporations. You mentioned the call center and other expenses."

"Expenses for Save America are the building overhead costs, some of Amy's time, the call center, and investigators used by Bill Webber."

"Bill Webber the reporter?" Gerald asked sounding impressed.

"Yes. We help him and he helps us."

"We have communication costs too," Thomas added.

"I'd like to get started today," Inez said.

"Gerald can take the car and I'll take you home later."

"I'd like to help in the shop if it's okay. I had an auto repair shop before I retired."

"I'm sure Cal would like help. Let's go tell Cal."

William took him into the shop and told Cal he had extra help. They started talking about cars and William was ignored. Thomas had taken Inez to her office and he was explaining everything about the computer network, the call center, and everything else. William was ignored again and left.

Amy was catching up on her work from yesterday so William returned to the chore of working on the Congressman's real estate list. He had finished putting his questions on the spreadsheet. There didn't seem to be a logical order or similarity to the list. The properties were located throughout the United States.

William called Michelle and told her he would start researching the list. She said she had been looking at all the contracts from the Transportation and Infrastructure Committee and hadn't worked on the real estate list since she talked to him.

Gerald was still in the shop. Cal loaned him some coveralls. William went into the shop but they didn't even look towards him. He had to go near them to remind them it was lunch time.

Amy had sandwiches for lunch. She bought bread, deli meat, cheeses, tomatoes, lettuce, pickles, and chips. They had condiments and drinks in the fridge. Inez and Gerald attended their first noon meeting.

William said, "We meet Monday through Friday at noon to discuss both the car business and Save America business. Amy has lunch for us each day."

Cal and Thomas had already fixed their plates. Inez and Gerald joined in. Amy and William were last in line. William made a Dagwood sandwich with no chips and a diet drink. Amy stared at his large sandwich and William smiled.

After everyone had consumed much of their lunch and William had consumed half of his, William said, "The first order of business is usually the car business but today we'll begin with Save America. The most important item is Inez's thoughts on our little endeavor."

"I'm impressed with what you have here. I'd still like the option to change my mind."

"I understand."

Gerald spoke, "I certainly like what you're doing with the cars and would like to stay involved. I'd also like to bring my cars in."

"It's nice to have someone knowledgeable like Gerald in the shop," Cal said. William was offended but didn't say anything about it. Thomas didn't look offended.

"I've reviewed all the financials this morning and everything seemed to be well documented. I may have some suggestions later but nothing is needed now. Thomas showed me all of the accounts and Amy showed me the payroll information. Amy also gave me a set of keys, gave me the code to the gate, and showed me how to use the alarm system."

Inez didn't mention William's name so he was offended again.

"It sounds like you're set," William said.

"Gerald and I have a commitment this afternoon so I plan to come back in the morning. Gerald will probably be with me too."

"I'm bringing my car tomorrow and checking it out in the shop." Gerald sounded more excited than Inez.

"I want to remind you that your association with Save America needs to be kept private for the benefit of all of us. One other minor detail is that you need to pick a different name to use when we deal with Bill Webber, the investigators and banks. We prefer to keep our real identities private," William explained.

"So Jeremy isn't your real name?" Inez asked.

"It isn't, as Thomas and Cal aren't their real names. Amy is Amy but if she had dealings outside the office for Save America, then she would need another name."

"I'd like to pick it now. Maybe Lola or Pandora. I'll also have to get a new wardrobe to go with my name. I'd expect Save America to pay for my new clothes," Amy teased.

"I was thinking Ethel or Bessie." William grinned.

"They sound like cow names."

"My grandmother is Ethel and she's a lovely lady."

"I was thinking of Giselle for me. I'd also need a new wardrobe. We can go shopping together. Zane or Gideon would be good for Gerald and he certainly needs a new wardrobe. Does Save America have a credit card we can use?" Inez asked.

"I certainly couldn't tell my girlfriend that I was working with Giselle and Lola," William said.

"I couldn't tell my wife either," Thomas added.

"Let's switch to cars," William said to get off the discussion of names.

"Just a second. You're using fake names for the bank accounts too." She saw our fake names on the accounts this morning.

"They are and they work fine. We'll get you the identification for your fake name as well," William said.

"Back to cars. Cal."

"Amy and I picked up a Mustang and Charger from Savannah yesterday. We put them on the rack today and both will need a good bit of work. We'll start taking them apart tomorrow. We'll also start working on the GTO this week. I don't plan to buy another car this week unless there's a great deal."

William didn't really want to think about the GTO since it made him think of Charlie. He was a great guy except for his desire to take the money and run.

"I need to tell you about lunch in Savannah. We ate at the Fiddler's Crab House and Oyster Bar on River Street. We were on the river. Cal had an oyster po'boy and I had a crab cake sandwich. We shared steamed oysters. It was great. We watched the boats on the river."

Cal added, "It was very good. I'd eat there again."

"I'm going to Savannah the next time too. So far we've eaten at two wonderful restaurants." Amy's excitement was evident.

William was still eating his monster sandwich while Amy was talking.

"We go over our financials in detail on Monday," William said.

"Thomas told me and showed me what's covered. I should have everything ready on Monday."

"Great. Anything else before we adjourn and I finish my sandwich?"

"Are you really going to eat all of that?" Amy asked while rolling her eyes.

"I am. It's now a challenge."

William made a copy of the Congressman's real estate list and took it to Amy after lunch.

William said, "See if you can find any pattern or details we need to add. I'll start researching each property deeper."

"Here are documents you need to review first. One is a contract and the other one is an offer."

William went back to his office and looked over the documents. He signed them and gave them back to Amy. He picked a property on the Congressman's list at random and started the research. The property was in Tennessee, which was odd since the Congressman's home state was Minnesota. The property was sold in 2012 under a corporate name. It was the CIT Investment Group, LLC and was registered in Washington, D.C. William's properties were in different names so it wasn't unusual. He found the county where the property was located and checked on the details. The purchase date was two years ago. The property was bought from an individual and that was also not unusual. The buyer of the property was the federal government, which was a little strange. He pulled up Google Earth and saw that the property still had a house on the property. He checked the Washington, D.C., corporate records and noted the names of the officers for the corporation. None were the Congressman. He added what he learned to the spreadsheet and told Amy. She hadn't started any work on the spreadsheet list.

William left the office, checked on properties, and got materials for one of the houses being worked on. He decided to help with the house being remodeled. He had new cabinet doors made and helped install them. The cabinets had been stained a dark color so the cabinets were painted the shade of white that the doors were painted. New hardware was also going to be installed on the doors and drawers.

It was late in the day when he finished helping. The house was near Aiken so he decided to go home. He was still exhausted after the past weekend so he poured a glass of wine and sat on the deck. He called Jessie and she agreed to come over for about thirty minutes. He told her he had leftovers and would heat them up. He was walking outside the house surveying the property and met her in the driveway. She was in her Impala with black jeans, a black shirt, and black boots. Her hair was dark, along with her eyes. He was reminded of the first time he saw her when the neighbors were murdered. He was a suspect for the murders. He didn't know he would be involved with a police investigator when he first saw her.

William opened her car door and kissed her while she was still in the car. "Can we use the back seat for a quickie?"

"I don't think so."

"You could handcuff me so it'd be official."

"No. I'm hungry."

"Hungry for my love or food?"

"Food."

"My insecurity has increased substantially between you and the office today."

"What happened at the office?"

"I'll tell you while we eat."

William poured her a glass of wine. He then heated up the leftovers and they sat at the dining room table.

"Tell Dr. Jessica about your insecurity."

"It started as a little boy when my older brothers abused me."

Jessie rolled her eyes and said, "Fast forward to today."

"Okay, but the long story is better. Before you affected my ego by rejecting my offer about the back seat, I was offended at the office."

"Please continue. Would you like to lie down?"

"No, Dr. Jessica. Anyway. With my unlimited charm, I convinced a retired accountant lady to help us with Save America. She started today and brought her husband, who had owned an automotive repair shop."

Jessie interrupted, "I see. Go on." I guess she thought a psychologist should interrupt.

"The first time I was offended was when Cal said he was glad to have someone in the shop who knew cars."

"I can see where that would have hurt. There's more?"

"The second time was in the noon meeting with the new lady accountant recognized everyone but me for helping her get up to speed and oriented."

"Did you state your dissatisfaction with either of them?"

"I didn't. Should I?"

"In my professional opinion, you should have fired both of them on the spot."

"I'll do it tomorrow."

"My charge for these services is two hours of sex. I'll expect it tomorrow night."

"Would you like a few minutes today? I've had a bad day." William used his most pitiful voice.

"Sorry pal. I've got to go. Duty calls."

"Work."

"My parents."

They had a long kiss before she departed. He cleaned up the house and went to bed early with a bruised ego and more insecurity.

William made it to the office at nine and all the others were there. He checked with Amy and she gave him a few items to do in the morning. He checked on Inez and she was busy on the computer and had papers across the desk.

"Good morning," William said with a cheery voice.

"Good morning."

"Do you have everything that you need?"

"Thomas and Amy are helping me."

William left thinking Dr. Jessica would need to provide more therapy. At least Amy needed him, although she could probably manage the business ventures by herself. William wondered if she could install cabinet doors and paint trim. He thought he better not ask. After finishing the Amy items, he returned to the spreadsheet. The next property he picked randomly was in Virginia. The corporate name was different. He checked on the purchase date from the county records. The county records showed the purchase to be fifty acres of land. He checked Google Earth and the property was still vacant land. The property was still owned by the corporation. He checked the corporate documents and the Congressman wasn't an officer. He made his notes on the spreadsheet.

William picked a third property at random. The property was in Washington, D.C., and the corporation was registered in Delaware. The corporation was in a third corporate name. Between the spreadsheet and the county records, he saw that the property was bought and sold by the corporation. The property was sold to the federal government in 2012. A Google Earth search showed a building on the property. He Googled the address and the building was a Department of Education building under construction.

William found two of three properties that were sold to the federal government. He wondered whether it was just good luck. He selected a fourth property. It was located in South Carolina. A fourth corporation had bought the property and still owned the property. A Google Earth search showed the property to be vacant. The property was in Aiken County so he'd take a look at the property. He made a note on the spreadsheet.

William made a few calls to check on his properties and see if additional materials were needed. There was a need for materials so he decided to leave after lunch.

Chapter 35

Amy had salads for lunch. There was deli meat and cheese left from yesterday so William added it to his salad. He also had chips since he didn't take chips yesterday. He did get a diet drink although he had heard diet drinks weren't good for you. The meeting started with Save America.

"How's everything, Inez?" William asked.

"I've almost caught up while I'm also trying to get ready for Monday. Payroll is today so I'm working on that too."

Thomas said, "The donations continue to be strong through the call center and lots of emails are being sent to Congressman Murphy. Anything from Bill, Mark, or Daniel?"

"I haven't heard from them lately. Amy and I are looking at real estate deals that Michelle sent me. The one weird thing is that a couple of properties were bought and then sold to the federal government."

They switched to the car business and Cal updated them on the progress. He told them he appreciated Gerald being in the shop. William couldn't remember Cal ever saying that about him. More therapy from Dr. Jessica tonight.

William sent Amy the spreadsheet on the Congressman's properties with his notes and then left to get materials for houses. Amy gave him a deposit to make at the bank. William used the gift cards he'd bought at a discount online to buy the materials. He helped with the house and came back to the offices about four thirty.

Inez had left shortly after lunch but Gerald was still there. He stuck his head in the shop door and saw the GTO had been moved into the shop area. He didn't go in so he didn't get ignored. Less therapy from Dr. Jessica.

Amy had left a couple of documents for William to review and sign. He signed them and left them on Amy's desk.

On his way home, William decided to cook. He thought that going out to dinner would take away from the time he needed to pay Jessie for his session yesterday. He decided on baked fish so he stopped to do his shopping. A nice salad along with the baked salmon and baked asparagus would be dinner. He thought he might have asparagus left from the other night but bought more just in case. He figured he could eat it later. He called Jessie and told her he was shopping for her dinner and asked if she had a preference. She didn't. William wasn't going to give her a choice anyway. She said she'd be over at six thirty but had to leave at nine. William thought he now had only thirty minutes to eat so he could pay Jessie the two hour debt.

William timed everything so it finished at six thirty. The salad and wine were on the table. He didn't have bread. Neither Jessie nor William typically had bread with dinner unless they were eating out. Jessie arrived on time and he ushered her to the table.

"What about small talk before dinner?"

"You don't do small talk and I have a debt to pay. You know how I like to pay my obligations."

"Since you're in a rush, I'll eat."

She put dressing on her salad and William poured her wine. The oven bell went off so he retrieved the salmon and asparagus. He put it on the plates directly from the grilling pan. William thought it smelled scrumptious. He ate most of his salmon and salad and started cleaning up as she was still eating.

"Do you have somewhere to go?" she asked.

"I do. I'm taking you to a pleasurable place."

"I'm ready as soon as I eat. I missed lunch."

William finished putting everything away except for Jessie's plate and salad bowl. After she ate all of her food, he placed the plate and bowl into the sink. He filled them with water to keep the grease and dressing soft. He pulled her up and took her to the bedroom. William had already taken the covers off the bed and only left the fitted sheet. He was taking her clothes off as he was directing her. He finished undressing her after he got her on the bed. He owed her two hours and wanted to pay his debt.

William had a logoed t-shirt with Garfield on the front. She pulled it off and then pulled off his pants. He rolled on top and kissed her French style. He had been to France. After he had her willing and ready, he had sex with her missionary style. He had been to a mission.

She flipped him so she was on top and continued in the cowgirl style. He tried to buck her off so she wouldn't last eight seconds but she held on. He would remind her later that her time on top counted as part of the two hours of debt.

They wrestled for position until both were spent. William got up and ran water in the spa tub. He figured a warm spa bath where he washed her could lead to another session. It did.

Jessie left after she was worn out. At least that was William's thoughts on the matter. He gave her a long kiss at the door to increase her longing for him.

William spent the weekend working on houses. Jessie and William had dinner on Saturday but no dessert at his house. On Sunday, he worked on houses and had lunch with Jessie and her parents. Her mother looked better each time he saw her. Her father looked the same from the last time. Jessie's mother was walking around the kitchen helping to fix lunch when he came in. He kissed Jessie on the mouth and her mother on the cheek.

William said, "You're getting around pretty good."

"The therapy has increased my stamina but I'll tire out soon."

She wasn't using a cane or walker so that was an improvement.

"Do you have to use the cane or walker anymore?"

"I do when I get tired."

"When you and Richard are healthy enough, we'll have the wedding."

When Jessie's mother and father were in the hospital, William had told them that Jessie and he would be getting married. It started out as a joke to cheer up Jessie's mother but it seemed like a great idea now.

"My best inspiration for getting better has been the wedding. Lots of relatives from Chicago will be coming down."

"After lunch, you and I will go get a mani-pedi. We can talk about the wedding then."

"That'd be great. I remember when you treated me in the hospital. That was a surprise."

"We'll leave after lunch. I have an appointment for us."

"What about me?" Jessie asked.

"Should we let her go, Wanda?"

"I suppose. Richard will be taking a nap after lunch and he's having a good day."

"Will I be ignored like last time?" Jessie looked at both of them.

"No." William shook his head. "You can sit between your mother and me."

"I don't think so. I know you'll be talking about me again."

In the hospital during the last mani-pedi, Wanda and William talked about the wedding and about Jessie.

"No, we won't." Wanda winked at William and William winked back.

Jessie and Wanda had cooked grilled chicken breasts, green beans, and macaroni and cheese. A tossed salad was made of mixed greens, tomatoes, carrots, and cheese. William helped Richard into the dining area and they had a family lunch.

Wanda said, "It's nice to eat together. We should do this every Sunday now that I'm feeling much better."

"I'd like that. I miss family meals," William said.

"It's settled then," Wanda stated.

Jessie and William cleaned up after lunch and he helped Wanda into his car. He didn't have the Cobra. They made it to the mani-pedi a few minutes early. Wanda had her cane but walked most of the way without needing it. Wanda sat in the middle of Jessie and William. William had ordered the full treatment for all of them except he didn't get the nail and toe polish. Jessie wanted a clear polish since she didn't want to look girly.

When they got in the chairs, Wanda said, "I was thinking the wedding should be in a couple of months. I think Richard and me will be well enough then." Wanda was looking at William and not Jessie.

"That'll work for me. We can start looking for a place to rent or we can have the wedding at my house."

"Jessie told me you had a nice house so maybe that'd be an option."

"I can take you to see it today."

"I'd better get home to check on Richard. Maybe we can go next Sunday."

"We can have Sunday lunch at my house if Richard is feeling okay."

William knew that Jessie did take her father to physical therapy so he should be able to travel to his house. The problem was he had steps going into every door of the house. He'd have a ramp built this week so they could use a wheel chair to get him into the house.

"That'd be great."

Wanda didn't look at her daughter while talking. Jessie sat quietly enjoying her mani-pedi. Jessie had acquired some patience since being in the south. Having to help her parents lately may have also influenced her increased patience.

"When would you like to shop for a dress to wear to the wedding?"

"I'd like to wait until I can get around better. Shopping is hard work."

"Did you and Jessie pick out a wedding dress?"

"I did but I can't get Jessie to go for a fitting."

"Would you like me to help convince her?"

"I would. She's very stubborn."

William looked at Jessie and she was staring at the ceiling.

"The wedding dress store is next to my restaurant downtown so I may be able to convince her to come to my house next Sunday."

Jessie stopped looking at the ceiling, leaned forward in her chair, and stared at William. She didn't say anything but William was sure she wasn't thinking happy thoughts.

"That would be perfect if you could arrange it."

"I'll try if you'll tell me more about Jessie when she was growing up."

"Jessie was a difficult child growing up. She was always into trouble. She was always beating up the boys." Wanda went on to tell William about her difficulties with Jessie growing up.

William looked at Jessie and he could see her lips moving as she counted. He was sure she'd get even with him somehow. He took them home and Jessie decided to stay with her parents. William was home alone again. He worked out in his home gym for a long time, which helped him sleep. He had gotten accustomed to Jessie spending the night when her parents were in the hospital. She also helped him sleep.

Monday morning came quickly and William was back in the office. Inez and Gerald were there along with everyone else. He didn't check to see if Inez needed anything since he didn't want a bruised ego at the beginning of the week. Amy and William sat down and planned the week. Amy had him pick out his lunch from a local restaurant's menu. She had renters moving out and renters moving in for two houses. Walkthroughs were scheduled for both houses. She had arranged a cleaning service for both although the tenants were supposed to leave them clean. The tenant's idea of being clean didn't agree with Amy's idea of being clean. Several people had called about the house William had just finished and Amy scheduled showings. William did all the showings since he knew what was done to the house. Most of the showings were after work hours but sometimes the potential buyers wanted to see the house during work hours. One showing was this morning and one was this afternoon. There was another auction this week and William needed to look at that house. He didn't need any more houses now and would have his bid ceiling lower than normal. He left to take another look at the house being auctioned on his way to the house showing. The house was in the north side of Aiken so it was a long drive.

It was the wife who looked at the house and really wanted it. She wanted to bring her husband back after work so William set a time an hour earlier than his other showing. He didn't get back to the office until noon.

The lunches from the local restaurant were great. Everyone had something different. William had a Reuben sandwich with fries. It was massive. He knew he'd be back in his home gym again tonight. Gerald had joined them for lunch too. William didn't consider him an official member but he was welcome.

William said between bites, "Let's start with the car business."

"We made progress on the cars in the shop. Amy has a buyer for our last car and it'll hopefully sell today. We'll know later today whether the buyer gets the loan. The buyer has an older Mustang so we may take it for trade. A little body and engine work, a new paint job, and some work on the interior and we can made a profit." Cal said.

"I thought we were only doing wrecked cars."

"Gerald wants to do the Mustang and I think it'll be good."

"I'm sure you know what you're doing."

Inez spoke, "Here's the spreadsheet for the cars. The numbers look good and the business is showing a profit. I'll be taking a Section 179 expense for the equipment this year and tax deductions for the startup costs. That'll offset some of the profits. We may also want to increase inventory at the end of the year to offset the profit."

William knew what she was talking about since he'd done the same thing on the businesses he'd started up.

Amy said, "I have my outfit if we buy enough cars for the car lot."

Inez and Gerald had a puzzled look on their faces but no one explained. Inez would probably ask Amy later.

William said, "Let's switch to Save America."

Inez handed out a spreadsheet for Save America. "The deposits for Save America continue and the balances for each account are shown on the spreadsheet. I don't see the need to create another nonprofit corporation yet. We do need to decide where the building and infrastructure expenses are deducted. I'd recommend including all the expenses in the car business rather than Save America. I don't think you want to list this building address as a deduction for the nonprofits since they could be traced to Save America."

"I hadn't thought of that. Maybe it was good we started the car business," William said.

"The call center may be different since it's all Save America," Thomas said.

"It is but it doesn't have a physical address in Augusta that we have to include on the tax forms," Inez said.

"What about the Aiken call center we had earlier?" Thomas asked.

"We should lump it into the present call center costs and I don't see us getting questioned."

"I agree with the approach," William said.

"I'll have more details with the spreadsheets next week."

William added, "Amy and I are looking at the Congressman's real estate transactions. I've got questions and may need help from Mark and Daniel."

William didn't explain his questions and nobody asked. He gave Amy credit although she hadn't found time to work on the list.

"The emails to the Congressman continue at a higher rate than expected. More people are viewing our website now. The number of website visitors has increased dramatically in the past few weeks. Our presence is well known. I've also noticed that a link to our website is being included on other websites," Thomas said.

"So what's next for the website?" William asked.

"Other websites show a number that represents the federal government's debt. I was thinking I'd like to show the federal debt with each Congressman's and Senator's part of the debt. I'll see if it's feasible this week."

"What do you think so far, Inez?" William asked.

"You're a great group of folks. My impression before I met you was that the group would consist of crazy opinionated idealists. I find you to be ordinary folk."

"Was that a compliment? I've never been called ordinary except for this one woman who had high expectations for me. That was my mother."

Everybody laughed including Gerald. William didn't know he was listening. William thought he'd just come for lunch.

"It was a compliment."

"We'll end the meeting with a compliment. Any other business can wait until tomorrow."

William decided to spend the rest of the afternoon until his showings working on the Congressman's list. He needed to hang around anyway since Amy would be at the two rental houses.

William picked another property at random from the Congressman's list. It was in North Carolina. The property was sold through another corporation to the federal government in 2012. The county records showed the purchase in 2010 and showed a building on the site now. William pulled it up on Google Earth and it was a post office. His suspicions increased.

He picked another property at random and it was in New York. The property was purchased in 2009 through another corporation and sold to the federal government. He pulled it up on Google Earth and it was an interchange for a highway. He was now sure he knew the scheme the Congressman had.

William called Bill Webber and he answered.

"Michelle sent me a list of properties Congressman Murphy bought and sold. I've been checking them and four of six properties I checked randomly were sold to the federal government. The properties that were developed are now a federal building, a post office, and a highway exchange. I suspect the other properties will end up being sold to the federal government. It's strange since each property was bought through a different corporation."

"Is Congressman Murphy shown as a corporate officer?"

"I checked four and he wasn't. I'll check the other two."

"Let me set up a time with Mark and Daniel and I'll call you back."

"I'll only be in the office for another hour. I have obligations with my own business."

"You mean Save America isn't your full time work?" Bill asked..

"No. I have another life and plan to keep it."

While William waited for Bill to call back, he checked the filings for the other two corporations and they didn't include the Congressman in any role. He picked another property at random. It was located in California. The property was bought through a different corporation from the others. The Congressman wasn't associated with the corporation. He checked the county records and it was purchased but not sold yet. This would be a good one for Daniel or Michelle to check out.

Bill called as William was making notes on the last property.

"I've got Mark, Daniel, and Michelle on the line."

"Hello folks," William said.

They said their hellos.

Bill spoke first, "Jeremy picked some of the properties on the list Michelle sent him and found that four out of six he randomly picked were sold to the federal government. One is now a federal building, one is a post office, and one is a highway interchange. It appears the Congressman is using his insider information to purchase properties that will be needed by the federal government. Since his committee selects the locations for the federal buildings, post offices, and highway interchanges, he can buy the properties in advance."

Mark asked, "Are there other congressmen involved?"

"I can't tell. The corporations could be just established for Congressman Murphy or could include other congressmen, senators, friends, or family. It'll take more searching to find out. I only looked at the names on the corporate filings and didn't dig any deeper."

Daniel asked, "Where are the properties you looked at?"

"I looked at another one this afternoon making a total of seven. They are in Tennessee, Virginia, Washington, D.C., South Carolina, New York, North Carolina, and California. The Washington, D.C., property is a Department of Education building, the North Carolina property is a post office, and the New York property is a highway interchange." William started to say that the one in South Carolina was near him but caught himself before saying it.

Bill said, "I'd like more details before confronting the Congressman."

Michelle said, "I can get more details if Jeremy will be available to answer questions."

"I'll be available. The hard part is finding out who's involved with the corporations. I can't access tax records so I don't know who received the funds from the corporations. Congressman Murphy is definitely involved since the properties show up in his disclosure form. My comparison of the purchase price and sales price in the county records versus the amount of gain shown on the Congressman's Financial Disclosure Form, tells me others are involved. You could look at all five hundred and thirty five Financial Disclosure Forms, Michelle."

"I could but it'll take some time," Michelle said.

"I'd like to know if it involves more than Congressman Murphy," Bill said.

"I'm guessing the Congressman obtained all the Federal Identification Numbers for the corporations in his name. I know that's what I'd do. I'd suggest making a Freedom of Information Act request for all corporations with a Federal Identification Number requested by the Congressman. It's a shame the Stock Act wasn't voted in until 2012."

"I have a contact in the IRS who'll provide me a listing of the Congressman's corporations if he did request the Federal Identification Numbers. I'll call him today and send the information to you Michelle," Bill said.

"I'll email you the spreadsheet with my notes, Michelle. I'd also suggest someone look at the properties still owned to see what's planned. I suspect it'll be a post office, a federal building, or a highway interchange."

They said their goodbyes. William emailed the spreadsheet back to Michelle and left for his showings.

Chapter 36

The wife that looked at the house in the morning had her husband with her this time. Her husband liked the house as well but wanted to think about it for a day or two. William was a low pressure salesman so he didn't try to push them into signing a contract.

The second couple came on time and also liked the house. They liked the updated kitchens and bathrooms, the tile floors, and the hardwood floors in the living and dining area. They liked the new lighting fixtures and fans. The house looked new with the fresh paint and new carpet in the bedrooms. The price was less than market value since William wasn't paying any real estate commission. They offered several thousand less. William accepted it after thinking about it for a few minutes and adding figures in a notepad he brought. He knew he would accept their offer as soon as they made it but didn't want to look too anxious. He had two contracts with him and he had them sign both. He gave them one and kept one. The contract allowed them to do a home inspection, which William agreed to pay for and William agreed to pay part of the closing costs. He included in the contract that closing would occur within thirty days.

It was late so William went home rather than going back to the office. He would give Amy the contract in the morning. He called Jessie and she said she was paying a conjugal visit tonight. He told her he'd fix dinner so that more of their time was spent horizontally this evening. She said she wanted to be home by nine. William felt like he was fifteen again and had to get his date home by a nine o'clock curfew.

William fixed grilled halibut and a seasoned corn dish with peppers, onions, and salsa. He also had a spinach salad with a little radicchio and sliced almonds. He had a bottle of Riesling in the fridge. He was drinking Pinot Blanc that was left from a couple of days ago. Jessie showed up before dinner was ready so he poured her a glass of wine and rubbed her shoulders.

She said, "I want my feet rubbed."

"I'm cooking so you'll have to earn a foot rub."

"You owe me after I had to endure my mother and you Sunday."

"I was just trying to learn about your childhood so I could understand you better." William was doing his best to sound truthful.

"Since you've never asked me about my childhood, I'm sure you just wanted to annoy me."

"Such a negative attitude. I haven't asked you since I was saving my questions for your mother."

"I'd be careful if you want dessert."

"Sorry. I was out of line with your mother and hope you'll accept my apology. I also have peanut butter pie to offer as my sign of my good faith."

"You're forgiven since you have peanut butter pie. I want it now." She got up from her stool, went to the freezer, took out the pie, and sliced a big hunk.

"You'll ruin your dinner."

"I'll just taste it." She returned to her stool and tasted the whole hunk.

The oven bell went off as she finished the last bite. William took the fish out and plated it with the corn. He placed the fish and salad on the table. She nibbled on her dinner and he ate his. Since she had her peanut butter pie, he cleaned up the kitchen quickly and took her to the bedroom. They wrestled for position and he let her win. He was on top when he finished so he won the bout. William then retrieved lotion and massaged her feet and calves. She was moaning more with the feet rub than the wrestling bout. William's ego was shattered. He stopped rubbing when she fell asleep. He left her and returned to the kitchen to complete the cleanup. He woke her up about eight thirty by nuzzling her neck and exploring her body. He was surprised when she didn't swing at him as she awoke. He needed to defend himself in the past. He convinced her to have a round two before she left. William slept well although it would've been great to wake up with her. The wedding sounded better every day.

The week was routine with a few calls from Michelle and a call from Diana. They were getting excited about their move back to Chicago. William could see them in Chicago after he married into Jessie's family. He kept checking the newspapers in Kingswood, New York, and he didn't see any news about the five murders.

Michelle had gotten the information from Bill on the corporations. William was right about the Federal Identification Numbers being requested by the Congressman. Michelle found a website that had all the properties bought by the federal government in the past twenty five years and checked county websites to see which ones were bought by the Congressman's corporations. It was a tedious task. Although she didn't want to, she also checked the five hundred and thirty five Financial Disclosure Forms filed since 2012. Another tedious task. She sent a spreadsheet to William with all the information.

She then called William.

"Did you get the spreadsheet?"

"I did but I haven't looked at it yet."

"Call me back after you review it."

William reviewed the spreadsheet and saw that Michelle had completed a search on all the properties. Most had been sold to the federal government. The corporations used were different for each purchase. The purchases went back twenty five years. She had included four other Congressmen who were involved.

William called her back.

"I see that you've been busy."

Michelle said, "I think I've included enough for Bill to see the situation. What do you think?"

"It's certainly obvious there was a scheme. How'd you get the names of the Congressmen that were involved?"

"I reviewed all five hundred and thirty five financial disclosure forms. My review only showed four congressmen that were involved. There were probably more before 2012 but I don't have a way to find them."

"Did you check the locations of the properties that the Congressman still owns?"

"No. I haven't yet."

"Bill may want that information too. It sounds like you have enough information for Bill. Call me when you set up a conference call."

Michelle went to see Daniel and showed him her results.

She said, "I talked to Jeremy and he thinks it's enough to show Bill."

"I'll call Bill to set up a time for a conference call."

Daniel called Bill and the conference call would be in one hour. Daniel called Mark and Michelle called William to let them know. Michelle emailed the information to Bill and Mark.

William went into the conference room and had Thomas join him for the conference call. He gave Thomas a copy of the spreadsheet. After the greetings, Michelle went through her spreadsheet and told everyone about checking county records and reviewing the Financial Disclosure Forms.

Bill asked, "How many more do you think were involved?"

"I don't know. The Financial Disclosure Forms were only required since 2012. I suspect some Senators and Congressmen that were involved have retired in the past twenty five years."

"I think I'll just concentrate on Congressman Murphy and let someone else sort out the rest," Bill said.

"How much profit did the Congressman make from his real estate deals?"

"So far he's made about thirty million in twenty five years. That doesn't count the property he owns that the federal government hasn't bought yet. The profit on those should be several millions," Michelle answered.

William looked at the spreadsheet she put together and it showed the Congressman making about thirty one million but there were real estate commissions and closing costs.

"I'd like to do my first report about the Congressman and just talk about the basics. I'll provide more details in later reports."

"I suggested to Michelle that you may want the expected usage of the properties still owned by the Congressman," William said.

"I may, but let's see how it plays out first. I'll start with the information Michelle put together. Thanks again for your help."

They said their goodbyes.

Bill arranged a meeting with his boss and the lawyer in an hour. Bill printed two more copies of the spreadsheets and took them to the meeting.

Bill handed a copy of the spreadsheet to his boss and the lawyer. "This is a spreadsheet showing the properties that Congressman Murphy bought and sold to the federal government in the past twenty five years using his knowledge from the Transportation and Infrastructure Committee. He has acquired about thirty million dollars and several million dollars in properties from this."

His boss and the lawyer looked over the spreadsheet.

"Did you get this information legally?" the lawyer asked thinking about the methods used by Bill to get previous information.

"Yes. Some of the information came from the Financial Disclosure Forms filed since 2012 and the rest of the information came from painstaking research in public records."

Bill figured that all the information could be acquired with enough research although he did shortcut the research with his friend in the IRS.

"Are there others involved?" the boss asked.

"Yes. I know of four Congressmen and there are probably more."

"Would you be able to do the research without the Stock Act?" the boss asked for his own information.

"I don't think so. The Congressman disguised his purchases through different corporations so it would've been very difficult to find without the Stock Act."

"So Congress actually passed an Act that helped the press?" the boss asked.

"It appears so."

"What's your plan?" the lawyer asked.

"I'll put a report together about Congressman Murphy."

"What about the others?" the lawyer quizzed.

"I'll mention that others are involved in my report and include their names in the follow-up reports. I need my air time."

"You've had lots of air time lately and we thank you."

William turned on CNN at five and watched the commercials prior to Bill's report.

Bill was looking at the camera when the talking head said Bill Webber was giving a live special report.

"This is Bill Webber and I'm in front of Congressman Murphy's house. We have learned that Congressman Murphy has been using the information from the Transportation and Infrastructure Committee to buy and sell properties to the federal government for over thirty million dollars in gain. These purchases were made using insider information."

The talking head asked, "Were these properties selected by the Transportation and Infrastructure Committee?"

"They were. It appears the Congressman purchased the properties as soon as the committee decided on a location for a federal building, post office, or highway interchange and then sold them to the federal government for a nice profit."

The talking head asked, "Didn't someone get suspicious when the Congressman sold the properties to the government?"

"The Congressman bought the properties through corporations that couldn't be traced to him."

"So the Congressman knew what he was doing was illegal and hid it?"

"It appears so."

"Where were the properties located?"

"They're located throughout the United States."

"Are there other Congressmen or Senators involved?"

"Yes. I know of four but there could be more."

The talking head said, "Thank you, Bill Webber, for the live report. I look forward to a follow-up report from you later."

William thought the report was well choreographed. William thought they now needed to pick the next person for the website. He suspected Congressman Murphy would be relieved of his duties in the House of Representatives soon. He suspected the FBI would be calling Bill and the Congressman to get details and to decide if a crime was committed. William knew a crime was committed since Congressman Murphy's scheme was just like insider stock trading.

Friday came and there wasn't anybody trying to kidnap William. He had been checking the news in New York and the Hummer was found. William was sure the contents of the trailer were a horrible site after a week. The newspapers did say that the five people in the trailer were part of a group in upstate New York that had been linked to several crimes. He'd keep checking the news each day for additional details.

Bill Webber appeared on CNN and other news and talk shows to discuss Congressman Murphy. He didn't call William probably because he was in demand again.

Jessie had agreed to stop by for a short visit. She came at six thirty but William couldn't get her to stay long. She ate with her mother so she wasn't hungry. She checked the freezer and did cut a piece of peanut butter pie.

William asked, "Did you come to see me or the pie."

It was hard for her to talk with her mouth full. "You and I needed my feet rubbed."

She placed her feet in his lap and William started rubbing.

"Can you come over tomorrow night?"

"I can and I may be able to spend the night if mom and dad are doing okay."

"You can have a second piece of pie then and I'll get lotion."

"No lotion for now. I may slip and fall again."

She stayed about thirty minutes and left.

William worked on a ramp to his house on Saturday so they could wheel Richard into the house for Sunday's lunch. He picked the back of the house near the pool since there were fewer steps. He finished, took a shower, and sat down with a beer to watch golf on TV.

Jessie wanted to go out to eat tonight so he took her to his restaurant in downtown Aiken. He had owned Aiken Brewing Company restaurant, microbrewery, and sports bar for several years and had ignored it since starting Save America. He'd hired a great person to run the restaurant and could trust her to do a great job managing the restaurant. He thought this was another expense he had due to Save America. William did miss brewing beer occasionally.

Jessie met William at six thirty and they sat at the bar. He had installed the bar himself and felt like it was part of his family. The bartender handed Jessie and him a beer when they came in the door. He always drank the Thoroughbred Red and this was Jessie's choice too. Everyone at the bar said hello to William as he came in and sat at the end of the bar near the servers' station. They ordered wings.

She asked, "How was your day?"

"It was good." William couldn't talk about Save America and the Congressman. "How was yours?"

"I didn't shoot anybody lately. I miss Chicago."

William wanted to tell her he had but a guy needs to keep some secrets from his future wife, especially if that future wife could arrest him.

"Maybe we could fly up there next week and shoot someone."

"I would except for my parents."

They chatted about her parents in between people interrupting to say hello to William. William introduced Jessie to about fifty people. They left about seven thirty.

"I'll race you to my house," William offered.

"I'm going to my parents' house."

"How about tomorrow night?"

"I can tomorrow night."

William kissed her and she left. He thought about another beer or two at the bar but went home.

Brewing was done on Sunday morning when the restaurant was closed and it was cooler. Brewing beer created a lot of heat and smell in the restaurant. The brewing system was located in the front of the restaurant behind plate glass windows. Two brewers were at the restaurant when he showed up. They questioned who he was since he'd been absent for many weeks. They let him stir in the mash and shovel out the grain. It was nice of them since those were the most strenuous tasks. He helped clean the fermenter and transfer yeast. He added the hops to the boil and helped transfer the wort. He let them finish all of the cleaning. He enjoyed the hours helping to brew.

Jessie called and told him she and her parents weren't coming over for lunch. Her father wasn't doing well.

On Sunday evening, Bill added details to his report about Congressman Murphy. He discussed many of the properties that were involved and showed pictures of the properties with the purchase dates with amount paid, the sales dates with selling price, and the profit made. He had twenty five properties that he displayed rather quickly. He said the Congressman hadn't responded to his request for an interview.

The talking head asked, "Have you been contacted by the FBI about the Congressman?"

"I have and I provided them a copy of my information."

"Did they indicate when they would be contacting the Congressman?"

"They didn't."

"Thank you, Bill Webber," the talking head said after his scripted questions. I'm sure the talking heads liked Bill since he gave them intelligent questions to ask.

William went to the office on Monday morning so Amy could discuss assignments for the week. Inez and Gerald also came in. Both were regulars now. Amy gave William several documents to review and sign. She told him to go to Aiken to file an eviction so he did. William was back for the noon meeting.

Amy cooked a pan of lasagna for lunch. It was a real treat. She must have known William had lost weight. He sweated a lot of liquid out brewing beer. Some of it was even added to the beer. William started with the car business.

Cal said, "We're making lots of progress with Gerald's help. The GTO and the Mustang we took in trade are almost done. The cars Amy and I picked up from Savannah are close too. We should have four cars ready to sell this week."

Inez said, "We're continuing to show a profit for the cars and it's keeping my husband happy." She passed out the car spreadsheet.

William said, "I'm sure you've seen the reports on Congressman Murphy. We'll need to replace him soon."

"The donations have increased since Bill's reports and the emails are going strong. Let's keep him on as long as we can," Thomas suggested.

Inez passed out the spreadsheet for Save America. "The amounts keep increasing, as you can see. We'll have a lot of money to buy ads for the election."

William asked, "Have you decided to stay with Save America? Your probation period is almost up."

"I have. You're a great group and Gerald is the happiest I've seen him in a long time."

Everybody told Inez they were elated she was staying. William knew his charm would be irresistible after she spent a little time with him.

Inez, Thomas, and William stayed in the conference room to chat a little more. Amy left and came back a few minutes later to tell us to watch CNN. A talking head said that Congressman Murphy had left the country.

The talking head said Bill Webber would be making a report shortly. In about ten minutes, Bill came on. He was in front of the Congressman's house and the FBI was carrying files and computers out of the house. Bill reported that the Congressman was seen at the airport early this morning heading to South America. Bill reported that the other four Congressmen involved were Congressman Rose, Congressman Sullivan, Congressman Hinton, and Congressman Crenshaw. He said that all four had served with Congressman Murphy on the Transportation and Infrastructure Committee.

The talking head asked, "Has Congressman Murphy been charged with a crime?"

"Not yet. The FBI is still obtaining information."

"Did you think the Congressman would flee?"

"I didn't."

"Have you talked to the FBI about the other four Congressmen?"

"Yes. I discussed the other four Congressmen with the FBI."

"When will the other four be charged?"

"I understand warrants are being issued today to confiscate files from them."

"Thank you, Bill Webber," the talking head said.

Congressman Crenshaw was William's next choice for the website so he'd need to make another choice. Amy had William run a couple of errands and he worked on a house until late in the day. Jessie wasn't coming over. It was a shame since he was going to ask her to marry him.

William worked on houses on Tuesday morning and made it to the office for the lunch meeting. Amy had ordered lunches from a restaurant. William's lunch was grouper with a shrimp sauce and a side of asparagus. Amy now knew what William liked to eat.

They talked about the car business and Save America.

Amy brought a cake from her office into the conference room with ten candles that were lit. She placed the cake in front of William. William was told by everyone to blow out the candles and he did. William's silent wish was that Jessie would agree to marry him.

Thomas gave William a box with an elaborate and decorative bow and ribbon. He opened it up and saw a framed ten dollar bill with an engraved plate that said "A Difference Maker".

Thomas patted William on the back. "I think you've made a difference with Save America."

Everyone applauded.